6

FULL-LENGTH PLAYS

VOLUME ONE

by
Edward Crosby Wells

CONTENTS

"The Playwright on the Playwright"	9
In The Venus Arms	17
West Texas Massacre	99
Flowers Out Of Season	205
The Moon Away	295
Desert Devils	413
The Proctologist's Daughter	507

To Ronald L. Perkins
for the journey of a lifetime.

Copyright © Edward Crosby Wells 2020.

All rights reserved. Except for brief passages quoted in newspaper, magazine, radio or television reviews, no part of this book may be reproduced in any form or by any means, electronics or mechanical, including photocopying or recording, or by an information storage and retrieval system, without permission in writing from the author.

This material is fully protected under the Copyright Laws of the United States of America and all other countries of the Berne and Universal Copyright Conventions and is subject to royalty. All rights including, but not limited to professional, amateur, recording, motion picture, recitation, lecturing, public reading, radio and television broadcasting, and the right of translation into foreign languages are expressly reserved.

No one shall commit or authorize any act or omission by which the copyright of, or the right to copyright, this play may be impaired.

No one shall make any changes in this play for the purpose of production.

Publication of this play does not imply availability for performance. Both amateurs and professionals considering a production are strongly advised in their own interests to apply to the author or the author's agent for written permission before starting rehearsals, advertising, or booking a theatre.

All producers of any play contained *6 Full-length Plays Volume ONE must* give credit to the Author of the Play in all programs distributed in connection with performances of the Play, and in all instances in which the title of the Play appears for the purposes of advertising, publicizing or otherwise exploiting the Play and/or a production. The name of the Author *must* appear on a separate line on which no other name appears, immediately following the title and *must* appear in size of type not less than fifty percent of the size of the title type.

THE PLAYWRIGHT ON THE PLAYWRIGHT
by Edward Crosby Wells

There was not a time when I did not want to write. My mother was a poet. So writing was probably in my blood, or perhaps it was infused into my blood by her way of punishing me whenever I did something not to her liking. When I did, which I did often, she would have me write a hundred or more times, "I will eat my vegetables," or "I will not lie," "I will not throw my clothes on the floor," or, "I will say my prayers every night," and so forth. When a little older, sentences became a bit more complex; "I will remember that an "an" comes before a vowel and an "a" comes before a consonant." And for God's sake, "a" comes before the words 'historical, hysterical and hippopotamus!" Yes, I learned very early by her and by some of the most blood-thirsty nuns I wish I'd never met. The common complaint from the nuns was, "Edward does not apply himself." They were right and I knew it. I hated school!

After years of serious health issues and a father who would disappear for weeks and months without an explanation, my mother committed suicide with sleeping pills. She died shortly before I turned twelve, so I can only imagine how the sentences would have been during my teen years, "I will not lock myself in the bathroom and masturbate?" I got my revenge; I flunked 7th grade English and then again in 9th grade. My father didn't return after my mother's death. I was orphaned and about to be put in foster home. Fortunately, my grandparents took me in.

I was born on October 19, 1944 at 11:10 AM in Suffern, New York. We lived on Greyridge Farms until 1951 when we moved a bit farther upstate to Arden Farms in Harriman, NY. We all—me, my mother and father—lived with my grandparents most of the time. My grandfather was a tenant farmer.

I knew I was a writer, but was yet to learn of what. It began with dreadful poetry and then moved on to equally dreadful fiction. I had written and re-written the first couple chapters —short chapters by anyone's standard—of a novel during my Junior and Senior year in public school. The novel was very Catholic and enigmatic. I couldn't get beyond what little I had written. I was too self-conscious and every word had to be just so. Thank you, mother! I'm still too self-conscious and will probably die that way.

I was a C and D student throughout high school. So, in the middle of my Senior year I had enough of it. I convinced my grandmother to sign the form that allowed me to quit school. She did and I quit. I wanted to go into the Air Force. When I tried to enlist they told me I was too fat and that I needed to finish high school. So, I went back after two weeks and begged the principal to let me return. After much reluctance on his part, he gave-in; no doubt thinking me too stupid to benefit from any further education. Shortly thereafter, a local family doctor prescribed diet pills for me and I lost over fifty pounds in my last semester of school and, with the amphetamines, I became an A student and found myself on the honor roll. No one was more shocked than I. Needless to say, I developed an unhealthy addiction to "speed" that would continue throughout my twenties and thirties.

After graduating high school I enlisted into the Navy and became a radioman on the USS Seawolf, a submarine and the second nuclear boat made, sister boat to the USS Nautilus. That was fun for awhile, but like everything else I grew bored. In the winter of 1964, I was stationed in New London, Connecticut and while on leave I went into the city. Being a native New Yorker, "The City" can only be one place—New York City. I met up with my best friend, who was still living on Arden Farms; forty-five miles north of Manhattan. We went to see a preview performance of Edward Albee's *Tiny Alice*. It was a life-altering experience. I had never heard words constructed in such a manner as to open places within me I never knew existed. It was as if I heard the voice of God. Years later, I was invited along with a few other playwrights, to a weekend retreat in Mister Albee's home, but due to circumstances I was forced to decline. I so much wanted to thank him for his inspiring me to become a playwright. Anyway, when *Tiny Alice* was over I remained in my seat, numb and exhausted. I turned to Bobby and simply said, because I knew, "I'm going to be a playwright." And so it began. Albee led me to Beckett, Ionesco and Sartre. They were my early influences. Later on, Williams and Orton would be important influences on me and on my future writing.

After being discharged from the navy, I was introduced to pot, more speed (my drug of choice) and LSD, while I was in the heart of the 1960s. Ten years turned into twenty years that went up in smoke and every drug I could get my hands on! Did you know Sartre wrote *Being and Nothingness* on speed? I wrote lists of things to do every morning, but never did them. "Edward does not apply himself."

I attempted to be an actor. I pounded the streets of "The City," and did some off-off Broadway, community, and dinner theatre. Along the way I acquired a working knowledge of just about every aspect of Theatre—most important for a playwright, who could not hold a day-job, and who came to know nothing about anything, except Theatre. I was a playwright in-name-only, who played at playwriting well into the 1970s when I was reading Proust and Gertrude Stein—amorphous and beautiful rambling, meets obscure, unpunctuated, literary cubism. If you haven't read Gertrude Stein, you must. As with the Cubists, she could show the front, sides and back of an idea all at once. She taught me how to read and how to think.

I enrolled in a community college. After three and a half semesters with a 4.0 cum, got bored—as I am wont to do—and quit. Went to four hairdressing schools and quit three of them, finally graduating from the fourth. After seven years of hairdressing I quit, after leaving a pair of scissors in the ceiling of the beauty parlor and went back to pursuing acting. After a summer of summer stock, I took a part-time and unbelievably low paying job writing theatre reviews for "Backstage," "Show Business" and other small papers and magazines including NYC cable television. Around then, during a weekend in Woodstock, NY, I met my future husband. With his support, I returned to playwrighting and finally wrote and finished my first play, *Willow Grove* of which no copy has survived the passing years. It is my "lost play," and the loss is still a source of sadness. After that, I wrote a series of short plays I referred to as "existential." I got that from Sartre and to this day I have no idea what "existential" means; although I am sure as the word is bounced around nowadays, the bouncers of the word haven't a clue either. Finally, in the latter half of the 1970s or early 1980s I found my "voice" and for the first time, took my writing seriously, and myself less so. My first surviving full-length play is the first play in Volume One in this anthology. It should be noted that Volumes One and Two of my full-length plays are in the order in which they were written.

In the Venus Arms is populated with some of my favorite writers: Gertrude Stein, Marcel Proust, Oscar Wilde and Franz Kafka. Alice B. Toklas is also one of the characters along with a character that also happens to have my name; a bold move for a beginner. The play is a farce about an inorcism (as opposed to an exorcism) and Gertrude Stein is the inorcist. Mister Robert Patrick, Drama Desk and OBIE Award-winning Playwright and author of Broadway's *Kennedy's Children*, wrote a lovely foreword to *In the Venus Arms*. It is included in this collection.

The second play in this first volume is a melodrama titled *West Texas Massacre*. Similar to Paul Zindel's revenge play, *Ladies of the Alamo*, *Massacre*, a play within a play, is about disillusionment and anger towards a theatre of amateurs. Mister Zindel is best known for his beautiful play, *The Effect of Gamma Rays on Man-in-the Moon Marigolds,* which I had the pleasure of directing at the theatre that inspired *West Texas Massacre*. Mister Zindel and I worked together at Circle Repertory Company while developing his new play, *Amulets Against the Dragon Forces*, while *Flowers Out of Season,* which is the third play in this anthology, was being developed. *West Texas Massacre* was written in a motel on Route 66 in Albuquerque, New Mexico. My partner and future husband, Ron Perkins, and I had left the scene where *West Texas Massacre* is set and I wrote it within a month on a portable typewriter. *Massacre* opened at the Raw Space—the Actors Studio in NYC under the direction of Frank Calo who would help develop my most financially successful play, *3 Guys in Drag Selling Their Stuff,* which is included in Volume Two.

The third play in Volume One, *Flowers Out of Season,* was written in a garage where we lived after leaving the motel. We were broke and rented the garage for one hundred dollars a month from a family that have become lifelong friends. *Flowers* is about a young couple in Southern New Mexico who have fallen on hard times. It is about America's working poor lost in a faltering social and healthcare system. *Flowers out of Season* was presented by Circle Repertory Company's Director's Lab under the direction of Michael Warren Powell on November 9, 1990. After undergoing another developmental phase at Denver's Changing Scene Theatre in June of 1993 under the direction of Jeremy Cole, it had its official world premiere produced by The PEOPLE*S Theater of Chicago under the direction of Madrid St. Angelo at the EP Theatre in Chicago, IL on January 11, 2008.

The Moon Away, the fourth play in Volume One, was also written in that garage in Albuquerque. It began as a Play of Catharsis but ended being what I consider one of two of my best plays (the other being *Flowers Out of Season).* The subject of *The Moon Away* remains the most painful experience in my lifetime, and the reason we landed in

Albuquerque flat broke. It is not strictly based on that experience. It is Theatre and Theatre is no place for autobiography. In the mid-1980s, hysteria swept the country. People in disproportionate numbers were using children to add fuel to what had become mass-hysteria to destroy the lives of others. Prosecutors and social workers coerced children to make false accusations of sexual molestation and satanic rituals involving the sacrificing of small animals. Day care workers, ex-marital partners and homosexuals became targets for shocking charges of rape, devil worshipping sodomites, etc. These were high profile cases that daily made the front pages of newspapers and the endless reports on evening TV. Parents wore buttons that warned "Believe the Children." "Listen to the children" and "children don't lie" became the mantra of the day. All the high-profile defendants, after months and years of hellish pain, were found not guilty. The number of children who would eventually recant was an alarmingly high percent. What began this hysteria is anybody's guess, but it grew—eventually making its way to Hobbs, New Mexico. It is against this backdrop the play is set. *The Moon Away* was developed and presented at the Greenwich House Theatre in NYC in February of 1995. After a further production at Mesa College in San Diego in March of 2000 and having undergone more fine-tuning, it had its official world premier at The Davenaughn Theatre in Boston, Massachusetts on September 1, 2006.

Winner of the Panhandle Playwrights Festival, *Desert Devils* directed by Boone Smith was produced by the Amarillo Repertory Company in Amarillo, TX where it premiered May 30, 2008. After that it would have a successful run at the Liberty Theatre in Yass, New South Wales, Australia under the direction of Alex Cuthbert. Set in the formerly oil-rich desert Southwest, *Desert Devils* explores the lives of three generations of women living under one roof. The play is, at once, outrageously funny and heart-breakingly tragic. These women tear and rip into one another's psyche with reckless abandon and something barely resembling love. Just beneath the surface these women hide a potent poison—the deadly venom accumulated over years of unfulfilled dreams mixed with the sudden and bitter acceptance of a life unrealized. .

The final play in Volume One is *The Proctologist's Daughter.* This wild spoof was commissioned by producer Frank Calo of Spotlight On Productions. Under the title of *Curse of the Snake Woman, The Proctologist's Daughter* opened at the Raw Space in NYC, on October 29, 2002 under the direction of Sean Cassels. I had a helluva time entertaining myself with this one. The play is set in the atmosphere of 1940s film noir. All the characters are pretty much Hollywood stock. In fact, there is not an once of realism, just cliché and a ton of fun-filled shtick inspired by Mel Brooks.

Every play in this collection was a labor of love. The bottom line is that everything I have ever written was a labor of love. For me, there is nothing more important than entertaining an audience. So, in the words of Baby June in the musical *Gypsy,* let me entertain you,

ECW, 2020
Denver, Colorado

IN THE VENUS ARMS

FOREWORD by Robert Patrick

To be a playwright in America today is unlike being one anywhere else at any other time in history. Jane Chambers was fond of saying, when asked if it was hard to be a Lesbian playwright, that it was much harder in America being a playwright than being gay. It has been socially difficult being an artist here in the land of machismo ever since the Oscar Wilde scandal identified artistry with homosexuality in the American mind. Till then, the growing new country had rather worshiped artists. They worshiped Wilde on his tour of America. The promise of this country was that the poor could earn everything which only the rich had had in Europe. One of those things was education. Isolated prairie farmers pitched in to hire schoolteachers, and let their sons off from harvesting work to attend school. Part of education was refinement through art. The first building in a new town after the tavern and the church was the Opera House. Shakespearean troupes toured the wildest frontiers. Children were given Roman names to prove that their proud parents had read the classics. After Wilde's disgrace, that changed, as any sensitive American boy discovered on the schoolyard. Sensitive boys avoided each other, lest they make a larger target. Their loneliness was immense. But at least there was the promise of a big-city career, success, fame, a circle of like-minded friends who shared one's interests and experience. Now even that hope is gone. Gore Vidal wrote to me in a letter dated November nineteenth, nineteen ninety-four, "I was lucky to have both a literary world & Broadway. Neither was much good, but compared to what faces you, mine was an age of gold, fool's or otherwise." Mister Vidal's generation had TV for which to write serious drama and audition it for Broadway and Hollywood. Now the only serious drama on TV is from The British Isles. We playwrights call PBS "The English Channel." In the nineteen sixties, there was Off-Off

Broadway and Bohemian camaraderie. That vanished as grant-grubbers and showcasers took over. And how many of the shows they grind out to get grants by the numbers ever move elsewhere? How many new American plays are commercially produced in any year today? How many published? Now for most U.S. dramatists, there is only invisible isolation in uncaring cities and towns, and the hideous feeling that their natural function is denied them, and its fruits denied to the culture that sees no individual perceptions of itself—no "brief chronicles of the time." All the drama America sees is the endlessly self-reflexive "genres" of TV and movies, relating to nothing but what was successful last year.

One must understand this situation to understand Mister Wells' unique and profoundly personal play. He does not "exposition" the world his play takes place in. He only exposes it. He sees the lonely situation I have described above so clearly every day that he assumes you see it, too, and only shows you what it is like to live in it. And here, at last, in this play that adheres to no genre's prerequisites, no academician's unities, you can see it. The loneliness of the high I.Q., caring, American artist is flung before you—the despair, the imagined acquaintance with admired artists of a bygone age, and, yes, the talking to one's self through them —all are here, in a form giving actors marvelous roles and marvelous challenges.

Welcome to Mister Wells'—my—our—and your world.

—Robert Patrick, Drama Desk and OBIE Award-winning Playwright and author of Broadway's *Kennedy's Children*

IN THE VENUS ARMS
a diabolical farce in 3 scenes

SYNOPSIS: 4M/2W. Written in three scenes. There is no intermission. This black comedy features the playwright himself. Spiritless, Wells is threatened by the night manager of *The Venus Arms*, a residential hotel, with permanent dispossession, leaving an empty, though very animated body. Four literati arrive to perform an "inorcism" (as opposed to an exorcism) to restore Wells' spirit. Gertrude Stein and Alice B. Toklas along with Oscar Wilde and Marcel Proust raise havoc while trying to raise the consciousness of the subject of their inorcism while Franz Kafka, the night manager, pops up in the form of a cockroach seemingly intent on the playwright's doom in this fun-filled, clever and diabolical farce

CHARACTERS IN ORDER OF APPEARANCE

WELLS: A playwright and a resident in The Venus Arms.
FRANZ KAFKA: The night manager for The Venus Arms.
GERTRUDE STEIN: A night visitor who comes to perform an inorcism.
MARCEL PROUST: A night visitor who has come to assist the inorcist.
OSCAR WILDE: A night visitor and party crasher.
ALICE B. TOKLAS: A night visitor and companion to Gertrude Stein.

THE SETTING of the farce takes place in a suite leased to Mr. Wells in a residential hotel known as The Venus Arms. Time has taken its toll on The Venus Arms, however the grandness of the Edwardian decor still lingers through a surreal atmosphere. There is a red velvet sofa. There is a tall bookcase somewhere. There is WELLS' desk which is downstage and facing the audience.

THE ACTION is continuous—from dusk till dawn.

THE TIME is the present.

Scene 1—*Cockroaches*

AT RISE: Complete darkness except for the LIGHTING that comes through a window. The sun is setting. As window LIGHTING slowly moves into twilight, the stage LIGHTING slowly RISES. There is a KNOCKING on the door. WELLS stops writing and rises from his desk, downstage facing audience, and begins to cross towards the door.

WELLS: Just a minute. *(Remembering something, he turns back to his desk and writes longhand, while speaking.)* If there were others I'm certain that—*(KNOCKING.)* Just a minute! *(Back to prior thought.)* Certain that … that … one of us would have heard or seen …. What? *(KNOCKING continues louder and faster as he crosses to answer the door.)* I'm coming! I'm coming! *(At the door.)* Who is it?

KAFKA'S VOICE: Kafka. Who else would it be? We don't allow night visitors, Mister Wells. Let me in.

WELLS: Why?

KAFKA'S VOICE: Open up and I'll tell you why.

WELLS: Why? *(Backs away as door slowly opens.)*

KAFKA: Because. *(Opening door with key, enters.)* Master key, Mister Wells.

WELLS: Look here, I could have you arrested for this, Mister Kafka … forcing yourself into a resident's home.

KAFKA: Beelzebub.

WELLS: What?

KAFKA: I said Beelzebub. Beelzebub! You are not going to have anybody arrested. *(Takes lease from pocket.)* Mister Wells, resident, do you see this *(Reads.)* "The party of the first part..." That is this establishment! "...agrees to lease to the party of the second part to be known as resident ..." that would be you. "The hotel staff..." of which I am one. "... is granted the unrestricted right of passage ..." That means to enter at will! You would do best, Wells, by keeping that in mind, *always*. You will not want to forget it. "...for purposes in the interest of the management of The Venus Arms. Said resident shall not deny free access to the authorized, known as Franz Kafka the night manager..." And we know who that is. "... under penalty of dispossession with neither prior notice nor reason." *(Stares menacingly at WELLS.)* Dispossession, Mister Wells. Shall I go on?

WELLS: Please, don't. We both know the bully you are. You'll win every time.

KAFKA: Of course. *(Puts lease back into his pocket.)* You wouldn't allow the exterminator in today. *(Eyeing the shelves of books in the bookcase.)* I see that you are a reader. One would think a writer would have no time for that sort of diversion.

WELLS: What do you want, Kafka?

KAFKA: *(Preoccupied with the books.)* Proust. *(Turns to WELLS, menacingly.)* I am not one for wasting words.

WELLS: Nor am I?

KAFKA: *(Continues browsing through books.)* Poetry. Poetry. More poetry. You have a good deal of poetry. Are you a poet, Mister Wells?

WELLS: A great many playwrights are—*were*. Those of us who are not now, nor have ever been, certainly appreciate the poet—and the poem. I ask you, Kafka, do you know the difference?

KAFKA: I know the difference between the poet and the poem and the playwright and the dilettante. There is a moment in time when they are one. Take Baudelaire, for instance ... the debility, the intoxication ... the spirit of self-sacrifice ... a lost soul who presses flowers the moment they bloom. What has he got against them?

WELLS: Against what?

KAFKA: Flowers, Wells, Flowers?

WELLS: I don't know that he has anything against them.

KAFKA: Then why murder them the moment they bloom?

WELLS: To capture their essence, I suppose.

KAFKA: You suppose far more than I. I am only a poor night manager ... a humble employee of the man downstairs. My nights are filled with more important matters so, naturally, I need a good part of the day for sleeping. *(Glances at another book.) Dorian Gray.* How difficult it must be learning to leave well enough alone.

WELLS: For some.

KAFKA: We'll see. *(Picking up a book here and there.)* Wilde. Goethe. Stein.. Kafka. *Ah,* I see you have one of my little tomes, *The Trial.* How sweet. *(Moves about the room lifting an object here and there and then tossing them back in a threatening manner.)* We mean exactly what we say in The Venus Arms. *Exactly.* Nothing more. Nothing less. I would keep that in mind. Break any of the rules and your stay will not be a pleasant one. We wouldn't like to find it necessary to have you dispossessed.

WELLS: Is that a threat?

KAFKA: Of course it's a threat, you silly goose. That's what I do. I am what I am and I do what I do and I love it, boy. I love it! The choice to remain or to move has always been yours. You're the one who wants to be a famous playwright. You're the one who chose to come to The Venus Arms and making a bargain with ... *God. (Pointing downward.)*

WELLS: I wouldn't call him God.

KAFKA: You will. In the meanwhile, you really must learn to follow the rules. There are no privileged few here. There are none for whom the rules do not apply. Life in The Venus Arms, as luxurious as it can be—for some—comes with a few well thought out rules; rules that must never be broken.

WELLS: *Please.* Rules are meant to be broken.

KAFKA: No tired adages on me, boy. Rules are not and never were meant to be broken. That's why they're rules, ninny. Breaking rules can be fatal. The Venus Arms is only concerned with the welfare of the chosen few who are its residents ... and, of course, with the collection of the rent. That's why there are rules, Mister Wells. *Rules* ... rules that are not meant to be broken.

WELLS: So say you.

KAFKA: Let the world go about its trivial pursuits. We, in The Venus Arms, do not concern ourselves with the world outside these walls. Forget about the world. Forget it ever existed. Otherwise, one should take up residence in something a bit more baroque. Something with a swimming pool. A Motel 6, perhaps.

WELLS: I find you a scary man, Mister Kafka.

KAFKA: Thank you, but I don't need to be found. It's my pleasure to serve. It is my purpose, Mister Wells. You should know I find you a lucky man.

WELLS: How's that?

KAFKA: We don't allow too many playwrights to take up residence here.

WELLS: Why is that?

KAFKA: You people are more trouble than you're worth. Goethe was the exception. But, most of the others didn't stay long. Management had to vacate their premises.

WELLS: Why?

KAFKA: *Why?* Because you playwrights think you're better than every other kind of writer. I blame that on Shakespeare.

WELLS: Did Shakespeare stay in The Venus Arms?

KAFKA: For one night only!

WELLS: Why only one night?

KAFKA: Because he *did* know better than every other kind of writer. He was a bad influence. We didn't want him discouraging all the other writers.

WELLS: You mean—

KAFKA: Exactly what I say. You didn't let the exterminator in today and I've been hearing reports about you upsetting other residents.

WELLS: For the love of God, what do you want?

KAFKA: "For the love of God." You're a funny man, Mister Wells.

WELLS: What do you want?

KAFKA: Peace ... quiet ... goodwill among men ... *(He laughs long and hideously.)* But, seriously ... the exterminator will have to come back just for you. That will cost you dearly. The Venus Arms will not subsidize a second extermination.

WELLS: *(Directing KAFKA toward the door.)* I only want to be left to my work. Is that too much to ask?
KAFKA: Depends on who you're asking.

WELLS: Leave. As long as I'm paying rent you have no right—

KAFKA: *Tut, tut, tut!* Not so soon. We've still this little matter concerning complaints from other residents.

WELLS: Complaints?

KAFKA: Some can't sleep nights.

WELLS: How is that my problem?

KAFKA: You've been entertaining guests after hours.

WELLS: Nonsense.

KAFKA: You've allowed all sorts of riff-raff into The Venus Arms. When you took up residence here, you agreed—in writing—to host only those approved by Management. Now, may I ask you a question?

WELLS: You're gonna anyway.

KAFKA: Of course. It is of a rather delicate nature, Wells. It pains me to ask, but ask I must. The question is: Have you any special affection for, or feel any particular fondness towards roaches?

WELLS: What?

KAFKA: Roaches! Roaches!

WELLS: What do I look like to you, Kafka?

KAFKA: That shouldn't matter, Mister Wells. It's totally irrelevant. I never even took your appearance into account.

WELLS: They're a life form. They have a right to exist. You exist ... I guess.

KAFKA: But I am not a cockroach. You didn't allow the exterminator in today! The rules of this establishment—

WELLS: *(Cutting him short.)* Please leave. You are cryptically frightening.

KAFKA: Now you sound like my mother. *(Pulls out lease and reads.)* "The hotel staff ..." That's me. Franz Kafka. "... in carrying out its ..."

WELLS: *(Interrupts. Close-up and staring.)* Hello. Is there anybody in there?

KAFKA: Nobody you want to anger. *(Backing toward the door, making placatory motions.)* You are speaking to a duly authorized representative of The Venus Arms. This may be your home for the time being, Mister Wells, but this is not your castle!

WELLS: You may be scary, but I'm not afraid of you. You can threaten all you like. Sticks and stones and all that.

KAFKA: Get off the playground, Wells. You will pay. You will pay in ways you could never imagine.

WELLS: You can put me on your menu, Kafka, but you can't eat me.

KAFKA: We'll see about that. You are an affront to the establishment!

WELLS: To Hell with the establishment.

KAFKA: To Hell, indeed.

(KAFKA has backed himself against the door with his hand behind his back fumbling with the knob. He manages to open the door and exit into the exterior hallway. He remains there in full view with the door ajar.)

KAFKA: *Alright.* I see you want to take me on. Be warned, you cannot beat the Devil, Mister Wells. Now, you get yourself some rest. Take good care of yourself and I won't bother you with the writ.

WELLS: Writ? What writ?

KAFKA: Don't you worry, Mister Wells, tomorrow is another night.

WELLS: *(Insisting.) Writ?* You said writ. What writ?

KAFKA: Something to do with search and seizure.

WELLS: Search and seizure?

KAFKA: They have been seen leaving your premises, Wells! They have been seen coming from your suite and making their way into the rooms of other residents.

WELLS: What in hell are you talking about, Kafka?

KAFKA: Roaches! Roaches! Roaches! You didn't let the exterminator in today. It is essential that you allow the exterminator in during his required rounds. There are others in The Venus Arms. Others we would not want you to infest.

(WELLS slams the door on KAFKA whose shouts are heard retreating down the hallway.)

KAFKA: *(Con't. Shouting from hallway.)* Never! Never! Never! You'll never beat the Devil, Mister Wells! *(KAFKA laughs.)*

WELLS: *(Momentarily stunned. Walks back and forth addressing the door as though it were KAFKA incarnate.)* I'll beat you and with your own game! *(Props nearby chair against door. Crosses downstage, looks out into the audience, takes his time to observe them.)* Who are you people? Are there any murderers out there? Just curious. You wouldn't tell me anyway. Certainly not in public. And you are the public. I just like to know who my neighbors are. One cannot be too careful. Especially when one has a bully for a landlord. I suppose I shouldn't have visitors, or let my characters loose in The Venus Arms without permission of the establishment. But I should be allowed to entertain whomever I like whether Kafka likes it or not. Don't you agree?

(A musical fanfare. A harp's glissando. The bookcase slowly swings open.)

WELLS: *(Con't.)* Did you hear that? It's time for me to write. *(Crosses to desk and sits. To the door.)* Okay, Kafka. *(He picks up a pen and begins to write in longhand.)* I'll write my own writ. Just watch me.

(GERTRUDE and MARCEL enter, leaving the bookcase to swing back into place.)

GERTRUDE: What is this? Where is this? What a dump!

WELLS: *(To ceiling.)* Hello. Hello. Anyone there?

MARCEL: Should we say "hello" back?

GERTRUDE: Quiet, Marcel. Say nothing. He's talking to himself.

WELLS: *(To audience.)* I'm talking to myself, aren't I? *(Arranges some paper on his desk, and continues to write.)*

MARCEL: *(Exploring the suite.)* Gertrude, can we help him? What do you think?

GERTRUDE: One can never say for certain what one thinks. At least one ought not. However, one should know whether one thinks one thing or another. Therefore, one should not abandon a thing altogether.

MARCEL: I hate it when you talk like that. It was just a simple question. Can we help him?

GERTRUDE: I just said so, did I not? So, quite naturally, I thought so. In fact, I remember telling Picasso … saying to Picasso … one never tells Picasso anything, "Pablo, you must give it a try."

WELLS: *(Writing and thinking aloud.)* I must give it a try.

MARCEL: Gertrude, he heard you!

GERTRUDE: Well, of course he heard me, Marcel. Sooner or later everybody will come to hear me.

WELLS: *(To audience.)* Can you hear me? Don't answer. I already know.

MARCEL: *(Startled.)* Oh, my! He's enough to raise the dead. Who is he talking to?

GERTRUDE: He believes he has an invisible audience.

MARCEL: Poor thing.

GERTRUDE: Well, anyway. *(Flops into an over-stuffed winged-back chair.)* We might as well make ourselves comfortable, Marcel. I think it is going to be a long, long night.

OSCAR: *(Entering through bookcase.)* Am I late? You're looking particularly well this evening, Marcel. Is that really you, Gertie, or just a vision of something inexplicable?

GERTRUDE: Are you late for what, Oscar?

OSCAR: Just being fashionable, dear one. *(Spies WELLS.)* Is there something foul in the air?

GERTRUDE: There is now.

OSCAR: Has he been done in?

MARCEL: He emptied out.

OSCAR: Emptied out?

GERTRUDE: *(With impatience.)* Unconscious, Oscar. There's no one home. Mister Wells has vacated the room.

WELLS: *(To audience.)* Do I appear to have vacated the room?

OSCAR: He's not unconscious. He's writing.

GERTRUDE: He's unconscious, Oscar. He only thinks he's conscious.

OSCAR: How can he think he is when he isn't? Or isn't when he thinks he is.

GERTRUDE: *Well, he isn't.*

OSCAR: That's just what I thought.

GERTRUDE: Oscar, are you here to help or what!?

OSCAR: Oh, dear. Am I induced?

GERTRUDE: We are all induced. *(Rises from chair, indicates WELLS.)* Now, let us put him on the divan.

MARCEL: Do you suppose the divan is best, Gertrude? I mean, look at him. He's still writing.

GERTRUDE: Marcel, you suppose. He, she, and it supposes. *I think.* Therefore, we will put him on the divan. He only imagines he's writing.

WELLS: *(To audience.)* I don't want to go on the divan.

GERTRUDE: *(Gertrude grabs a vase, crosses to WELLS and breaks it on his head. WELLS slips to the floor.)* Now he's unconscious.

OSCAR: Wouldn't want to meet you in a dark alley, Gertie.

GERTRUDE: Well, Marcel, legs or arms?

MARCEL: Legs. No. Arms. No. Legs—

GERTRUDE: Marcel! Make up your mind!

MARCEL: Legs.

GERTRUDE: *(Takes WELLS' wrists while MARCEL takes his ankles. BOTH start to lift him but they don't get far.)* Marcel, you are letting down your end.

MARCEL: I am not letting my end down. Oscar, would you be so kind?

OSCAR: *(Takes one of WELLS' legs.)* Upsy-daisy. He's a right plump porker he is. How's your end, Gertie?

GERTRUDE: *Gertrude's* end is just fine, Oscar!

OSCAR: Good. There seemed to be some doubt about it, as I recall.

(ALL struggle to maneuver WELLS onto the divan.)

OSCAR *(Con't.)* Now, let me see. Where was it I heard something about Gertrude's end? No matter, who listens to rumors anyway? Gertrude, I wouldn't let it trouble me for a moment, were I you. But, then I'm not you and you are. More's the pity. Besides, I'm certain your end is picture perfect. *(GERTRUDE grunts with hostility.)* Gertrude, you're letting your end sag. *(GERTRUDE glares, letting WELLS' arms drop as they finish piling him onto the divan.)* Honestly, Gertrude, have you no respect for the unconscious?

GERTRUDE: *Humph! (Crossing to armchair.)*

OSCAR: Think of the nasty bruises the poor thing is going to get.

GERTRUDE: *(Flops into chair. Warning.)* Better you think of them.

OSCAR: Did I say something wrong, Marcel? *(MARCEL shrugs ignorance and sits on corner of divan nearest GERTRUDE. OSCAR crosses to desk, removes a sheet of paper from a pile, looks it over with astonishment before exclaiming:)* What a mess! *(GERTRUDE and MARCEL, having been sitting in an abstracted state, are startled.)*

GERTRUDE: Oscar, this is not a matter for farce! You will please stop adding insult to Wells' condition.

OSCAR: Wells' condition? Gertrude, his condition seems to be suffering an eclipse! Listen to this letter. At least, it has the appearance of one. *(Reads.)* "To whom it may concern or to whomever can find a reason for making it of concern."

MARCEL: It doesn't concern you, Oscar.

OSCAR: I've no doubt. *(Reads.)* "It is a mystery to me, also. I, too, have detected more bodies uninhabited than I have been able to detect with somebody in them. Furthermore, I suspect that there are a great number of bodies that come in an empty condition right from the get-go." *(Aside.)* What, pray tell, is a "get-go"? *(Reads.)* "From when they are born, they come that way." So that's a get-go. Americans … hmm. *(Reads.)* "Others are beginning to shut down and a slowing of their operational ability is an early symptom for a complete evacuation soon to follow. What is worse … " *(Aside.)* What could possibly be worse? He certainly entertains a very adequate respect for nothing.

GERTRUDE: Put in down, Oscar.

OSCAR: *(Ignoring GERTRUDE. Reads.)* "What is worse, decapitation seems to have little or no effect on mobility since one was heard to tiptoe on the roof while I tried *without success to sleep." (Replaces paper on desk.)* The man indirectly goes neither here nor there simultaneously.

GERTRUDE: We are already fully aware of his problem.

OSCAR: We? By that you mean, of course, you and Monsieur Proust?

MARCEL: *(More weary than irritated.)* Who else?

OSCAR: Who else indeed? How totally selfish of me to even consider the possibility that I may or may not exist. In your presence, Monsieur Verbosity and Miss Forgot-to-punctuate, I am nothing, a naught, a superfluous gathering of negative ventilation.

GERTRUDE: Don't flatter yourself! You're something ... *else.*

OSCAR: How kind. I hope to return the compliment.

GERTRUDE: *(Pressing on.)* We must see ourselves clear to solving that which is the problem.

OSCAR: I see your problematic insight can be as much admired as your modesty.

MARCEL: I feel Oscar hasn't grasped the gravity of the situation.

OSCAR: Oscar has grasped the gravity of the situation and it is firmly in the palm of my hand. However, in the other hand, hearing tiptoeing decapitatees seems more a matter of levitation, don't you agree?

GERTRUDE: Well anyway, we will never accomplish anything while Oscar persists in his drawing room manner.

OSCAR: This *is* a drawing room, is it not?

GERTRUDE: Yes. And as usual you're doing what you do best in one

OSCAR: And that would be?

GERTRUDE: Farce.

OSCAR: You flatter me.

GERTRUDE: Not as much as you flatter yourself. Are you going to approach our problem with the respect it deserves? We are here to do a job. There is much to be done.

MARCEL: Your failure to be serious, Oscar, will only create a further complication in Wells' condition.

OSCAR: He certainly is a condition.

GERTRUDE: We like to think of him as the symptom.

OSCAR: Well, I like to think of that as a problem.

GERTRUDE: *(To herself.)* Why? Why? Why do I bother?

OSCAR: What's the answer, Gertie?

GERTRUDE: *(Sharply.)* What is the question!

OSCAR: Where's Miss Toklas?

GERTRUDE: Sitting.

OSCAR: Sitting? Sitting where?

GERTRUDE: Where one usually sits, Oscar. Down. Alice is sitting down.

OSCAR: Where is Alice sitting down, Gertrude?

GERTRUDE: *(Motions to bookcase.)* Out there ... about halfway here.

OSCAR: Neither here nor there, I see. I don't suppose you could be more specific?

GERTRUDE: I could.

OSCAR: *(After a pause.)* Marcel, why is Alice sitting down out there about half way here?

MARCEL: Tired.

GERTRUDE: From the weight.

OSCAR: The weight?

MARCEL: Our picnic I imagine. Wouldn't you say so, Gertrude?

GERTRUDE: I would say the weight, I think.

OSCAR: I see. I guess. What are you two talking about?

GERTRUDE: Your question, Oscar.

OSCAR: My question?

MARCEL: Miss Toklas.

OSCAR: *Ah,* Alice and the grub. I love a picnic.

GERTRUDE: Well anyway. You didn't think we were going to spend the night in this dreary asylum without sustenance, did you?

OSCAR: Gertrude, you don't strike me as one who has ever gone without sustenance. Poor Alice. How she must suffer.

GERTRUDE: *Fool.*

WELLS: *(Raises his head and shouts.)* Of course! You mustn't let temporary residents to take over your body. Don't trust a single soul. Only your own. *Oh,* how I love a picnic! *(Blacks out.)*

(Startled, MARCEL jumps and seeks refuge on GERTRUDE'S footstool.)

OSCAR: *(Casually.)* I agree with you, kiddo. See? He likes picnics, too.

MARCEL: *Mon Dieu!* He nearly frightened me to death. I wish he would warn us, Gertrude. Oh, I'm faint! My heart. My nerves. I deplore sudden outbursts.

GERTRUDE: *(Mild chiding.)* Really, Marcel. Aren't we being somewhat extravagant?

MARCEL: I wish he had warned us, that's all ... just a little warning ... a sign that something big was soon to follow.

WELLS: *(Raised on an elbow, interrupts.)* To be or not? What *is* the question.

OSCAR: Ah, that has an air of twisted familiarity.

MARCEL: He did it again, Gertrude.

GERTRUDE: *There, there,* Marcel.

WELLS: From inside out the dispossessed fall. Hollow moans in endless space. Cobwebs cover their dusty tongues and worse—

OSCAR: What, pray tell, could be worse?

WELLS: They're evil. Their every act is motivated by ancient reptilian senses!

OSCAR: That's a crock. Definitely worse. Hey, Gertie, thought you conked him out.

GERTRUDE: He's more thick-headed than I thought.

WELLS: Suppose we all are guilty? What then? *(Rises and goes back to his desk and sits. To audience.)* How many of you are not here. Put your hands up. *Hmm* ... quite a few of you are missing, I see. Miss Stein conked me out, didn't she?. Boy, did that hurt. I don't remember inviting night visitors, but I always like a bit of company ... for inspiration, you know. She really hit me over the head, didn't she? Gertrude can be a brute sometimes. I'm in pain! *(Slumps over desk, exhausted.)*

(GERTRUDE, MARCEL and OSCAR are fascinated, bewildered and amazed—an abstracted pause to study the slumped body of WELLS.)

GERTRUDE: Well! Are you satisfied, Oscar? Now that you have made our work here that much more difficult with your careless and reckless disregard for Wells' condition, our symptom has yet another problem to add to its syndrome!

OSCAR: God only knows where he'll put it!

GERTRUDE: Fortunately for Wells, Marcel and I are here to tend to the symptom's condition.

MARCEL: Very fortunate, indeed ... for both of you, Oscar.

OSCAR: By that, I assume you mean the plague and I? How capital of you to put us both in the same boat, Marcel.

MARCEL: Were that the case, you would not find yourselves in the same boat.

OSCAR: How fortunate.

MARCEL: Not at all fortunate. The truth is, to use your metaphor, Oscar, generally speaking, you would ...

OSCAR: *(Interrupts.)* Nautically speaking.

MARCEL: I beg your pardon?

OSCAR: To use my metaphor, you would be "nautically" speaking.

MARCEL: *Oui. Excuser-moi de vous déranger.* Nautically speaking, you would each be so preoccupied with trying to maintain balance, neither of you would be good company for the other. Furthermore, you each would be doing everything humanly possible just to keep your footing ... and you will only find yourselves going nowhere.
OSCAR: Nonsense. I'd simply sit and row myself ashore.

MARCEL: Ah, but here is the unfortunate truth of the situation: Wells' condition means having one of your legs in one boat and your other leg in another boat, nautically speaking.

OSCAR: Nicely put, Marcel, but a strain on the inseam. I may fish from the shore from now on.

GERTRUDE: You do that, Oscar! *(Remembering something important.)* Fish! Nearly slipped my mind!

OSCAR: Fish, Gertrude?

GERTRUDE: Well, not fish. Food. Alice. Where is Alice?

OSCAR: Sitting, no doubt. Probably still sitting on her down.

GERTRUDE: *Humph!* Well! She cannot stay sitting in one place forever! *(Rises and crosses toward bookcase.)*

OSCAR: That's what I've always felt—sitting in one place forever is worse than sitting nowhere at all ... or maybe I mean the other way around. Something like that.

GERTRUDE: *(Swings bookcase open. Calling.)* Alice ... Alice ....

OSCAR: Were I you, I'd tell her good, Gertie. Let her know you won't stand for all her sitting.

GERTRUDE: *Humph! (Gertrude exits.and soon she is heard retreating:)* Alice. Alice. *Alice!*

OSCAR: *(Moving closer to MARCEL, in a chummy manner.)* Do tell, Marcel, what brings you out on a night like this?

MARCEL: *(Coolly.)* Wells' condition, of course.

OSCAR: Come, come, tell the truth. You and Miss Stein are not exactly a match made in Heaven.

MARCEL: *Tout au contraire.* That is exactly from where we got our orders.

OSCAR: Really? You've been sent by some heavenly agency to look after our dear confused playwright? The two of you? Like celestial nannies?

MARCEL: And who, may I be so bold to ask, might have sent you here?

OSCAR: No one. I came of my own accord. I fear I am neither heaven-sent nor sent from elsewhere, my dear Marcel. I am mine own just reward.

MARCEL: How novel.

OSCAR: Yes. So, why have you gotten yourself mixed up with Gertrude Stein?

MARCEL: I have not gotten myself "mixed up" with Mademoiselle Stein.

OSCAR: Maybe I've gotten you mixed up with somebody else.

MARCEL: I don't know why you're here, Oscar.

OSCAR: For the picnic, darling.

MARCEL: This is a very serious matter and your being here could jeopardize the mission. Mademoiselle Stein and I are here to help our dear Mister Wells … not to complicate his condition.

OSCAR: "*Mademoiselle Stein*" is it? I have never known Gertie to come with a prefix. Marcel, tell me something … doesn't Wells strike you as gaga?

MARCEL: Gaga?

OSCAR: Gaga. Bughouse. Blithe as a haberdasher.

MARCEL: He will be just fine after the inorcism.

OSCAR: Inorcism? You mean like an exorcism?

MARCEL: No, not like an exorcism at all. In fact, it is quite the opposite. Don't fret, Oscar. Gertrude and I know exactly what we are doing.

OSCAR: Do you now? How fortunate, indeed, for you and Gertrude and, of course, our dearly dispossessed.

MARCEL: Very fortunate, *Monsieur* Wilde.

OSCAR: Let me see if I have this clear. When somebody gets outside of somebody and that somebody outside of somebody doesn't belong outside of that certain somebody, you call an inorcist?

MARCEL: Naturally. Unless, somebody gets inside of somebody and that somebody inside of somebody doesn't belong inside that certain somebody, then you call an exorcist.

OSCAR: Precisely. That's something entirely different, right?

MARCEL: Quite, and that can get rather messy.

(There is a KNOCKING on the hotel door.)

OSCAR: *(Rises. Crossing to door.)* That must be the inorcist! Or, Alice delivering the fish.

MARCEL: *(Jumps up in a panic.)* NO! They wouldn't use that door! They couldn't!

OSCAR: Who could ... *(Removes chair from under knob.)* ... with this here? *(Opens door.)* Good eve ... *(Slams door.)* GOOD GOD!

MARCEL: Who is it?

OSCAR: *(Gropes to speak – sotto voce.)* Nobody.

MARCEL: Who?

OSCAR: Nobody—just a problem.

MARCEL: A problem?

OSCAR: A big problem.

MARCEL: A problem with what?

OSCAR: With a problem.

MARCEL: Well? What does he want?

OSCAR: *(Indicating WELLS.)* To give unto him! A writ, I think. *(The KNOCKING continues.)* Oh, Mr. Wells, I think it's for you.

WELLS: *(Rises and crosses towards the door.)* Just a minute. I'm coming. *(KNOCKING.)* Hello? Hello? Who is it? *(KNOCKING.)* Hello? Is anybody there?

OSCAR: I'll say!

OSCAR throws open the door. KAFKA steps into the room. He has been transformed into a giant cockroach. He is carrying a large canister with a hose attached; the type used by professional exterminators.

ALL freeze.

BLACK OUT.

End Scene 1

Scene 2—*birds and cucumber sandwiches*

A short while later.

AT RISE: The door to the outer hallway is blocked with something bulky—a credenza, perhaps. WELLS is at his desk, writing. OSCAR and MARCEL are involved in a conversation in progress.

MARCEL: And so our cat ate most anything.

OSCAR: Fish, yes. Every cat loves fish. *Pâté de Foie Gras,* most certainly, but madeleines, my dear? Why do I suspect that I am being wooed with ambiguity, Marcel?

MARCEL: Your nature, perhaps. I assure you cats love cookies, as well. And certainly my mother's madeleines.

OSCAR: An odd sense of detachment comes over me, my dear Marcel, when trying to follow one of your stories. There is a bewitching duplicity about them. Tryplicity. Quadplicity. Blah blah and blahplicity! I am never quite certain whether I am drowning in your rhetoric or floating off into your oratory.

MARCEL: I merely want the reader to reflect upon themselves.

OSCAR: I find that terrifyingly provocative.

MARCEL: Of course you do, Oscar. Shall I continue?

OSCAR: By all means, do continue.

MARCEL: In spite of her protest, my father continued dropping bits of madeleines under the table. Meanwhile, my mother continued with an attitude that took the face none could mistake for anything other than disapproval.

OSCAR: How well I know that face. Have you taken a good, hard look at Gertrude Stein lately?

MARCEL: *Merde.*

OSCAR: Merde, indeed. I will not tell her you said that.

MARCEL: I did not say that about her face. Shame on you. I meant it was your disapproval of Madame Stein that was *merde.*

OSCAR: Are you calling me *merde* directly to my face.

MARCEL: Not directly to your face. No.

WELLS: *(To the audience.)* You're still here. Good. Thank you. *Young.* I was young once. We all were, of course. When I was young. Once. There were visitors in the night. They would come and I would capture them. Put them down on paper and play with them. My friends. The night visitors. Kafka is my nemeses. He loves to threaten me. And he does a good job of it. All the others who have come and gone. So many. I capture them for another time. For instance ... *(He picks a sheet of paper from off the desk.)* ... allow me to read to you a bit of what I'm working on now. *(He reads.)* "OSCAR: How well I know that face. Have you taken a good, hard look at Gertrude Stein lately? MARCEL: Merde. OSCAR: Merde, indeed. I will not tell her you said that. MARCEL: I did not say that about her face. Shame on you. I meant it was your disapproval of Madame Stein that was merde. OSCAR: Are you calling me merde directly to my face. MARCEL: Not directly to your face. No."

WELLS: *(Continues. To the audience.)* You're still here. Good. Thank you. *Young.* I was young once. We all were, of course. When I was young. Once. There were visitors in the night. They would come and I would capture them. Put them down on paper and play with them. My friends. The night visitors. For instance ... *(He sits behind his desk and writes.)* "OSCAR: You can disarm the severest...." *(Returns to writing.)*

OSCAR: *(Continues sentence).* ...critic. Had the good doctor the good sense not to share his biscuit with the pussy, the good doctor would never have met with your mother's disapproval.

MARCEL: Precisely. You would do better to observe the feline.

OSCAR: I'm not a pussy watcher, Marcel, and neither are you! A positively demonic endeavor—to say the least. I'm sure there's a hidden meaning in there somewhere. I promise not to think about it. It can remain hidden for all I care. You probably never had a cat, anyway! You're making it up. I don't want to talk about it anymore. You're tiresome.

WELLS: *(Lifts his head and speaks directly to audience.)* Mister Proust can certainly be tiresome. Although, I find that to be the case when it is I who am the one who is tiresome. Things work that way, you know. If I am to be honest, I tend to project whatever it is I am feeling upon others. Perhaps we all do that, to one degree or another. I don't think we can ever hide our feelings completely. It would be like hiding ourselves completely. Mister Wilde, on the other hand, has always been the greatest of fun. He has given me countless hours of pleasure. However, as time goes by, I am finding it more and more difficult not to see that behind his mask lies a certain sadness. Behind the clever and quick wit there is a terrible pain...a dolefulness. Maybe that too has more to do with me than with the man himself. Sorry to butt in. I can't help my little asides. I'll try to keep them brief. Anyway, I guess it is now time for Alice's big entrance. *(He returns to his writing.)*

GERTRUDE: *(From other side of bookcase.)* Come along, Alice.

OSCAR: And speaking of something overblown and long-winded.

GERTRUDE: *(Entering through bookcase.)* Do watch out. Step lively. Oh Alice, don't be afraid to step on them. They're just clothes hangers for Pete's sake.

ALICE: *(Enters. She is weighted down like a packhorse with wine bottles, cheeses, long loaves of French bread and an over-sized picnic basket. Tripping, stumbling, exhausted and disheveled—she makes an uncertain announcement.)* Well ... here I am.

OSCAR: *(To MARCEL, referring to ALICE.).* That remains to be seen. I did see our darling *Mademoiselle* Gertie was totally empty-handed *(To ALICE, crossing to help her unload.)* Let me help you, dearest one. You must be positively exhausted. *(Gives GERTRUDE the evil-eye.)* From all that sitting, no doubt. One ought not sit too long. Tends to wear one out, you know. My, you are looking a bit jaded, aren't you, dearest one?

ALICE: Oh, I am, Oscar. I really, really am.

OSCAR: Of course you really, really are. What you need is help.

ALICE: Help?

OSCAR: *Help.* Gertie, did you hear that melancholic cry for help? Dear Alice has been sitting much too much. We wouldn't want our poor dear to come to a dreary conclusion.

GERTRUDE: *(Piqued.) Humph!*

OSCAR: *Humph?* Was that a *humph,* Gertie? Or was it gas?

GERTRUDE: *Humph!* You should sharpen that dull-wit of yours before you become yet more tedious than you already are.

OSCAR: You will not go unpunished, dear one.

(GERTRUDE flops into chair. OSCAR and ALICE unload and spread foodstuff on an upstage table or countertop, then busy themselves with opening wine bottles and preparing a tray of hors d'oeuvres. OSCAR peels the skin from off cucumbers and makes cucumber sandwiches. OSCAR and ALICE appear to be having a good time and every so often a giggle is heard. GERTRUDE, on the other hand, appears quite the contrary—she is not having a good time at all.)

MARCEL: *(Sitting on one of two large footstools on either side of GERTRUDE.)* You mustn't allow yourself to be provoked by one so devoid of interest, Gertrude. Remember why it is we are here.

GERTRUDE: I'd enjoy throttling him, Marcel—with my own two hands!

OSCAR: I'm ravished!

GERTRUDE: Good. Eat something.

OSCAR: I will in a minute, Gertie. *(To ALICE.)* You really should have come a bit sooner. Gertrude is positively chomping.

ALICE: Guillaume was supposed to have our auto repaired. But, he didn't … so we had to walk all the way.

OSCAR: In those shoes?

ALICE: Oh, yes.

OSCAR: Oh my. You should have come by taxi, Alice ... something with wheels.

ALICE: Gertrude? Gertrude? *(Having her attention.)* Why didn't we come by something with wheels?

GERTRUDE: *What?*

ALICE: A taxi.

GERTRUDE: Why on Earth would you want to take a taxi when we have a lovely auto, dearest Alice..

ALICE: But, it doesn't work.

GERTRUDE: Of course it works.

ALICE: But, it doesn't now.

GERTRUDE: Yet. here we are. When it is repaired it will.

ALICE: But, until it is, I think we ought to come and go by taxi.

GERTRUDE: Alice, one takes a taxi when one does not own an automobile. When one owns an automobile in need of service one walks.

ALICE: *Hmm.*Okay.

OSCAR: And so it is written. *Okay. (To GERTRUDE.)* Is that the consensus of your vast experience with things mechanical?

GERTRUDE: The proof of my experience has been convincingly demonstrated in the past.

OSCAR: You don't say? Water under the bridge. *(To ALICE.)* You see, that all goes to prove that one must learn to walk before one rides. *(To GERTRUDE.)* On the other hand, one should learn the mechanics for the thing one drives.

GERTRUDE: I know perfectly well the mechanics. However, Guillaume wanted to discover for himself that he knew nothing and—having made that discovery—his experience has totaled into an unremarkable sum. Do you drive, Oscar?

OSCAR: Certainly not! I have no gift for handling machinery. The fact is I am terrified of finding myself the victim of a head-on collision. Or, my muffler caught in the wheel like my dear friend Isodora. Quite painful, indeed, she said. Did you happen to catch Miss Duncan dance at Saki's little soiree?

GERTRUDE: No, Oscar, I did not. And, for the benefit of all concerned, I suggest you stay off the road—especially one shared by a booming carriage trade. Surely, you must agree.

OSCAR: I must and I do. In fact, I told Marcel a short while ago how it was I felt about this very matter.

MARCEL: Gertrude, hadn't we better give time to more important matters?

OSCAR: How one gets to where one has gotten is important, Marcel. The more thought I give to the matter, the more important it becomes.

MARCEL: Really?

OSCAR: Oh, yes. And the more important it becomes, the more attracted I am to the art of balloonery.

GERTRUDE: Indeed.

ALICE: What's balloonery?

OSCAR: It is a marvelous vehicle, dearheart. You see, generally, economy is the proof of a thing's worth. And though it is quite impossible for me to say, since I've never actually gone off in one, I am told that ballooneryists are of the consensus that efficient function can be achieved with merely an ample supply of hot air.

GERTRUDE: *Humph!*

OSCAR: *(To Gertrude)* And I raise you one. *(To Alice.)* Isn't that interesting?

ALICE: Oh, yes. Think of the time Gertrude could have saved not waiting for Guillaume to discover what he already plainly did not know.

OSCAR: Think of it.

ALICE: *(To GERTRUDE.)* Wouldn't you just love balloonery!. We'd never have to take a taxi and we'd never be in need of service. So, we'd never have to walk. Think of it. No need for wheels. Just think of it, Gertrude!

GERTRUDE: Alice, don't think of it! The world is confused enough. You're only making a spectacle of yourself for others to not know what to think.

OSCAR: She's got you there, Alice. Thoughtless of you not to think what others won't think of you soaring off into the ether.

ALICE: *(Apologetic.)* I guess you're right. Sometimes I just can't seem to help myself.

OSCAR: Of course you can't. Even if it feels good, my dear, you mustn't allow yourself a moment's pleasure without first consulting the great oracle of Baltimore, our own expatriate and sulfur-sniffing Gertrude Stein.

ALICE: Thank you, Oscar.

GERTRUDE: You are so kind.

OSCAR: Any time.

GERTRUDE: This is all too tedious for conscious appreciation. I know perfectly well the mechanics needed to keep a vehicle in proper working order. When Guillaume is satisfied with what little he knows, I'll make a few minor adjustments on the universal and tighten the suspension.

OSCAR: I've never been one for garage-talk.

GERTRUDE: Should anybody consider the efficacy of auto-ing versus the practicality of balloonery as it pertains to human life, somebody could wonder of the potential destructive capacity of a bird's beak. In fact, one should.

OSCAR: *(To GERTRUDE.)* You certainly have a distinctive knack for disproving what so many have proved by proof positive. Besides, the only thing more terrifying than a head-on collision or my neck snapped like poor Isodora's, is finding myself plummeting through midair.

MARCEL: May I add something of import to this exchange?

OSCAR: By all means. We've been hoping somebody would.

MARCEL: We are forgetting our purpose for being here. However or whatever it was that brought us here, or takes us back, is of little consequence.

OSCAR: That's easy for you to say. Alice here carried all the goodies.

ALICE: And then some.

MARCEL: *(To GERTRUDE.)* Why did you ask him here in the first place?

OSCAR: Really, Marcel! Come down from your tuffet!

MARCEL: *(Ignoring the last.)* Well?

GERTRUDE: Well, what?

MARCEL: Why did you ask him here in the first place?

GERTRUDE: I didn't. I never asked him here in the first place to this place nor, in the second place, to anyplace. I thought you did. Though I did think your judgment was suffering a terrible calamity. Perhaps, thought I, it was out of some sense of unspeakable brotherhood you asked him here. I wanted another genius. Certainly not that ... that Victorian viper.

OSCAR: *(To ALICE.)* She did? *(ALICE giggles.)* She didn't? *(Ibid.)* She did! *(ALICE whispers something into OSCAR'S ear. BOTH giggle.)*

GERTRUDE: Are we to wait all night before you and Alice are through with whatever it is you are doing?

OSCAR: Hurry it along, Alice, before she ravages us all. *(ALICE giggles. BOTH continue with the foodstuff.)*

GERTRUDE: *(Sotto voce.)* Viper.

WELLS: Viper. Period. I want to be a genius like Gertrude Stein! Where is my genius?

OSCAR: It speaks. *(To WELLS.)* Did you lose it? *(To GERTRUDE.)* Better keep your voice down, Gertie. You're confusing our dispirited scribe. He thinks you're a genius. Will false rumors never cease?*(Takes a glass of wine to WELLS, sets it on desk.)* Here you go. Oh, my! Don't you look a sight! *(Returns to ALICE who is sipping wine. Indicating WELLS.)* You see what sitting does? *(ALICE giggles.)* Alice, nobody likes a girl who titters in her wine. *(To GERTRUDE.)* Isn't that right, Gertrude?

WELLS: Right!

OSCAR: That's right. Write. Write your little heart out.

(OSCAR goes back to preparing the tray of foodstuff with ALICE and engages her in a silent conversation. Every so often a giggle is heard.)

GERTRUDE: *(To MARCEL. Sotto voce.)* Viper. I'll throttle him.

MARCEL: We are here to perform an inorcism. Remember Wells' condition.

GERTRUDE: You remember Wells' condition. My God, Marcel, you remember everything else!

MARCEL: You needn't misdirect your anger, *Mon ami.*

GERTRUDE: *Mon ami* your ass! Why did you ask Oscar here in the first place? Everywhere he goes he is bound to make a farce of it. Can you answer me that?

MARCEL: Answer you what?

GERTRUDE: Your remembrance of things past is not quite so good as we've all been led to believe. Why did you ask him here?

MARCEL: I distinctly remember asking you why it was you who did the asking.

GERTRUDE: Because it is I who is wanting for an answer.

MARCEL: And I am trying to give you one. I did not ask him here. I never asked hime here. Period.

GERTRUDE: You didn't?

MARCEL: I didn't. I was sure I had made myself clear on that point.

GERTRUDE: You didn't.

OSCAR: *(To ALICE.)* She did!

MARCEL: *(To GERTRUDE.)* I certainly did…

OSCAR: *(To ALICE.)* She didn't?

MARCEL: *(To GERTRUDE.)* …earlier when asking why you asked Oscar here in the first place.

GERTRUDE: You did?

MARCEL: I did.

GERTRUDE: *(Remembering.)* You did! I do recall you did.

MARCEL: Then, what is the answer, I wonder.

GERTRUDE: And the question is who, since we know it was neither you nor I who did.

MARCEL: I know.

GERTRUDE: You do?

MARCEL: I don't. I mean, I know who didn't.

OSCAR: *(To ALICE.)* She didn't. *(ALICE sips wine and giggles.)*

GERTRUDE: Well, who did?

MARCEL: Alice?

ALICE: *(Giggling.)* She didn't!

GERTRUDE: It could not have been Alice, Marcel. I never told Alice where we were going until we got here.

OSCAR: *(To ALICE.)* She didn't?

ALICE: Not a word.

MARCEL: Then who?

ALICE: *(With a negative nod to OSCAR.)* She didn't.

GERTRUDE: Good question. Everybody knows anybody who would ask Oscar anywhere must have deliberate intentions of doing subversion.

MARCEL: You mean …

GERTRUDE: I do.

OSCAR: *(To ALICE.)* She did.

GERTRUDE: I understand somebody has undertaken the overthrow of this undertaking! There is one who does not want this inorcism to take place.

MARCEL: But who? And why?

WELLS: Kafka ...

GERTRUDE: I mean to find this out.

(GERTRUDE and MARCEL pay no attention to WELLS as they are far too absorbed with themselves at present.)

MARCEL: A discouraging moment.

WELLS: Kafka ...

GERTRUDE: A dark foreboding.

OSCAR: *(Turns from what he is doing and answers WELLS as though a game had been signaled to begin.)* Kafka! *(To ALICE.)* Did you know that in Czechoslovakian Kafka means Raven?

ALICE: News to me. *(A beat.)* Sapsucker.

WELLS: Kafka...

GERTRUDE: Who?

MARCEL: Who?

OSCAR: Hoot owl!

GERTRUDE: Let us think.

WELLS: Kafka ...

OSCAR: *(Nudges ALICE.)* Well?

ALICE: *Umm* …titmouse!

OSCAR: Good, Alice. Toucan!

WELLS: Kafka!

ALICE: *Umm* …cuckoo!

OSCAR: Loon!

WELLS: Kafka!

ALICE: Cockatoo!

OSCAR: Bobwhite!

ALICE: Redpole!

OSCAR: You're out of turn, Alice.

WELLS: Kafka.

OSCAR: Now, Alice.

ALICE: Magpie!

GERTRUDE: *(Suddenly aware of the goings-on.)* What do you two think you are doing?

OSCAR: *(To ALICE.)* What do you think? *(ALICE shrugs and giggles.)*

WELLS: Kafka!

OSCAR: Nuthatch!

GERTRUDE: WHAT IS THIS?

OSCAR: Bird calling?

GERTRUDE: Well stop it! Marcel and I are trying to think!

OSCAR: Then try you must.

WELLS: Kafka!

OSCAR: *(To WELLS.)* Quiet. You're ruffling Gertie's feathers. *(Sneaks one in.)* Albatross.

GERTRUDE: Have you quite finished with your parlor game, Oscar?

OSCAR: *(Nudges ALICE.)* Alice, have you learned some Czechoslovakian today? *(ALICE nods a fearful "yes.")* Quite finished, Gertie.

GERTRUDE: *(Turning back to MARCEL who is resting his chin in his hand and looking thoroughly bored with everything. Referring to OSCAR.)* Bird brain.

OSCAR: Did you say something, Gertie?

GERTRUDE: Nothing! I said nothing!

OSCAR: That's what I thought, too ...and you're very good at that. *(To ALICE.)* You see, my dear, she didn't. *(Goes back to what he was doing. ALICE is seen sipping wine more than doing anything else.)*

GERTRUDE: *(To MARCEL.)* He'd turn Medea into a farce!

MARCEL: I thought he had. *(Remembering.)* We had a minor incident while you were gone looking for Alice. Did you happen to notice the door?

GERTRUDE: *(Takes note.)* Oh, are we keeping somebody in or out?

MARCEL: Out. After you left there was a knocking so, naturally, at first we thought it was Alice and the inorcist. I mean, you and Alice.

GERTRUDE: Do you mean you and Oscar thought it was Alice and I or do you mean you thought it was me and Alice?

MARCEL: I knew it wasn't.

GERTRUDE: Naturally it was not because it could not have been Alice nor could it have been me, unless you were mistaken. You should have thought better and known we would have known better than to use that door. Well anyway, who was it?

MARCEL: A cockroach exterminator.

GERTRUDE: *Ah* ...the exterminator.

MARCEL: Well, yes and no. It was more cockroach than exterminator.

GERTRUDE: What are you saying?

MARCEL: It was a cockroach disguised as an exterminator who knocked on the door.

GERTRUDE: A disguised cockroach? Knocked on the door?

MARCEL: It was a very big cockroach. Nearly six feet.

GERTRUDE: Precisely. Six feet. Spiders, I believe, have eight.

MARCEL: No, no, no. It stood nearly six feet tall.

GERTRUDE: Oh, I see. That is something altogether different, isn't it? Well what did it want?

MARCEL: Wells.

GERTRUDE: If that is what it came for it never got what it wanted.

MARCEL: No. But it was a close encounter. Had Mister Wells not been so quick to shut the door in time who could say what might have happened?

GERTRUDE: Not a very fair question if you are asking me. I wasn't here.

OSCAR: *(Aside.)* Tell me about it.

MARCEL: I'll tell you, it did give us cause for more than a bit of alarm.

GERTRUDE: It must. Don't you think it rather odd that Wells would open the door?

MARCEL: It needn't. It doesn't. He didn't.

GERTRUDE: He didn't?

MARCEL: There's something you should know.

GERTRUDE: *(Bracing for the worst.)* Then give it to me quickly.

MARCEL: *(He does.)* It was Oscar who opened the door and almost let in the exterminating cockroach!

(ALICE is approaching with a tray of hors d'oeuvers—cheeses, crackers, cakes, cucumber sandwiches, etc.)

GERTRUDE: OH ...OH ...OH!   WORSE THAN I THOUGHT!

OSCAR: Nothing's that bad, Gertrude.

ALICE: *(Extending tray to GERTRUDE.)* But you didn't even taste them yet. Oscar thought everything looked delicious.

GERTRUDE: Who cares what Oscar thought?

OSCAR: *(While bringing four glasses of wine and serving them.)* Someone must, Gertie.

(GERTRUDE braces herself. She is fit to kill.)

OSCAR: *(Con't.)* In fact, I'm sure of it. I seem to remember someone who did, but I was never too sure about him. And then of course there was ... *(To MARCEL, indicating wine.)* Vin rosé ...or is it *vin ordinaire?* Anyway, it's French. You'll love it! *(Hands MARCEL a bottle cork.)* Here's more cork for you, my dear. I know you are a man of discreet fetishes. I hope it helps put a smile on your face. No, they had to drag that one away. Poor boy. Poor, sweet, very stupid boy. And screaming like a maniac. Then he was, wasn't he? He had an enormous—appetite. Got big as a house, he did ... from that appetite. *(Offering wine to ALICE.)* Pity. We seem to be all out of cooking sherry, *Mon cheri.* *(ALICE giggles.)* What a pity. We never heard from that one again. *(About to offer GERTRUDE a glass.)* Dreadful sight it was ... watching that boy get carried away. And the scandal it caused! But that's another story. Well, there must have been someone, Gertie. I'm sure I'll think of one who did, or does, or is willing to give some consideration to what I think—or thought.

GERTRUDE: *(Takes wine. Booms.)* DULLARD!

ALICE: *(Sitting on the other footstool beside GERTRUDE. Sheepishly speaks:)* No, he's not, Gertrude.

OSCAR: There you go, Gertie. Someone cares what Oscar thinks.

GERTRUDE: *(Sotto voce.)* Dullard.

OSCAR: Come along, Alice. Gertrude is beginning to repeat herself. Besides, one must not sit too long.

GERTRUDE: *(Ibid.)* Dullard.

OSCAR: Marcel?

MARCEL: *(Coolly cautious.)* Oui?

OSCAR: Surely, you must have heard of Dr. Peter Mark Roget who wrote a simply marvelous book just filled with all sorts of marvelously simple synonymy.

MARCEL: Is that a question?

OSCAR: It could be. Would you like it to be?

GERTRUDE: Dullard.

OSCAR: *(Continues to MARCEL.)* There! You see? Gertrude may get herself a reputation for repetition. *(GERTRUDE snarls.)* Now, let me see. *(A thoughtful pause.)* A dullard is a dolt ...is a dunce ...is a donkey ...is an ass ...is ...

MARCEL: *(Irritated. Interrupts.)* Cul ennuyeux stupide

OSCAR: That's the spirit! You help save Gertie's reputation.

GERTRUDE: *Humph!*

OSCAR: Ever have a cucumber sandwich, Alice?

ALICE: *(Giggles.)* I don't think so.

OSCAR: You have been sitting far too long. Try one, my dear.

ALICE: *(Takes a cucumber sandwich from off the tray and begins nibbling while rising and going for an opened bottle of wine.)* This is simply delicious! Gertrude, you really must give Oscar's cucumber sandwiches a try. I've never tasted anything quite so—delicious.

GERTRUDE: *(Scoffs.)* Delicious.

ALICE: Yes—delicious. *(Returns to footstool with bottle, sits and refills her glass.)*

OSCAR: Exactly what I thought.

GERTRUDE: *(Beside herself.)* Oscar, what are you doing here?

OSCAR: Marcel said I was to help the inorcist.

GERTRUDE: He did?

MARCEL: *(Resigned)* I did.

(ALICE giggles. GERTRUDE kicks her. ALICE drinks. GERTRUDE sighs.)

OSCAR: *(To GERTRUDE.)* So are you going to tell me?

GERTRUDE: Tell you what?

OSCAR: What I am to do.

GERTRUDE: First you tell me what you are doing here!

OSCAR: Being the perfect host. Serving wine. Making sandwiches. I didn't see you lifting a finger all night. Oh ... and while you were gone looking for our dear little Alice, Marcel told a most remarkable story. All about a cookie-eating cat and a green plum-eating Marcel. Regurgitated for days!

ALICE: The plum?

OSCAR: Marcel. However, the cat, being quite clever, did not. Seems the Proust household wasn't all it was cracked up to be. Don't you just love a good story, Gertie?

GERTRUDE: Gertrude! And Gertrude deplores stories! Good or otherwise!

OSCAR: *(To ALICE.)* Good heavens! Is that true?

ALICE: Oh yes. Gertrude deplores. She likes faces.

OSCAR: I know exactly what you mean. I've never been able to deny a pretty face, either.

ALICE: Have I a pretty face?

GERTRUDE: Alice! *(Kicks ALICE.)* Sit!

ALICE: I am.

GERTRUDE: In silence.

ALICE: *(Guzzles some wine. Timidly.)* Gertrude, you always said you liked faces.

GERTRUDE: Yes, Alice. Faces. Faces with something new and something different seen in every line wrinkling and molding their character into something more behind those lines than just another story. Faces don't tell stories ... they are stories. That is the difference between fiction and autobiography; between story and faces. And that is the difference between a genius, such as myself, and that clever overgrown imp of a sandwich maker Oscar Wilde!

ALICE: *(Disturbed.)* Oscar's not a genius?

GERTRUDE: Certainly not! He's a clever sandwich maker!

MARCEL: Stay calm, Gertrude. He is not worth the bother. You will only get out of sorts and make yourself sick like you did over that ungrateful Hemingway creature.

GERTRUDE: *(Snaps.)* SANDWICH MAKER!

OSCAR: You did it. Now you have done it. You have finally gone and done what you wanted to do and you have done it.

GERTRUDE: Marcel, do you know what he is talking about?

MARCEL: I have long since forfeited all hope.

GERTRUDE: What is your problem, Oscar?

OSCAR: You call yourself a genius and then you have the colossal audacity to call me a "sandwich maker!"

GERTRUDE: I call myself a genius because a genius I am. And, I am well aware that you have always been the perfect model of blameless mediocrity ...

ALICE: *(Interrupts.)* I have something to say.

GERTRUDE: Save it, Alice! Then you'll always have something to say.

OSCAR: Good advice, Gertie. You should take that advice yourself. By the time you reach old age you'll have yourself a whole short story.

GERTRUDE: Sandwich maker!

OSCAR: You've done it again! You have an exceptionally superior, superfluous quality for doing it again!

GERTRUDE: I refuse to listen to your senseless drawing room theatrics and your mindless parlor games anymore.

OSCAR: Why? Because you're a self-dubbed genius who thinks that gives her the privilege to discredit my well-made cucumber sandwiches? A genius or not, Gertrude, nobody but another genius would know enough to give you the recognition you so brazenly demand, or maybe only desire as some lonely wanton beast. Given the nature of the beast, one genius is not about to acknowledge another as being one also; it tends to diminish ones sense of magnitude. So, as not to lessen the importance of being genuine, genii, generally speaking, gravitate towards obscurity. However, being obscure for obscurity's sake does not now nor will it ever make one a genius! Besides—as genii go—you, Miss Stein, are the most splendidly ineffective.

GERTRUDE: How dare you—

OSCAR: I dare because I speak truth.

ALICE: I have something to say.

OSCAR: Out with it, Alice. But don't spend all your life's savings in one sentence.

ALICE: I don't mind if you're not a genius, Oscar. I think your sandwiches are perfectly delicious. *(She sees that she has everybody's attention and continues nervously.)* Well ... I guess that is all I have to say. And, thank you. *(Bites into cucumber sandwich and chews while making "yummy" sounds.)*

GERTRUDE: Who cares! A sandwich maker is a sandwich maker is a sandwich maker!

OSCAR: *Ah,* but that was not what you meant! So, allow me to assure you that under these lovely slices of cucumber, *(Holds up a slice.)*, right down to where the bread is giving them their support. *(Examines, sniffs, takes a bite.)* Delicious. And should you find yourself one day examining that all-supportive bread—the bedrock upon which rests the savory delights of heavenly ambrosia—you could find it a bedazzling experience to discover that aside from it being well made, *(Holding up a piece of crust.)*, there is a great deal more to digest than just its outer crust! *(Pops the crust into his mouth.)* And, Gertrude, as we all know, it is often difficult to chew and sometimes impossible to swallow.

GERTRUDE: *(After a pause.)* Thank you so much for your gastronomical interlude. I am sure you found yourself quite profound. *Obscurest! Insignificant! Pompous oaf!*

OSCAR: Indeed. I shall think of those words as cud for thought.

WELLS: *(Screams.)* Franz Kafka!

MARCEL: *(Startled. Jumps)* Ahhhhhhhhhhhhhh! Oh, God! He did it
again!

GERTRUDE: Calm yourself, Marcel, and sit down!

WELLS: Satan. The Devil. God. Kafka. Who?

OSCAR: I think he's trying to communicate.

GERTRUDE: Aren't we all? Only some of us know how to do it better than others.

OSCAR: I imagine.

GERTRUDE: And I imagine the door opened itself while I was gone looking for Alice.

OSCAR: The door? We're back to that, are we? Well, to tell you the truth, Gertrude, you needn't imagine anything because it was I who opened the door.

GERTRUDE: I know.

OSCAR: Then why did you ask?

GERTRUDE: It is your reason for opening the door that occupies my immediate interest. What was your reasoning? You do have a reason, don't you?

OSCAR: There was a knocking.

GERTRUDE: So?

OSCAR: So? Is that not reason enough?

GERTRUDE: No, it is not. Answer every knock and one day you will find yourself standing vis-à-vis a do-harm.

OSCAR: Vis-à-vis?

ALICE: A do-harm?

GERTRUDE: *(To ALICE.)* Sit!

OSCAR: I couldn't stop myself. Nobody knocks on my door anymore.

GERTRUDE: Oscar, if anybody knocked on your door they'd be too late!

MARCEL: Speaking of being too late—

GERTRUDE: Right you are, Marcel. We had better hurry along with the inorcism or else the entire process could reverse itself.

OSCAR: Really?

GERTRUDE: One could find oneself inside a body in which one does not belong; finding oneself a prisoner of circumstance and then....

ALICE: *(While going for another bottle of wine.)* And then what, Gertrude?

GERTRUDE: And then what what, Alice?

ALICE: Suppose one should find oneself inside a body one doesn't belong in as the process reverses itself because we didn't hurry along with the inorcism and one finds oneself a prisoner of ...a prisoner of—

GERTRUDE: Circumstance. A prisoner of circumstance.

ALICE: *(Returning with a full bottle of wine.)* Yes, circumstance. Suppose one finds oneself a prisoner to it. Then what?

GERTRUDE: Then it is no longer our affair.

(WELLS crosses to window and leans out. He seems to be struggling with something immediately below the window's sill.)

ALICE: Whose affair is it?

GERTRUDE: *(Losing patience.)* It is somebody else's, Alice.

ALICE: Whose? If it is not our affair, then whose affair is it?

GERTRUDE: It's the Pope's!

OSCAR: The Pope is having an affair?

ALICE: The Pope? Oh my God!

OSCAR: *(Catches a glimpse of WELLS struggling with what can now clearly be seen as KAFKA, still a cockroach, trying to pull him out of the window.)* What the devil?

GERTRUDE: No! The Pope is not having an affair! The Pope doesn't concern himself with cases of dispossession and we shouldn't concern ourselves with the contrary. Now, unless we wish to be of concern to the Pope, we had better hurry along with what's-his-face's inorcism.

WELLS: *Help! Help!*

OSCAR: *(Dividing his attention between what is happening at the window and the conversation taking place.)* What's-his-face's? Small wonder the poor soul is alienated. *(Steals another look towards window.)* What do you guess causes alienation?

GERTRUDE: Consciousness, Oscar. Consciousness.

WELLS: *Help! Help!*

OSCAR: One would think not being conscious.

GERTRUDE: One shouldn't, and not being conscious, one couldn't.

OSCAR: The poor alienated soul.

WELLS: *Help!*

MARCEL: He's not alienated. Wells is in danger of becoming dispossessed. There's a world of difference. One might say that he feels meaningless, deserted and without purpose.

WELLS: *(Still fighting off KAFKA.) Beelzebub!*

MARCEL: He experiences a feeling of nothingness.

GERTRUDE: *(Matter-of-factly.)* The real tragedy is that the one who is dispossessed generally projects his emptiness on the world at large. Since most find themselves in others, when finding nothing in others is—quite naturally—to experience a severely negative sensation. You might say he sees others as dead men walking, wandering aimlessly about. And, he questions whether or not he could be one, himself.

WELLS: Does anyone hear me? *Help!*

OSCAR: Interesting. *(Glancing towards the window.)* What do you say when all that you have worked for—the purpose of our little gathering—is about to fly out the window?

GERTRUDE: I would say if you don't have a firm grasp on the matter at hand you've bitten off more than you can chew.

OSCAR: Would you really? *(Takes another glance towards the window. WELLS is dangling half out and is desperately trying to fight off KAFKA who continues trying to pull him out altogether.)* The poor devil. I'd say, what a tragedy.

MARCEL: It isn't a tragedy, Oscar. In fact, there's nothing tragic about it.

ALICE: If the Pope wants to have an affair, I say let him have it. *(She's obviously had her limit of wine.)* For God's sake let him have his affairs.

OSCAR: If this isn't a tragedy, I don't know what is. *(Glances towards window.)* What story are we on?

GERTRUDE: I don't follow.

OSCAR: Here, in The Venus Arms, are we very high up?

WELLS: *Help!*

GERTRUDE: The top floor, I believe.

OSCAR: Then we have a bit of a sticky situation.

GERTRUDE: You're wasting our time. What is it?

OSCAR: A very dubious looking character out on the ledge appears to want a rather nasty end to the subject of our inorcism.

GERTRUDE: You're not making any sense. *(Turns and sees what is going on at the window.)* WHAT IS THIS?

WELLS: *Help!*

(ALICE, GERTRUDE, and MARCEL jump to their feet. OSCAR remains sitting and pops a cucumber sandwich into his mouth. MARCEL faints. GERTRUDE rushes to the

window to help WELLS free himself from KAFKA the cockroach. ALICE screams!)

OSCAR: *(Eating a cucumber sandwich. Aside.)* Consciousness is it?

BLACK OUT.

End Scene 2

Scene 3—*the metamorphosis*

A short while later.

AT RISE: WELLS is back at his desk, writing. ALICE is sitting on the floor with several wine bottles trying to find one with something still in it; she is obviously quite tipsy. OSCAR is still where he was last seen and he is eating a cucumber sandwich. MARCEL is looking weak.

GERTRUDE: *(Returning from window.)* What a drama!

MARCEL: *(Shaken.)* Never. The last. Never again. I haven't the strength for this sort of thing. Oh, Gertrude, I think I'm dying. I'm dying, Gertrude. I'm dying!

GERTRUDE: Again?

OSCAR: You're already dead, Marcel. Or have you forgotten?

MARCEL: But, I'm still here.

OSCAR: Then what are you worried about? When you're not still here is when there'll be plenty of time to worry.

MARCEL: I think I'm losing my mind.

OSCAR: Well, that's a possibility. Somewhere along Swann's Way, I should imagine. To be possessed or to be dispossessed cannot compare to the thrill of being self-possessed.

MARCEL: *(With vengeance.)* You ... you ... you pompous *provocateur!*

OSCAR: *(Shocked.)* Indeed.

MARCEL: Who do you think you are? What right have you to come here and make a mockery of what you obviously know nothing about? *(To ALICE, equally hostile.)* And you ... you simple sow ...

GERTRUDE: *(Rising to it—angered.)* Marcel, unless you are really dying and intend doing it within the next minute, you would do best to recover quickly from this amnesia you appear to be suffering.

WELLS: *(To audience.)* Kafka nearly killed me.

MARCEL: I'm not suffering from amnesia.

GERTRUDE: You're not? How else can you explain your forgetting your place?

MARCEL: I didn't forget. *(Thinks better of it.)* I seem to have forgotten.

GERTRUDE: Good. Glad to see you've made a speedy recovery.

ALICE: Did he mean, "cow?" *(She rises from the floor with bottle and glass in hand, sits on the footstool, pours herself another glass of wine.)* Because if he did I'll ... I'll—*(Too drunk to continue.)*

OSCAR: And you'd be in your right if you did, Alice.

MARCEL: I don't know what came over me.

OSCAR: A vision of nothingness—of existence without meaning? Cramps? Heartburn? A boil on the arse?

MARCEL: *(A mean look at OSCAR, before a more gentle, contrite demeanor toward GERTRUDE.)* I was confused. Will you ever forgive me, *Mon ami?*

GERTRUDE: I do not remember you doing anything for which you need to be forgiven. Do you, *Mon ami?*

MARCEL: *(After a pause.)* No. I must not have been myself.

ALICE: If you're dying I guess it doesn't really matter who you are—or were.

OSCAR: *Ah.* I heard a little fox in the tender vines.

GERTRUDE: He isn't dying, Alice. At least, not at the moment.

ALICE: That's good news ... for Marcel. *(Pause to look around the room.)* Then who is?

GERTRUDE: Everybody.

ALICE: Everybody is dying? *(Puzzles, then lifts her glass in a toast.)* Well, that's life! *(Chug-a-lugs the wine.)*

OSCAR: Alice, that wine should be of so rare a vintage.

WELLS: *(To audience.)* Night visitors. Kafka wants to possess me all to himself. He is my nemesis. My Professor Moriarty. My demon. Night visitors make him angry. He hates people, but that's because he's jealous. He's jealous because he's not one. I checked into The Venus Arms for inspiration. Without visitors in the night there would be no inspiration come daylight. They bring it to me. They give me something to think about—to write about. So, Kafka is getting a writ of dispossession. Afraid my thoughts will reach the others; confuse and contaminate their thinking. I won't leave. Not until my work is done. He is the king of petty devils and I will beat him. *(Goes back to writing.)*

MARCEL: Oscar?

OSCAR: Yes, Marcel?

MARCEL: I want you to know ... in all the excitement ... I never really meant to ... I mean I regret ....

OSCAR: Frog feet! Don't wither on the vine, my dear. We all regret ... regret that we can't know everything we say. Perhaps after we're through with this bit of business here—I know a fabulous hotel in Morocco where we can drown ourselves in Absinthe and ruddy young ....

GERTRUDE: *(Interrupts. To OSCAR.)* Why? Why don't you know everything you say?

OSCAR: Because I say so much, my dear.

GERTRUDE: You say so much of what?

OSCAR: So much.

GERTRUDE: So what!

ALICE: *(To herself.)* So what? Lots and lots of Popes had affairs.

GERTRUDE: Alice, this isn't the time.

ALICE: You said it was the Pope's affair. *(Belches.)*

MARCEL: Disgusting.

ALICE: I know. I read all about it. Upside down. In a pit. Fire licking their feet. How do you suppose they got upside down? *(No reply.)* I don't know either, but there they were—all those upside down Popes in a pit. Isn't that peculiar? *(No reply.)* And you know what else? *(GERTRUDE, MARCEL and OSCAR are speechless. Each looks to the other to say something.)* Well? Know what else?

GERTRUDE: *(Concerned.)* You have become very tired, Alice.

ALICE: Nope! I am very, very disgusted. *(Swaying sideways.)* I read all about them ... upside down in a ... a ....

OSCAR: Pit?

ALICE: Right! In a pit! I read a little Dante.

GERTRUDE: You read a little what?

ALICE: Dante. I read a little ... *(Hiccups.)* ... Dante.

GERTRUDE: Oh, my poor Alice. I knew someday something like this would happen.

MARCEL: I read some Dante once.

OSCAR: Did you now?

MARCEL: Oh, yes. The Italians have such a poetic sense for earthly matters, and the torment of men's souls.

OSCAR: All that pasta, no doubt, and all those statues.

MARCEL: Quite so. We French have always been so much more cerebral.

OSCAR: *Snails.* They go right to the brain. *(To ALICE.)* One shouldn't read perfect strangers. There's no telling where one could be led.

ALICE: It was Hell, Oscar. That's where they put ... put ... put ....

OSCAR: My dear, if you can't get it going, don't begin with a putsch.

ALICE: What's ... *putsch?*

OSCAR: Humpty Dumpty falling from the window ledge of The Venus Arms—with a little outside assistance.

ALICE: Oh—

OSCAR: *(To GERTRUDE.)* Who was that strange being? One would think closing the door in his face the first time would have sent a clear and irrefutable message.

WELLS: *(Looks up from his writing. Speaks more to himself than to anyone else.)* I have a message for you. Do you hear me? You can lead Humpty Dumpty into Hell, but you can't hang him in a pit! It's irrefutable! You will never get what you come for. I will not make a bargain with you or any other. Never and never again. Nevermore. That strange being is Franz Kafka!.

OSCAR: He reads a little of everything, a lot.

ALICE: So does Gertrude.

OSCAR: Does she now?

ALICE: Yes, most of it to Pablo.

OSCAR: *(To GERTRUDE.)* You do? While Alice reads a little Dante?

ALICE: Well, it's more fun than reading Pablo the funny papers.

WELLS: *(Staring at his night visitors.)* People! There's nobody in you to make you work. Yet, here you come as the dead to wander through the fog of the streets as mere projections, background to your own story. The subjects of mine.

GERTRUDE: *(Crossing to WELLS.)* Enough is enough. You are going to sit there and write something constructive and stop acting like a ninny!

WELLS: *(Writing.)* You are going to sit and write something constructive and stop acting like a ninny!

GERTRUDE: I am going to sit and write something constructive and stop acting like a ninny.

OSCAR: That will be a first.

WELLS: *I am.*

GERTRUDE: Thank you.

ALICE: Hump-tee Dump-tee. *(She giggles.)*

GERTRUDE: *(Returning.)* Much worse than I thought. Much worse. Still, a most interesting case. *(To MARCEL.)* You know, not every dispossession affords one such an opportunity to examine what usually remains buried deep beneath the surface.

MARCEL: How true. He is a rare specimen.

OSCAR: *(Aside.)* I had a frog once.

GERTRUDE: *(To MARCEL.)* He is indeed. Not often are we summoned to a task of such significance and as you well know I love a challenge.

OSCAR: *(Ibid.)* I loved that frog. We got on so famously— the frog and I.

GERTRUDE: *And me.*

OSCAR: You had a frog? *(GERTRUDE humphs.)*

MARCEL: Learning is always worth the effort.

GERTRUDE: Precisely. Provided we are endowed with the spirit to follow the quest and the ability to rise to the occasion.

MARCEL: Only you could have said it so *précisément*.

OSCAR: *(Ibid.)* Until the day came when I decided to get to know him better.

GERTRUDE: Genius is but a tool, Marcel. It is my hands around the tool of genius that so many so much admire.

MARCEL: In your hands the tool of genius is but putty.

OSCAR: *(Aside.)* I won't even go there. Anyway, in an effort to explore this loving relationship with my frog to the very paramount of its pinnacle, I took that poor little creature ... *(GERTRUDE and MARCEL are now aware of OSCAR speaking. They listen.)* ...by its green, leathery neck, and not knowing what I had in mind, he croaked his last croak loving me with those big watery, froggy eyes. I was not even vaguely conscious of any knowledge of how this interest to explore our loving relationship would end with my bludgeoning him. With something scientific, as I recall. One, two, three, squish! It was over. Finished. But, who's the wiser, I ask you? Who is the wiser?

ALICE: I'm going to be sick.

OSCAR: No, you're not. Just tell yourself you will only go as far as nausea and no further.

MARCEL: Oh, my God.

OSCAR: My exact words and I have never dissected a frog since. Much less, eaten one.

GERTRUDE: Oh, my God.

OSCAR: Alice, care to join the divine chorus?

ALICE: *Huh?*

MARCEL: I think we had better hurry and finish what we came here to do.

OSCAR: Humpty Dumpty's inorcism, wasn't it?

GERTRUDE: Would you rather we left Humpty Dumpty as we found him?

OSCAR: Of course not, but I would like to know the reason he was found in that condition. What causes a body to suddenly up and empty out?

MARCEL: What does that matter to Humpty Dumpty? All that matters to him is that he is put back together again— back straddling the wall, in one piece and in back in the flux of things.

OSCAR: If we know the reason for Wells' condition we may then be able to foresee any future reoccurrence.

MARCEL: Impossible. One never knows what choices he will make. After the inorcism he will be free to make the choices that will create his history, his past and his future.

OSCAR: You're quickly becoming as obscure as Gertie. What I want to know is the cause of Wells' condition.

GERTRUDE: The cause? There is only one cause and that cause is essential and primal. It is the force behind creation itself. It is that pristine and vital cause which creates and is what is created. It is the force deep within that connects all of life to a single Animator that some call God and what others call themselves.

OSCAR: *(After a pause.)* My dear Gertrude Stein, I am in awe. I may never call you Gertie, again.

GERTRUDE: Good idea.

ALICE: *(Pops up.)* I may!

GERTRUDE: Of course, my dear Alice, you may call me whatever you fancy.

ALICE: You mean ... Baby Woojums?

GERTRUDE: *(Touching ALICE in some gentle way.)* Yes, Mama Woojums, I'm here watching over you. You go to sleep and Baby Woojums will wake you when it is all over.

ALICE: All over?

GERTRUDE: *Shhh ... (ALICE appears to have gone to sleep.)*

OSCAR: You do that so well, Baby Woojums.

GERTRUDE: Careful, Oscar. Gertrude does it by being very, very careful.

OSCAR: Apparently.

(There is a strange CLICKING SOUND coming from the adjoining bedroom.)

MARCEL: What the—Gertrude, I think we are about to have company.

GERTRUDE: Oh, no. The bedroom! Did anybody think to check the bedroom window?

(The CLICKING SOUND of our giant cockroach continues. There is a sense of panic in the atmosphere. GERTRUDE jumps up and is followed by MARCEL. They seem to be looking for something.)

OSCAR: What's going on? You two are beginning to frighten me.

WELLS: *Beelzebub! He's coming!*

GERTRUDE: Quick! We need a hiding place!

OSCAR: *(Panics. Runs around the room and comes to an armoire and opens the door.)* An armoire! I've always found armoires a safe place! God knows I spent many a day in one of these!

MARCEL: Oh, Gertrude. What are we going to do?

OSCAR: Care to join me in the armoire? *(Enters the armoire and closes the door behind him.)*

GERTRUDE: Quickly! We've got to hide the playwright!

MARCEL: Where? Where?

GERTRUDE: *(Rushing over to WELLS.)* I don't know where! First we've got to shut him up. Give me something to gag him with. *Quick! Quick!*

MARCEL: *What? What?*

(In a panic, MARCEL grabs a handful of cucumber sandwiches and hands them to GERTRUDE.)

GERTRUDE: What is this?

MARCEL: Cucumber sandwiches.

WELLS: I'll beat you yet, Beelzebub! *(GERTRUDE shoves the cucumber sandwiches into Wells' mouth.)* Bee...arghhh.

(The CLICKING SOUND of the cockroach KAFKA continues in the next room. GERTRUDE grabs WELLS and frantically leads him around the room looking for a hiding place. MARCEL jumps upon one of the footstools and covers his eyes with his hands. ALICE is passed out on the floor.)

GERTRUDE: *(Opens the armoire door. OSCAR screams.)* Shut up!*(Pushes WELLS into the armoire with OSCAR.)* And stay shut up. *(Slams door shut. Runs over to MARCEL and yanks him from off the footstool and leads him to the armoire. She attempts to open the door but it will not open.)* Oscar?

OSCAR: *(From inside the armoire.)* Yes?

GERTRUDE: Open this door, please.

OSCAR: *(Ibid.)* No.

GERTRUDE: Oscar.

OSCAR: I will not be intimidated. There's no room. Go someplace else.

MARCEL: We're going to be trapped like rats, Gertrude. We'll never get out of here now. I knew it! I just knew it!

GERTRUDE: Oh, shut up, Marcel! Oscar, open this door right now or Reading Gaol will have seemed like a weekend in the country compared to what I may do to you. Have I made myself clear?

OSCAR: *(Slowly opening the door.)* Crystal.

(GERTRUDE pushes MARCEL into the armoire and follows him in, closing the door behind her. There is SILENCE and then the SILENCE is broken by the SOUND of the CLICKING—and the SOUND of ALICE snoring. Suddenly, the armoire door swings open and GERTRUDE, MARCEL and OSCAR run on tiptoes to ALICE and drag her back into the armoire with them. The CLICKING SOUND grows louder until KAFKA, still a cockroach, ENTERS. KAFKA searches about the room and appears quite angry to discover he cannot find WELLS. He then crosses to the door that opens in from the hallway and removes the obstruction that was placed there to keep him out. KAFKA then crosses to the tray of cucumber sandwiches and begins eating while making loud "yummy'" sounds. The armoire door slowly opens and GERTRUDE, MARCEL and OSCAR poke their heads out to see what KAFKA is up to.)

MARCEL: *(Whispers.)* Trapped like rats.

GERTRUDE: *Shhh.*

OSCAR: Look at that! The bug is eating all my sandwiches.

GERTRUDE & MARCEL: *Shhh.*

GERTRUDE: *(Whispers.)* We've got to get him out of here.

MARCEL: *(Ibid.)* How?

GERTRUDE: Follow me.

(Like a conga line on tiptoe, GERTRUDE followed by MARCEL and OSCAR sneak out of the armoire and quietly cross behind KAFKA toward the bedroom. When they reach the bedroom door KAFKA rises causing them to make a quick maneuver into the bedroom and quickly close the door

behind them. KAFKA crosses to get a bottle of wine and returns to the cucumber sandwiches, eating and drinking and making grotesque "yummy" sounds. The bedroom door slowly opens and GERTRUDE, MARCEL and OSCAR stick their heads out while at the same time the armoire door slowly opens and ALICE staggers out looking lost and confused. GERTRUDE darts out of the bedroom on tiptoe and quickly crosses to ALICE in time to catch her as she faints and then drags her back into the armoire, closing the door. MARCEL and OSCAR withdraw back into the bedroom closing the door behind them. KAFKA starts sniffing the air as if smelling something foul. He rises, crosses to the window and opens it. Slowly, the bedroom door opens and MARCEL and OSCAR poke their heads out while, at the same time, the armoire door opens and GERTRUDE pokes her head out. They signal to one another and hurl themselves toward KAFKA, pushing him out the window. WELLS comes out of the armoire and crosses over to the cucumber sandwiches and takes a handful. He then crosses to his desk and sits. GERTRUDE, MARCEL and OSCAR all breathe a big sigh of relief.)

MARCEL: We've got to get out of here.

OSCAR: You're telling me?

MARCEL: This is serious. He'll be back.

OSCAR: We just dumped him from the top floor of The Venus Arms. Nobody could survive that fall.

GERTRUDE: I have seen cockroaches survive falls from far more stories than there are to The Venus Arms.

MARCEL: Quite so, Oscar. We're on borrowed time now.

OSCAR: What about the inorcism?

MARCEL: What about it?

OSCAR: Well? Aren't we going to do it?

MARCEL: We did it.

OSCAR: We did?

GERTRUDE: It is done and it is over and now all that remains is for us to depart before it becomes too late.

OSCAR: What about the screams, the furniture smashing against the walls, the thrills, the chills, the spills, the excitement—the split-pea porridge?

GERTRUDE: What on Earth are you talking about?

MARCEL: I don't remember any of that?

OSCAR: Nor I. That's my point.

GERTRUDE: Oscar, an inorcism is not an exorcism nor is an inorcist an exorcist.

OSCAR: Splendid logic there, but where does it leave us?

MARCEL: Out of here and soon, I hope.

OSCAR: Not so quick! I'd say this inorcism has been a crashing disappointment.

GERTRUDE: I say it has been a success.

OSCAR: A success? A lot of bloody talk if you ask me. I say we spin Wells' head around a few times, throw in some inexplicable paranormal phenomena, a few poltergeists and what not and call it a night!

GERTRUDE: You are becoming tiresome, Oscar. The inorcism is over. I declare it a *fait accompli*. Furthermore, if we do not get out of here in short order I fear the subject of our inorcism might decide to possess us.

OSCAR: What are you saying? Are you saying that Wells can keep us here against our will?

MARCEL: And force us into servitude.

OSCAR: That could be fun.

GERTRUDE: It is not a pretty prospect, Oscar!

OSCAR: Then what are we waiting for?

WELLS: *(Looking up from his desk.)* I am not unique.

MARCEL: Hurry, Gertrude.

WELLS: I am not unique! *(LIGHTING change: Outside the window the sun can be seen beginning to rise.)* I am not unique!

(GERTRUDE, MARCEL and OSCAR gasp and recoil in horror.)

GERTRUDE: What a night!

(There is a KNOCKING on the hallway door.)

MARCEL: Quickly! Let us depart!

WELLS: *(Calling to door.)* Just a minute!

MARCEL: I don't want to spend eternity in The Venus Arms!

OSCAR: I don't want to spend another minute in The Venus Arms!

(The KNOCKING continues.)

WELLS: Just a minute. I'm coming. *(Rises.)*

(GERTRUDE, MARCEL and OSCAR make a quick exit through the bookcase. WELLS starts to cross towards the door. The bookcase swings back open and GERTRUDE, MARCEL and OSCAR make a mad dash for the armoire.)

GERTRUDE: How could you be so forgetful, Marcel? Alice? Alice? Wake up, Alice! Quickly, Marcel! Legs or arms?

MARCEL: *Uh ....*

GERTRUDE: Never mind!

(GERTRUDE takes ALICE'S arms while MARCEL and OSCAR take her legs and begin to carry her towards the bookcase. Meanwhile, WELLS has just about reached the door.)

WELLS: I'm coming! I'm coming!

GERTRUDE: *(About to enter the bookcase.)* Poor Alice. How did I get her into this? Quickly! Oscar, you are letting down your end!

OSCAR: I certainly am not!

(KNOCKING!)

WELLS: Who is it?

GERTRUDE: Marcel?

KAFKA'S VOICE: Let me in there, Mister Wells.

MARCEL: It isn't me, Gertrude.

GERTRUDE: Then who is it?

KAFKA'S VOICE: It's Mister Kafka and you'd better open up!

(Carrying ALICE, GERTRUDE, MARCEL and OSCAR exit through the bookcase just as the door opens and KAFKA, no longer a cockroach, enters.)

KAFKA: *(Holding up his key.)* Master key, Mister Wells. I saw a light under your door. I've been meaning to have a talk with you all night, but you know how it is sometimes.

WELLS: How what is?

KAFKA: Being the night manager for The Venus Arms leaves little time for social amenities. What with all the work required of my position, combined with a shortage of manpower, my nights are filled with more responsibility than a night manager ought to have.

WELLS: But you do. You manage quite well.

KAFKA: Of course I do. I have no choice, but I go on. I do. We all do. Don't think that there haven't been times when I've thought how nice it must be just to sit and do little more than to throw up my hands, or fold my arms and feel my own inertia. However, if I didn't do all that I am responsible for, who would?

WELLS: *(Curt.)* Hire some help.

KAFKA: *Ah.* That is exactly what I have come to see you about.

WELLS: You want me to help you? *(Snorts at the ridiculousness of such a suggestion)* You want me to help the Devil?

KAFKA: By helping to make his work a bit more easy.

WELLS: It isn't easy enough?

KAFKA: Far from it, Mister Wells.

WELLS: You who have done nothing but threaten me now want my help?

KAFKA: Yes. Can I count on you?

WELLS: Certainly not!

KAFKA: I haven't much time remaining. *(Walks around room, turning off the lamps.)* I was hoping you'd find it within yourself to overlook our differences and do something that could help all the other residents, as well. *(Browsing through the papers on the desk.)* But, I see you don't care for the welfare of others. Self-possessed! You'd rather stay up all night and keep yourself entertained without concern for our other residents who too must pass the night in The Venus Arms.

WELLS: What do you want?

KAFKA: *(Seeing the sun rising.)* The sun, my sweet! The sun! *(Crosses to window.)* What do I want? I want to rest. I want to sleep, perchance to dream. As I have already said, my nights are filled with as much responsibility as one can handle. *(Picks up and eats a cucumber sandwich.)* It's no picnic being me, Kafka the night manager. I'll be going off duty soon and I would like very much to leave knowing that when today is over and I come back on duty tonight, there will be no need to threaten you again with dispossession. We despise having to take such extreme measures here in The Venus Arms. I really want to help you, my sweet.

WELLS: By threatening me with dispossession? You might as well kill me once and for all, for all the good your helping does.

KAFKA: Help me.

WELLS: How?

KAFKA: By letting in the exterminator whenever it is necessary—by not creating a disturbance for those who do not wish to be disturbed. By allowing others to pass the night in sleep if that is what they so choose to do. By not entertaining dead souls. By managing during the daylight hours. *(Pause.)* Tell me, dear heart, what exactly is it that frightens you?

WELLS: Nothing.

KAFKA: Then let him in. There's nothing to fear unless you are a cockroach. You're not a cockroach, are you?

WELLS: *(Sitting on divan.)* Of course not.

KAFKA: Then what is it?

WELLS: Nothing. Nothing, Kafka—*nothing.*

KAFKA: *(Crosses to WELLS and stands over him behind the divan.)* Let him in, Mister Wells. Let him in. Be my day manager.

WELLS: *(Becoming drowsy.)* I'm afraid of....of...nothing.

KAFKA: Relax. The exterminator is essential. I only want to help you, my pet. Will you help me help you?

WELLS: *(Very drowsy.)* I'm afraid. Afraid.

KAFKA: Of course you are. Relax. It will pass. Everything passes.

WELLS: *(Lies across divan.)* I'm afraid of dispossession. Of nothingness.

KAFKA: *(Places a hand on WELLS' forehead. Speaks softly, gently.)* Relax, my sweet. Relax. All is right. You'll see.

WELLS: *(Sotto voce.)* I'll see.

KAFKA: *(Comforting.)* Shhh, don't be afraid. Sleep now. You needn't be afraid any longer. *Shhh,* let him in, dear one. Let him in and I will help you. Accept me. Let me enter, my beautiful Mister Wells, let me enter. I will help you to live without fear of nothingness, without fear of dispossession. I'll help you. Help me. Help me help you. I want tp possess you.

WELLS: *(Can hardly lift himself to speak.)* Possess me.

KAFKA: *(A long sigh of pleasure.)* Yes, I will. *(Bends over and gently kisses WELLS on the forehead.)* Thy will is done! *(WELLS stirs.) Shhh*—dream, dream something, anything. Dream. Dreaming is something—something better than nothing. Sleep. Sleep, my dear, and I will leave you with a dream. *(WELLS stirs.) Shhh. (Crosses to bookcase.) Shhh.*

WELLS: *(With great effort, he raises his head.)* Too soon, too late. There's an audience watching. I know. I've spoken with them

KAFKA: *Shhh.*

(WELLS closes his eyes and sinks into SILENCE.)

KAFKA: *(After a pause. To the audience.)* Sometimes, when we refuse to bargain, to compromise, we find ourselves living life backwards. Dream now. Dream a dream of something better and nothing anybody could imagine. Take good care of the day, my son. *(Exits, closing the bookcase slowly behind him.)*
(SUNLIGHT floods the room before the LIGHTING slowly dims.)

BLACK OUT.

END OF PLAY

WEST TEXAS MASSACRE

SYNOPSIS: 6W/4M, One Set, Full Length. In this melodrama within a melodrama Marsha is the Queen of a West Texas community theatre. With her, it is always about Marsha – Marsha, Marsha, Marsha! Marsha is having an affair with Dr. Hal. Marsha's husband, Mike, is having an affair with Alyson. Alyson, Botoxed and liposuctioned, is the pretender to the Queen's throne. Is Bill the teacher having an affair with one of his students? Marsha's world is filled with intrigue, back-stabbing, secret board meetings and double-dealings. We learn all about the actors and their diabolical plots as they perform Massacre at Dirty Gulch, a rootin'-tootin' old-time melodrama, written, directed and starring none other than – Marsha! Marsha plays Mary Holiday whose illegitimate daughter is abducted by Indians. The Indian Princess Desert Flower, played by Alyson, sheds her feathers and we discover her to be none other than Mean Mabel Wiggens, the She-Scourge of the West. Marsha's husband plays Bad Bart Blackey who is in cahoots with Mean Mabel. Marsha's daughter plays Mary's daughter who returns to be reunited with her mother after many years of back-aching work in a house of ill repute. Was it the Bible or a bullet that done-in Madam Lillie? The two melodramas quickly become intermingled with enough devious-doings to curl the mustache on Fu Manchu. And then, of course, there is a massacre. Oh, what bloody fun!

West Texas Massacre opened at Raw Space – the Actors Studio, 529 W. 42nd St., NYC under the direction of Frank Calo with assistance by Elias Stimac and with the following cast:

MILES COHEN — O.T. Taylor/Sheriff Upstringer
MARJORIE CONN — Doris Powell/Polly Upstringer
DAVID DOTTERER — Bill Walker/Judge Sweets
DANA LETOWSKY — Rita Pipes/ Sally Sweets
LESLIE C. NEMET — Miss Lulu/Lori
NATASHA PETERSON — Alyson Barrett/ Princess Desert Flower
LAURA RAYNORVL — Marsha Cornell-Simmons/ Mary Holiday
JOHN RUSSO — Hal/Grover
JAMES SADLER — Mike Simmons/Bart Blackey
JULIE ZIMMERMANN — Evelyn Forester/ Widow Deere

THE ACTION of the play takes place on the stage of The Playhouse, a community theatre in the fictional town of Derrick, Texas. The action takes place during a performance of *Massacre at Dirty Gulch*: a rootin'-tootin', old-time, wild west melodrama set in The Horse's Mouth, a West Texas saloon in Dirty Gulch, Texas in the late 1880s.

THE SETTING is the interior of The Horse's Mouth Saloon as executed by the Derrick Community Players. There are swinging doors leading to the street. There are steps leading to a landing that leads to the upstairs living quarters. There is a window unit. There is the bar counter and stools. There is a piano and bench. There is another exit. Two or three tables with three chairs each finish off the set.

THE TIME is the present.

THE CHARACTERS *(in order of appearance)*: Names in parenthesis are the roles the characters take on in the melodrama, *Massacre at Dirty Gulch*, within the play:

MARSHA CORNELL-SIMMONS (Mary Holiday): The Grande Dame of American community theatre. She is in her forties to fifties, lean and attractive.

DR. HAL LUCE (Grover Oats): Middle aged. He takes good care of himself, shrewd and somewhat aloof.

O.T. TAYLOR (Sheriff Upstringer): Middle aged or older. A good old boy one could find amusing were something about him not so menacing.

MIKE SIMMONS (Bart Blackey): One is never quite certain as to the depth of his character. He is Marsha's husband.

RITA PIPES (Sally Sweets): Twenties to thirties. A Texas Princess with a let's-play- dumb-blond-because-I-can-get-what-I-want-with-this-act-but-I'm-really-the-smartest- woman-in-the-world attitude.

ALYSON BARRETT (Princess Desert Flower/Mean Mabel Wiggens): Lean and attractive. She is in line to the Grande Dame's throne.

BILL WALKER (Judge Sweets): A schoolteacher, somewhat intense.

EVELYN FORESTER (Widow Deere): A woman of means gained from hard work. Relaxed, simple and a born arbiter.

LORI SIMMONS (Miss Lulu): The daughter of Mike and Marsha.

DORIS POWELL (Polly Upstringer): Plump to obese, coarse and loud. She would like to vie for the title of Grande Dame but has neither the grace nor charm.

PROLOGUE—"Pep Talk"

As the House LIGHTING dims we hear the RECORDED VOICE of MARSHA:

MARSHA *(Recorded voice.)*: Okay, gang! Listen up! As your director, I just want to say that you all have every reason to feel proud of yourselves. We've put a lot of time and work into this and, yes, we've had our little ups and downs . . . but . . . all in all, we've got ourselves a good little show. Now, if you'll all take your places we're about to start. The audience is in and it looks like we've got ourselves a pretty good opening night house.

Thanks again, gang . . . for everything. And remember those new blocking changes. Let's make *Massacre at Dirty Gulch* the melodrama that Derrick, Texas will not soon forget!

Places everybody! And break a leg!

ACT ONE—*Scene 1*

AT RISE: GROVER OATS, behind bar, is pouring out a whiskey for MARY HOLIDAY who is lavishly posed on a barstool wearing a slinky dance hall dress, circa 1880. PERFORMANCE LIGHTING.

NOTE: ALL ACTORS are in period costume, since what we are watching is a performance of the melodrama within the play. We do, however, travel back and forth through time to witness prior rehearsals and the personal interactions between the actors performing the melodrama. These changes of time will be noted in the text of the script by calling for either PERFORMANCE LIGHTING or REHEARSAL LIGHTING.

ALSO NOTE: The character name before the backslash is the character speaking. For example: MARY/MARSHA followed by dialogue or stage directions belongs to the character of MARY in the melodrama within the play.

MARY/MARSHA: *(A very broad character as played by MARSHA.)* This ol' bug juice shoor hits the spot, Grover, but I ain't a-gonna tell ya jest where that spot is. *Ha, ha, ha!*

GROVER/HAL: *(HAL, likewise.)* You're a good-un, Mary Holiday. You're a good-un!

MARY/MARSHA: Any news from that thare brother o' yours what got hisself dee-tained by that thare sheriff up in Ok-lee-homa?

GROVER/HAL: 'Fraid they're gonna throw the key away on that one, Mary.

MARY/MARSHA: Dear me.

GROVER/HAL: 'Sides, he ain't no full-brother anyhow.

MARY/MARSHA: He ain't?

GROVER/HAL: Nope! I'm an Oats and he's a Blackey. Ya see, his ol' man, Bad Billy Blackey, took advantage o' my mother, rest her soul.

MARY/MARSHA: Rest her soul.

GROVER/HAL: while m' pa was off doin' his duty.

MARY/MARSHA: Yor pa was in the cavalry?

GROVER/HAL: Nope. He was in the outhouse.

MARY/MARSHA: He wasn't only bad, Grover. He was quick.

GROVER/HAL: That he was, Mary. Bad Billy Blackey, curse his soul.

MARY/MARSHA: Curse his soul.

GROVER/HAL: Snuck up on m' ma whiles she was a-stuffin' the bird.

MARY/MARSHA: A-stuffin' the bird, Grover?

GROVER/HAL: It was Christmas.

MARY/MARSHA: Ya say it was Christmas and yor ma was a-stuffin' the bird whiles yor pa was in the outhouse?

GROVER/HAL: Right you are, little lady. Only m' pa was a-stuck.

MARY/MARSHA: A-stuck?

GROVER/HAL: In the outhouse.

MARY/MARSHA: Yor ma was a-stuffin' whiles yor pa was a-stuck?

GROVER/HAL: And Bad Billy Blackey was a-sneakin'!

MARY/MARSHA: Ya mean ta tell me that whiles yor ma was a-stuffin' and Bart Blackey's pa was a-sneakin', yor pa was a-stuck?

GROVER/HAL: Yup. In the outhouse.

MARY/MARSHA: Oh dear.

GROVER/HAL: But, Bad Billy Blackey weren't Bart's daddy yet.

MARY/MARSHA: He weren't?

GROVER/HAL: Nope. That happened after Ma dropped the bird.

MARY/MARSHA: She dropped the bird?

GROVER/HAL: And screamed.

MARY/MARSHA: Well, why didn't yor pa come a-runnin'?

GROVER/HAL: 'Cause he was a-stuck.

MARY/MARSHA: In the outhouse.

GROVER/HAL: Sure 'nough! 'Twas the coldest December anybody could remember. So, when he sat down he got hisself frozified.

MARY/MARSHA: Frozified?

GROVER/HAL: Sure 'nough! Ma had ta crawl in under the outhouse and set a fire under 'im.

MARY/MARSHA: That must o' smarted, Grover.

GROVER/HAL: Not as much as what she had ta tell Pa 'bout what Bad Billy Blackey went and did after she dropped the bird.

MARY/MARSHA: Fo' shame, Grover. Fo' shame!

GROVER/HAL: So, ya see, Bart's a Blackey. He ain't a Oats at all. He was conceived in sin and he's mean as rusty nails through and through.

MARY/MARSHA: That's the saddest story I ever did hear. Still, he's kin, Grover. And you know what they say about blood and water. Pour me another shot o' that amber lightnin'. I feel a faint comin' on.

GROVER/HAL: Now, you take 'er easy, little lady. I don't want no harm ta come to m' little angel.

MARY/MARSHA: Am I really yor little angel, Grover?

GROVER/HAL: Why, you jest say the word, sugar pie, and I'm all yours.

MARY/MARSHA: Even though I, too, have a child conceived in sin?

GROVER/HAL: Now, don't you fret, little Mary.

MARY/MARSHA: Oh, booo-hooo, booo-hooo. Guess talkin' 'bout kin made me think o' my long lost daughter, Louise . . . abductafied by Injuns fifteen years ago today. Stolen on her third birthday.

GROVER/HAL: Fo' shame.

MARY/MARSHA: Yup. She'd be eighteen today, Grover. Eighteen. Booo-hooo.

GROVER/HAL: *(Pouring her another drink.)* Now, don't you cry, little lady. Here. Drink up.

MARY/MARSHA: Here's to a frog in your corset! *(Swigs drink.)*

(REHEARSAL LIGHTING).

HAL: *(A major transition from the character of GROVER.)* A frog in your corset? This is fucking garbage, Marsha.

MARSHA: *(Ibid.)* Garbage? I'll have you know that Mike and I did a thorough research and "a frog in your corset" was definitely an eighteen-eighty West Texas colloquialism.

HAL: I don't think so.

MARSHA: Mike and I spent a year working on this script, Hal, so we could save the theatre some royalty money. And it was approved by the board, as you doubtless recall, *unanimously.*

HAL: That doesn't make every word the two of you write sacrosanct.

MARSHA: *Unanimously,* Hal. This is a melodrama. *Massacre at Dirty Gulch.* Not bloody *Long Day's Journey Into Night!*

HAL: I'm certain O'Neill would be the first to point that out.

MARSHA: Well, what the hell did he know about entertaining people?

HAL: You're not serious?

MARSHA: Of course I'm serious. People don't want depression. They want entertainment. We did that *Electra* thing here and it was as boring as a cow patty.

HAL: I'm not surprised.

MARSHA: Suppose you let me direct my script. All right?

HAL: Fine. Direct away.

MARSHA: How else do you think we can afford to put on everything else we do around here? *Huh?* Melodramas make money. *Money, money, money.* And as the new president of our board of directors it would behoove you to keep that in mind.

HAL: *(Sarcastic.)* I'll make a mental note.

MARSHA: You do that, Hal.

HAL: Can we get on with rehearsal, Marsha?

MARSHA: I don't bust my buns every summer with these goddamned melodramas for my health. You don't really think anybody gives a rat's ass about what you consider "good" theatre, do you? They're here for the beer and the popcorn. And if that is what it takes to pay the bills around here and then maybe subsidize some O'Neill, Williams, Miller, Albee, whomever, then that is what it takes! Understand? *(The SOUND of HAMMERING.)* What the hell is all that noise? We're trying to rehearse here!

MIKE: *(Popping his head in from upstage landing.)* Hi-ho! Just securing the escape behind the landing, Marsha.

MARSHA: Well, secure it somewhere else!

MIKE: I can't secure it somewhere else. I've got to secure it here.

MARSHA: *(Strained.)* Then secure it some other time, Michael.

MIKE: But I need to do it now before somebody gets hurt.

MARSHA: Then, for God's sake, do it quietly!

MIKE: Yes . . . right . . . quietly . . . sorry . . . *(Disappears.)*

SHERIFF/O.T.: *(Rushing on.)* Did-ja hear the news? Did-ja?

MARSHA: Not now, O.T.!

O.T.: Oh. I thought I heard Hal say "fo' shame."

MARSHA: No. Hal didn't say "fo' shame," damn it!

O.T.: *(Fingering his ear.)* Battery must be low on my hearing aid. I thought he did.

MARSHA: Well, he didn't! Besides, it's not "did-ja hear the news? Did-ja?" It's three did-jas and you left out the "Ok-lee-homa."

O.T.: Three did-jas and put back the Ok-lee-homa. Right. Got it.

MARSHA: Then let me hear it, O.T.

O.T.: Well, now. Let me see . . . . Did-ja hear the news, did-ja, did-ja, from Ok-lee-homa?

MARSHA: NO! Did-ja hear the news from Ok-lee-homa? Did-ja! Did-ja! Did-ja!

O.T.: Right. Got it, Marsha. *(While exiting.)* Did-ja, did-ja, did-ja . . . .

MARSHA: *(To HAL.)* Honest to God! Every time that man opens his mouth his brain leaks. Now, can we get on with this *today?*

(PERFORMANCE LIGHTING.)

GROVER/HAL: Today, huh?

MARY/MARSHA: Yup! My poor little Louise would be eighteen today.

GROVER/HAL Fo' shame. Fo' shame.

SHERIFF/O.T.: *(Rushing in.)* Did-ja hear the news from Ok-lee-homa? Did-ja? *(There is a long pause. MARY flashes a tight-lipped smile. Suddenly, he remembers and quickly adds:)* Did-ja? Did-ja?

GROVER/HAL: Now calm down, set a spell, have a drink and fill us in, Sheriff Upstringer.

SHERIFF/O.T.: Ol' Blackey's escaped!

GROVER/HAL & MARY/MARSHA: No?!

SHERIFF/O.T.: Yup! And that ain't the worst!

GROVER/HAL: It ain't?

SHERIFF/O.T.: Nope! *(Fingering his ear.)* Did you just say "it ain't," Grover?

GROVER/HAL: *(Sotto voce.)* Yup. *(MARY looks panicked.)*

SHERIFF/O.T.: Did-ja? Did-ja?

GROVER/HAL: *(Something is wrong.)* Yup!

SHERIFF/O.T.: *(Fingering his ear.)* What's that?

MARY/MARSHA: *(Through clenched teeth.)* He said "IT AIN'T," Sheriff.

SHERIFF/O.T.: *(A couple taps on hearing aid. Removes finger from his ear.)* Gotcha. *(A long pause. Taps hearing aid.)* Nope. *(A pause to tap hearing aid, again.)* Nope, that ain't the worst!

GROVER/HAL & MARY/MARSHA: IT AIN'T?!

SHERIFF/O.T.: Nope. He's here in Dirty Gulch.

MARY/MARSHA: He is?

SHERIFF/O.T.: Yup. *(Again, he's forgotten his line.)* Yup . . . yup . . . .

MARY/MARSHA: *(Helping him out.)* You saw him, Sheriff?

SHERIFF/O.T.: *(Remembering.)* Right! Yup! I saw him, Miss Mary . . . behind the livery stable, playin' one-eyed jacks.

GROVER/HAL: He always did like a good game o' cards.

SHERIFF/O.T.: And who do ya think was a-sweepin' in all o' the winnin's?

MARY/MARSHA: Pray tell, Sheriff.

SHERIFF/O.T.: Bart Blackey!

GROVER/HAL & MARY/MARSHA: No!

SHERIFF/O.T.: Yup. *(A long pause.)* Yup.

MARY/MARSHA: *(Feeding SHERIFF his line.)* Was he as big as life, Sheriff?

SHERIFF/O.T.: Huh? Oh! Right . . . *Yup.* Big as life. Ol' Blackey hisself, The meanest, baddest varmint ever to set foot in Dirty Gulch.

GROVER/HAL: Why didn't ya put the cuffs on him, Sheriff?

SHERIFF/O.T.: Cain't! Long as he don't break the law here in . . . in . . . .

MARY/MARSHA: Dirty Gulch.

SHERIFF/O.T.: Right. Dirty Gulch. Long as he don't break the law here in Dirty Gulch, it's outta my hands.

GROVER/HAL: But he's wanted for murderin' and rustlin' in Ok-lee-homa.

SHERIFF/O.T.: But not in Texas, boy. I'm a-feared my hands is tied. But if he so much as spits on the sidewalk here in . . . in . . . Dirty Gulch.

MARY/MARSHA: Thare ain't no sidewalks here in Dirty Gulch.

SHERIFF/O.T.: Well, on the ground. If he so much as spits on the ground here in . . . Dirty Gulch, I'll run him in sure as shootin'. Now, give me a shot o' that snake venom, Grover.
GROVER/HAL: One snake venom comin' up. The venom's on The Horse's Mouth, Sheriff. *(Gives whiskey to SHERIFF.)*

MARY/MARSHA: Fill 'er up again, Grover. I feel another faint comin' on.

GROVER/HAL: You better be careful, little lady. That thare scorpion juice will sneak up behind ya and strangulate ya.

MARY/MARSHA: My poor Louise. My poor little Louise.

SHERIFF/O.T.: By the way. Ol' Blackey's got hisself a purty young squaw by the name o' Princess Desert Flower. Said he won her in a poker game up in Tulsa. *(Moving toward exit.)* Shor is purty. *(Exits and quickly re-enters.)* Well, I better mosey on over to the jailhouse and see what's a-stirrin'. *(Exits.)*

GROVER/HAL: *(Calling after him.)* Say hello to the little woman, Sheriff!

SHERIFF/O.T.: *(Re-entering.)* Say what?

GROVER/HAL: *(Through clenched teeth.)* Hello to the little woman, Sheriff.

SHERIFF/O.T.: Right. Sure 'nough, Grover. *(He exits. From backstage we hear:)* Did-ja, did-ja, did-ja . . . .

(REHEARSAL LIGHTING)

MARSHA: Hal, O.T. is never going to get that right. So, you've got to get your line out before he exits.
HAL: I'll do my best.

MARSHA: So far, your best hasn't been good enough, Hal.

HAL: Sorry.

MARSHA: "Sorry" doesn't cut it. It doesn't look good. You've got to stop him with your line before he gets offstage. Didn't they teach you anything down in Dallas?

HAL: Yes. How to be a good doctor.

MARSHA: You know perfectly well what I mean.

HAL: There's no need for you to be abusive.

MARSHA: When I'm abusive you'll know it, Dr. Luce.

HAL: Marsha, what exactly is your problem? Whenever the least little thing doesn't go exactly the way you think it ought to, you go off the deep end.

MARSHA: I'm trying to direct a show here. Now, if you can't take direction, then I'll just have to find somebody who can.

HAL: From where? You came crying to the board about how nobody turned out for your auditions.

MARSHA: I didn't come crying.

HAL: Demanding we take parts in this stinking melodrama or the collapse of The Derrick Community Playhouse would be on our heads.

MARSHA: I don't recall.

HAL: Marsha, the entire board of directors of The Derrick Community Playhouse, including your husband and daughter, are in this show—not to mention yourself both acting and directing. It's not our problem if you've run everybody off and can't get anyone to audition for your shows anymore.

MARSHA: You don't know what you're talking about. You come blowing into town thinking you're the Almighty Savior from Dallas and you don't know a thing!

HAL: I know this is a volunteer organization and people have better things to do than to put up with your abuse.

MARSHA: Bad timing, Hal. It's just bad timing! May I remind you, Mr. President, that everybody got burned-out on that last abomination we did?

HAL: *Charley's Aunt* made money.

MARSHA: It was an embarrassment!

HAL: Why? Because neither you nor your husband directed it?

MARSHA: Correct me if I'm wrong. But, I have the distinct impression you're trying to tell me something.

HAL: I'm not some idiot you dragged in from the oil field.

MARSHA: Then, stop acting like one.

HAL: A little civility. Is that asking for too much?

MARSHA: Why don't you just take a hike . . . like back to big `D'.

HAL: I never asked to play this part, Marsha.

MARSHA: Then quit! We'll cancel the show. That'll look good, won't it? Prima donna board president, obstetrician, community leader of Derrick, America walks out on little old melodrama because he thinks he's above us all. *Abortionist.* Put that on your resume and stuff it!

HAL: *What?*

MARSHA: You heard me. Don't think I didn't do some checking up on you. How many babies have you murdered, Doctor?

HAL: I volunteered one day a month at a women's health

clinic. Strictly in a supervisory position, I might add.

MARSHA: They ran you out of town with death threats, baby killer!

HAL: There's no reasoning with you.

MARSHA: So, why don't you just pack up all your dirty little tools of death and get the hell out of Dodge!

HAL: *(After a pondering pause.)* Funny. Baby's changed her spots.

MARSHA: What is that? Some kind of obscure, pediatric allusion?

HAL: "Harder, Hal. Oh, God! Harder, harder! Michael doesn't do it anymore—not like you do, baby. Not like you do at all."

MARSHA: You son of a bitch! That was a one shot deal.

HAL: Changed your tune, have you?

MARSHA: A one-shot deal! So, zip up your manhood and go home.

HAL: One of these days, Marsha, somebody's going to run you and your husband right out of this theatre.

MARSHA: Oh, really? Well, it won't be you!

HAL: Won't it?

MARSHA: Try it, buster! You just friggin' try it.

BLACK OUT.

END ACT ONE—*Scene 1*

ACT ONE—*Scene 2*

AT RISE: GROVER OATS is behind the bar pouring drinks for BART BLACKEY, MARY HOLIDAY and SHERIFF UPSTRINGER. SALLY SWEETS is playing the piano and singing "I'm Only A Bird In A Gilded Cage." SALLY finishes her tune and ALL applaud and cheer. PERFORMANCE LIGHTING.

BART/MIKE: *(Villain that he is, struts over to SALLY.)* Right powerful pair o' tonsils you got thare, little lady.

SALLY/RITA: *(To say she is somewhat scatter-brained could be construed as a compliment.)* Thank you, Mr. Blackey.

BART/MIKE: Can I buys ya a drink?

SALLY/RITA: What'll I have?

BART/MIKE: What does ya want?

SALLY/RITA: What can I git?

BART/MIKE: Your heart's desire.

SALLY/RITA: Then, that's what I'll have.

BART/MIKE: And what'll that be?

SALLY/RITA: Whatever that is.

BART/MIKE: Whatever what is?

SALLY/RITA: Whatever you want, Mr. Blackey.

BART/MIKE: I gots what I want, m' little nightingale.

SALLY/RITA: And what'll that be?

BART/MIKE: Tarantula juice.

SALLY/RITA: Then, that's what it is.

BART/MIKE: I like a gal who knows her mind!

SALLY/RITA: Well, I certainly don't want to hear about it! *(Sits at table.)*

BART/MIKE: *(Sits next to her. Calling to bar:)* Hey, Grove! Bring us a bottle o' that tarantula poizzon o' yorn and hop-to, little brother! I gots me here the valedictorian of Dirty Gulch.

SALLY/RITA: *(Giggles. Playfully slaps his arm.)* Hesh up! You want them all t' know? You can shows it to me later. Out behind the livery stable. *(Giggles.)*

BART/MIKE: *(Aside. Curling his mustache.)* Looks ta me like this little ol' gal is ripe fer learnin', and I'm the one gonna teach her a thang or two! *Ha, ha, ha!*

SHERIFF/O.T.: *(To GROVER.)* Ya got 'im in yor line o' vision?

GROVER/HAL: I'm a-eyein' him like a snake, Sheriff.

SHERIFF/O.T.: Good boy. One wrong move and I'm runnin' him in.

GROVER/HAL: Sally's a-eyein' him like a snake, too.

SHERIFF/O.T.: Watch yor mouth, boy!

PRINCESS/ALYSON: *(Rushes in. She is wearing moccasins, a suede Indian dress with beads and she is crowned with a feathered headpiece more befitting an Indian chief than a princess.)* Messie Blackey! Messie Blackey!

SHERIFF/O.T.: Hold on a minute! Whoa, girlie! Thare ain't no Injuns allowed in The Horse's Mouth Saloon.

PRINCESS/ALYSON: Me princess!

SHERIFF/O.T.: Goes double fer princesses. Right, Grover?

GROVER/HAL: Yup. We don't put no stock in that blue blood stuff 'round these parts.

PRINCESS/ALYSON: Me Princess Desert Flower. Me no got blue blood.

SHERIFF/O.T.: Ya better flap yor feathers and fly outta here afore ya git what fer.

BART/MIKE: Ya heard the sheriff! Git outside and keep m' saddle warm!

PRINCESS/ALYSON: Me got message.

BART/MIKE: Git out fors I de-featherfy ya!

GROVER/HAL: Well, I reckon we can make an exception in this case. Waddaya say, Sheriff?

MARY/MARSHA: *Yeah.* Let's hear what she's got to say.

SHERIFF/O.T.: All right. But make it quick. Talk and walk.

BART/MIKE: Well, waddaya want? Speak up! Stop standin' thare like ya just swallowed a horney toad!

PRINCESS/ALYSON: Me got message for tin badge.

BART/MIKE: Well, spit it out, bird brain! *(SALLY giggles.)*

PRINCESS/ALYSON: Heap big fat lady get off stagecoach ask me see why sheriff not meet fat lady. Fat lady break Sheriff back if he in dirty saloon.

SHERIFF/O.T.: *(Fingering ear.)* Huh?

MARY/MARSHA: I think she means yor wife's a-gonna hatchetate ya if-n ya don't git on home, Sheriff.

SHERIFF/O.T.: *(Tapping on hearing aid.)* Huh?

MARY/MARSHA: YOUR WIFE!

SHERIFF/O.T.: *(Jumps up.)* Moses in the bull rushes! The little lady is home from visitin' her sickly mom up north, rest her soul.

ALL: Rest her soul.

GROVER/HAL: Now hold on a minute, Sheriff. Her ma ain't dead.

SHERIFF/O.T.: She ain't? Well, I'll keep a-prayin'. *(He exits, re-enters, crosses back to GROVER.)* Grover, you keep an eye on ol' Bart whiles I sneaks out the back door. *(Crosses to exit.)*

GROVER/HAL: Right, Sheriff. *(The SHERIFF exits.)*

SHERIFF/O.T.: *(Re-enters.)* What's that?

GROVER/HAL: Right, Sheriff.

SHERIFF/O.T.: Uh . . . right. *(Exits.)*

(REHEARSAL LIGHTING).

ALYSON: *(Standing somewhere.)* Marsha, don't you think it looks a little awkward for me to just stand here during the entire scene?

MARSHA: No.

ALYSON: Well, it feels awkward. What if I crossed over to the piano bench and sat down?

MARSHA: This is eighteen-eighty, Alyson, and Indians do not sit on piano benches.

ALYSON: Well, couldn't I have just a little bit of business?

MARSHA: Why? So you can upstage everybody?

ALYSON: I'm burning up, Marsha. These lights are killing me!

MARSHA: Would you prefer we did your scenes in the dark?

ALYSON: It's this headdress, Marsha. Why couldn't I have just one feather? Whoever heard of a whole headdress for a princess? If I don't die of heat stroke, my neck's going to snap from the weight of the feathers!

MARSHA: That would be a pity, wouldn't it, Alyson?

ALYSON: *Yeah,* a real tragedy.

MARSHA: Is this going to be another *Streetcar*, Alyson? Are you going to cause dissension among the ranks here as well?

ALYSON: I didn't cause dissension, Marsha. All I said was that Blanche was supposed to be crazy in that last scene and that you would have looked more in character if you came out of that bathroom a little more frumpy, instead of coming out in your mink and wearing more makeup and looking more glamorous, as it were, than when you first set foot in New Orleans.

MARSHA: I like to look good for curtain calls. Besides, it was silver fox and it was what the director wanted. Michael is a genius when it comes to theatre.

ALYSON: Really, Marsha? You don't think his being your husband has just an itsy-bitsy, little something to do with it?

MARSHA: It might interest you to know that I had to beg and plead with Michael to give you the part of Stella, in spite of your age. He wanted Sharon Martin.

ALYSON: Sharon Martin! My God, Marsha! Sharon Martin can't act her way out of that proverbial paper bag and she weighs over two hundred pounds!

MARSHA: Have you seen her lately? She's lost at least sixty pounds.

ALYSON: And she's boxed-out of her mind on speed!

MARSHA: Nonetheless, you've got me to thank, Alyson. Now, can we get on with the show?

(PERFORMANCE LIGHTING.)

JUDGE/BILL: *(Entering with WIDOW DEERE.)* Howdy, folks!

GROVER/HAL & MARY/MARSHA: Howdy, Judge Sweets. Widow Deere.

WIDOW/EVELYN: *(Turning to SALLY who is sitting in BART'S lap.)* Sally Sweets! You better high-tail it on home!

SALLY/RITA: I ain't a-doin' nuthin'.

WIDOW/EVELYN: Ya ain't? Who's that man a-sittin' under ya?

SALLY/RITA: Ain't nobody.

BART/MIKE: Pleased ta meet ya, madam.

WIDOW/EVELYN: I ain't no madam! You wanna talk like that you go over ta Lillie's place, young man! *(To SALLY.)* Now, I ain't a-gonna tell ya agin. *Git on home!*

SALLY/RITA: *(To JUDGE.)* Do I gotta, Pa?

JUDGE/BILL: She's gonna be yor Ma mighty soon, so's ya better start gittin' used ta heedin' her now.

SALLY/RITA: *(To BART.)* I'll meet ya later behind the livery stable.

WIDOW/EVELYN: Sally!

SALLY/RITA: *(Rises. Crossing to exit.)* Going. Going . . . .

WIDOW/EVELYN: *Git!*

SALLY/RITA: Gone. *(Exits.)*

GROVER/HAL: What'll ya have, Judge? Widow Deere?

JUDGE/BILL: *(Sitting at table with WIDOW DEERE.)* I'll have a shot o' vinegaroonaide and a sass-per-elli fer the little lady.

GROVER/HAL: Comin' up.

WIDOW/EVELYN: *(After a pause. To JUDGE.)* Thare's an

Injun standin' by the door.

JUDGE/BILL: *(Turns to look at the PRINCESS who appears to be about to topple over.)* So thare is.

WIDOW/EVELYN: Well? What's she doin' thare?

JUDGE/BILL: I don't know. Maybe she's passin' out cigars. *(GROVER delivers drinks.)* Thank ya, Grover. Say, what's that thare Injun a-doin' over thare?

GROVER/HAL: Standin'.

JUDGE/BILL: I can see she's a-standin'. But, why is she a-standin'?

GROVER/HAL: 'Cause we don't allow no injuns ta sit in saloons. It's territorial law. *(Flashes glance to MARY who smiles back through clenched teeth.)* Or somethin' like that. Anyways, we don't allow no sittin' Injuns in The Horse's Mouth.

WIDOW/EVELYN: It looks bad, Grover Oats. It looks bad. In my day Injuns knew thare place. Ya know what I mean?

GROVER/HAL: Oh, she's a-keepin' it. *(The PRINCESS looks very unhappy.)*

WIDOW/EVELYN: Where'd she come from?

GROVER/HAL: Tulsa.

JUDGE/BILL: Tulsa? What tribe is that?

GROVER/HAL: Don't rightly know. The sheriff says ol' Bart Blackey won her in a poker game.

WIDOW/EVELYN: Looks like he lost the game, if-n ya ask

me. Dirty Gulch is a God-fearin' town. I hope he doesn't take ta sittin' under her, too.

GROVER/HAL: I'll keep m' eye on 'im. *(Returns to bar.)*

MARY/MARSHA: *(Crosses to table where BART is sitting and sits.)* Are you as bad as they say you is?

BART/MIKE: Badder, lady. Badder.

MARY/MARSHA: *(Fans herself. Impressed.)* Oh, my!

BART/MIKE: Yup! I'm the meanest, toughest, roughest, nastiest, most mendacious, malicious, cantankerous, treacherous varmint ever to walk this earth!

MARY/MARSHA: *(Very impressed.)* Good heavens! I'm Mary Holiday. I live upstairs over the saloon. If-n anybody cares ta know.

BART/MIKE: Well, somebody jest might, little lady. Somebody jest might. Ha, ha, ha! *(Aside. Curling mustache.)* Looks ta me like it's a-gonna be a real busy night. Mighty busy, if ya know what I mean. *Ha, ha, ha!*

(REHEARSAL LIGHTING illuminates the table where MIKE and MARSHA are seated.)

MARSHA: *(To MIKE.)* I'm going to kill that bitch! She's been nothing but trouble from day one.

MIKE: Let it go.

MARSHA: I don't know how you put up with her all through *Streetcar*. Honestly, Michael! If you had cast Sharon Martin as I suggested, we might be rid of Mrs. Douglas Barrett by now!

MIKE: Sharon Martin can't act her way out of a paper bag. Besides, she's as big as a house and strung-out on diet pills.

MARSHA: Oh, that seems to be everybody's excuse.

MIKE: Alyson did raise over twenty thousand for the building fund this year.

MARSHA: *(Correcting him.) Nearly.*

MIKE: What?

MARSHA: *Nearly, nearly.* Alyson Barrett raised *nearly* twenty thousand dollars, not over.

MIKE: Nearly. Over. Close enough, Marsha.

MARSHA: Well, I could raise more than that were I married to her money.

MIKE: I'm sorry you're not.

MARSHA: I didn't mean it that way, Michael. I mean, look at all her connections. I hold this place together year after year and look at the thanks I get. Don't forget it was daddy who donated the land for this den of despots!

MIKE: Nobody's forgotten, Marsha. You won't let them.

MARSHA: They're trying to take it over.

MIKE: What? Who?

MARSHA: The Playhouse. The board is trying to push me out and take over The Playhouse.

MIKE: Marsha, would you listen to yourself.

MARSHA: They are, Michael, they are! They're trying to takeover the whole goddamned shooting match!

MIKE: Maybe, that's what they think *you're* trying to do.

MARSHA: I just love this place more than anybody could possibly imagine. My life is here. Nobody loves theatre more than I do. I *am* theatre.

MIKE: *(Comforting.)* I know . . . and that's why I want you to stop making yourself sick over nothing.

MARSHA: Nothing? All the years of labor, the love I have poured into this theatre, *nothing?*

MIKE: That's not what I was talking about.

MARSHA: I have dedicated my life and my soul for The Playhouse. That's something. Not nothing. *Something.* Don't you understand that this is all I've got? Oh, God! There must be something better.

MIKE: Ease off a little. Let them have their way with all the petty things.

MARSHA: What petty things?

MIKE: Petty things. Things that don't really matter. Give in once in a while. Throw people a bone every so often and let them think you're on their side.

MARSHA: *(Finding this very interesting.)* You're right. You are perfectly right. What would I do without you, Michael?

(REHEARSAL LIGHTING rises where ALYSON is standing. MARSHA rises and crosses into the light.)

MARSHA: Al, I was thinking . . .

ALYSON: *(Curt.)* That could be dangerous, Marsha.

MARSHA: *(Ignoring the remark.)* Suppose the next time I'm in Midland, I hunt you down one of those cute little beaded Indian headbands with one little old feather sticking out of it? Any color you'd like. What would you say to that?

ALYSON: I'd say, you're putting me on.

MARSHA: Seriously, Alyson.

ALYSON: Seriously? I'd say, it would be a damned-sight better than these twenty pounds of molting turkey feathers that are giving me such a freaking headache!

MARSHA: Then, that's just what I'll do. Oh, by the way, guess what I saw today?

ALYSON: I can't imagine, Marsha.

MARSHA: Well, I was in the library doing some research. Looking for some inspiration for adding some authenticity to *our* little production.   Note that I say *our,* Al. *Our* production. For it is, isn't it? I mean, we're all in this together. Each a little cog in the big wheel we call theatre Each with our separate little duty. Pulling together. Working together.

ALYSON: *(Cutting her off.)* And your point is?

MARSHA: Well, there in the Derrick Public Library, what do you think I saw?

ALYSON: Your life flashing before your eyes?

MARSHA: Don't lose that sense of humor, Alyson. It may well be your best trait. What I saw was a photograph. A very old photograph, circa eighteen-eighty. And what do you think it was a photograph of?

ALYSON: Your prom night?

MARSHA: Really, Alyson, your repartee is quite remarkable. It was a photograph of a sweet little Indian maiden seated as plain as day on what I detected to be a piano bench. So you may sit! *(Indicates bench.)* You may sit through the entire scene over there on the piano bench!

ALYSON: *(Crossing to bench. To MIKE as she passes behind him.)* How do you live with that bitch?

MARSHA: What was that, Alyson?

ALYSON: I said, these freaking feathers make me itch! *(Sits on bench.)*

MARSHA: Then scratch in character, dear. Remember, you're an actress. *(Crosses to bar and sits on barstool.)*

(REHEARSAL LIGHTING rises around the table where EVELYN and BILL are seated. The rest of the stage goes into darkness. ALYSON should remove her headdress at this time, dropping it behind the piano, and replacing it with a single feather in a headband.)

EVELYN: Poor Marsha, she works so hard. What would The Playhouse do without her?

BILL: Oh, give me a break, Evelyn. We'd do what we always do and we'd all be a lot better off.

EVELYN: Poo.

BILL: Unless the board takes some sort of action, we won't have a playhouse. She's run off every actor, director and every volunteer of any sort. And the audiences are dwindling, too.

EVELYN: Poo.

BILL: It's not poo.

EVELYN: Poo, Bill, poo. I'm sure if we all sat down together and talked this all out we could clear the air.

BILL: Now, that's poo! We've tried and you know it.

EVELYN: Not hard enough. *(MARSHA suddenly appears at the edge of the light where she can be seen eavesdropping on this conversation. BILL and EVELYN continue unaware of her presence.)* You weren't here when we used to get together at old Tom Cornell's house and put together plays that we'd perform in a hangar over on the old air base.

BILL: I know. I know.

EVELYN: All the time it was Marsha holding us together. Dreaming and scheming about how one day we'd have a theatre of our own. You weren't there, Bill. She worked and begged and pleaded until old Tom finally gave in and donated this land and enough money to get The Playhouse going.

BILL: That was then, Evelyn. This is now. Did you know I wrote that one-woman show she's running around doing for whomever will have her. Getting herself ready for her "big opening" at the country club. *"Marsha Cornell-Simmons are Great Ladies of the Theatre."* Marsha Cornell-Simmons *are*. How absurd!

EVELYN: How could you have written it, Bill? I thought it was excerpts from Shakespeare and things like that.

BILL: Well, it is. But somebody had to do all the research

and put it all together.

EVELYN: That's hardly the same thing. You know, Bill, I think you're jealous.

BILL: No, I'm not. I just want credit where credit's due.

EVELYN: Poo.

BILL: I propose we call an emergency meeting of the board to discuss how we can handle this situation.

EVELYN: And what situation would that be?

BILL: I'm talking about poor attendance, low turn-out for auditions, the gossip, the rumors, the back-stabbing, all the people who have come and gone and won't come back to The Playhouse until she's out.

EVELYN: Mike and Marsha are members of the board. We'll have to inform them of any meeting.

BILL: No, we won't. We'll have a quorum without them.

EVELYN: I don't like this and I don't think you're being fair. This is no way to run an organization. Our bylaws specifically state that all members must be informed of any meeting where any official business is to take place.

BILL: I'm talking about the welfare of The Playhouse.

EVELYN: You're not talking about any such thing.

(BILL looks up and catches a glimpse of MARSHA as she moves out of the light and back to the barstool.)

BILL: *(Obviously shaken.)* All that work, just for her because I loved her and she never even said "thank you."

EVELYN: Poo.

(PERFORMANCE LIGHTING.)

WIDOW/EVELYN: *(Rising.)* Come along, Judge. I got a might load o' chores fer ya ta be a-doin'.

JUDGE/BILL: *(Rises.)* Ain't even tied da knot and she's a-workin' me ta death!

WIDOW/EVELYN: *(Pushing JUDGE toward exit.)* Hesh up and let's git a-goin'. That mouth o' yours is gonna git ya in a might load o' trouble one o' these days.

JUDGE/BILL: *(At door. To GROVER.)* Let this be a lesson to ya, boy!

WIDOW/EVELYN: Move it!

GROVER/HAL: Take 'er easy, Judge . . . Widow Deere.
(JUDGE and WIDOW exit.)

MARY/MARSHA: Lemme have another shot o' that thare red-eye, Grover.
(The RECORDED SOUND of a barrage of GUNFIRE.)

SHERIFF/O.T.: (Rushes in and announces:) Thare's a gunfight goin' on over at Madam Lillie's!

ALL A gunfight?!

(The SHERIFF exits, followed by MARY and GROVER with his shotgun taken from under the bar-counter. BART and PRINCESS DESERT FLOWER are left alone onstage.)

BART/MIKE: *(Rises. Crosses to PRINCESS.)* They fell right into m' trap. While they's all over at Madam Lillie's, the rest o' m' boys is relievin' the bank o' all its assets. *Ha, ha, ha!*

PRINCESS/ALYSON: You heap bad, Blackey.

BART/MIKE: Shedd-up, ya redskin heathen! If'n I want a squawk outta you I'll pluck yor feather!

PRINCESS/ALYSON: Me like it when you talk bad to Princess.

BART/MIKE: Gimme a kiss, you red devil in buckskin! *(He reaches down, gathers her up into his arms. THEY embrace and kiss.)*

(REHEARSAL LIGHTING, leaving the stage dark except for area surrounding MIKE and ALYSON.)

ALYSON: *(Pulling away.)* No.

MIKE: No?

ALYSON: Marsha knows.

MIKE: She doesn't even suspect. Believe me.

ALYSON: I'm certain of it, Mike. Nothing gets by her, nothing. You see how she treats me? Like a bug!

MIKE: Marsha treats everybody like a bug.

ALYSON: I'm telling you she knows—and God only knows what she's capable of.

MIKE: Trust me. *(THEY embrace and kiss.)*

BLACKOUT.

END ACT ONE—*Scene 2*

ACT ONE—*Scene 3*

AT RISE: MARY HOLIDAY and MISS LULU are alone onstage and seated at table. PERFORMANCE LIGHTING.

LULU/LORI: *(Dressed in the manner of a "working girl" employed by Madam Lillie.)* Terrible! Terrible! The house is all shot up. The girls have all run away. Madam Lillie's as dead as dead can be.

MARY/MARSHA: Fo' shame. Fo' shame. Did ya see the man what shot her?

LULU/LORI: Nobody shot her, Miss Mary. She got herself Sodom and Go-mori-fied!

MARY/MARSHA: Sodom and Go-mori-fied?

LULU/LORI: Yep! The Bible done did her in.

MARY/MARSHA: The poor woman. In her time of trouble she went fer the Bible.

LULU/LORI: No. She went fer the gun what she kept a-hidden 'tween the covers of the Bible. Ya see, she cut a hole in the pages of the Old Testament and that's where she kept her little pearl-handle.

MARY/MARSHA: But, how'd she git herself done in?

LULU/LORI: Well, when she opened the Bible she got ta readin' 'bout Sodom and Go-mori and got herself so riled up and angry she slammed shut the covers of the Good Book with such a wallop it triggered her little pearl-handle.

MARY/MARSHA: Fo' shame. Fo' shame.

LULU/LORI: Yup. The bullet came right through the bindin' and hit her square 'tween the eyes! And that's how she got herself Sodom and Go-mori-fied.

MARY/MARSHA: My-o-my. The Lord works in strange ways.

LULU/LORI: That He does.

MARY/MARSHA: You poor baby. You jest sit right here and I'll bring ya a shot o' Grover's guaranteed pick-me-upper. *(Rises. Crosses to bar.)*

(REHEARSAL LIGHTING.)

MARSHA: *(At bar, pouring drink.)* Lori.

LORI: Yeah, Ma?

MARSHA: Are you sure the Cooper boy isn't making all this up?

LORI: Blake Cooper wouldn't make up a thing like that. He's on the football team, Mother.

MARSHA: Is there some sort of connection between sports and honesty?

LORI: He's an Armadillo, Mother!

MARSHA: *(Incredulous.)* Well, I guess that puts him above scrutiny, doesn't it? I mean, if you can't trust an Armadillo, who can you trust? No trouble getting into the Supreme Court for him.

LORI: The Armadillos have the highest quad-A rating in the state.

MARSHA: I'm sure that must mean something, Lori. Still, that's a pretty serious accusation, even for an Armadillo.

LORI: Mother, it's common knowledge what Mr. Walker is.

MARSHA: *(Returning with glass.)* Well, I know Bill's different, Lori.
LORI: A fag, Mother. Bill Walker's queer bait.

MARSHA: That doesn't mean he's a bad teacher.

LORI: Oh, Mother, you're such an innocent?

MARSHA: *(Innocently demure.)* Well, maybe. You know me, sweetheart—another time, another generation. I'm old-fashioned, I admit it. My innocence blushes.

LORI: Mother, are you rehearsing something? I mean, is that from something

MARSHA: From my heart, Lori.

LORI: Besides, it's only the cute boys he keeps after school. Ask anybody.

MARSHA: Well, maybe it's the cute boys who've got the most to learn.

LORI: Mother, really. Be serious.

MARSHA: So, why didn't the boy's mother go to the police or the Superintendent of Schools?

LORI: I don't know. Maybe, he didn't tell his mother. I mean, there are things I don't tell you.

MARSHA: What kind of things?

LORI: Things, just things. Sometimes I think you're from the Stone Age. Like really Paleozoic, you know? He's going to Texas A and M in the fall.

MARSHA: Who is?

LORI: Blake Cooper.

MARSHA: *Ah*, the Armadillo. I thought you said he's on the football team?

LORI: He is. Well, he was. You're so literal, Mother. He sat right in front of me during graduation. I don't know how you could have missed him. What a hunk! It's a wonder Mr. Walker didn't rip his jeans off right there in class and perform fellatio on him.

MARSHA: LORI! Where on earth did you ever learn such a thing?

LORI: Honestly, Mother. You're still in the Twentieth Century. Lighten up.

MARSHA: When I was your age, Missy, I was . . .

LORI: Still a virgin, right?

MARSHA: *(Shocked.)* WHAT?! You don't mean to tell me that you're—

LORI: *(Cutting her off.)* I don't mean to tell you anything, Mother.

MARSHA: Get upstairs!

LORI: Why?

(PERFORMANCE LIGHTING.)

MARY/MARSHA: Go on, Miss Lulu. You git along upstairs and rest a spell.

LULU/LORI: I could do with a rest, Miss Mary. You're so kind to me. *(Rises.)* You know, most women wouldn't walk across the street with a girl like me . . . what with the kind o' business I'm in and all. You're a good woman, Mary Holiday. I can almost see the glow of purity radiatin' all around you. *(Exits upstairs.)*

(There is a long pause while MARY paces back and forth. Suddenly, POLLY UPSTRINGER enters, wearing a bonnet and bouncing through the swinging doors – looking like a plump Bo-Peep.)

POLLY/DORIS: Mary Holiday! Mary Holiday!

MARY/MARSHA: Why, Polly Upstringer, the sheriff's wife! Whatever brings you in here? To what do I owe the pleasure?

(REHEARSAL LIGHTING.)

DORIS: *(She plops into a chair at a table. The flighty sweetness of her entrance quickly turns sour.)* Cut the bullshit, Marsha! You know perfectly well why I'm here. If that sorry, sick, fag sonofabitch is going to remain in this play, I want to know why!

MARSHA: Well, I can't very well throw him out now . . . can I, Doris? Who else can we get to play the Judge?

DORIS: Then, what do you plan to do about it?

MARSHA: That's why I phoned you, Doris. I thought I could bounce a few things off you, so to speak. Correct me if I'm wrong, but we don't really want that sort of character on our board of directors, do we?

DORIS: Can you prove any of this?

MARSHA: Oh, I'd say I had enough information to make it rather hot for him.

DORIS: Pervert!

MARSHA: Now, let's not be too harsh . . . or too quick to judge.

DORIS: Marsha, you're the one who said he was screwing around with his students. You can't throw a cow patty without getting a little stink on you. Now, was he or wasn't he?

MARSHA: I was only repeating what I heard, Doris. Although, it did come from a very reliable source. Still, we mustn't jump to conclusions.

DORIS: I'd like to run his sorry ass out of town. I knew there was something sleazy about that man!

MARSHA: We all did, Doris. But first, let's concentrate on replacing him on our board of directors. That is, if you think he should be replaced.

DORIS: Of course I do!

MARSHA: Well, I was thinking . . . who would be the best choice?

DORIS: And?

MARSHA: When Daddy donated the land—you did know that the land The Playhouse sits on was donated by my father, didn't you?

DORIS: *(Impatient.)* Yes, Marsha. From here to El Paso they know it.

MARSHA: You don't have to be rude about it.

DORIS: *Tch. (Slaps her own wrist.)* Sorry.

MARSHA: When daddy donated the land he said, "Marshmallow"—he called me Marshmallow—Marshmallow, you see that everybody takes good care of everything. You wanted your little playhouse, now it's up to you to take good care of it.

DORIS: *(Growing more impatient.)* Get on with it, Marsha!

MARSHA: On his deathbed he said it.

DORIS: That's very nice. Really, it is. But who was it you were thinking would be the best choice?

MARSHA: *(Coy.)* The best choice? The best choice for what, Doris?
DORIS: For the board, Marsha. The goddamned board!

MARSHA: Oh, well, it would have to be someone who knows what The Playhouse is all about. Its roots, so to speak.

DORIS: And?

MARSHA: And someone who cares enough to see that management doesn't fall into the wrong hands, if you know what I mean.

DORIS: I think I've got the gist, Marsha.

MARSHA: Well?

DORIS: Well, what?

MARSHA: It's you, Doris, you.

DORIS: *(All saccharine.)* No? Me? Really? Oh, I couldn't!

MARSHA: Of course you could.

DORIS: All right. Now that I think about it . . . *(Remembers something.)* Oh! *Oh, oh, oh!*

MARSHA: What is it?

DORIS: Evelyn Forester said that that fag was talking about getting together some sort of secret board meeting.

MARSHA: I know.

DORIS: You do? You're not supposed to. How did you find out?

MARSHA: I've my ways. Anything else?

DORIS: That's all I know. Besides, I'm not privy—like some of us we know—to all the intrigue and espionage that goes on around here.

MARSHA: I wouldn't exactly call it that, Doris.

DORIS: You wouldn't? Good God Almighty, Marsha! The doings around here would make the CIA blush. This place is like a training camp for the Taliban!

MARSHA: Now, Doris, we're only volunteers, working *gratis,* doing our best to run a little ol' community theatre.

DORIS: Well, thank God none of you are nuclear armed.

MARSHA: Can I count on you, Doris?

DORIS: Honey, you can always count on me.

MARSHA: And Evelyn? Where does she stand?

DORIS: In the middle of the road. Where else has she ever been known to stand?

MARSHA: And Hal?

DORIS: Hal? Marsha, you ought to know better than I about Hal.

MARSHA: What ever do you mean?

DORIS: Cut the bull, Marsha. Everybody knows the two of you have a thing going.

MARSHA: A thing?

DORIS: A thing. A thing. You do know what *a thing* is, don't you?

MARSHA: Well, that depends.

DORIS Marsha, let's make a deal. You cut the bull and the games and I'll deal you a straight hand. You know what I'm saying?

MARSHA: *(After a pause.) Everybody?*

DORIS: Maybe not everybody. But, since I'm usually the last to find out anything around this rifle range, I think it's safe to assume that Rita knows, and O.T. knows, and Alyson knows, and of course the fruit knows. But I don't think Evelyn knows, or if she does, she's keeping quiet. And certainly not Mike because if he knew then you'd know. So, I think it's safe to assume that he's pretty much left in the dark. Well, I don't want to seem pushy, Marsha, but how do you propose going about getting me on the board?

MARSHA: Leave it to me. I can handle it.

DORIS: *(Crossing to piano.)* I've no doubt. And the pervert?

MARSHA: When I'm done with Mr. William Walker, that sonofabitch will wish he'd never heard of Derrick, Texas!

DORIS: That's what I like about you, Marsha . . . you're so demure.

MARSHA: *(Quotes Lady Macbeth.)* "Give me the daggers. The sleeping and the dead are but as pictures; 'tis the eye of childhood that fears a painted devil. If he do bleed I'll gild the faces of the grooms withal, for it must seem their guilt."

(DORIS begins to play the piano.)

DORIS & MARSHA: *(Sing.)* THERE'S NO BUSINESS LIKE SHOW BUSINESS

(While they are singing, BILL enters. DORIS and MARSHA quickly become aware of his presence and stop singing.)

DORIS: *(Rising. Nervously.)* Well, Marsha, I've got to study my lines. It's such an enormous part for me. *(Crossing to exit.)* Oh, hello, Bill.

BILL: Doris.
DORIS: *Um.* Bye, everybody. *(Exits.)*

BILL: I've got to talk to you.

MARSHA: Sure, Bill. What's up?

BILL: It's delicate.

MARSHA: Well, you can tell me, Bill. I'm your friend.

BILL: Someone's been calling members of the school board and accusing me of immoral turpitude.

MARSHA: You're not serious?

BILL: I'm afraid I am. You don't know anything about who might be making those calls, do you?

MARSHA: How could I possibly, Bill? This is the first I've heard of it. How awful this must be for you.

BILL: If I give them my resignation it will be handled quietly. We can avoid a public scandal.

MARSHA: But of course you're innocent. You'll fight it, won't you?

BILL: They'd never believe me, Marsha. Most already know I'm gay. At least, they suspect it. In a little West Texas town like Derrick the accusation alone is tantamount to a conviction.

MARSHA: I'm stunned. People can be so vicious, can't they? If there's anything I can do to be of help just let me know.

BILL: What are they saying about this around The Playhouse?

MARSHA: As I said, this is the first I've heard of it. Although, Doris Powell did make a disparaging remark about you being, you know.

BILL: What I know is, somebody is really out to get me.

MARSHA: It does look like that, doesn't it? It's appalling,

the level some people will sink to. But I wouldn't put too much stock into anything Doris Powell might say. She just takes her religion very literally.

BILL: What did I do, Marsha? What would make someone so angry they'd do this to me?

MARSHA: I'm sure I can't say, Bill. I guess you'll have to search your soul for an answer. I don't want to sound cold, but I'm wondering if this is going to affect our little melodrama in any way?

BILL: I don't see how. I'm committed to it.

MARSHA: Oh, good.

BILL: Christ! I'd rather be accused of robbing a bank, or good ol' heterosexual rape. Even a mass murderer would get more sympathy in this town!

MARSHA: You don't think that's a bit melodramatic? *(After a pause.)* By the way, did I ever say thank you for all your help with *Great Ladies of the Theatre?* I'm sure I must have. Wouldn't you agree?

BILL: *(A scrutinizing pause before it dawn on him.)* You were there, weren't you? Behind the flats listening from backstage?

MARSHA: Listening from backstage? I assure you that I have no idea what you're talking about, sweetie.

BLACK OUT.

END ACT ONE—*Scene 3*

ACT ONE—*Scene 4*

GROVER OATS is behind the bar, MARY HOLIDAY is posed on a barstool, PRINCESS DESERT FLOWER is seated on the piano bench, BART BLACKEY and SALLY SWEETS are seated at a table, SHERIFF UPSTRINGER and the WIDOW DEERE are seated at another table. There is an argument in progress. PERFORMANCE LIGHTING.

GROVER/HAL: Hold it down! Hold it down! *(He pulls out his shotgun and points it heavenward.)* Quiet! Don't make me pull the trigger on this here thing! The Sheriff he's got somethin' ta say! *(A long pause.)* I said, the Sheriff he's got somethin' ta say!

MARY/MARSHA: *(Getting SHERIFF'S attention.)* Sheriff!

SHERIFF/O.T. *(Fingering ear.)* Right! Well, as ya'll know they got away with the whole . . . whole . . . whole . . . *(Looking about, panicked.)* . . . whole . . .

MARY/MARSHA: *(Helping him out.)* Do ya mean the kittinkaboodle?

SHERIFF/O.T.: Sure 'nough! The whole kittinkaboodle and the whole enchilada, too! And poor Madam Nellie's stretched out on her back for the very last time. Rest her soul.

ALL: Rest her soul.

SHERIFF/O.T.: Blowed away by the word o' God!

ALL: Amen.

MARY/MARSHA: Waddaya gonna do about it, Sheriff?

SHERIFF/O.T.: Bury her, I reckon.

MARY/MARSHA: I mean, waddaya gonna do about them that's got away?

ALL: *(General ad lib.)* Yeah, waddaya gonna do about them that's got away?

GROVER/HAL: Quiet down! Quiet down! Ya'll hesh up so's-n the Sheriff can talk! *(A long SILENCE. Repeats SHERIFF'S cue.)* So's-n the sheriff can talk!

SHERIFF/O.T.: Ain't nothin' we can do 'bout it till mornin'. They's got away in the sandstorm wid all da hosses.

MARY/MARSHA: All da hosses, ya say?

SHERIFF/O.T.: *Yup.* And thare ain't a hoss ta be had.

ALL: *(General ad lib.)* Ain't no hosses. Not a one. No hosses . . . .

GROVER/HAL: Quiet down!

(REHEARSAL LIGHTING.)

HAL: Quiet down, please. Ms. Pipes, as you all know, is secretary to the Superintendent of Schools. So, why don't we all listen to what she has to say. Rita, you've got the floor.

RITA: As I was saying, the boy was questioned by our office and, at present, there seems to be no hard evidence for legal action.

O.T.: Where there's smoke there's fire.

RITA: The boy himself never made the accusation.

HAL: So, all we have to go on are a series of anonymous phone calls to the office of the Superintendent of Schools and, of course, our knowledge of Bill's sexual preference.

RITA: We always knew that.

HAL: But it sure doesn't go in his favor now, does it?

O.T.: Now that we all know how the man swings, I say we got an open and shut case.

HAL: This isn't a jury, Mr. Taylor. As it is, I seriously doubt that Mr. Walker will have a job to return to in the fall.

O.T.: I would hope, for the good of our community and the welfare of our children, that Mr. Walker has the common human decency to tender his resignation. I would also be mighty careful, if I was him, about who I turned my back on. There ain't no telling what somebody's libel to go and do. Ya'll know what the Bible has to say about his kind. A man could go and get himself shot, if you know what I mean.

HAL: All right, all right. Let's all calm down. We don't need to get into that. I appreciate your position, Mr. Taylor. But, this isn't the proper forum for that kind of discussion.

O.T.: *(Tapping hearing aid.)* What? What?

HAL: I said, this isn't the place for that kind of discussion.

O.T.: Are you telling me that the Word of God has no place in The Playhouse?

HAL: All I'm saying is that I appreciate that this is an emotionally charged issue. Rita has prepared a letter informing Bill of our intent to dismiss him from the board of directors, and which we have unanimously approved. *(ALYSON raises her hand.)* I stand corrected. Will the secretary note one abstention: Alyson Barrett.

RITA: Noted.

HAL: Now, concerning the nomination of Doris Powell, any further discussion? *(Silence.)* All in favor signify by saying aye.

ALL: *(Except ALYSON.)* Aye.

HAL: Opposed? *(Silence.)* Motion carried. Any new business?

MARSHA: Yes. Who will we get to play the Judge?

ALYSON: Why don't you play it, Marsha?

MARSHA: I don't see how that's possible, dear heart.

ALYSON: You don't? Why with all your faces I'm sure you'll figure something out.

MARSHA: You give me far too much credit.

ALYSON: You know something, Mrs. Cornell-Simmons, you're a regular farce! A goddamned, one-woman, bona fide tragic extravaganza!

MARSHA: I'm sure you've misunderstood some act of kindness.

ALYSON: Get real! You staged this whole little fiasco. I just want to be here when the karma comes back around, bitch.

O.T.: Now, Mrs. Barrett, you really don't mean to say such—

ALYSON: *(Cutting him off - sharply.)* Shut up! Don't you freaking tell me what I mean or don't mean, you Bible thumping sonofabitch! Who the hell do you think you are!? *(Turning on everyone.)* Where in hell do all you people get off, *huh?* What a bunch of hypocrites!

MARSHA: *(Calmly.)* Alyson?

ALYSON: WHAT?

MARSHA: Does this mean we'll have to find ourselves another Princess Desert Flower?

ALYSON You're priceless, Marsha. You really are. In fact, you're altogether something else. Other-worldly. It's uncanny to think you really have blood flowing through those veins of yours. The thought of you as really belonging to the human race frightens the shit out of me.

MARSHA: So, what are you saying? Is that a yes or a no?

ALYSON: Don't worry, honey. I'm going to play this through to the bitter end. I'll be a Princess you'll never forget!

MARSHA: You already are, dear.

ALYSON: *(She loses it.)* I'll kill you!

(Rushing MARSHA, ALYSON attacks her. MARSHA screams. They fall to the floor, fists flying. HAL and O.T. rush over to separate them.)

ALYSON: *(Continues.)* You sorry bitch!

(HAL and O.T. get caught-up in the fight and take a few punches from the ladies. ALYSON shakes herself loose of O.T.'S grip.)

ALYSON: *(Continues.)* You sorry sonsofbitches! I'd check the bullets in the prop guns were I any of you! *(Exits.)*

*(Smalltalk follows with phrases such as: "What got into

her?" and "What did she mean by that?" . . . etc.)

MARSHA: *(To MIKE, over the din of chatter.)* You were certainly a big help, Michael!

MIKE: It all happened so fast. What could I do?

MARSHA: I don't know. Something better than your bump on a log impression!

HAL: Let's have some order, please! *(Pause for order.)* I propose that in the light of our current situation we cancel the melodrama.

MARSHA: No! *No, no, no, no, no!* Michael, say something!

MIKE Do you really think that will be necessary, Hal?

HAL: I don't see any alternative. We don't have a Judge and it now looks like we don't have a Princess, either.

MARSHA: Of course we do. You all heard Alyson say she was going to see it through "to the bitter end." Regardless of what some of you may think of Alyson, she is not a quitter.

RITA: Nobody said anything about—

MARSHA: *(Stopping her.)* And that's to everybody's credit. Now, hear me out. *(Extravagantly noble.)* I certainly hope none of you are thinking about asking Alyson for her resignation just because of one little old outburst, even if it wasn't her first.

O.T.: What about that stunt she pulled at the *Charley's Aunt* cast party?

MARSHA: And you'd be in your right to hold a grudge, O.T. Was Leota Ruth able to get all that guacamole out of your suit?

O.T.: Well, yes.

MARSHA: See? No damage done. Please, let's not make any hasty decisions. Alyson Barrett has been one of our most dedicated workers. Remember, it was Alyson who, almost single-handedly, raised nearly twenty thousand dollars for our little theatre.

RITA: I think it was over twenty thousand, Marsha.

MARSHA: Rita, if you check your books, you'll see that it was *nearly,* not over.

O.T.: *(A bit put-out.)* Well, I helped a little, Marsha.

MARSHA: And didn't we all? In fact, I supplied her with all the contacts. Michael and I spent hours upon hours compiling that list, but that's neither here nor there. Let's give credit where credit is due.

O.T.: If you ask me, you're too kind.

MARSHA: I can't help myself, O.T. It's just my nature.

RITA: Maybe we should hold off on Alyson's plaque of appreciation.

HAL: It's already been voted on and passed, Rita.

RITA: Since when has that ever meant anything around here?

EVELYN: What does she mean by that? *(Looking around and getting no response from anyone.)* O.T., what does she mean by that?

MARSHA: Evelyn, I'm sure Rita meant that in the best possible sense. It's a compliment to us as the governing body to be flexible, open minded, willing and able to change directions when the need arises.

RITA: That's exactly what I meant, Marsha.

MARSHA: Of course it was.

EVELYN: *(To herself.)* Poo.

MARSHA: Now, about that "check the bullets in the prop guns" remark. Who could possibly take that seriously? But, in case anybody's worried, I, personally, will be responsible for props from now on.

O.T.: Still—

MARSHA: I know, O.T., I know. That Bible-thumping-you-know-what remark didn't set well with me, either. But you know theatre people. Always on stage. God love us. That's show biz. I know that I'm certainly willing to forgive and forget if it's for the good of The Playhouse.

HAL: Rita, has that plaque been sent to the engraver yet?

RITA: No, sir.

HAL: All in favor of holding off on the plaque until we've given it further consideration signify by saying aye.

ALL: Aye.

HAL: Motion carried.

O.T.: That still leaves us without a Judge.

MARSHA: Not necessarily. As far as Bill Walker is

concerned, we can hold off on his dismissal until after *Massacre* closes. Why change horses in mid-stream? You all heard Rita say that the office of the Superintendent of Schools had "no hard evidence."

O.T.: *(To himself.)* Pervert.

MARSHA: Who are we to judge? God knows we're all guilty of something.

EVELYN: Poo.

MARSHA: Come on, Evelyn. I've seen you parking in those spaces reserved for cripples. None of us are innocent. However, when his name first went into nomination I had my doubts. Remember?O.T.: It was a big mistake!

MARSHA: We're all entitled to one, O.T. *(Turning.)* Rita, who was it nominated him?

RITA: *(Reluctantly.)* It was you, Marsha.

MARSHA: No, no, no. That was just a formality in the due process of Parliamentary Procedure. I mean, whose idea was it to have him on the board in the first place?

RITA: *(Uncertain. Hesitant.)* Alyson's?

MARSHA: Of course! How could I have forgotten. For goodness sake, who among us isn't guilty of being a bad judge of character one time or another?

O.T.: But Marsha—

MARSHA: *(Holding up her hand, cutting O.T. off. Magnanimously.)* No, no, no. Let's be practical. I, for one, do not want to do anything to bring disgrace down upon our little theatre, or our little melodrama. As they say, the show must go on.

O.T.: But, Marsha—

MARSHA: Let me finish, O.T. God knows how I'm torn-up about this whole affair. I don't know how these rumors got started about poor Mr. Walker. They seem to have a life of their own, but it also seems to me that—

O.T.: Marsha, it was you who called this emergency meeting!

MARSHA: ME?! *(Looking about innocently.)* Good heavens, no! I just wanted us all to sit down together over a friendly cup of coffee so we could put an end to all those vicious rumors; however grounded in fact they may or may not be. Why, my phone's been buzzing all week! All those people who come to see our little plays calling me. Calling me because they don't know anybody else to call.

O.T.: Then who?

MARSHA: What does it matter now. I say the show must go on.

MIKE: *Hear, hear!*

MARSHA: Thank you, Michael.

HAL: Rita, perhaps we should hold off sending that letter to Mr. Walker until after the melodrama closes.

RITA: Yes, sir.

HAL: And I will inform Doris Powell of our decision to place her on our board of directors right after we adjourn.

MARSHA: Then it's settled? *Massacre At Dirty Gulch* goes

on as planned?

HAL: All in favor signify by saying aye.

ALL: Aye.

HAL: Motion carried. Now, about who's bringing what to the cast party.

(PERFORMANCE LIGHTING. JUDGE enters with gun in hand. A sudden SILENCE. ALL eyes are on JUDGE.)

GROVER/HAL: Wait a minute!

BART/MIKE: *(Jumping up from chair.)* Everybody stay calm!

BLACK OUT.

END ACT ONE

ACT TWO—*Scene 1*

AT RISE: ALL are as they were at end of ACT ONE. PERFORMANCE LIGHTING.

JUDGE/BILL: *(With gun in hand.)* Don't a one o' ya move!

SHERIFF/O.T.: What's the matter, Judge?

JUDGE/BILL: Where's that Injun gal?

SHERIFF/O.T.: *(Crossing to JUDGE.)* She went on the warpath, Judge. Attacked poor little ol' Mary Holiday. Then she scooted off like greased lightnin'.

MARY/MARSHA: It was un-pre-voked, Your Honor. I detected eyes as blue as robin's eggs. Ain't never saw no Injun with blue eyes before. So, I told her so and then she went all wild and crazy.

JUDGE/BILL: 'Cause she ain't no Injun! Sheriff, that thare gal is the notorious Mean Mabel Wiggens!

ALL: NO?!

JUDGE/BILL: Yup! The she-scourge of The West!

ALL: NO?!

JUDGE/BILL: Yup! The hatchetatin' hussy!

ALL No?!

JUDGE/BILL: Yup! The mistress o' murder!

ALL: No?!

JUDGE/BILL: Yup! The gun-slingin' slut!

ALL NO?!

JUDGE/BILL: Yup, she's a bad one. *(Turns to BART.)* And I'm accusin' you, Bart Blackey, o' bein' in cahoots. *(To Sheriff.)* Put the cuffs on him, Sheriff.

BART/MIKE: *(Buying time.)* Me?

JUDGE/BILL: Yup.

BART/MIKE: I'm as innocent as a new-born babe.

JUDGE/BILL: Nope.

BART/MIKE: As honest as Abe.

JUDGE/BILL: Nope.

BART/MIKE: As pure as the driven snow.

JUDGE/BILL: Nope.

BART/MIKE: As good as gold.

JUDGE/BILL: Nope. I don't think so.

BART/MIKE: Well, I ain't all bad.

ALL: *(Except BART.) Yup!*

BART/MIKE: I'm a-tellin' ya, ya got me all wrong.

JUDGE/BILL: Nope!

BART/MIKE: Yup!

JUDGE/BILL: Don't ya go a-yuppin' me, Blackey. I gots me two o' yor boys over at the courthouse a-willin' ta testify agin ya. Whaddya say ta that?

BART/MIKE: Curses! I reckon ya leaves me no choice. *(Grabs SALLY SWEETS, pulls out his gun and holds it to her head.)* Everybody, stay calm! Drop yor guns, boys, or I'll blow this little gal's head from here ta Tucson!

SALLY/RITA: Oh, Mr. Blackey, ya wouldn't?

BART/MIKE: Yup!

SALLY/RITA: Do as he says, Pa. I think he means it.

JUDGE/BILL: Well, I reckon since that's how ya put it, Blackey, ya leaves me with no choice.

(JUDGE and SHERIFF drop their guns.)

BART/MIKE: *(Moving toward exit, taking SALLY as his hostage.)* Back off! Back off! And if-n any o' ya come a followin' after me, this little ol' gal will be a-singin' with the angels!

SALLY/RITA: Oh! Curse you, Bart Blackey! Curse you! You can have my body but you'll never have my respect!

BART/MIKE: Got no need for yor respect, girlie. *Ha, ha, ha!*

SALLY/RITA: *No, no, no!* A thousand times no!

BART/MIKE: *Yup, yup, yup!* And jest as many!

SALLY/RITA: Do as he says, Pa! Do as he says!

(Holding SALLY with gun to her head, BART exits dragging

her along.)

SHERIFF/O.T.: Fo' shame. Fo' shame. And thare ain't a hoss ta be had.

JUDGE/BILL: Ain't a fact, Sheriff.

SHERIFF/O.T.: It ain't?

JUDGE/BILL: Nope.

ALL: Nope?

JUDGE/BILL: Nope. Found 'em all a-huddled down in the gulch. Rounded 'em all up m'self.

SHERIFF/O.T.: *(Fingering ear.)* Ya say ya found the hosses?

ALL: YUP!

SHERIFF/O.T.: *(Rushes to swinging doors.)* Then, wadda we waitin' fer? *(Exits.)*

JUDGE/BILL: *(To WIDOW DEERE.)* Come along, m' sweet. We'll git our little girl back. Don't ya fret.

MARY/MARSHA: She's already in m' prayers, Judge.

JUDGE/BILL: Thank you, Mary Holiday. You're a good woman. *(To WIDOW DEERE, arms around her.)* Ain't she a good woman, m' precious?

WIDOW/EVELYN: If-n ya say so, Judge. If-n ya say so. *(Exits with JUDGE.)*

MARY/MARSHA: *(At bar. Alone with GROVER.)* That thare brother o' yor's sure is a mean one.

GROVER/HAL: That he is, Mary. That he is.

MARY/MARSHA: Yor pa never should o' went to the outhouse.

GROVER/HAL: He never did agin.

MARY/MARSHA: *Never?*

GROVER/HAL: Nope. Ma burned it to the ground.

MARY/MARSHA: Well, what did ya'll do after that?

GROVER/HAL: I'd rather not say.

MARY/MARSHA: Better let me have another shot o' yor bug juice, Grover. I feel a faint comin' on.

(REHEARSAL LIGHTING.)

HAL: Don't you think you've had enough, Marsha?

MARSHA: You'll know when I've had enough. And if you think you're going to run me out of The Playhouse, you've got another think coming.

HAL: Marsha, I believe you need professional help.

MARSHA: That's rich; coming from an abortionist! Why don't you just pack up your bloody forceps and crawl back to Dallas?

HAL: You need a rest, Marsha.

MARSHA: I know what I need and what I need is this theatre! Daddy gave The Playhouse to me! Not to you or to anybody else on that board of butchers!

HAL: You've been under a lot of pressure lately.

MARSHA: You bet I've been under pressure and you and your gang of thugs are the cause.

HAL: You've done this to yourself. You railroaded that entire board meeting.

MARSHA: I didn't railroad anything!

HAL: Marsha, it was a sham designed solely for your benefit so you could get Doris Powell on the board.

MARSHA: That bitch!

HAL: She was your friend not so long ago.

MARSHA: Some friend. So, you all went ahead and had your secret meeting after all in your little smoke-filled room caucus of assassins!

HAL: Are you aware that Bill Walker's tenure has been terminated?

MARSHA: What has that got to do with me?

HAL: This isn't a game, Marsha. We're talking about a man's life!

MARSHA: I'm sorry for him. But, he did do it with one of his students, didn't he?

HAL: There's no proof of that. Just gossip started by who? Who, Marsha?

MARSHA: Who? Who? How in hell do I know who?

HAL: Doris Powell says you.

MARSHA: That traitor! Who can believe a word she says?

HAL: Enough on the board to ask for your resignation.

MARSHA: You're throwing me off the board?

HAL: And from all further activities connected with The Playhouse.

MARSHA: *(Disbelief.)* What?

HAL: Until you've had sufficient time to rest.

MARSHA: No. No!

HAL: You left us with no alternative.

MARSHA: Look. Right after *Massacre* closes I'll do my one-woman show. It'll be a big money maker, Hal. I'll call the club and tell them we've decided to do it here instead. I'll donate all the proceeds to The Playhouse. What a way to end the

HAL: Haven't you been listening, Marsha?

MARSHA: It could be a wine and cheese affair. Everybody will come all decked out – tuxedos, gowns, glitter!

HAL: No.

MARSHA: We'll pack the house. Standing room only!

HAL: I'm sorry, Marsha.

MARSHA: You can't do this, Hal.

HAL: *(Touches her shoulder.)* It's for your own good.

MARSHA: *(Withdraws to piano.)* Don't touch me!

HAL: Marsha, please . . .

MARSHA: Don't ever touch me again. Never!

HAL: Marsha . . .
MARSHA: *(Banging helter-skelter on keyboard.)* I can't hear you . . .

HAL: Marsha!

MARSHA: *(Sings wildly.)*
THERE'S NO BUSINESS LIKE SHOW BUSINESS
THERE'S NO BUSINESS I KNOW

HAL: *(Grabs her.)* Stop it!

MARSHA Don't touch me! Don't touch me, I said! *(Runs to chair. Sits.)*

HAL: Will you pull yourself together!

MARSHA: You can't do this. Don't you understand? You can't do this.

HAL: It's already been done. The board met and that was our decision.

MARSHA: No.

HAL: Everyone is very concerned about you, Marsha.

MARSHA: No.

HAL: You really left us no choice.

MARSHA: No.

HAL: Are you going to be all right?

MARSHA: What the hell do you think, Hal? Would you be all right?

HAL: I'm sorry. Really, I am.

MARSHA: Really? How sorry are you, Hal?

HAL: I hate to leave it this way!
MARSHA: Just go. You're not going to wash off any of your guilt around here, Hal. So, take your guilt and go.

HAL: *(Crosses to exit.)* If you need anything. *(No response. After a pause.)* I'm sorry. *(Exits.)*

MARSHA: *(After a pause. Looking about.)* Daddy. Daddy? They want to take my playhouse away. What are we going to do, Daddy? What are we going to do?

BLACK OUT.

END ACT TWO – *Scene 1*

ACT TWO—*Scene 2*

There is no one onstage. The RECORDED SOUND of HORSES GALLOPING off into the distance is heard. The WIDOW DEERE and POLLY UPSTRINGER enter through swinging doors. PERFORMANCE LIGHTING.

POLLY/DORIS: We'll be safe if-n we waits in here till the posse returns.

WIDOW/EVELYN: Poor little Sally. Abductified by such a mean ol' villain.

POLLY/DORIS: It's a sin what this world is comin' to nowadays. *(Fanning herself.)* Oh, it is. It is. Reverend Gudger gave a whole sermon last Sunday on the wages of sin. I love sermons on sin. Don't ya just love sermons on sin? Oh my! There's nothin' like a sin sermon ta put the fear in ya. Don't ya love it when The Reverend Gudger fills ya with fear?

WIDOW/EVELYN: He was a-sittin' under m' poor Sally.

POLLY/DORIS: Oh, that's just his way, honey. He likes ta git close ta his flock.

WIDOW/EVELYN: Does he minister, too?

POLLY/DORIS: Does he ever!

WIDOW/EVELYN: I didn't know that. Oh dear, this sinful world is comin' to its brink! When a man the likes o' him takes to the pulpit the end has gotta be near.

POLLY/DORIS: Whatever are ya talkin' 'bout, child?

WIDOW/EVELYN: Bart Blackey a-sittin' under m' innocent

little, soon-ta-be-stepdaughter, a man of the cloth. The world's comin' to an end, I tell ya. Comin' to an end.

POLLY/DORIS: Oh, him! I thought you was talkin' 'bout The Reverend Gudger.

WIDOW/EVELYN: No. I was talkin' 'bout Bad Bart who went and abductified poor little Sally Sweets.

POLLY/DORIS: Don't ya worry, Widow Deere. The men folk'll git her back safe and sound.

WIDOW/EVELYN: I hopes so, Polly Upstringer. I sure do hopes so.

POLLY/DORIS: *(Fans herself.)* My, I'm burnin' up.

WIDOW/EVELYN: Must be somethin' ya et.

POLLY/DORIS: No. It's talkin' 'bout sin. Talkin' about sin just lights a fire under me. Does it do that ta you?

WIDOW/EVELYN: Nope. Maybe, yor standin' in a hot draft.

POLLY/DORIS: No, no! It's sin! Sin'll do it ta ya every time. Just thinkin' 'bout it makes a body start ta burn. And thare's sin all around us, ain't thare? Ya can't go anywhere nowadays without thare bein' sin just around the corner. *(Fanning herself.)* Oh, I tell ya, I can smell sin a mile off!

WIDOW/EVELYN: Sure that ain't a dead heifer down in the gulch?

PRINCESS/ALYSON: *(Enters with gun in hand.)* Stick 'em up, ladies! Looks ta me likes I gotta coupla pigeons!

WIDOW/EVELYN & POLLY/DORIS: Princess Desert

Flower!

PRINCESS/ALYSON: (Removing headband, feather and wig.) It's Mabel Wiggens to you, ladies! Now, ya'll jest stay calm and maybe ol' mean Mabel will shows ya a little mercy! 'Though I wouldn't count on it! *Ha, ha, ha!*

(REHEARSAL LIGHTING.)

DORIS: Mercy? Mercy, Alyson?

ALYSON: That's right. She did all right by you. Didn't she, Doris?

DORIS: What, exactly, is your point?

ALYSON: My point is you're on the board, aren't you? That is what you wanted. Wasn't it, Doris?

DORIS: For your information, 'though I don't see what business it is of yours, Marsha approached me as regards the board. It was never solicited.

EVELYN: Ladies, ladies, let's not quarrel and say things we'll regret.

ALYSON: It's a little late for that, Evelyn.

EVELYN: Well, I think we ought to sit down and behave like the adults we are. *(Sits.)*

DORIS: I quite agree. *(Goes to bar. Removes box of pizza from under counter.)*

ALYSON: Oh? You quite agree, do you?

DORIS: What do you want from me, Alyson?

ALYSON: I'm not sure yet, Doris. But, when I figure it out you'll be the first to know.

DORIS: While you're figuring it out you don't mind if I have my supper, do you?

ALYSON: Eat away. It's what you do best.

DORIS: *(Chewing on pizza.)* If you're trying to be provocative, Alyson, you're on the brink of success.

EVELYN: Ladies, ladies. Shouldn't we be rehearsing our lines?

ALYSON: Later, Evelyn.

EVELYN: We don't want to let Marsha down. Now, do we? *(No response.)* All right. Let's take it from our entrance, Doris.

DORIS: *(Chewing on pizza. Not getting fully into character.)* "We'll be safe if we wait in here until the posse returns."

EVELYN: *(Likewise. Not getting fully into character.)* "Poor little Sally. Abductified by such a mean old man."

DORIS: Villain.

EVELYN: What?

DORIS: "Abductified by such a mean old villain."

EVELYN: Oh, poo. Villain. "Poor little Sally. Abductified by such a mean old villain."

DORIS: "It's a sin what this world is coming to nowadays." *(Fans herself with a slice of pizza.)* "It is, it is.

Reverend Gudger gave a whole sermon last Sunday on the wages of sin. I love sermons on sin. " Alyson, this is an example of the mind of the woman whom you would defend. Listen up. "Don't you just love sermons on sin? Oh my! There is nothing like a sin sermon to put the fear in you. Don't you love it when The Reverend Gudger fills you with fear?"

EVELYN: "He was sitting under my poor Sally."

DORIS: "Oh, that's just his way, honey. He likes to get close to his flock." So, he can fill you with something else and it ain't God! Can you imagine actually sitting down and writing this kind of shit?

EVELYN: "Does he minister, too?"

DORIS: "Does he ever." Alyson, did it ever occur to you that Mike and Marsha may actually be one person?

ALYSON: I'm sure I don't know what you're talking about, Doris.

EVELYN: "I didn't know that. Oh dear, this sinful world is coming to its brink. When a man the likes of him takes to the pulpit the end has got to be near."

DORIS: *(To ALYSON.)* When have you ever known Mike to have an idea of his own? He's hardly a man. More like a wimp, I'd say. *(To EVELYN.)* "Whatever are you talking about, child?" *(To ALYSON.)* Nope. Mike's something Marsha winds up every morning and sends out to do her bidding. Well, I suppose if you like the zombie type, he's your man.

ALYSON: Well, no one is really asking you.

EVELYN: "Bart Blackey sitting, sittin', a-sittin' under my

innocent little, soon to be stepdaughter, a man of the cloth. The world's coming to an end, I tell you. Coming to an end." Did I get that all right?

DORIS: Sounded good to me. "Oh, him. I thought you was talking about The Reverend Gudger."

EVELYN: "No. I was talking about Bad Bart who went and abductified poor little Sally Sweets."

ALYSON: I don't know what you're talking about, Doris. I happen to think Mike has a wonderful mind of his own.

DORIS: You would. "Don't you worry, Widow Deere. The men folk'll get her back safe and sound."

EVELYN: "I hope so, Polly Upstringer. I sure do hope so."

DORIS: "My, I'm burning up." *(Fans herself with a slice of pizza.)*

EVELYN: "Must be somethin' ya et."

ALYSON: We know who Marsha had in mind when she wrote that line.

DORIS: Very funny, Alyson. You know I have hypoglycemia. If I don't eat something every couple hours I get very ill. If attacking me for something I can't help is the best you know, then you are to be pitied. *(To EVELYN.)* "No. It's talking about sin. Talking about sin just lights a fire under me. Does it do that to you?"

ALYSON: She walks into rehearsal every night with her double cheese pizza and two Big Macs and she has the gall to tell us she's feeding her hypoglycemia.

EVELYN: "Nope. Maybe your standing in a hot draft."

DORIS: "No, it's sin! Sin will do it to you every time. Just thinking about it makes a body start to burn. And there's sin all around us, ain't there? You can't go anywhere nowadays without there being sin just around the corner." Right, Alyson? *(Fanning herself.)* "Oh, I tell ya, I can smell sin a mile off!"

EVELYN: "Sure that ain't a dead heifer down in the gulch?"

ALYSON: "Stick 'em up, ladies. Looks to me likes I got a coupla pigeons."

EVELYN & DORIS: "Princess Desert Flower!"

ALYSON: "It's Mabel Wiggens to you, ladies. Now, ya'll just stay calm and maybe ol' Mean Mabel will shows ya a little mercy! Though I wouldn't count on it. *Ha, ha, ha.*"

EVELYN & DORIS: "Mercy, mercy!"

ALYSON: "Hush up!"

EVELYN & DORIS: "Mercy, mercy!"

ALYSON: "If I told you once I told you twice to hush up! You're my hostages till I know Bart's clean clear of that there posse." That's where Lulu enters. "You pigeons is wearin' down my patience!" And that's all we can do without a Lulu.

DORIS: No. I wouldn't count on mercy, Alyson.

ALYSON: You're really something. You're not on the board five minutes and you're stabbing Marsha in the back.

DORIS: She had it coming. And don't you stand there looking so innocent. You didn't put up much of a fight, as I recall. *(Takes bite of pizza.)*

ALYSON: How could I? You were all out for blood. I certainly didn't want it to be mine.

DORIS: See how you are?

EVELYN: Ladies, ladies.

DORIS: Oh, shut up, Evelyn!

EVELYN: *Poo!*

DORIS: Well, Alyson, from what I heard about your little tantrum at the meeting before last, you ought to be grateful it wasn't your blood on the boardroom floor.

ALYSON: Aren't you going to offer anybody some of that pizza?

DORIS: *(Holds up box and indicates that it is empty.)* Sorry, you should have asked sooner. *(Puts box under counter.)*
ALYSON: You know what, Doris? You look like you just came from a famine . . . and you caused it! *(EVELYN laughs.)*

DORIS: Shut up, Evelyn! *(To ALYSON.)* Let me tell you a thing or two, Princess Spread Eagle! *(Swigs drink.)* Stop pretending you care so much for poor little shat-upon Marsha who's tried to cut every one of our throats at one time or another. Poor helpless Marsha, who'd have you for breakfast if she could stomach your vile, disgusting, aging flesh!

EVELYN: *Ladies, ladies.*

DORIS: *(Ignoring EVELYN.)* Don't think we don't all know about that little tummy tuck you had in Dallas last year. By the way, it's too bad you can't get frequent flier mileage on all those Botox injections! Not to mention all that electrolysis to keep you from looking like Mighty Joe Young!

ALYSON: You fat lump of buffalo shit!

EVELYN: *Ladies, ladies.*

DORIS: *(Still ignoring EVELYN.)* That's cute coming from the black hole of the universe.

ALYSON: You've made your point!

DORIS: Not yet I haven't!

EVELYN: *Ladies, ladies.*

ALYSON: *(To DORIS. Ignoring EVELYN.)* Have another bourbon. You're still half a gallon away from your daily quota.

DORIS: Alyson, making fun of me is not going to get Marsha back on the board. Nor do I need you to remind me of my shortcomings. So, do me a favor and get the hell off my case!

EVELYN: *Ladies, ladies.*

DORIS & ALYSON: Shut up, Evelyn!

EVELYN: *Poo!*

DORIS: *(Pouring herself another drink.)* Alyson, you can save your bleeding heart act for somebody who cares. Marsha got what she deserved. *(Swigs drink.)* By the way . . . *(Pours herself another drink.)* . . . are you still fucking Marsha's husband?

(MARSHA enters from upstairs and stands posed on landing.

She appears tired and dazed. ALL eyes are on her.)

ALYSON: Marsha? Are you okay?

MARSHA: Yes, of course. Am I interrupting something?

DORIS: Not at all, Marsha. We were just discussing the climate around here. Fair to Midland, I'd say. Want a drink?

MARSHA: No, not now. Maybe later. Thank you for asking, Doris.

DORIS: *(Uneasy.)* Sure. You're welcome, Marsha.

MARSHA: Have you girls been rehearsing your lines?

EVELYN: *(With concern.)* Yes, Marsha.

MARSHA: Good, good. If this is to be my last show, let's make it a good one.

EVELYN: It will be, Marsha. We've gone through all our lines and we didn't miss a one.

MARSHA: *(Oddly elsewhere.)* Good, good.

ALYSON: Look, I'm really sorry, Marsha.

MARSHA: No, no, no, Al. It's all right. Really, it is. I know you were all thinking of my good.

DORIS: Right. We were only thinking of what's good for Marsha.*(ALYSON throws DORIS a mean glance.)* What? Did I say something wrong?

MARSHA: The rest will do me good. We have a cabin in Cloudcroft.

EVELYN: I didn't know that.

MARSHA: Michael and I bought it a long time ago. Just a few hours into New Mexico. Deep in the mountains. Beautiful climate. Not like here at all.

DORIS: *Yeah,* the climate's a little rough around here. Never know when a sand storm is going to sneak up on you.

EVELYN: That sounds nice, Marsha.

MARSHA: Oh, it is. Green trees. Pine. The scent of pine! Don't you all just love the scent of pine? *(No response.)* Not the stink of gas and oil. Don't you all just hate the stink of gas and oil? *(No response.)* Michael says that it's the smell of money, but I think it just stinks. And flat! Flat as a tortilla.

ALYSON: This dump has never been known for its scenic beauty.

DORIS: So, when are you leaving, Marsha?

MARSHA: Right after the show closes. Lori will be taking an apartment in Lubbock. She'll be going to school there.

EVELYN: *(As if talking to a child.)* Isn't that nice? Lubbock of all places. *(To DORIS and ALYSON.)* Isn't that nice?
DORIS: Oh, yes. One of my favorite places. Lubbock. *(She turns her head away and holds her nose.)*

ALYSON: *(To MARSHA.)* Are you sure you're all right? Is there anything we can do?

MARSHA: What is the matter with all of you? I'm just fine. Tired, that's all. There's no need for any of you to feel guilty.

DORIS: Guilty? I don't feel guilty. Do you feel guilty, Evelyn?

EVELYN: Poo.

DORIS: Alyson, are you feeling guilty?

ALYSON: *(Through clenched teeth.)* For God's sake, Doris!

DORIS: Don't worry about us, Marsha.

MARSHA: You're very kind, Doris. All of you. I know you all did me a favor. I'm grateful. Honestly.

DORIS: *(Snide.)* Honestly?

MARSHA: Yes. To every single one of you. Michael and I were thinking about taking a sabbatical, anyway. It's time to let some fresh blood take care of The Playhouse. You know what I mean?

DORIS: Ain't nothing like fresh blood. Is there, Alyson?

ALYSON: *(Warning.)* Shut up, Doris.

DORIS: Marsha, are you putting us on?

MARSHA: Putting you on? I don't know what you mean.

DORIS: All this Girl Scout stuff.
ALYSON: *(Snapping.)* Doris, I'm warning you. You keep this up and you're going to regret it!

DORIS: Don't get your silicon tits in a twist, Missy!

MARSHA: I don't understand. *(Looking around. Confused.)* Is something wrong?

ALYSON: No. Nothing, Marsha.

MARSHA: *(To no one in particular.)* Ants are incredible,

aren't they?

(A long SILENCE while ALL eyes dart to one another.)

DORIS: *(Clearing her throat.)* Ants, Marsha?

EVELYN: You mean like fire ants and flying ants?

MARSHA: I'm not sure.

EVELYN: *(Trying to liven things up. To ALL in general.)* Remember when all those flying ants got into The Playhouse last year?

DORIS: Who could forget that! The stage was crawling with them and ol' O.T. went stomping around trying to kill them as quick as they dropped! God, I thought I'd bust a gut laughing! Just bust a gut!

(ALL laugh except MARSHA who stares blankly about as if in another time, another place.)

ALYSON: Well, we're all glad you didn't, Doris. *(To EVELYN.)* What show was that?

EVELYN: Ah . . . ah . . . oh, poo! The one about the two men. You know. One was real neat and the other one wasn't.

ALYSON: *(Remembering.)* *The Odd Couple.*
EVELYN: That's the one.

DORIS: *(Coming from behind the bar and demonstrating.)* "Well, I'm tellin' ya, Felix." STOMP. STOMP. STOMP. *(Stomps about.)* "This here place don't need cleanin', it needs a fumigator!" STOMP. STOMP. STOMP.

EVELYN: He didn't?!

DORIS: He sure did! And in that Texas twang of his trying to sound like New York City!

EVELYN: That was a good one, that was!

(ALL laugh except MARSHA. Suddenly, they remember her sitting there and end their laughs rather nervously. DORIS goes back behind the bar and pours herself another drink.)

DORIS: Well, so much for ant stories.

MARSHA: Michael calls them piss ants. They don't let go. They're mean and unpredictable. They grab hold and they'd rather die than give it up.

ALYSON: Marsha, what are you talking about?

MARSHA: Ants. On the patio.

DORIS: *(A snide aside.)* Is that like bats in the belfry? *(Swigs drink.)*

EVELYN: *(Throws DORIS a mean glance. To MARSHA.)* What about them, honey? What about the ants on the patio?

MARSHA: They're all over. Big ones. Little ones. The big black ones live in a hole just off the cement. The little ones hide where you can't see them. Michael wants to pour some poison on them, but I won't let him. And the little ones . . . they wait. They can crawl up your leg and you don't even know they're there.

EVELYN: Better get rid of them if you know what's good for you.

MARSHA: Once, I saw a big one wander into where all the little ones were busy working, and before he had a chance to get out, one of the little piss ants got hold of him by the leg and wouldn't let go. That big black ant went round and round, dragging that little piss ant with him. I watched for the longest time while he went in circles trying to shake loose that little piss ant. He must have been in terrible pain and the piss ant must have been dead by now, but he wouldn't let go! I took a little piece of paper and tried to flick the piss ant off, but I was afraid that I'd tear the big ant's leg off with it.

DORIS: *(Aside.)* Give me a break.

EVELYN: If you know what's good for you you'll get rid of those suckers before they tear up your whole patio.

MARSHA: "Watch," He said. "Don't interfere, Marsha! Just watch," He said.

ALYSON: Who?

MARSHA: God, of course.

DORIS: God spoke to you, Marsha? *(ALYSON throws DORIS a mean glance.)*

MARSHA: He told me to watch and learn. I know it has something to do with something more than just ants. But, I don't know what. I just don't know what.

ALYSON: *Shhhhh.* It'll come to you Marsha. If God wants you to know, it'll come to you.

MARSHA: I just can't see it. What is it I'm supposed to learn?

ALYSON: I don't know, Marsha.

DORIS: Oh, come on, Alyson! You're not buying any of this, are you? My God! It's straight out of Tennessee Williams.

And bad Williams at that!

ALYSON: Doris, I'm going to give you a choice. You can either drink that bottle of bourbon or you can eat it!

MARSHA I'm sorry. I seem to be upsetting you, Doris. *(Crossing to exit.)* I'll just leave you alone and you can get on with running your lines.

ALYSON: If you need anything, Marsha, just call. All right?

MARSHA: Sure. *(Exits.)*

DORIS: What a crock! *(Swigs drink.)*

EVELYN: *Poo.*

(PERFORMANCE LIGHTING.)

WIDOW/EVELYN & POLLY/DORIS: *Mercy! Mercy!*

MABEL/ALYSON: Hesh up!

WIDOW/EVELYN & POLLY/DORIS: *Mercy! Mercy!*

MABEL/ALYSON: If-n I told ya once I told ya twice ta hesh up! You's m' hostages till I knows Bart's clean clear o' that thare posse. *(LULU enters from upstairs and stands on the landing pointing her gun at MABEL.)* You pigeons is wearin' down m' patience!

LULU/LORI: Drop yor gun, Mean Mabel!

MABEL/ALYSON: Curses! Ya ain't a-gonna use that thang are ya, girlie?
LULU/LORI: Ya wanna find out?

MABEL/ALYSON: Now, hold off a spell. *(Backs toward*

exit.)

LULU/LORI: I said drop it and I means drop it!

MABEL/ALYSON: *(Still backing away.)* Now a little pussycat likes you shouldna be a-playin' wid firearms. *(At door.)* Ya wouldn't shoot a lady, would ya? *(She backs toward exit and escapes.)*

(MABEL escapes. MARY enters from upstairs and rushes to LULU.)

MARY/MARSHA: Pray tell! What's goin' on?

POLLY/DORIS: Miss Lulu done saved our lives. Princess Desert Flower done turned out ta be Mean Mabel Wiggens.

MARY/MARSHA: No.

ALL: *(Except MARY.)* Yup!

WIDOW/EVELYN: And if it weren't fer Miss Lulu we'd be goners fer sure.

LULU/LORI: It's the least I coulda done.

POLLY/DORIS: Oh! Sin, sin, sin! It just makes m' blood boil!

WIDOW/EVELYN: I still thinks yor standin' in a hot draft, Polly Upstringer.

MARY/MARSHA: What the hey! Drinks is on The Horse's Mouth, ladies! Git on over to the bar, Widow Deere, thare's time enough ta be tea-total!

(WIDOW DEERE crosses to bar. POLLY pours a round of drinks. The WIDOW and POLLY drink heartily while LULU

and MARY have the following exchange.)

LULU/LORI: I know ya'll think I'm a bad girl what with m' profession and all.

MARY/MARSHA: Why no, Miss Lulu. It is not in my nature to cast disparagement upon another's reputation. The Good Lord knows how I, too, have sinned.

LULU/LORI: No.

MARY/MARSHA: Oh yes, Miss Lulu. I, too, have my little faults. Judge not and ye shall not be judged, I always say.

LULU/LORI: Oh, you're such a good woman, Miss Mary. A saint among sinners. I don't deserve your kindness.

MARY/MARSHA: Of course you do.

LULU/LORI: If you say so, Miss Mary.

MARY/MARSHA: *(Recognizes something on LULU's arm.)* WAIT!

LULU/LORI: WHAT?!

MARY/MARSHA: *(Pointing to arm.)* This!

LULU/LORI: *(Looking at arm.)* This?

MARY/MARSHA: That!

LULU/LORI: That?

MARY/MARSHA: Thare!

LULU/LORI: Thare? Why that thare ain't nothin' but m' strawberry birthmark, Miss Mary.

MARY/MARSHA: Good Lord in heaven! My daughter what got abductified by Injuns had a strawberry birthmark jest like that one.

LULU/LORI: Ya don't say?

MARY/MARSHA: I do say, Miss Lulu.

LULU/LORI: I, too, was abductified by Injuns. I never knowed no parents but the Injuns what abductified me. They was real nice, though.

MARY/MARSHA: You don't say?

LULU/LORI: I do say, Miss Mary.

MARY/MARSHA: Louise!

LULU/LORI: Who's Louise?

MARY/MARSHA: That's you, darlin'. That's you! *(THEY embrace.)* M' baby! M' baby's been returned ta me!

LULU/LORI: Mama?

POLLY/DORIS: *(At bar. To WIDOW.)* It's like a fire in yor underthings.

WIDOW/EVELYN: Ya sure it ain't heat rash?

BLACK OUT.

END ACT TWO – *Scene 2*

ACT TWO—*Scene 3*

(POLLY UPSTRINGER is behind the bar. The WIDOW DEERE, MARY HOLIDAY and LOUISE are sitting on barstools. ALL are obviously quite drunk. It is evening. The RECORDED SOUND of approaching horses is heard. PERFORMANCE LIGHTING.)

WIDOW/EVELYN: *(Swaying on barstool.)* Hark.

POLLY/DORIS: *(Putting a finger to her mouth.)* Shhhh. *(ALL giggle.)*

WIDOW/EVELYN: *Shhhh.* Sounds like the men is returnin'.

(The SHERIFF and GROVER enter and dust themselves off.)

GROVER/HAL: *(Crosses to bar.)* We've recovered the money!

MARY/MARSHA: Oh, that's good news, Grover.

SHERIFF/O.T.: And Sally's back wid her pa! *(Crosses to table and sits.)*

POLLY/DORIS: Oh, that's good news! *(Hands GROVER his bartender's apron.)*

WIDOW/EVELYN: *(Very drunk.)* Good news! I'll drink to that! *(Swigs drink.)*

POLLY/DORIS: *(Crossing to table. To SHERIFF.)* What about that varmint Bart Blackey?

SHERIFF/O.T.: What?

POLLY/DORIS: What about that varmint Bart Blackey?

SHERIFF/O.T.: *(Tapping on hearing aid.)* What?

POLLY/DORIS: BART BLACKEY!

SHERIFF/O.T.: That varmint Bart Blackey got away!

POLLY/DORIS: Oh, that's bad news.

WIDOW/EVELYN: Bad news! I'll drink to that! *(Swigs drink.)*

SHERIFF/O.T.: And that ain't the worst.

POLLY/DORIS: What's the worst?

SHERIFF/O.T.: The varmint swore a curse on us.

MARY/MARSHA & POLLY/DORIS: Swore a curse on us?

SHERIFF/O.T.: Yup.

POLLY/DORIS: Oh, dear. That is bad news.

WIDOW/EVELYN: Curses! I'll drink to that! *(Swigs drink.)*

GROVER/HAL: Said he was a-puttin' a curse on Dirty Gulch and he'd be avenged by sunrise.

POLLY/DORIS: Seems ta me like thare's already a curse on Dirty Gulch.

MARY/MARSHA: That don't sound good, Grover.

WIDOW/EVEYLN: Curses on yor curses, Blad Blarkey . . . Blark Blattey . . . Bark Battey . . . Bartty Blark. *Poo.* What's his name?

MARY/MARSHA: *(Helping WIDOW off stool and*

maneuvering her over to a chair by a table.) Come along, Widow Deere. You'll be a-might safer sittin' over here.

WIDOW/EVELYN: What's his name?

MARY/MARSHA: *(Positioning WIDOW into chair.)* Downsy-daisy. Thare ya go. *(WIDOW looks around, sways a bit and tries, once more, to say 'Bart Blackey' before passing out, face down, on the table. MARY returns to the bar.)* She had a might more than she's used to what with bein' tea-total all her life.(To LOUISE.)* Would ya go upstairs and git my shawl? I'm a wee bit chilly, darlin'.

LOUISE/LORI: Be m' pleasure, Miss Mary. I mean, Mama. *(She staggers up the stairs and exits as JUDGE and SALLY enter.)*

SALLY/RITA: (Carrying two big sacks with dollar signs on them.) I'm home!

POLLY/DORIS: So you is! Praise the Lord!

ALL: Praise the Lord!

WIDOW/EVELYN: *(Raises head and sings.)* AMAZING GRACE. *Her head falls back onto table.)*

SALLY/RITA: *(Holding up bags.)* Where ya want me ta put 'em, Pa?

JUDGE/BILL: Behind the bar. If-n ol' Bart Blackey decides ta return, theys oughta be where we can keep an eye on 'em. *(Sits next to WIDOW DEERE.)*

SALLY/RITA: *(Giving money bags to GROVER.)* Here ya go, Grover. *(Crosses to table where the JUDGE and WIDOW are sitting.)* Well, I'm back. Here I am. *(Shrugs, giggles and sits. To WIDOW.)* It's me, Widow Deere. Safe and sound. Guess what. Thare's a curse on us. Isn't that exciting? *(No response.)* Well, I think it's exciting. Hello? Hello? *(To JUDGE.)* Am I sitting next to a dead person?

MARY/MARSHA: Listen up, everybody! I gots good news! My little Louise what got herself abductified by the Injuns has been returned ta me.

GROVER/HAL: That is good news, Miss Mary. Praise the Lord!

ALL: *(Except WIDOW.)* Praise the Lord!

MARY/MARSHA: However, I ain't too awful wild 'bout the line o' work she done chose fer herself.

SHERIFF/O.T.: Well, whatever it is, it cain't be as bad as workin' fer Madam Lillie. Rest her soul.

ALL: *(Except WIDOW.)* Rest her soul.

(LOUISE enters. While standing on the landing she hands MARY her shawl.)

MARY/MARSHA: Ladies and gentlemen, my little Louise! *(In shock and with open mouths, the MEN stare.)* Louise, I wants ya ta meet yor new family. *(The MEN slowly turn away and hang their heads in shame.)*

LOUISE/LORI: I already have, Mama.

MARY/MARSHA: Oh . . . well . . . I see.

POLLY/DORIS: I got some really bad news.

SHERIFF/O.T.: C'mon let's have it 'for it gets any worse!

POLLY/DORIS: Mean Mabel's a-stalkin' about and I thinks

she means ta make trouble. If-n it hadn'ta been fer little Louise we'd all be in that big saloon in the sky.

(ALL ad lib their shock and concern. There is general din of orchestrated chaos. Fade into REHEARSAL LIGHTING.)

MARSHA: *(Much more composed than in her last scene, but still a bit restrained.)* Okay, gang, listen up! When Bart and Mabel make their entrance, I want to create the dramatic tension of that moment by juxtaposing it with the merriment of your celebrating. *(RITA raises her hand.)* Yes, Rita?

RITA: Well, since there's a curse on us, why are we celebrating?

MARSHA: Your return, for one thing, Rita. The return of the money and, of course, Louise's return to her mother.

RITA: Well, wouldn't the curse still make us all a bit reserved?

MARSHA: No. *(To ALL in general.)* Any further questions? *(RITA raises her hand.)* Yes, Rita?

RITA: Who's Louise's father?

MARSHA: I don't know. There's nothing in the script to indicate. It's just one more of those mysteries that make life interesting.

RITA: But, you wrote it.

MARSHA: Indeed, I did. Anybody else? Any further questions? *(O.T. raises his hand.)* Yes, O.T.?

O.T.: Well . . . uh . . . I just wanted to say . . . uh . . . well, Marsha, I think you've been big about this and . . . uh . . . I wanted to say thank you. *(The sentiment is echoed, mixed with applause, except BILL who remains still.)*

MARSHA: Thank you.] Thank you all, very much. But, as you know, I'm only doing my job. Now, unless there are any further questions, *(No response.)* Good. *(MARSHA turns to LORI and engages in a silent conversation.)*

(The stage goes dark except for area REHEARSAL LIGHTING around the table where RITA, BILL and EVELYN are seated.)

RITA: San Francisco?

BILL: Yes. I have some friends out there I can stay with while I'm getting myself situated.

EVELYN: We're sure going to miss you around here, Bill.

RITA: San Francisco. Hollywood. Maybe, when ya'll get situated out there I can come out and stay with you while I try to break into the movies.

BILL: Hollywood is in Los Angeles, Rita.

RITA: Of course it is. I knew that. But, it can't be that far of a commute.

BILL: It's pretty far.

EVELYN: What's makes you think you could get into the movies, Rita? You have a hard enough time getting cast by the Derrick Community Players.

RITA: I'm sure you didn't mean that the way it sounded, Evelyn.

EVELYN: We live in a very uncertain world, Rita.

BILL: In a way, I suppose I ought to be grateful.

EVELYN: How's that, Bill?

BILL: It took something like this to get me to do what I should have done years ago - get the hell out of Texas.
(REHEARSAL LIGHTING fades out and fades in on table where DORIS and O.T. are seated.)

DORIS: I still don't trust her. I liked her better when she was a bitch.

O.T.: What makes you say that?

DORIS: I don't know. I can't put my finger on it. But, something around here smells pretty fishy to me.
O.T.: Everything's been going along nice and smooth, if you ask me.

DORIS: Too smooth. I'm telling you she's up to something.

O.T.: Can't you see she wants to leave on a good note? This is her last chance to show us her good side.

DORIS: As many sides as she has, "good" is not one of them.

O.T.: I think you just want to make trouble, Doris.

DORIS: No, I don't, O.T. I just want to get to the bottom of whatever's going on. I'm telling you she's up to something. And unless we figure it out, and quick, we're just liable to find ourselves on the shit-end of her stick, again! And what's with all the blocking changes?

(REHEARSAL LIGHTING fades out and fades in on the area surrounding LORI and MARSHA.)

LORI: Do I have to?

MARSHA: Yes. You have to, Lori.

LORI: But, why are you changing the blocking? God knows I'm onstage little enough as it is!

MARSHA: I'm not going to argue with you, Lori. When you hear Grover's cue for Bart's and Mabel's entrance, you get up those stairs.

LORI: But, that's not the way we've been doing it.

MARSHA: That's the way we're doing it now! Do you understand me, Missy?

LORI: *(Sulking.)* Yes, Mother.

(REHEARSAL LIGHTING rises in all areas.)

MARSHA: Listen up, cast! *(Calling to backstage.)* Mike, can you hear me?

MIKE: *(Poking his head in.)* Yup.

MARSHA: Al?

ALYSON: *(Poking her head in.)* I hear you, Marsha.

MARSHA: After you enter, take time to size things up. This will give the audience time to focus on your presence before the fireworks begin. And make certain you don't start shooting until I'm on the landing. Is that understood?

MIKE & ALYSON: *(Poking their heads in.)* Yes, Marsha.

MARSHA: Or else, it will throw off the entire balance of the tableau effect we're going for. Does everybody understand

that? *(Some nod 'yes' and some say it.)* Good.
DORIS: Marsha?

MARSHA: Yes, Doris?

DORIS: Aren't we all taking this a bit too seriously?

MARSHA: What exactly, do you mean?

DORIS: I mean, all this re-blocking of yours. After all, it's only a silly little melodrama.

MARSHA: I beg to differ, Doris. This is my last play in this theatre and if I have been inspired to make a few changes for the good of the production, then why would you want to begrudge me that?

DORIS: I don't want to begrudge you anything, Marsha. I'm . . .

MARSHA: And I'm only doing this for you. All of you. I want to make you all so very, very proud of yourselves. *Massacre At Dirty Gulch* will be a triumph! I'm sorry, Doris. I don't mean to scold. If you have a better idea, please share it with us.

DORIS: No, no. Let's do it your way. *(Sinking into chair. To O.T.)* That bitch is up to something. I used to think she was perfectly sane pretending to be crazy. Now, I think she's perfectly crazy pretending to be sane!

MARSHA: Okay, gang! Listen up! As your director, I just want to say that you all have every reason to feel proud of yourselves. We've put a lot of time and work into this and, yes, we've had our little ups and downs. But, all in all, we've got ourselves a good show. Now, if you'll all take your places we're about to start. The audience is in and it looks like we've got ourselves a pretty good opening night house.

Thanks again, gang . . . *for everything.* And remember those new blocking changes. Let's make *Massacre at Dirty Gulch* the melodrama that Derrick, Texas will not soon forget! Places everybody! And break a leg!

MIKE: *(Popping his head in.)* Hear, hear! Let's hear it for Marsha! Hip-hip hurray!

ALL: *(Joining in and cheering.)* Hip-hip hurray! Hip-hip hurray!

(PERFORMANCE LIGHTING.)

ALL: *(Cheering.)* Hip-hip hurray! Hip-hip hurray!

GROVER/HAL: *(Shoots gun into air. Lighting fixture crashes to stage floor.)* Quiet down! Quiet down! Hesh up, ya bunch o' varmints! Drinks is on The Horse's Mouth!

WIDOW/EVELYN: *(Sings over the raucous din being made by ALL celebrating.)* AMAZING GRACE . . . .

DORIS: *(Breaking character. She is the only one who noticed the fallen fixture. Panic-stricken, she yells over the chatter.)* Oh my God! She's in charge of the props!

(The SOUND of celebration grows louder.) SALLY/RITA: What about the curse?

GROVER/HAL: Curses on the curse!

(ALL laugh. MARSHA steps up on the landing as LORI exits upstairs. BART enters through swinging doors as MABEL enters through side door.)

DORIS: *(Jumping up. Out of character.)* WAIT!!!

GROVER/HAL: It's Bart Blackey and Mean Mabel

Wiggens!

(ALL pull out their guns.)

DORIS: STOP!!! THE GUNS!!!

(BLACK OUT. A barrage of gunfire, screams and shouts, the SOUND of tables and chairs falling over, glass shattering, moans and cries. Then, SILENCE. The PERFORMANCE LIGHTING slowly rises. Bodies, blood-soaked, lay stretched helter-skelter about the stage. Standing on the landing, alone, overlooking the rubble and carnage, wearing a twisted and deranged smile, is MARSHA.)

MARSHA: *(Steps down from the landing.)* Done. Exit all. You did it to yourselves.

LORI: *(Enters onto landing. Confused and frightened.)* Mama?

MARSHA: *(Totally spaced-out. In a southern accent she quotes Blanche from A Streetcar Named Desire.)* "Tarantula was the name of it! I stayed in a hotel called The Tarantula Arms! Yes, a big spider! That's where I brought my victims." *(Looking upward.)* Daddy?

LORI: *(Crosses to MARSHA.)* Mama. Mama?

MARSHA: *(Looks at LORI blankly. Quotes from Streetcar.)* "Whoever you are, I have always depended on the kindness of strangers." *(Slowly, LORI leads MARSHA towards exit. MARSHA surveys her handiwork and, with an air of injured innocence, her voice floats across the stage.)* Piss ants!

MARSHA and LORI exit. LIGHTING fades to BLACK.

END OF PLAY

FLOWERS
OUT OF SEASON

A FEW REVIEWS

"[Flowers Out Of Season] throws together sex, religion and suicide in a fresh, original and transcendent way . . . I think I have just seen the future of American Theatre." —Michael Bourne, Circle Repertory Company

"Spiritually barren lives given meaning by fundamentalist religion. Comfortable lifestyles devoid of passion. And the finality of the gun. All reflect what happened to American values . . . and they form the subject of Edward Crosby Wells' challenging new play, Flowers out of Season . . . one of the best things this theatre [Changing Scene, Denver] has done." —Jeff Bradley, Denver Post

"Powerful stuff . . . riveting . . . thought-provoking . . . Flowers Out of Season is a production that promises revelations regarding working rural poverty, American health care, and religion as well as a healthy dose of dangerous eroticism . . . the show delivers on all of these promises – brilliantly at times . . ."
—Randy Hardwick, The Chicago Critic

"Edward Crosby Wells' play hails from the Nick Cave School of magic realism: set in the same sort of vaguely southwestern, vaguely antediluvian, lightning-driven flood plain of the mind, it has a Murder Ballads-style hero who may literally be the devil in disguise. The expressionism and outright fantasy of Wells' audacious, borderline supernatural scenario are well matched by director Madrid St. Angelo's stylized, sensual staging . . ." —Brian Nemtusak, Chicago Reader

"Something significant . . . be advised that this is the show that will soon make the journey worth the effort." —Mary Shen Barnidge, Windy City Times

THE CHARACTERS:

DAWN ROSE—Early to late-twenties.
BUCK ROSE—Early to late-twenties.
DAISY WINTER—Mid-forties to mid-fifties.

SYNOPSIS:

1/M, 2/W, 2 simple sets easily changed out, full-length drama.

A young couple, Buck and Dawn, in Southern New Mexico have fallen on hard times. They are America's working poor—lost in a faltering social and healthcare system. We meet them early one morning on the day that will change their lives forever. Their conversation reveals the political, religious and social underpinnings of the disenfranchised in America. Later that same day Buck meets Daisy, a much older woman. They come together for a stormy, dangerous and frightening afternoon encounter. The tension erupts into the unleashing of Nature's fury, perhaps brought about through the power of magic. Sensuous and seductive, the plot twists and turns leading to a shattering conclusion.

ACT ONE begins at 4:30 AM on a Thursday in October.

ACT TWO is later that same day.

TIME is the present.

SETTING is Hobbs, a small city in southeastern New Mexico, a mile from the West Texas border.

ACT ONE

AT RISE: The living room of the Rose residence; a sad tumbledown adobe. Clothes in piles scattered here and there. An ironing board holds yet more clothes belonging to their three children (an eight month old boy and two girls, ages four and six) and on the floor beneath the ironing board there is a woven-plastic laundry basket, cracked, torn and bulging with yet more laundry. Food-stained dishes, empty soda and beer cans fill those places where knick-knacks, in a more traditional home, might be found. Sheer, rust-stained curtains hang unevenly over a window where a strip of black electrical tape mends a crack in its dirt and smoke-stained pane. There is but one piece of art to be seen and that is of Jesus painted on black velvet and it is hanging on the wall for all to plainly see. Somewhere a child's tricycle is parked along with other toys belonging to their children.

(DAWN enters from the bedroom. She is dressed in a pink chenille bathrobe, time-worn and faded. She wears no visible make-up and her hair is pinned back and in disarray. Tired and drawn, appearing older than her years, one senses that under the best of circumstances DAWN'S mirror would reflect little more to enhance the uncomely image we now have of her. She walks in her worn-thin scuffs with heavy, dragging-steps, switches on the living room lights and then scuffs off into the kitchen. A rattling of pots is heard.)

DAWN: *(From offstage, over the SOUND of the water running from the kitchen faucet.)* Git! You give me a headache! Go on! Git outta here! *(Pause.)* GIT! You hear me? *(Pause.)* Go ahead and drown, you stupid know-nothing! What do I care, huh? *(Pause.)* You want an aspirin? Go ahead! Take it. Take them all! Gimme two and you can have the rest. Won't be needing them no more. Not after today. Go ahead. Take them!

(BUCK, shirtless, enters from the bedroom with a cigarette in his mouth, wearing cowboy boots and jeans. He zippers the fly on his jeans leaving the belt unbuckled, sits on the couch and pulls at some of the stuffing exploding through the threaded-fabric of its arm. BUCK is ruggedly attractive and often displays a boyish grin. He is a chain-smoker.)

DAWN: *(Con't.)* What the hell! You want the Sno-Ball? Take it! *(The SOUND of the water running from the kitchen faucet stops.)* Here. Have a cyanide Tylenol. Good for you. No? How about a little Comet cleanser on your Sno-Ball? Huh? Draino? Boy, that'll do you good. Do me good. *(A short laugh.)* Here. Have a little Draino on your Sno-Ball. *(Pause.)* Ugh, ugh, ugh! He's eating it! Oh, God, he's starting to bubble!

BUCK: Shouldn't have left the Sno-Balls out.

DAWN: Didn't. Jessie did.

BUCK: There's some fresh packages in the fridge.

DAWN: Pink or white?

BUCK: Don't matter.

DAWN: All we got is pink.

BUCK: I'd rather have pink.

DAWN: Good. *(A beat.)* Why don't ya'll just high-tail it?

BUCK: You talkin' to me?

DAWN: Why would I be talking to you? *(She enters with two mugs of hot water with a spoon in each mug. She puts the mugs down on the coffee table and withdraws from a pocket of her bathrobe two cellophane-wrapped cream-filled chocolate cupcakes covered with a sticky pink marshmallow coating sprinkled with grated coconut.)* Roaches. I was talking to the roaches. There's a big ol' fat one who's gonna have one bad plumbing problem— *(Handing BUCK the package of cupcakes.)* Pink, right?

BUCK: Right. *(Tears open the package and begins to eat.)* Good.

DAWN: Junk.

BUCK: Right. Bad. *(With a full mouth.)* But good.

DAWN: A thing can't be bad but good.

BUCK: Course it can.

DAWN: *(Searching about the room, lifting clothes here and there; in the drawer of the telephone table, one place and then another; everywhere she searches. Exasperated.)* Garbage.

BUCK: Well, I got this here theory and that ain't garbage.

DAWN: 'Bout what?

BUCK: Junk food.

DAWN: *(Still searching.)* What about the Maxwell House? Got a theory about that?

BUCK: On the shelf over the kitchen sink.

DAWN: No. *(A beat.)* Well, maybe. *(Exits into kitchen and returns with jar of instant Maxwell House coffee.)* Well, how'd it get there? Don't tell me! Jessie.

BUCK: Nope. Can't reach. *Me.* Ain't that where it belongs?

DAWN: *(Enters with jar of instant coffee.)* Mammaw says that sill over the sink ought to hold Ivory soap and Comet cleanser and stuff like that. Some people says to keep your coffee in the fridge to keep it fresh, don'tcha know. *(NOTE: Mammaw is pronounced ma'am-ah.)*

BUCK: Sounds good to me.

DAWN: *(Dumping huge spoonfuls of instant coffee into the mugs.)* Maybe it does. Maybe not. When all's said and done that's a body's business, isn't it? *(Exits into kitchen.)*

BUCK: I hear that.

DAWN: *(From kitchen.)* 'Though plants always did look nice in a kitchen window. *(Returns from kitchen with sugar bowl and proceeds to dump five large spoonfuls of sugar into each mug.)* Well, what's your theory?

BUCK: 'Bout what?

DAWN: How do I know? It's your theory, ain't it?

BUCK: *Naah,* you don't want to hear it.

DAWN: Probably not, but tell me anyway.

BUCK: You sure you want to hear it?

DAWN: Nope.

BUCK: Then, what are you asking for?

DAWN: 'Cause you'll bust if you don't tell it.

BUCK: I ain't gonna bust.

DAWN: Tell it!

BUCK: Eat all the junk food you can.

DAWN: *(After a pause to ponder.)* That's it?

BUCK: That's it.

DAWN: You do. *(Remembering.)* You know they got a theory about evolution, but that's the workings of the anti-Christ, don'tcha know. And then there's that theory about relatives, but you got to be an Einstein to understand it. But I never heard one about junk food except to say that it's junk food and junk is junk.

BUCK: Forget it. If I was a doctor you'd listen.

DAWN: If you was a doctor you'd still be talking silly.

BUCK: You're just mean as all get-out this morning. You wouldn't know a good theory if it came up and bit you on the . . . *(Sneaks up and pinches her on the buttocks.)*

DAWN: OUCH!

BUCK: Or on the . . . *(Playfully goes to pinch her breasts.)* Beep! Beep!

DAWN: Buck Rose, you are sinful!

BUCK: Just having some fun, darlin'.

DAWN: *(Glances at painting of Jesus.)* Well, not in front of Jesus. It ain't right to have fun in front of Jesus. You just sit back down there and behave yourself. *(Hesitant.)* You changed your mind?

BUCK: No. You?

DAWN: Nope. I'm ready. In fact, I picked out something real special to wear just for the occasion.

BUCK: What?

DAWN: You'll see. It's a surprise.

BUCK: What kind of surprise?

DAWN: The kind that surprises! Gonna wear make-up, too. Got it in a going-out-of-business sale in the mall. Seems like everybody's going out of business nowadays. Want more Sno-Balls?

BUCK: Beer nuts.

DAWN: *(Indicates beer nuts on the coffee table.)* In front of you.

BUCK: *(Picks up package of salted peanuts from coffee table—opens them and begins to pop them into his mouth. Sips coffee.)* Coffee's cold.

DAWN: I let it run.

BUCK: Not long enough. *(Takes a long drag on his cigarette and then puts it out by pinching it between his fingers.)*

DAWN: As long as it takes.

BUCK: Takes longer.

DAWN: It don't. You turned it down.

BUCK: When?

DAWN: When they turned the gas back on.

BUCK: *(Sips coffee.)* Should've boiled the water.

DAWN: Should've left the thermostat where it was.

BUCK: Maybe.

DAWN: Ain't no maybe about it! All has to do with money anyway, don't it?

BUCK: Money or bullshit. *(Going through pile of clothes.)* These clean?

DAWN: Ought to be. Jessie was here when I did them, if you need a witness.

BUCK: *(Finds shirt and puts it on. Buckles belt.)* She'd get around better if she had new braces.

DAWN: Insurance went up too high after that last operation.

BUCK: They didn't pay up.

DAWN: Welfare won't buy her braces.

BUCK: I make too much.

DAWN: Crippled.
(A long SILENCE.)

BUCK: *(At imaginary downstage window.)* She's a good kid. Jenny and Josh too.

DAWN: Yeah. Mammaw wanted to know where we was going. I don't mind telling you it was difficult.

BUCK: What did you tell her?

DAWN: We was going to a junk food convention in Dallas.

BUCK: Believe you?

DAWN: I don't think so. But, you know how she loves those kids. Spoils them to death, don'tcha know.

BUCK: Yeah, I know. *(Looking out window. After a pause.)* That flare—never really saw the flame before.

DAWN: You see that old oil patch flare every day.

BUCK: Not the flame. Not like today.

DAWN: It's the same. Every day it's the same. Nothing changes.

BUCK: Everythang changes. Sooner or later—everythang changes.

DAWN: Maybe.

BUCK: *(Watching the flame.)* It just licks up that there dark piece o' sky like it was the tongue o' Satan.

DAWN: Satan brings darkness to where there's light. He don't put light where there ain't none.

BUCK: I wouldn't be too sure 'bout that.

DAWN: It's in the Bible, don'tcha know.

BUCK: Maybe some thangs are best left in the dark.

DAWN: Like what?

BUCK: Dark thangs. Evil thangs. Thangs no God-fearin' soul ought to see.

DAWN: We got Jesus. Jesus will save us. *(She crosses to the painting of Jesus, kisses her fingertips and then presses her fingertips to the lips of Jesus.)* Now we're safe. Satan can't enter a house where Jesus lives. He can't cross the threshold without being invited.

BUCK: *(Turning from window.)* I thought that was vampires.

DAWN: Vampires? What's vampires got to do with anything?

BUCK: You got to invite them in or they can't enter.

DAWN: Sure they can.

BUCK: Nope, not unless you invite 'em.

DAWN: They come at night through the bedroom window. Nobody has to invite them. They come in all on their own and that's why you need Jesus and garlic.

BUCK: That's right, but not the front door. They can't come in through the front door. Least, not unless you invite them.

DAWN: Well, who is gonna invite a vampire into their house?

BUCK: Somebody who don't know it's a vampire.

DAWN: Well, you can't go around asking everybody who comes to the door whether he's a vampire or not.

BUCK: Guess not.

DAWN: Ain't no guess about it. *(Remembering.)* Mammaw had a run-in with a witch.

BUCK: What?

DAWN: When she was livin' down in Eunice.

BUCK: There ain't no witches down in Eunice.

DAWN: Not anymore, but in the old days there was a whole coven of them.

BUCK: So? What happened to them?

DAWN: Mammaw run them off.

BUCK: How?

DAWN: With the help of Jesus. You can do anything when you got Jesus.

BUCK: Amen.

DAWN: Praise the Lord.

BUCK: When?

DAWN: When she was carrying my mother. Lived in the next house over.

BUCK: The witch?

DAWN: The whole coven.

BUCK: Lord Almighty.

DAWN: Said they was Roman Catholic.

BUCK: Well . . . that was a sign right there.

DAWN: And they put a mark on my mother right there in Mammaw's womb.

BUCK: Powerful.

DAWN: Telepathic, don'tcha know. Big and purple. Right on her head. Covered her right eye. Or, maybe her left. It wasn't givin' birth to me what killed my mother. No sirree. It wasn't me. It was 'cause she was marked before she was ever born. A big purple mark of the devil.

BUCK: That'll do it. What about the run-in?

DAWN: After my mother was born and Mammaw saw that big ol' purple mark she knew who it was put it there, 'cause in the night she could hear them chantin' Latin.

BUCK: Ain't that what Catholics do?

DAWN: Yeah, but not backwards. They was chantin' Latin backwards, don'tcha know. That's what gived them away.

BUCK: How'd she know?

DAWN: What? It was Latin?

BUCK: It was backwards.

DAWN: Who are you? Judge Judy? She knew, that's all. Mammaw has a way with just knowing things. It's a gift . . . like second vision and stuff like that.

BUCK: Stuff like that sure comes in handy, don't it?

DAWN: You bet it does. Anyway, Mammaw prayed and prayed to Jesus until he finally appeared to her and told her what to do.

BUCK: *(Incredulous.)* Jesus appeared to your Mammaw?

DAWN: Sure. Why not?

BUCK: In the flesh?

DAWN: Well, no. Not exactly. He was wearing a white robe. All shiney and vibrating. Blinding, don'tcha know.

BUCK: What did he say to her?

DAWN: Burn 'em out! What else do you do with witches?

BUCK: She burned their house down?

DAWN: In the night. Whiles they was sleeping.

BUCK: Your Mammaw?

DAWN: *Yessiree.* Burned every one of them. The whole coven. Cat too.

BUCK: Cat, too?

DAWN: Possessed.

BUCK: But, that's arson . . . and murder.

DAWN: No it's not. Not when you're dealing with witches.

BUCK: She could've been mistaken.

DAWN: Mammaw? Don't be silly.

BUCK: She could've gone to prison.

DAWN: I ain't gonna tell if you don't. 'Sides, Jesus told her to do it. You don't think Jesus is gonna tell a body to do something and then go and let 'em go to prison, do you?

BUCK: Guess not.

DAWN: There ain't no guess about it.

BUCK: Powerful.

DAWN: Sally-by-the-pump-jack said she saw Satan in the all-you-can-eat last Thanksgiving.

BUCK: Eatin'?

DAWN: Standing in line whiles she was getting herself checked out at the register.

BUCK: What did he look like?

DAWN: Just your everyday-person. 'Though she said he did remind her a bit of a Hollywood movie star.

BUCK: Satan's from Hollywood?

DAWN: No, the movie star. Anyway, Satan can just pop in and out of everyday-people whenever he wants. Just like . . . *(She snaps her fingers.)* . . . that!

(A flash of LIGHTNING. The SOUND of THUNDER. The painting of Jesus falls to the floor. BUCK and DAWN stare at each other with wide-eyed wonder. In the ensuing SILENCE, BUCK hangs the painting back in its place. DAWN shudders.)

BUCK: You better watch that.

DAWN: Well . . . anyway, she and the other Sally was on their way out with the whole clan from Lovington when Satan came up and whispered in her ear.

BUCK: Sally-with-the-ranch's?

DAWN: Sally-by-the-pump-jack's. He told her that if she didn't bow down and worship him right then and there—right there in the all-you-can-eat—disaster would befall her on the Lovington Highway.

BUCK: Did she?

DAWN: Bow down? Course not! She ain't as big a fool as all that.

BUCK: Did it?

DAWN: *Yup.* Disaster befell all right. That's how she lost her teeth. They all piled into that old Mercury of Sally-with-the-ranch's brother-in-law and hit a chuck-hole headin' out for Lovington. Knocked her teeth out. Chuck-hole big enough to bury a horse in.

BUCK: Powerful. Terrible thangs happen when you least expect 'em.

DAWN: It was all for the best. She got herself new teeth from J.B.'s insurance and she found Jesus. New teeth and Jesus. What more could a body ask for?

BUCK: Praise the Lord! *(Looks out window. With urgency.)* Be dawn soon. Time to go.

DAWN: No! I'm not ready. *(Searches about the room.)*

BUCK: What are you lookin' for?

DAWN: Dawn Marie Rose ain't goin' no place without her make-up! *(She finds the paper bag containing the make-up —foundation, lipstick, mascara, eye shadow and blush.)* And you ought to put on clean underwear, Buck Rose.

BUCK: Ain't wearin' none.

DAWN: That'll be a fine howdy-do.

BUCK: The shirt's clean, ain't it?

DAWN: Ought to be. Jessie was here when I washed it, if you need a witness.

BUCK: Nope. Take your word. Shoe box under the bed?

DAWN: No.

BUCK: Well?

DAWN: Top of the closet. Jenny plays under the bed. Practically lives there if you ask me. Hope Mammaw can do somethin' about that shyness of hers. When the gas man came she hid out under your dirty clothes and I couldn't find her for the longest time and when I did I kept smellin' somethin' foul—like an armpit.

BUCK: Poor Jenny. *(Exits into bedroom.)*

DAWN: Poor nothin'! She seemed to like it. *(She hunts down a hand mirror, then sits and dumps the contents of the paper bag onto the coffee table.)* I sniffed and sniffed for hours trying to figure out where that armpit was comin' from. Checked Josh's Pampers. You know what big ones he can lay . . . but, it wasn't him. God knows what the gas man thought! *(She begins to apply make-up foundation.)* He kept lookin' at me like I went and laid a big fart or somethin'.

(BUCK enters with a shoebox, places it on the coffee table and removes a handgun.)

BUCK: Sweet Jesus, ain't she a beaut?

DAWN: They're supposed to have something to do with your penis.

BUCK: Who's supposed to have something to do with my penis?

DAWN: Guns.

BUCK: Now where'd you hear that?

DAWN: I don't know. A long time ago. It's psychology.

BUCK: That explains it.

DAWN: When a man holds a gun he's supposed to be holding his penis.

BUCK: Psychology.

DAWN: *Yup.*

BUCK: You mean like this? *(Cups his crotch with one hand while holding the gun in the other.)*

DAWN: No, I don't mean like that! Men who play with guns like to play with their penis.

BUCK: That's sick!

DAWN: I'm only telling you psychology. They got studies about that sort of thing.

BUCK: You're tellin' me that this here gun is really my wacker?

DAWN: Course it ain't your wacker!

BUCK: You bet it ain't. I ought to know my own wacker.

DAWN: It's your ersatz.

BUCK: My ersatz? What the hell's a ersatz?

DAWN: It's your penis.

BUCK: My penis ain't no such thang! And this here gun ain't my wacker! I don't care what psychology says!

DAWN: Do you wanna learn something or not?

BUCK: I know I don't keep my wacker in a shoebox!

DAWN: You don't keep it in your pants half the time.

BUCK: *(Starts to undo his pants.)* You wanna see the difference for yourself?

DAWN: Stop it—not in front of Jesus. You're not wearing any underwear.

BUCK: *(Lays gun on end table, crosses to painting of Jesus and removes it from the wall, places it on the floor, facing the wall.)* There. Now he can't see.

DAWN: *(Jumps up and rushes to painting.)* That's a terrible thing, Buck Rose. You could burn for that. *(Hangs painting back in its place.)*

BUCK: It's as natural as pie, darlin'.

DAWN: *(Crosses back to couch.)* We're not talking about baking. *(Begins to apply eye shadow.)*

BUCK: Who was the one talkin' 'bout my wacker?

DAWN: I was referring to that there pistol. I was telling you what that there doctor said.

BUCK: What doctor?

DAWN: On the TV. He made a study of it.

BUCK: Wackers? Some doctor made a study of wackers? You been watchin' too much television, if you ask me.

DAWN: What else am I supposed to do while you're off delivering your junk food?

BUCK: It ain't junk food.

DAWN: What else could you call it?

BUCK: Candy, crackers, chips, jerky—but it ain't junk food. *(Shrewdly.)* Must be somethin' wrong with that doctor's wacker. Probably got a little one.

DAWN: Nope. It's a real big one.

BUCK: You seen it?

DAWN: Everyday I look for it and I see it. Big as day! He's got the biggest, best wacker on TV! Need one of them big screens to see it all. *Now.* Will you shut up about it and let me get this here make-up on straight?

BUCK: *(After a pause to consider.)* Dawn?

DAWN: Yes, Buck?

BUCK: *(Snuggles up to her. Boyishly.)* Did you really see the doctor's wacker?

DAWN: *(Playfully.)* Yup.

BUCK: Yup?

DAWN: Plain as day.

BUCK: Big as . . . me?

DAWN: Bigger.

BUCK: Go on. They don't show wackers on TV.

DAWN: They do now.

BUCK: Since when?

DAWN: All the time. Saw one last week.

BUCK: Go on.

DAWN: Ask Sally. She saw it, too.

BUCK: Sally-by-the-pump-jack?

DAWN: Sally-with-the-ranch. She got cable. They show wackers all the time on cable.

BUCK: That's a fine thang. While I'm off tryin' to make a buck you're over at Sally's watchin' wackers!

DAWN: Yeah . . . but, you know what?

BUCK: What?

DAWN: It's like they say: There ain't nothin' like the real thing.

(DAWN tickles BUCK playfully. BOTH laugh while playfully wrestling until they roll off onto the floor and laugh some more. Suddenly, DAWN jerks her head violently and lets out a terrible shriek. Her body begins to convulse with an epileptic seizure. BUCK jumps to his feet and frantically searches the room for the hard rubber device to put in her mouth).

BUCK: *(In a panic.)* Oh, Jesus! Jesus, Jesus! Don't let this happen! *(Searching.)* Where is it? Oh, God! Where is it? *(Ad lib, etc. He cannot find it and rushes back to DAWN and inserts the side of his hand into her mouth. He cries for her and he cries in pain.)* Baby, baby, it's okay. It's okay. Oh, please, Jesus. Please— *(DAWN continues to convulse.)* Oh, Jesus! Stop it! Stop it! *(Then, conspicuously, he raises his free hand and snaps his fingers.)* NOW!

(A flash of LIGHTNING. The SOUND of THUNDER. Suddenly, DAWN'S body goes limp and there is a long SILENCE.)

BUCK: *(Continues. Removes his hand from her mouth. Cradling her head in his arms.)* Baby, baby. Daddy's here. Daddy's not gonna let this happen no more. No more, baby. Ah, Jesus—*(He gathers her tightly into his arms.)* No more, baby—no more. *(Looking Heavenward.)* This is the last time, Jesus.

(DAWN slowly regains consciousness.)

BUCK: *(Con't.)* Shhhh . . . it's okay. Everythang's okay. Shhhh—

DAWN: Buck?

BUCK: *Shhhh—*
DAWN: How long?

BUCK: Not long. A few seconds, that's all. Not long at all. You'll be good as new in no time.

DAWN: I went to see my Pappaw. *(Pronounced pap-pah.)*

BUCK: *(Comforting her.)* Shhhh—

DAWN: He was in the garden. "Plantin' taters," he said. "Watch those bare feet, Dawn Marie! You're up to your ankles in Earth and you'll be growin' taters 'tween your toes, child!"

BUCK: That sounds like your Pappaw all right.

DAWN: And there was angels. Beautiful angels all around him. God, they were beautiful. All shiny—like the light was inside them, don'tcha know.

BUCK: *Shhhh—*

DAWN: And he said he was waiting for me. He's been waiting for me all this time.

BUCK: That's 'cause he loves you.

DAWN: Oh, he does, Buck. He really does.

BUCK: Course he does. Just like me, darlin'.

DAWN: You know what else he said?

BUCK: What else?

DAWN: He said that if I stayed with him we'd go and get Mammaw and the kids. He'd teach us all how to fly, he said. Then, he rose up off the ground and spun around a few times while all the time the angels sang the most beautiful song I ever heard. It reminded me of you.

BUCK: Did it?

DAWN: Oh, yes. It reminded me of you all right . . . beautiful . . . from the heart—kind of country, you know. And I told Pappaw that Buck Rose loves me, too. And that I couldn't stay until my husband was at my side.

BUCK: And what did he say to that?

DAWN: He said he'd wait. He said that he's got all the time in the world. And he said winter's coming—nuclear winter. Nuclear winter's coming and there ain't no immunity to that.

BUCK: There is to death though.

DAWN: How can you be sure?

BUCK: Like your Pappaw said, we'll have all the time in the world.

DAWN: What are we going to do with it, Buck?

BUCK: We'll think of something.

DAWN: I want to leave now.

BUCK: Not yet.

DAWN: Yes. Now . . . *please.*

BUCK: Soon. *"Dawn Marie Rose don't go no place without her make-up."* Remember?

DAWN: I remember. *(She picks up her mirror and begins to apply some blush.)* Why couldn't I be pretty?

BUCK: But, you are pretty.

DAWN: No. You're just saying that.

BUCK: I'm not. It's the truth. You're the prettiest gal I ever set eyes on.

DAWN: Buck Rose, you could burn for lying so.

BUCK: Honest.

DAWN: I know what I look like. You don't have to lie for me, Buck. It's all right. I accepted the way I look a long time ago. I'm not pretty and we both know it.

BUCK: That's just not true, darlin'.

DAWN: *(Hesitantly.)* Buck, can I ask you a real serious question?

BUCK: Sure.

DAWN: You'll tell me the truth? The absolute truth?

BUCK: Of course.

DAWN: Swear it.

BUCK: I swear it.

DAWN: Swear it on Jesus.

BUCK: I swear it on Jesus.

DAWN: Would you have married me anyway—even without Jessie on the way?

BUCK: Yes. I would.

DAWN: And if you knew that Jessie was going to be born crippled, would you still have?

BUCK: But, I didn't know.

DAWN: But if you did?

BUCK: If I did, I'd still have married you.

DAWN: Is that the truth?

BUCK: Yes. *(A beat.)* That is, if you would've had me.

DAWN: Of course I would.

BUCK: Then, it's settled.

DAWN: Thank you. *(She begins to apply mascara.)* The drugstore in the mall's going out of business.

BUCK: So you said.

DAWN: Sally bought a load of make-up, too.

BUCK: Sally?

DAWN: By-the-pump-jack. J.B. finally got himself some work.

BUCK: I thought he already had work rough neckin'.

DAWN: He lost that months ago when that there sink-hole liked to take him and the rig clear to China. 'Sides, Sally said he never liked rough neckin'.

BUCK: There's big money in the oil fields.

DAWN: Sometimes there is and sometimes there ain't. Too much of a see-saw, if you ask me. Now he's working for Hobbs Parks and Recreation. That's civil service, ain't it?

BUCK: Don't rightly know.

DAWN: Yeah, that's what it is. Civil service. Government work.

(BUCK withdraws to the imaginary downstage window and stares out at the flare and the pre-dawn darkness.)

DAWN: *(Continues.)* Ol' J.B. the civil servant.

BUCK: *(To himself.)* Black as sin.

DAWN: I have a great idea.

BUCK: *(Still at window and speaking to himself—into the distance—until further noted.)* Satan's tongue.

DAWN: *(In her own world.)* Why can't all the parks be filled with fruit and nut trees? Wouldn't that be nice?

BUCK: Maybe God needs Satan.

DAWN: Just like in the Garden of Eden.

BUCK: Maybe Satan is really doin' what God had planned for him all the time.

DAWN: I mean, they got to pay J.B. to do whatever it is he does anyway.

BUCK: I mean, God is all-powerful. That's the nature of God. He could make Satan disappear like . . . *(Conspicuously, he snaps his fingers.)* . . . that!

(LIGHTNING strikes somewhere outside the window. The LIGHTS inside flicker off and then back on again. A distant rumble of THUNDER.)

DAWN: It can't be that much more trouble to have him plant a few fruit and nut trees.

BUCK: Maybe Satan has a purpose.

DAWN: Maybe some beans and squash, too. No . . . I don't like squash.

BUCK: Maybe Satan is really God when He wants to teach us somethin'.

DAWN: Maybe, corn and carrots and pinto beans—

BUCK: One and the same.

DAWN: Instead of going to the store, you just walk on over to the park and pick what you need.

BUCK & DAWN: *I wonder.*

BUCK: God, is that You lickin' up the darkness?

DAWN: Wouldn't that be nice?

BUCK: *(Turning from the window. To DAWN.)* What?

DAWN: Planting stuff in the park for everybody to eat.

BUCK: *Naah.* People will pick 'em all 'fore you got a chance to get any for yourself.

DAWN: No they wouldn't. Not if you filled all the parks and lined all the streets. There'd be enough for everybody. Why? If everybody in Hobbs planted just one thing wherever there was space we could turn Hobbs, New Mexico into the Garden of Eden.

BUCK: Wouldn't work.

DAWN: Course it would. And before you know it, Eunice would do it. Lovington would do it—and Jal and Tatum. Pretty soon all America would be covered with good things to eat and nobody would ever go hungry. Wouldn't be no trouble at all once everybody set their minds to it.

BUCK: What about the farmers and the canners and the stores you'd be puttin' outta business?

DAWN: Well, they could all find work doing something else. 'Sides, think of all the money people would be saving on groceries. Might even do away with money altogether.

BUCK: That's called communism, Dawn.

DAWN: Then Jesus was a communist.

BUCK: That's a terrible thang to say.

DAWN: Since when has the truth been a terrible thing to say?

BUCK: You're confused.

DAWN: Am not. All I'm saying is, if planting fruit and nut trees all over for every body to pick from is wrong, then America ain't never been Christian at all.

BUCK: Then what is it?

DAWN: I don't know. Something else. Just a bunch of poor souls who call themselves Christians, but don't know a thing about the mercy and the love of Jesus. They just wanna tell other people what to do. That's all.

BUCK: Ain't nothin' new in that. Everybody likes to tell everybody else what to do.

DAWN: That don't make it right.

BUCK: It's the American way.

DAWN: Well, that's about as sad a thing as I ever heard. Nuclear winter's coming.

BUCK: Nuclear winter ain't coming. That's somethin' you dreamed.

DAWN: Pappaw showed me.

BUCK: Your Pappaw's dead, Dawn.

DAWN: I know that. But, that don't stop him from showing me things. He showed me nuclear winter and it was awful. The sky was all gray. Trees and grass were black and brown and there was this terrible silence. It was like all the sounds you never think to listen to just up and disappeared. That's an awful sound—that silence. And those who were not yet dead just sat quietly staring up into that gray sky while their flesh peeled away from their bones. Oh, God, it was awful. And, you know, I don't think it was from bombs being dropped. No. It was something else. Something worse. Something we did to ourselves.

BUCK: Maybe your Pappaw was just showing you what might happen.

DAWN: It'll happen. The Kingdom of God is at hand. And what's the Kingdom of God if it ain't the Garden of Eden? Don'tcha see it, Buck?

BUCK: I guess.

DAWN: Ain't no guess about it. God helps those who help themselves.

BUCK: It ain't that simple, Dawn.

DAWN: It could be.

BUCK: *(Angry.)* Yeah? Well, what could be and what is is two different thangs!

DAWN: *(Visibly shaken.)* It was just an idea. Just a nice idea. You don't have to yell at me.

BUCK: All the nice ideas in the world ain't gonna change a thang!

DAWN: I don't wanna believe that.

BUCK: Believe what you will! It don't change a fucking thing!

DAWN: No. *(Breaking down.)* It don't got to be that way.

BUCK: Well, it is! And the sooner you see it the better! *Shit! Fucking shit!* Ain't nothin' but shit!

DAWN: Stop it! Stop it! You're hurting me.

BUCK: The world's a evil place, Dawn!

DAWN: *(Covering her ears.)* No. I don't want to hear it anymore!

BUCK: Pain and suffering everywhere you look. LOOK!

DAWN: *(With eyes tightly closed, in obvious pain.)* NO! No, no, no—

BUCK: Yes, yes, yes! LOOK! Look at you! You're dyin', Dawn.

DAWN: I know.

BUCK: You heard what the doctor said!

DAWN: I know—

BUCK: Kidney won't last another six months!

DAWN: Oh, God! Why do you want to hurt me?

BUCK: I don't want to hurt you. I want you to see.

DAWN: I see. I see all right.

BUCK: Then look! Look at me! A nothing! Nobody! A goddamn nobody. Wake up for Christ's sake! We're both fucking nobodies and nobody gives a shit!

DAWN: That ain't true!

BUCK: Look at little Jessie fallin' over, bangin' her head against the floor!

DAWN: *(Crying with pain.)* She needs new braces, that's all.

BUCK: And your Mammaw—burnin' out a family in the dead of night whiles they was sleepin'!

DAWN: They was witches! What else was she supposed to do?

BUCK: Plantin' fruit trees ain't gonna do nothin'! MONEY! Money's what does it—what makes the heart beat! The crippled walk! The kidney work! MONEY! Without it you're nothin'! Nothin' but a great big pile of shit!

DAWN: No!

BUCK: NOTHIN'. Without money they leave you in the street to die!

DAWN: There's good people, Buck. You know that. There's plenty of good people and they care.

BUCK: All in business for money. Without it you can rot in hell for all they care.

DAWN: No. Oh, God! I can't take the pain anymore! *(A mournful cry.)* Love! Some people care because they love!

BUCK: *Bullshit! (Grabs her and shakes her.)* Wake up for Christ's sake!

DAWN: Love!

BUCK: There ain't no love!

DAWN: Stop it! You're hurting me!

BUCK: Wake up! *(Shakes her harder.)* People cover each other in shit and call it love!

DAWN: No. *(Breaking free.)* Some people would die for love.

BUCK: That's right. There's people dyin' for love everyday.

DAWN: They ain't hurting anybody. There's people killing for money everyday, too.

BUCK: That's right. Everyday there's people dyin' for love and people killin' for money. What's the difference?

DAWN: Big difference.

BUCK: Ain't no difference.

DAWN: Yes. There's gotta be.

BUCK: Nope. There don't gotta be, at all.

(DAWN breaks down in tears.)

BUCK: *(Continues in a more quiet, soothing tone.)* Either way there's people dyin'. It's shit, Dawn. Don't you see it? Ain't nothin' but shit. That's the price you pay for gettin' yourself born.

DAWN: *(Crosses to couch and sits.)* I didn't get myself born. It just happened, that's all.

BUCK: *(Staring into the distance beyond the window. Sotto voce.)* You'll be back. *(Crosses to Dawn, picks up hairbrush and carefully begins to brush DAWN'S hair.)* Thangs don't just happen, Dawn.

DAWN: Yes. They do. Lots o' things just happen and it ain't nobody's fault.

BUCK: Nope. There's a plan to everythang. *(Slowly brushes her hair.)* Be dawn soon. Time to go.

DAWN: I want to call my Mammaw.

BUCK: Too early.

DAWN: I want to say goodbye.

BUCK: Too late.

DAWN: *(Puts on lipstick. After an anticipatory pause.)* Maybe she'll call me.

(LIGHTNING flashes outside the window, followed by the dull rumble of THUNDER.)

BUCK: *(Warning.)* Dawn—don't even think it.

DAWN: *(She raises her hand and is about to snap her fingers.)* Just maybe—

BUCK: *Don't!*

(DAWN snaps her fingers and they stare at each other in SILENCE. Then they look towards the telephone. Suddenly, the SOUND of the telephone ringing.)

BUCK: *(Continues.)* You shouldn't have done that. Everythang was just fine the way it was. Be dawn soon. Not much time.

DAWN: *(Crossing to telephone.)* I just want to talk to Mammaw before we leave.

BUCK: Sky's startin' to lighten up.

DAWN: I know. I'll just be a minute. *(Picks up phone.)* Hello, Mammaw. I had a feeling it was you . . . Well, of course I know what time it is . . . Yes, Mammaw, I know it's early. You called me, remember? *(BUCK crosses to tricycle and sits on it. To no one in particular.)* Be dawn soon.

DAWN: Yes. We're both up. Had our coffee already. How are the kids? No, I don't. I don't, Mammaw . . . I know. I've tried to break her of it. I don't know why she likes to bury herself in dirty clothes! No, I don't think Doctor Spock does, either. She just does, that's all. Keep them in the hamper . . . *Oh.* In that case, I don't know what to tell you. You'll figure something out. Right here—on Jessie's tricycle.

(BUCK pedals tricycle around the room.)

DAWN: *(Continues.)* I know she's crippled. Sally thought it might be good exercise . . . No. Sally-with-the-ranch . . . For her birthday . . . No. The one coming up. *(To BUCK.)* Would you get off that before you break it! *(Into phone.)* No,

Mammaw. I was talking to Buck. That's what I told him . . . Dallas. In a few minutes . . . No, Mammaw. There's no girls jumping out of cakes. Mammaw, it's not that kind of convention. What? Okay. Let me talk to her. *(To BUCK.)* Would you please get off that tricycle before you break it! *(Into phone.)* Jenny? Slow down, honey. Mommy can't understand what you're saying . . . Well, because . . . because . . . just because. Because it makes you smell funny, Jenny . . . I know you do. But, other people don't like to smell poop, baby. *(To BUCK.)* Get off! *(Into phone.)* Jenny . . . Oh, Mammaw. Well, just—just—just wash it off for God's sake! Okay. Let me talk to her . . . Jessie? Did you give Jenny Josh's dirty Pampers? I know she does, honey, but you hadn't ought to do that. I love you, too, sweetheart. Daddy does, too. You be a good girl, okay? Do as your Mammaw says. Okay? Now, let me talk to Mammaw . . . Soon, baby. I love you. Bye bye. *(After a pause.)* Mammaw? Listen. I got to go now . . . Yes—yes, I will. We know the way. I love you, too. *(After a pause.)* Goodbye, Mammaw. *(She slowly places the receiver back in its cradle.)*

BUCK: Everythang okay?

DAWN: The usual.

BUCK: I told you not to.

DAWN: I just wanted to say goodbye.

BUCK: Happy?

DAWN: Yes.

BUCK: Scared?

DAWN: No.

BUCK: *(Extremely solemn.)* Dawn's breaking. Sun's rising.

DAWN: So soon?

BUCK: Yes.

DAWN: *(Also solemn. A long sigh.)* Red?

BUCK: *(Looking out window.)* Yes.

DAWN: Sailors take warning.

BUCK: *(Still looking out window.)* Be light soon—time to go. *(Crosses to end table and picks up the gun.)*

DAWN: Yes . . . Wait! I almost forgot.
BUCK: The sun's startin' to break through. Dawn's passing.

(DAWN crosses to where she has a pair of bright red high heel shoes hidden. She kicks off her scuffs and puts on the shoes. She removes her robe. She is wearing a bright blue one-piece bathing suit with a white sash that reads: MISS CONGENIALITY. Suddenly, she is radiant. She is beautiful. She is America.)

DAWN: Surprise. Like it?

BUCK: Yes. "Miss Congeniality."

DAWN: Kept it all these years.

BUCK: I remember that night.

DAWN: So do I. Like it was yesterday. Knew I wasn't gonna win.

BUCK: I thought you was.

DAWN: Well, maybe for a moment. For a moment, I felt pretty.

BUCK: You always was.

DAWN: Well, it doesn't hurt to try.

BUCK: No, it doesn't hurt to try. *(After a pause.)* Dawn, I . . . I . . .

DAWN: *(Not letting him finish.)* No. No goodbyes. I'll see you on the other side.

BUCK: *(Looking around the room.)* Where?

DAWN: *(Indicates couch.)* There—on the couch.

(DAWN crosses to one of the piles of clothes and uncovers a large plastic bag and removes a bouquet of dead and dried roses. She then crosses to the couch and sits.)

BUCK: *(Placing a throw-pillow behind her head.)* Here.

DAWN: Thank you, Buck. Would you sing for me?

BUCK: *(Places the point of the gun directly on the pillow, aimed directly at her head.)* What do you want me to sing?

DAWN: "Here She Comes."

BUCK: I don't know that one.

DAWN: Yes you do. *(Sings.)*
Here she comes, Miss America...

BUCK: Now?

DAWN: Yes. Now.

(BUCK leans over and kisses her gently.)

BUCK: *(Sings.) Here she comes, Miss—*
(BUCK pulls the trigger. DAWN's body jerks forward with the SOUND of the gunshot.)

BUCK: *(Continues. There is a disturbing mix of sadness and anger in his voice. He speaks.)* America.

(LIGHTNING strikes somewhere outside the window. A distant rumble of THUNDER. The LIGHTING slowly dims to BLACK OUT.)

END ACT ONE

ACT TWO

AT RISE: BUCK is standing behind the sofa exactly as he was last seen at the end of Act One. Only his face is illuminated. Slowly, the LIGHTING rises to show us that we are now in another living room on the other side of town. BUCK stretches, looks around the room and then examines the gun for a moment or two before placing it under a cushion of the sofa. Then, BUCK takes a cigarette from out his shirt pocket and moves about the room searching for some matches. After a while, he picks up DAISY'S purse and removes a gold lighter, puts the purse back on the coffee table and lights his cigarette; putting the lighter in his pocket, casually – not the deliberate act of a thief. DAISY is offstage preparing tea in the kitchen and will remain there until noted.

BUCK: Do you hear me?

DAISY: Yes. I do now. Go on.

BUCK: Gotta eat. Three kids. Mind if I take m' boots off?

DAISY: Not at all. Make yourself comfortable.

BUCK: *(Sits on sofa – removes boots.)* One, boy—eight months. Girl, four. Don't be ashamed to tell me if you smell somethin' ripe. Ain't had these here boots off in nearly two years. *(Sniffs his boots and puts them back on. Once on, he rises and cases the room.)*

DAISY: Two years?

BUCK: Just joking. The other, six. Crippled. Had two operations. Needs another. Can't walk too good without her braces. Needs new ones. Out-growed 'em.   Insurance canceled. If I was to disappear, welfare might kick in—

DAISY: I can't hear you.

BUCK: Wife . . . gets these here headaches, you see. And fits. Terrible fits. Only one kidney and that's gone bad. All over now.

DAISY: How sad. I'm sorry to hear that.

BUCK: No need. Nope. Gotta eat. Know what I mean? *(Looking at watercolors.)* Four-thirty in the morning comes early, you know. Gotta eat. Three kids. You?

DAISY: Me?

BUCK: Kids?

DAISY: One. He and his wife live in California. He's studying to be an architect. She's a social worker.

BUCK: That's like welfare, ain't it?

DAISY: She works for the Department of Welfare—or Social Services—if that is what you mean.

BUCK: Givin' handouts to the wrong people.

DAISY: You'll have to speak louder.

BUCK: He's in college, right?

DAISY: Berkeley.

BUCK: Pretty smart, huh?

DAISY: He certainly thinks so.

BUCK: And what do you do?

(DAISY enters from the kitchen with a tray of tea things. She is dressed plainly, yet smartly – skirt, blouse, practical shoes. Not unattractive, DAISY is a haunting and haunted woman with that kind of quality that always leaves one wondering whether she is younger than her age seems to be or does she simply look older than she is.)

DAISY: *(Placing tray on coffee table.)* Oh, keep house. Do my watercolors. Read. Volunteer at the hospital on Mondays. That sort of thing. *(Crosses to imaginary downstage window and looks out.)* Looks bad. Looks like we got inside just in time.

BUCK: In time?

DAISY: For the storm.

BUCK: Yeah. We're due for a good one.

DAISY: A bad one, you mean.

BUCK: Right. That's what I was fixin' to say. Bad. Somethin' wicked.

DAISY: Not too wicked, I hope.

BUCK: Wicked enough.

DAISY: Enough?

BUCK: To be exciting.

DAISY: Oh, well, I can handle that.

BUCK: Maybe. Terrible thang—tornado. And rain—hard and heavy rain.

DAISY: *(Looking out window.)* Oh, my! Look at those clouds. Brown. Brown as brown can be.

BUCK: That's good ol' West Texas dirt sneakin' over the New Mexico border. Probably rain mud all over Hobbs. *(Referring to the watercolors.)* Those yours?

DAISY: *(Turning from window.)* Excuse me?

BUCK: Them paintin's—you do 'em?

DAISY: The watercolors. Yes, I did.

BUCK: Nice. Flowers. Sunset on the mesa. More flowers. An artist. Nice.

DAISY: Thank you. *(Indicating tea.)* Strong?

BUCK: Yes.

DAISY: Then, we'll just let it steep. *(A long, uncomfortable SILENCE.)* Where did you park?

BUCK: Around the corner.

DAISY: *(Nervously.)* Good.

(A fidgeting SILENCE.)

BUCK: How old are ya—if you don't mind m' askin'?

DAISY: *(She does mind. A forced smile.)* No. No, I don't mind. I don't mind at all. Forty—something.

BUCK: Don't look it.

DAISY: Thank you.

BUCK: Naah, I'da taken you for 'bout thirty—somethin'.

DAISY: *(Flattered.)* Thank you.

BUCK: Twenty—somethin'. Would be havin' a birthday in two weeks.

DAISY: Happy birthday. *(A beat.)* Would be?

BUCK: If I was to live that long.

DAISY: Of course you'll live that long.

BUCK: Will I? You don't know that.

DAISY: Well, no—but, I think it's safe to assume—

BUCK: It ain't safe to assume nothin'. Ain't safe no way.

DAISY: I only meant—

BUCK: I know what you meant. *(After a pause.)* I'm what you call your Libra. You?

DAISY: Aquarius.

BUCK: Put much stock into that kind o' thang?

DAISY: I suppose there may be something to it. I don't know, really.

BUCK: Yeah, I feel the same way. I don't know . . . *really.*
(After a pause - sings.)
This is the dawning of the Age of Aquarius
Age of Aquarius
Ahh-quar-ree-us. *(Speaks.)* That's an old hippy song.

DAISY: Not so old. *(A nervous attempt at making conversation.)* You sing.

BUCK: All my life. You?

DAISY: No. Like to though.

BUCK: Then, why don'tcha?

DAISY: Can't.

BUCK: Course you can. Everybody can.

DAISY: But not well.

BUCK: *Well* . . . that's a whole other matter. Sing somethin'.

DAISY: No. Really. I can't.

BUCK: Come on. There's nobody here.

DAISY: *(Embarrassed.)* No. Please.

BUCK: Come on. Ain't nobody to hear you now.

DAISY: There's you.

BUCK: Ain't nobody, I say. Sing.

DAISY: No. I can't sing.

BUCK: *Sing.*

DAISY: *(Firmly.)* I don't want to.

BUCK: That's different. If you don't want to, I understand. *(After a pause – with a big, boyish grin.)* You sure?

DAISY: *(Softening.)* As sure as sure gets.

BUCK: That won't fill a thimble, ma'am. *(He shrugs.)* Suit yourself. *(Sings.)*
This is the dawning of the Age of Aquarius
Ah-quar-ree-us
AHHH-QUAAA-REEE-UUUS *(A beat. Speaks.)* Like movies?

DAISY: Used to.

BUCK: Don't make 'em like they used to, huh?

DAISY: I mean, I don't get out much.

BUCK: Should. There's more out there than the eye can see.

DAISY: Is there?

BUCK: Worlds and worlds.

DAISY: Really?

BUCK: You'd be surprised.

DAISY: Would I?

BUCK: Guarantee it.

DAISY: *(Uncomfortable. Guarded.)* I don't like to go alone.

BUCK: What about your ol' man?

DAISY: My husband? He doesn't like to go out much—anymore.

BUCK: Sick?

DAISY: No. He works long hours.

BUCK: I don't get out much myself. 'Cept to make my deliveries. Junk food, she calls it.

DAISY: Oh?

BUCK: The ol' lady. Never know when one o' those fits is gonna come upon her. *(He lights a cigarette with the gold lighter, but DAISY does not notice it. He pockets the lighter. After a pause.)* Almost forgot.

DAISY: What?

BUCK: Nothin'. She went to live with her Pappaw this mornin'.

DAISY: Left you?

BUCK: We had this arrangement.

DAISY: I hope it works out for you.

BUCK: It will. *(Another uncomfortable pause.)* Three kids make you older. Know what I mean?

DAISY: I know *one* does.

BUCK: How's that?

DAISY: Well . . . ah . . . on birthdays. On his birthday, I mean. My son's. They always seem more traumatic than my own.

BUCK: Traumatic?

DAISY: I feel my age more . . . my youth . . . or rather, lack of it.

BUCK: I wouldn't worry 'bout that, ma'am.

DAISY: I'm not exactly worried. *(Indicating tea.)* I think it's about ready. *(Pours tea.)*

BUCK: Your husband . . . what does he do?

DAISY: Insurance. House, car, life. You know.

BUCK: Yeah, it don't always pay up.

DAISY: Well, I'm sure if you had a policy with my husband . .

BUCK: You're right, ma'am. *(A beat.)* He's uptown, right?

DAISY: His office is on North Dal Paso, if that's what you—

BUCK: *(Cutting her off.)* Thought he was in the oil business.

DAISY: Oil? Good heavens, no. Insurance. *(Indicating the tea.)* How would you like it?

BUCK: Honey. Bees make it . From flowers. *(Referring to a watercolor of daisies.)* Like them in the paintin'. *(A beat.)* He older than you?

DAISY: I beg your pardon?

BUCK: The ol' man—he older than you?

DAISY: Yes . . . twenty years . . . older.

BUCK: Twenty years. I figured somethin' like that.

DAISY: How? How did you figure something like that?

BUCK: I've a nose for people. A natural gift. What's 'is name?

DAISY: Phil. Philip. Philip Winter.

BUCK: Yours?

DAISY: Daisy. Daisy Winter.

BUCK: *(Indicating watercolor of daisies.)* Like them flowers in the paintin'.

DAISY: Actually, they're watercolors.

BUCK: Watercolors . . . right. Jessie has a little box of—*(A reflective pause.)* Daisy Winter. Alone among the scrub pine and the cactus in a field of dying pump jacks.

DAISY: Excuse me?

BUCK: Daisy Winter. She holds her head high in the desert where she leans into the sun—this flower, this blossom—alone among the scrub pine and the cactus in a field of dying pump jacks. Daisy Winter. Your name . . . and you.

DAISY: And me?

BUCK: You give me that impression.

DAISY: I never thought— How beautiful . . . yet sad.

BUCK: Yes. *(After a pause.)* Buck.

DAISY: I beg your pardon?

BUCK: Buck. That's m' name. Buck Rose.

DAISY: Nice to meet you. *(A conservative laugh.)* That's really silly. I mean, after all this time. It's like, "Have a nice day," isn't it? *(Stiffening.)* I'm sorry. *(Relaxes.)* Buck Rose. That's a flower, too. I mean, the Rose is.

BUCK: That's it then! We're two flowers all alone . . . holding our heads high into the sun . . . wondering whether we've blossomed too soon or too late. Daisy Winter and Buck Rose . . . slow dancing in the winter desert.

DAISY: *(After a pause.)* Oh, my. That's very poetic—beautiful really.

BUCK: *(After a pause.)* So, he's twenty years older. Works long hours. *(A pause.)* Nice house.

DAISY: *(With renewed caution.)* Yes. Thank you.

BUCK: When's he get home?

DAISY: About five, six, seven, sometimes later. *(She looks at her watch and in the process she spills tea in her lap.)* Damn. *(With a vengeance she goes at the spot of spilled tea with her napkin, just above her knee.)*

BUCK: Burn yourself?

DAISY: It'll be all right.

BUCK: *(Places his hand just above her knee.)* Can't never be sure. *(Rubs the spot, sensuously.)*

DAISY: *(Nervously.)* No . . . one can never . . . be. *(A pause as BUCK's fingers caress her leg just above her knee.)* I'm always so afraid. . . .

BUCK: Of getting burned?

DAISY: Yes.

BUCK: It could smart real bad.

DAISY: Yes. You'd think I would have learned by now. Clumsy me.

(BUCK raises her skirt and leans over, pressing his lips against the place where she had spilled the tea. DAISY releases a long sigh – then, nervously, pushes him away.)

BUCK: I can make it feel better.

DAISY: All the years. . . ?

BUCK: Now—just now.

DAISY: I'm sorry. I 'm really not certain that we—

BUCK: *(Putting a finger to her lips. Not letting her finish.)* Shhh. Don't say anything that you won't have a way out of later on. *(After a pause.)* You ain't from these parts, are you, Daisy?

DAISY: No. We came down from Madison, Wisconsin . . . just after Phil Junior was born.

BUCK: Been a long time.

DAISY: Over twenty-two years.

BUCK: Almost a native. You oughta be talkin' like one o' us by now.

DAISY: Yes. *(A beat.)* You mean, I don't?

BUCK: Hell no! Excuse me, ma'am. Don't mean to go cussin' in your house.

DAISY: *(Amused.)* It's all right.

BUCK: Is it?

DAISY: Really, it is.

BUCK: *(After a pause.)* Like the great Southwest?

DAISY: It's all right, I guess.

BUCK: You guess?

DAISY: I'd prefer it better upstate, I think. Maybe Albuquerque. Santa Fe, perhaps. I don't know. Philip has his business and—

BUCK: Insurance, right?

DAISY: Winter Insurance Agency, yes.

BUCK: Winter Insurance Agency. Sounds like it means somethin' different from what it says. But then . . . a lot does, don't it?

DAISY: I'm sorry. I don't follow you.

BUCK: Some hear one thing—some another.

DAISY: I'm afraid . . . I'm really confused.

BUCK: I was makin' a joke, ma'am. I mean, there's fire insurance, life, health, theft . . . but, whoever heard of insurance against winter?

DAISY: Oh, yes. *(Chuckles.)* A lot of claims to pay there.

BUCK: That's the spirit! *(A beat.)* I'm a vendor. Candy. Crackers. Chips. Jerky.

DAISY: That sounds interesting.

BUCK: It is. You get to meet a lot of interesting people. Take *you,* for instance.

DAISY: Me?

BUCK: *Very interesting. (A beat.)* You'll be needing a honey dip for that honey jar.

DAISY: *(Remembering.)* Isn't that a coincidence? That's what I was doing just before we met.

BUCK: Fixin' to buy yourself a honey dip?
DAISY: *(Rises – goes to get paper bag.)* I did. I went to that little health food store on Turner to get just that. A honey dip. *(Returns and takes the honey dip out of the bag and plunges it into the jar of honey.)* Oh, dear! I should've washed it first.

BUCK: It's just fine. Sides, ain't nothin' compared to what the bees must've walked through collectin' their honey.

DAISY: *(Laughs.)* You're probably right.

BUCK: It's a fact. Bees ain't as clean as you might think. No way! Uncle Kirby used to keep bees and the thangs they got into around the ranch just ain't fittin' to say. That there honey dip ain't seen the places Uncle Kirby's bees been!

DAISY: *(Laughs.)* And then, of course, there's all those flowers covered with God knows what.

BUCK: Yes. There's all those flowers covered with God knows what.

DAISY: Well, it is a coincidence, isn't it? *(She looks to BUCK for a response and gets none.)* I mean, two things happening at once. You know, you mentioning the very thing that was the very reason for my being out today . . . what brought us together.

BUCK: The honey dip. *(Pause.)* You into health food?

DAISY: No. Not really. Although, I was a vegetarian once. *(BUCK stares at her blankly.)* I mean, I didn't eat meat.

BUCK: Why?

DAISY: I don't know, really. *(Pause.)* Well, I suppose I do. I mean, there's the obvious—the price of meat nowadays.

BUCK: The price of meat. *(He stretches his legs out in front of him.)* I hear that.

DAISY: It's very easy to tell yourself you're doing something for some great and noble principle when, in fact, you're doing it out of necessity.
BUCK: *(Glancing around the room.)* Necessity?

DAISY: We had hard times, struggles. Don't think we didn't.

BUCK: Times change.

DAISY: Yes. Times change.

BUCK: *(Arches his back, stretches, lets his hands rest in the vicinity of his thighs – smiles.)* No meat, huh?

DAISY: *(Watches BUCK, nervously.)* No.

(BUCK stiffens his legs, arches his back, runs his hands, palm down, along the outer seam of his jeans, then back along the inner seam until his thumbs come to rest hooked over his belt buckle. DAISY watches nervously.)

BUCK: Ain't never knowed nobody what didn't like a taste of meat every now and again.

DAISY: *(Aware of BUCK's body language, but too nervous and too insecure to acknowledge it in an overt way.)* Well, I do . . . now. But, then . . . I asked myself what I would do were I stranded on an island and actually had to kill for a meal. Would I do it? No. You go to the supermarket and you pay somebody else to do it for you—your killing.

BUCK: It ain't murder to kill if you got a good cause.

DAISY: At the meat case you don't really make the same connection.

BUCK: What connection is that?

DAISY: The one you'd make if you were stranded on an island.

BUCK: Or, in the desert.

DAISY: Yes. Or in the desert . . . face to face with the thing whose ground flesh you just threw into the shopping cart without question.

BUCK: Sounds serious. *(Hooks his thumbs over his belt buckle, letting his fingers dangle over his crotch.)* Powerful serious.

DAISY: Well, I suppose if there were no alternatives . . . I mean, eat meat or die—I owe it to myself to survive.

BUCK: That's the bottom line, ain't it?

DAISY: It seems that way.

BUCK: There's a killer in all of us.

DAISY: Perhaps, to a certain extent. Something carried over from the old days. But, I couldn't do it for pleasure. Not like some hunters seem to do.

BUCK: Not for sport, huh?

DAISY: I see nothing sporting about it. *(A beat.)* Anyway, I gave it up.

BUCK: *(Running his hands down his thighs, then back to his belt buckle.)* Meat.

DAISY: No. I gave up giving up, so to speak. I realized that my giving up meat wasn't going to stop the slaughter of livestock, was it?

BUCK: S'pose not. But, when you got five mouths to feed, you'd kill. A rabbit here, there—and any man that tries to keep you from it. You'd kill. I promise.

DAISY: Surely, you don't mean that?

BUCK: When a man gets hungry he gotta eat.

DAISY: Nothing is so important that I'd kill another human being for it. I'd rather die first.

BUCK: You think so?

DAISY: I believe so, yes. I couldn't hate that much.

BUCK: Hate? Off the ranch altogether! Hate ain't got nothin' to do with it. People who hate don't kill nothin', 'cept maybe themselves. You gotta love to kill, Daisy.

DAISY: I don't see the sense of that.

BUCK: No? You gotta love yourself enough when you're hungry. You gotta protect the thangs and the people you love, don'tcha know. When somebody you love is in pain and dyin' right before your eyes, you gotta kill and take the misery away.

DAISY: Ah, you mean euthanasia.

BUCK: I mean knowin' what love is all about—really about.

DAISY: *(Shivers. Crosses to window.)* I'm cold. You frighten me with this talk.

BUCK: Don't mean to.

DAISY *(At window – looking out.)* All heaven is about to break open. Strange. All that sand and water up in those clouds. You wonder how it all stays up there. My God, the sheer weight of it!

BUCK: It don't.

DAISY: *(Turning from window.)* What?

BUCK: It don't. When all that sky gets heavy enough it just busts open and lets loose. Like widow's tears at a funeral. Pourin' down to beat all. 'Fore you know it, the rain and a little bit o' Texas will come down a-pourin'.

DAISY: *(Sotto voce.)* A little bit o' Texas.

BUCK: It's 'cause o' all those cotton farmers and peanut farmers turnin' up all that land 'cross the border, and the wind whippin' it up into the skies. 'Fore you know it, there's a little bit o' Texas here, there. Why, darlin', I bet there's a little bit o' Texas comin' down on Wisconsin right this minute.

DAISY: *(A long, wistful sigh.)* Wisconsin. *(After a pause.)* We just take what comes along and we make the best of it. At least, we should, shouldn't we?

BUCK: What else is there?

DAISY: Something better. There must be something better.

BUCK: There's magic.

DAISY: Not in my life.

BUCK: It ain't over, yet.

DAISY: No, not over.

BUCK: Maybe magic is all around you hidin' in plain sight.

DAISY: I don't see it.

BUCK: *(Moving in on her, facing her.)* That don't mean it ain't there. You gotta have faith. And then you gotta reach out and grab it. Take it in your hands, Daisy. Go ahead. Grab it, Daisy. Make it yours. It's right in front of you waitin' to be touched. Come on. Touch it, Daisy. *Touch it.*

DAISY: *(Confused. After a pause.)* What exactly are we talking about?

BUCK: Magic. Magic, darlin', magic.

DAISY: Oh . . . I thought . . . never mind. *(After a long, reflective pause.)* You know, there's something hypocritical about it all.

BUCK: Hypocritical?

DAISY: My not eating meat. After a year of vegetarianism, I ended it with a hot dog in the lobby of K-Mart. That's a laugh, isn't it? No, I'm not much into health food. I was all over Hobbs looking for a honey dip and ended up at that little store on Turner where, sure enough, there were honey dips—and you.

BUCK: Me?

DAISY: In Allsup's parking lot.

BUCK: Makin' my last delivery.

DAISY: Coincidence.

BUCK: Two thangs happenin' at once.

(BUCK snuffs out his cigarette between his index finger and thumb, then drops it into the ashtray.)

DAISY: You'll burn yourself!

BUCK: *(Showing her his thick, dark-stained fingertips.)* Callused.

DAISY: *(Sitting – sips tea.)* Strong.

BUCK: Yes.

(In the SILENCE that follows, BUCK starts to light another cigarette using the gold lighter he had earlier removed from DAISY'S purse. DAISY recognizes it, but checks her purse to make certain. The cigarette doesn't get lit.)

DAISY: How did you . . . that was in my . . . look, I think you'd better—

BUCK: *(Cutting her off. Putting on his charm.)* Wait a minute! Now, hold on. It ain't how it seems.

DAISY: Oh, it's how it seems, all right.

BUCK: No, ma'am. You're jumping the gun.

DAISY: Am I?

BUCK: Yes, ma'am. Thangs ain't what they seem. I promise. Thangs ain't at all what they seem, ma'am.

DAISY: I know that lighter was in my purse because I just picked it up from being repaired at the jeweler's. That lighter belongs to my husband, Mr. Rose.

BUCK: I wasn't gonna keep it.

DAISY: Oh?

BUCK: You thought I was . . . well, shame on you, darlin'. I was just lookin' for a light, that's all. And you was in the kitchen busy as a bee . . . makin' all this nice tea, and I couldn't find a match to save my life. So, I took a little peek *(Picks up her purse and takes a playful peek.)* . . . as little as that . . . and lo and behold! What do you think I saw?

DAISY: *(Amused by his boyish manner.)* The lighter?

BUCK: Plain as day.

DAISY: I'm sorry.

BUCK: No. I'm the one who's sorry, ma'am.

DAISY: Really, it's all right.

BUCK: Oh, no. It's not all right. Not by a long shot. *(Handing her the lighter.)* Take it. I'm sorry. My mother brought me up better than that. I'm really, truly sorry.

DAISY: I'm sure you didn't mean to—

BUCK: No, ma'am. *(After a pause.)* I don't suppose you have a book o' matches around?

DAISY: *(Handing him back the lighter.)* Here. Use this. It was really very silly of me.

BUCK: Weren't silly at all. Thank you, ma'am. *(Lights cigarette, and with an obvious gesture, he places the lighter on the coffee table.)* If ever I took somethin' what didn't belong to me, may God cut my hands off as quick as *(Raises his arm.)* . . . that! *(Snaps his fingers. A great bolt of LIGHTNING flashes just outside the window. In a moment – THUNDER.)*

DAISY: *(Startled.)* Oh, my.

BUCK: *(Moving closer to her.)* It's all right, darlin'.

DAISY: *(Recovering.)* Oh, dear.

BUCK: Just a coincidence. Two thangs happenin' at once.

DAISY: Oh, my. *(Takes a deep breath.)* One would think you were Thor himself.

BUCK: Thor?

DAISY: A god in Norse mythology, dealing out lightning and thunder with a snap of his fingers.

BUCK: Powerful.

DAISY: Indeed. In fact, today is Thor's day—Thursday.

BUCK: Thursday . . . *Thorsday.* That's a new one on me. That goes back a ways, don't it?

DAISY: A long way. Are you interested in things mythological?

BUCK: What do you mean?

DAISY: Myths, creation stories. Like Genesis in the Bible.

BUCK: I believe in Jesus.

DAISY: Yes, of course. But, there are other cultures, civilizations. Some with as many gods as—

BUCK: *(Cutting her off.)* I believe in Jesus.

DAISY: But, before Jesus there was—

BUCK: *(Stopping her - firmly.)* I said, I believe in Jesus. Jesus is for sinners.

DAISY: *(Uncomfortable.)* Sinners—yes. *(A pause to collect herself.)* I was only making reference to the lightning when you snapped your fingers.

BUCK: Like this? *(Snaps his fingers.)*

(LIGHTNING.)

DAISY: *(Frightened.)* Stop it! Stop it!

BUCK: *(Comforting.)* It weren't nothin' but one o' them coincidences.

(The SOUND of THUNDER.)

DAISY: *(On the verge of tears.)* It frightens me. You—

BUCK: *Shhh.* Buck's here.

DAISY: Frightens—

BUCK: Just a little ol' lightnin' and thunder. Mother nature havin' herself a little hissy-fit.

DAISY: It just frightens me—

BUCK: *(Comforting.)* Ain't nothin'.

DAISY: I know. I know I'm silly. I've always been like this. I feel I'm connected to it.

BUCK: To what? Thunder and lightnin'?

DAISY: To the weather in general. It's like the weather outside and I, in here, are one. Does that sound crazy?

BUCK: Is it the truth?

DAISY: I don't know. It's my truth, I guess.

BUCK: Do you know how you feel?

DAISY: How I feel? Yes. I know how I feel.

BUCK: *(Reassuring.)* That's it then. That's all you need to know, Daisy. That's all there is to know.

DAISY: *(After a thoughtful pause.)* Do you really think a tornado is coming?

BUCK: *Yup.* There's a tornado comin' all right.

DAISY: Then, you see, I feel responsible.

BUCK: How's that?

DAISY: That it's my fault somehow. My doing.

BUCK: Don't seem possible.

DAISY: I know it doesn't. But, that's how I feel.

BUCK: *Shhh.* You just got worked into a state.

DAISY: Sometimes, I'm in the supermarket, or just walking in the mall when it happens. I'm connected to them. All these people and events. They're pieces of me and I'm a piece of them. Connected. Deep inside. And, I'm thinking that they can hear what I'm thinking! And, I'm hearing what they're saying as what I'm thinking.

BUCK: *(Comforting.)* It's all right, darlin'.

DAISY: No! It's not all right. I'm connected to the whole of everything. We all are. And I can't free myself of it.

BUCK: Then, why try?
DAISY: I want my own will! Don't you understand what I'm saying?

BUCK: Sure. You're scared o' bein' alone.

DAISY: *No.* I want to be alone.

BUCK: That's a lonely place to be, darlin'.

DAISY: Yes. Yes, it is.

BUCK: Best you relax. *(Comforting.)* *Shhh.* Buck's here.

DAISY: And when I try to talk to somebody I hear—no, feel —feel an exchange of information which has nothing to do with the actual words themselves. *God!* I don't know what I'm saying anymore. What are you doing to me?

BUCK: Ain't doin' nothin', darlin'. *Honest.*

DAISY: Honest?

BUCK: Injun.

DAISY: *(Takes a long, deep breath.)* I suppose you're not afraid of anything. You've got youth, looks, strength, charm. Afraid of nothing and nobody, right?

BUCK: That's not true. Ain't true at all.

DAISY: *(Teasing.)* What's a strapping young man like you afraid of?

BUCK: Lots o' thangs.

DAISY: What kind of things?

BUCK: Dark thangs. Evil thangs. The devil's thangs.

DAISY: The devil's thing? *(Unsure.)* You're joking—

BUCK: No, ma'am. There ain't nothin' funny 'bout the dark powers. That's why I accepted Jesus as my Savior. I am born again.

DAISY: Born again? What exactly do you mean by that?

BUCK: What I mean is what I say.

DAISY: You needn't be defensive.

BUCK: I'm not.

DAISY: It's just that I've heard that phrase—born again—used so often, so loosely, I don't have a sense for it. I don't know what it means.

BUCK: I guess you gotta be to know. Before I was born again I was a dead man walkin' the Earth without the breath of Jesus. I was a dead man walkin' in the darkness. *(After a pause.)* I know somebody who ran into the Satan when he was pretendin' to be some big Hollywood movie star. He's real all right.

DAISY: Surely, you mean that figuratively.

BUCK: No ma'am. He's real. And you never know whose eyes he's gonna show up behind next.

DAISY: You make it sound so frightening.

BUCK: It oughta frighten you, ma'am.

DAISY: Oh, my—

BUCK: I wouldn't worry though. Buck's here. You'll be safe. Bein' born again has its advantages. If you was to be born again, what would you do with your new life?

DAISY: I don't know. *(Beat.)* A park ranger.

BUCK: You? A lady park ranger?

DAISY: Why not? I'd be a good one. Taking care of the plants and animals. Planting fruit and nut trees wherever I could so everybody would have something good to eat. Wouldn't that be nice? You wouldn't have to bring your picnic to the park. You could just pick it right off the trees. Wouldn't that be nice?

BUCK: *(Thinking he is hearing the voice of Dawn.)* What?

DAISY: Why can't all the parks be filled with fruit and nut trees? Just like in the Garden of Eden. Wouldn't that be nice?

BUCK: Yes, nice.

DAISY: Everybody could just pick whatever they wanted. I planted a pecan tree in the park across the way last year, but someone from the Parks Department dug it up no sooner than it began to take root.

BUCK: *(Sotto voce.)* I'm sorry.

DAISY: I wrote a letter to the city council, but I'm still waiting for a reply. Got them on the phone, they put me on hold and then disconnected me.

BUCK: *(Sotto voce.)* I'm truly sorry.

DAISY: Said they'd get right back to me. Left me holding a disconnected phone, waiting . . . and then it went dead.

BUCK: Did you wait . . . long?

DAISY: I'm still waiting.

BUCK: I'm sorry.

DAISY: Waiting for some kind of satisfaction. They don't kill you with kindness, that's for sure. They might as well take a gun to your head. Know what I mean?

BUCK: I'm sorry.

DAISY: It seems there is a law against people planting anything in the city parks. Sharing is not encouraged in our society. People are starving and there's no Earthly reason for it.

BUCK: I'm sorry. I'm really, truly sorry.

DAISY: Stop saying you're sorry. It's not your fault. It's the system. It lacks Humanity. Surely, you'd agree with that.

BUCK: I can't rightly say.

DAISY: Saying one thing, doing another. People seldom live up to their promises. Well, there's a better world coming, you'll see. *(Pauses to take him in.)* You're not drinking your tea.

BUCK: *(Sips tea.)* Nice.

DAISY: *(Sips tea.)* Yes. Nice.

BUCK: *(Remembering.)* Transmigration of spirit.

DAISY: *What?*

BUCK: Just somethin' I heard. Had this here radio talk show on whiles I was parked over by Allsup's.

DAISY: While I was in the health food store.

BUCK: Right. *(A beat.)* Coincidence? *(He snaps his fingers – a sudden flash of LIGHTNING.)* Two thangs happening at once!

(The LIGHTING from the lamps go out. This should not affect the LIGHTING too much, as it is still mid-afternoon. It is, however, darker outside than would otherwise be normal for this time of day–this time of year. Every so often throughout the remainder of the play, the SOUND of gusts of wind can be heard howling, accompanied by the SOUND of a tree's branch scratching against the windowpane.)

DAISY: *(Rises. Crosses to window.)* Oh, my! The electricity's out!

BUCK: *(Rises and follows her.)* It'll be back on in no time.

DAISY: *(Looking out window.)* I don't think—

(Suddenly, the LIGHTS flash back on, followed by the SOUND of THUNDER.)

DAISY *(Continues. Startled.)* Oh, dear!

BUCK: *(Looking out the window from over her shoulder.)* They come in hard and fast. Go out the same way. *(While standing behind DAISY, he has unbuttoned his shirt. As he turns from the window, he pulls his shirt out of his jeans. His chest is bare.)* You don't mind if I get comfortable?

DAISY: *(Turning from window. Getting a good, hard look at him and liking what she sees.)* No . . . not at all. *(Moving away, nervously.)* More tea?

BUCK: Take tea and pee. *(Removes his shirt.)*

DAISY: What?

BUCK: Just somethin' I heard once. Five o'clock. *(He unbuttons her blouse.)* He comes home.

DAISY: Yes.

BUCK: Storm's makin' it dark out there.

DAISY: Yes.

BUCK: There's a lot of lonely out there.

DAISY: Yes.

BUCK: Yes. *(Lifting away her blouse.)* All the time in the world.

DAISY: Time?

BUCK: Still time.

DAISY: Yes.

BUCK: Yes.

DAISY: I never did anything like this before.

BUCK: Before?

DAISY: Now.

BUCK: Like what? *(Facing her, cupping his hands on her buttocks.)*

DAISY: This.

BUCK: This?

DAISY: You know.

BUCK: Yes. I know, Daisy.

DAISY: I never asked a stranger home before.

BUCK: I ain't no stranger. We been gettin' on 'bout all kinds o' thangs all afternoon.

DAISY: You know what I mean.

BUCK: Yes. I picked myself a daisy.

DAISY: I don't know what possessed me.

BUCK: A beautiful daisy. Lovers make wishes on daisies.

DAISY: Yes, by tearing off their petals.

BUCK: That's how it's done, Daisy. *(Running his hands down along her arms. After a pause.)* Do you hate him?

DAISY: *(Shudders.)* Him?

BUCK: Your husband—the old man.

DAISY: No. I love my husband. Do you love your wife?

BUCK: Love's funny. It comes. It goes. Is he bald?

DAISY: *(A bit put-off.)* No.

BUCK: Gray? *(He undoes her skirt and it drops to the floor. DAISY is wearing a slip.)*

DAISY: Yes.

BUCK: He's sixty-something, right?

DAISY: Yes.

BUCK: *(Running his hands down along her body, slowly.)* Do it much?

DAISY: *(Sadly, expectantly.)* No.

BUCK: Been a long time—

DAISY: Yes. A very long time.

BUCK: Yes.

DAISY: *(Having second thoughts.)* Your wife—

BUCK: Dawn.

DAISY: Dawn. That's a pretty name. Pretty.

BUCK: Was.

DAISY: Was?

BUCK: There's some question about us gettin' back together.

DAISY: I hope it works out for you.

BUCK: It will . . . like Miss America.

DAISY: Excuse me?

BUCK: Beautiful like Miss America. *(Sings.) Here she comes, Miss America (After a pause. Speaks.)* Like music?

DAISY: Yes. Would you like to hear some?

BUCK: I wouldn't mind.

(DAISY turns on the radio and it is most likely tuned to the station she usually listens to—FM easy listening—and the MUSIC is a slow, sensuous tango.)

DAISY: How's this? It's the Roswell station.

BUCK: *(Moving close to her.)* Not bad.

DAISY: Want to hear something else? I can change it.

BUCK: No. Leave it on. *(A pause to listen.)* It's one o' them tangos.

DAISY: Yes. Yes, it is.

BUCK: Can you do it?

DAISY: The tango? *(BUCK nods "yes.")* I haven't danced in years.

BUCK: Me neither. Wanna try?

DAISY: It's been a long time.

BUCK: I'm game.

DAISY: *(Hesitant.)* Yes. Why not?

(BUCK and DAISY begin to dance a slow, sensuous tango. Their dialogue should be stretched out over periods of dancing. The passion of the dance and the dialogue should be both evident and erotic—as though this were sexual intercourse itself. To quote a phrase used by a director friend, "It should burn a hole in the stage!")

DAISY: *(Continues.)* Oh, my. You've done this before.

BUCK: Never.

DAISY: It's been years. Wherever did you learn . . . to dance . . . the tango?

BUCK: Just picked it up . . . somewhere. Just picked it up.

DAISY: It's a kind of . . . passion . . . dancing . . . the tango.

BUCK: Yes.

DAISY: Yes.

BUCK: A kind of . . . passion . . . dancing—

DAISY: Yes.

BUCK: Yes.

DAISY: Dangerous . . . mysterious . . . seductive . . . precise.

BUCK: Powerful.

DAISY: Yes.

BUCK: The tango.

DAISY: The tango.

BUCK: Yes.

DAISY: Yes.

BUCK: Dangerous.

DAISY: Yes . . . yes.

BUCK: Seductive.

DAISY: Yes . . . yes.

BUCK: Precise.

DAISY: Yes . . . yes.

BUCK: Powerful!

DAISY: *Yes.*

(LIGHTNING.)

DAISY: *(Continuing.)* Yes! Yes!

BUCK: Yes!

(LIGHTNING.)

BUCK: *(Continues.)* Yes! Yes!

(The SOUND of THUNDER.)

BUCK: *(Continues.)* YES.

DAISY: YES.

(The SOUND of THUNDER.)

BUCK: *(Ibid.)* YES! YES! . . . *The tango.*

(LIGHTNING.)

DAISY: *The tango.*

(They have worked their way behind the sofa, BUCK, naked, has his back up against the sofa. DAISY goes down on her knees and begins to perform fellatio on BUCK. Passionate SOUNDS. The SOUND of THUNDER. The MUSIC and the LIGHTS go out. More passionate SOUNDS until BUCK climaxes.)

DAISY: *(Stands.)* The electricity—

BUCK: *Shhh—*

DAISY: *(Crosses to window.)* The storm—

BUCK: That was nice, darlin'. Real nice. *(Goes for a cigarette.)* Sweet Jesus, that was beautiful

DAISY: *(Disturbed.)* How can you say such a thing?

BUCK: *(Lighting a cigarette, slipping the lighter into his pocket.)* Such a thang as what, darlin'?

DAISY: *(Reluctantly.)* "Sweet Jesus."

BUCK: Ain't he sweet?

DAISY: I don't know. I just don't think it's appropriate. *(Realizes that BUCK has, once again, pocketed her husband's lighter.)* Please give me the lighter, Mr. Rose.

BUCK: Huh?

DAISY: The lighter. You just put it in your pocket.

BUCK: *(Feeling his pocket.)* So I did. Why don'tcha come on over here and get it? Just reach your hand down in there and lift it out, darlin'.

DAISY: No.

BUCK: Your warm hand—

DAISY: No.

BUCK: Slidin' hot. Slippin' it out.
DAISY: Stop it!

BUCK: C'mon. *(He extends his arms outward from his sides, pushing his pelvis forward.)* Slip your little hand down there and feel around for it.

DAISY: *(Standing firm.)* Give me the lighter, Mr. Rose.

BUCK: Buck. Nobody calls me Mister Rose. That's m' daddy.

DAISY: *(After a pause.)* Buck, please. It's getting late. Please give me the lighter and leave.

BUCK: Leave? Just like that? *(He snaps his fingers.)*

(LIGHTNING.)

DAISY: *(Panicked.)* Oh, my God!

BUCK: Yes, Daisy. Yes.

(The SOUND of THUNDER.)

DAISY: Oh, God! *(Backing away.)* Don't hurt me. Please don't hurt me.

BUCK: *(Moving toward her.)* Ain't nobody gonna hurt you, darlin'.

DAISY: *(Backing away. On the verge of tears.)* You can have the lighter. Keep it. Just leave me alone, please.

BUCK: *(Grabbing her hand, forcing it to his pants' pocket.)* You want it? *Huh?* Dig for it!

DAISY: No!

BUCK: I said, dig for it!

DAISY: *(Pulls away. Slaps him hard on the face.)* Get out!

(LIGHTNING.)

BUCK: It ain't polite to slap a gentleman, ma'am.

(SOUND of THUNDER.)

DAISY: *(Frightened.)* Oh, my God. Please. I'm sorry. Please. Look, if it's money you want—

BUCK: I don't want none o' your money, lady. I just saw a woman gettin' old. Nothin' but old.

DAISY: Shut up.

BUCK: And lonely.

DAISY: Shut up!

BUCK: Ain't had a real time in years.

DAISY: *Stop it!*

BUCK: So, I says to myself, "Buck boy, we're gonna show this ol' gal some real time." Real time, Daisy.

DAISY: *Please—*

BUCK: *(Removes the lighter from his pocket.)* Here! Here's your lighter. *(Extends it to her. She backs away.)* Here. Take it. Go on now. Take it! Take it! *(Following her as she backs away.)* You wanted it. Now take it. It's yours, Daisy. All yours.

DAISY: *(Grabs it out of his hand.)* Thank you. Now, please put your clothes on and leave, Mr. Rose.

BUCK: Buck. Say it.

DAISY: What?

BUCK: I said, say it!

DAISY: What? What do you want me to say?

BUCK: BUCK. BUCK. My name is Buck. Say it, woman. Say it!

DAISY: *(With renewed fear. Sotto voce.)* Buck.

BUCK: Again!

DAISY: *(A little louder.)* Buck.

BUCK: AGAIN.

DAISY: Buck!

BUCK: That's better. Again.

DAISY: Buck! Buck, Buck, Buck! All right?

BUCK: *(A big, boyish grin.)* That's m' name, darlin'. That's m' name.

DAISY: *(Regaining composure. Truly alarmed.)* Yes.

BUCK: Yes? Yes what?

DAISY: Yes, Buck.

BUCK: Yes . . . that's nice, Daisy. My little flower . . . all alone.

DAISY: *(Placating.)* Yes, Buck. Your little flower all alone, Buck.

BUCK: All alone. Without love. *(Sadly.)* There ain't no love. *(Forcefully.)* Y'all better leave now.

DAISY: *(Stunned.)* What?

BUCK: I said, it's time for you to go.

DAISY: Go? Go where?

BUCK: Git!

DAISY: What are you talking about? You're the one who needs to leave.

BUCK: *(Sternly.)* Git outta this house.

DAISY: *(Dumbfounded.)* What?

BUCK: *(Resonating in a deep, threatening voice.)* GET . . . OUT . . . OF . . . THIS . . . HOUSE.

DAISY: This is my house, Mr. Rose!

BUCK: BUCK!

DAISY: Buck, this is my house. You don't order me about in my house.

BUCK: Does he?

DAISY: Who?

BUCK: Ol' man Winter. Does he order you about?

DAISY: That's none of your business!

BUCK: No. I bet not. I bet he don't got three words to say to you. Not three! Not the three you want to hear.

DAISY: That's none of your—

BUCK: *(Cutting her off.)* Old. Old. Old nothin' man. *Git out!*

DAISY: No! This is my house!

BUCK: This ain't your house. It's his house. Ol' man Winter's house. You're just a daisy hangin' on the wall like in one o' them watercolors. *(He pulls a watercolor off the wall and throws it to the floor.)* Dead! No more! All over!

DAISY: Stop it!

BUCK: Dead, Daisy. All your petals plucked.

DAISY: Stop it!

BUCK: Buried in here with your dead flowers. Roses from a lost beauty contest. Cold, dead, brittle. *(He snaps his fingers.)* Go!

(LIGHTNING and HOWLING WIND.)

DAISY: No.

BUCK: You ain't nothin' but a dead thang hangin' on the wall. His wall.

(The SOUND of THUNDER.)

DAISY: No.

BUCK: A trophy!

DAISY: *(Breaking down, realizing that there may be some truth to this—a truth she does not want to hear—much less, face.)* No! That's not true! Not true at all!

BUCK: Dead and stuffed and still walkin'.

DAISY: No.

BUCK: You gotta be born again!

DAISY: No! I don't want to be. *(Pause.)* It's a lie.

BUCK: What is? What's a lie, Daisy?

DAISY: You . . . Jesus . . . everybody! It's all a lie. My—

BUCK: What, Daisy? What?

DAISY: My life, goddamnit! My life!

BUCK: He owns you.

DAISY: No.

BUCK: *(Softly.)* It's time to leave, Daisy.

DAISY: No. You have no right. I'm calling the police! *(Crosses to telephone.)*

(BUCK crosses to sofa and removes the handgun from where it was hidden.)

BUCK: *(Crossing to DAISY.)* Run, Daisy. *(Rips cord off telephone.)*

DAISY: *(Sees gun.)* Oh, my God!

BUCK: Run. You don't love him.

DAISY: *(Backing away.)* I do! I do love him!

BUCK: You're trapped, Daisy. Trapped.

DAISY: No.

BUCK: Like a flower without sunshine.

DAISY: I love him! I love him!

BUCK: Bullshit!

DAISY: Don't hurt me . . . please.

BUCK: You're trapped, Daisy. M' little flower is trapped.

DAISY: Please, don't kill me.

BUCK: Run while you can, Daisy. Git away from him. He's old man Winter.

DAISY: No! He's my husband. *(A cry of agony.)* He's my husband and I love him.

BUCK: Bullshit! He's dark. He's evil. The son o' Satan.

DAISY: Stop it! You're crazy!

BUCK: You never know whose eyes Satan's gonna show up behind.

DAISY: You're crazy!

(BUCK grabs her.)

DAISY: *(Continues. Struggling.)* Let me go! Leave me alone!

BUCK: You're a flower, darlin'. *A flower.* Run! Run! Run while ya still got a chance.

DAISY: *(Struggling, breaks free and falls to the floor.)* HELP!

BUCK: *(Straddling her.)* Shhh. You've been alone too long.

DAISY: *(On her back, resigned.)* Shoot me! Shoot me! Go ahead. S hoot me you sonofabitch! Shoot me if you're going to. Shoot me.

BUCK: *(Tracing her face with the barrel of the gun.)* I'm sorry, darlin'. It's time for you to leave.

DAISY: Why?

BUCK: It just is. *(Sticks the gun in her mouth.)* Now it is time to get the fuck out of here. You don't love him. *(He removes the gun from DAISY'S mouth.)*

DAISY: *(Resigned.)* No. No, I don't love him.

BUCK: You should've left while you had the chance, darlin'.

DAISY: I have nowhere to go. *Oh, God. Help me.* I'm trapped. I have nowhere to go. *Help me. Help me.*

BUCK: *(Resigning.)* Me, too, darlin'. Me, too. Two flowers in the desert. All alone. Trapped. Trapped and nowhere to go. *(Pauses to listen.)* Listen.

DAISY: What?

BUCK: *Shhh. Listen. (He kneels beside her.)*

(The SOUND of the TORNADO, like a freight train, moving slowly toward the house.)

BUCK: *(Continues.)* Listen.

DAISY: *(Rises to her knees.)* What? What is it?

BUCK: The voice of God. *Tornado.*

DAISY: Oh, my God!

BUCK: He's coming, Daisy. He's coming to wash away the sins of the world.

DAISY: Stop it! Stop it!

BUCK: I can't.

DAISY: Yes! Yes, you can. I know you can.

BUCK: No, Daisy. Only you can stop him now.

(The SOUND of the TORNADO grows louder.)

DAISY: How?

BUCK: Here. *(He offers her the gun.)* Take it.

DAISY: No.

BUCK: Take it.

DAISY: *(Grabs the gun and points it at him.)* Please. Please leave. I'm afraid—

BUCK: Me, too, darlin'. Me, too. *Shhh.* Listen.

(The SOUND of the TORNADO grows louder.)
BUCK: *(Continues. Sings.)* Here she comes, Miss A-mer-i-ca. *(After a pause. Speaks.)* You're a beauty, Daisy. Like a Miss America.

DAISY: Thank you, Buck.

BUCK: Sweet Jesus! Save these poor servants. Trapped with nowhere to go! Save us, Lord! Save us! Show us the way, Sweet Jesus! Show us the way!

DAISY: Stop it!

(The SOUND of the TORNADO grows louder.)

BUCK: Show us the way! Show us the way!

DAISY: We're going to die!

BUCK: We're all going to die!

DAISY: I don't want to.

BUCK: Are you born again!?

DAISY: I don't believe!

BUCK: We're here, Lord! Come and get us!

DAISY: No! You can stop it. You can stop the tornado now.

BUCK: Too late. *(Backing away from where DAISY kneels on the floor, stretching out his arms as if crucified.)* Dear Lord, there ain't nothin' on this ol' planet of yours but sinfulness and shit, Lord. Evil and shit!

DAISY: *Please.*

BUCK: Can you love?

DAISY: Yes.

BUCK: You hear that, Lord? She can love!

DAISY: Yes, yes!

BUCK: Love me! Kill me!

DAISY: NO!

BUCK: Let me fly, Daisy! Let me fly!

DAISY: I can't!

BUCK: Show her the way, Sweet Jesus. Show her the way!

DAISY: Oh, God! Help me!

BUCK: *(Wails.)* Do you hear me, Lord? *(He turns toward DAISY with his arms outstretched as if crucified.)* I said, do you hear me
(The TORNADO has reached the house. The SOUND is a deafening rumble.)

BUCK: *(Continues.)* DO YOU HEAR ME?

(DAISY pulls the trigger. SILENCE. The TORNADO is gone. BUCK stands stunned with a contented look on his face—blood splattered on his t-shirt.)
BUCK: *(Continues. Softly. At peace.)* The world is yours, Daisy. *(He falls to his knees.)* Sweet, sweet Daisy. *(He keels over, dead.)*

(LIGHTNING and the far off rumble of THUNDER. The electricity returns and the LIGHT of the lamps and the MUSIC of the tango resumes. DAISY kneels paralyzed in place, horrified with the realization of what she's done. The SOUND of a gentle rain beginning to fall.)

DAISY: Oh . . . my . . . God.

(The LIGHTING slowly dims to the MUSIC of the tango. BLACK OUT and CURTAIN.)

END OF PLAY

THE MOON AWAY

"*The Moon Away, which is based on an actual event, examines the dreams, memories, and emotional confinement of Joe, a homosexual photographer in southern New Mexico, wrongfully accused of sexual contact with a minor. Afraid, angry, and hiding himself from a community that judges him, Joe delves into a world of lost hopes and bitter resentment. His ideals, identity, and future are all in question as he struggles to find the voice hidden within his dreams and memories.* The Moon Away *is more than a play about homosexuality. It is an exploration into the elements (loves, fears, etc) that make a person complete. That search for one's self is a shared experience by all people, regardless of sexuality. That is what makes us human. It is amazing and beautiful. It feels real. It is a show that challenges, engages, moves, and uplifts the viewer. I have never seen an audience hold their breath like they have for this piece. The audience hangs on every word and image. This comes from great writing . . . passion permeates throughout* The Moon Away.*"*
—Braden Weeks, Boston Producing Director

THE MOON AWAY was developed and presented at the Greenwich House Theatre in NYC in February of 1995. It was the first play to be produced at that theatre. After a further production at Mesa College in San Diego in March of 2000 and having undergone more fine-tuning, it had its official world premier at The Davenaughn Theatre in Boston, Massachusetts on September 1, 2006 with the following cast and crew:

JAMES TAMBINI—Joe
JOHN BOWEN—Lawyer, Convict, Pope, Tormentor 1
ELIZABETH OLSON—Psychologist, Mother Superior, Junior's Mother, Tormentor 3
MICHAEL HADDAD—Conrad, Junior, Tormentor 2
Director—Dawn M. Simmons,
Stage Manager—Katie Toohil
Set Designer—Nina Sokoler
Lighting Designer—Chris Fournich
Costume Designer—Mildred Louis
Technical Director—Karen D. Weeks

THE CHARACTERS

JOE—age forty.
CONRAD—age forty. Joe's lover. Doubles as TORMENTOR 2, JUNIOR.
THE PSYCHOLOGIST—a woman between thirty and forty. Doubles as TORMENTOR 3, THE MOTHER, THE MOTHER SUPERIOR.
THE LAWYER—a "no nonsense" man over the age of thirty and under the age of fifty. Doubles as TORMENTOR 1, THE POPE, PRISONER.

The **TIME** is the mid-1980s.
The **ACTION** takes place in a small city in Lea County, New Mexico, a few miles from the West Texas border.
The **SETTING** is in the abstract—the time-space of the mind—the landscape of dreams.

NOTE: There is doubling. This play is written to be performed by 3 men and 1 woman.

NOTE: The play is broken down into 22 scenes for technical reasons only. Unless noted, there should be no visible break in the action of the play. The actual design of the set is dictated only by an emphasis on the word "surreal" in the sense of style, a suggestion for having the actors seem to appear and disappear, and by the necessity for a functional bridge—dream-like and surreal. This bridge must support the actors who walk upon it from time to time throughout the course of the play. Furthermore, whatever the design of the set pieces, we shall need places to sit and a place to take our stand.

ACT ONE:

Scene 1—a bridge in Joe's dream.
Scene 2—a visiting room in the city jail.
Scene 3—the same.
Scene 4—the same.
Scene 5—the photography studio.
Scene 6—a visiting room in the city jail.
Scene 7—the photography studio.
Scene 8—a visiting room in the city jail.
Scene 9—the same.
Scene 10—the same.
Scene 11—the bridge.
Scene 12—a visiting room in the city jail.
Scene 13—the psychologist's office.
Scene 14—a cell in the county jail.

ACT TWO:

Scene 1—the bridge.
Scene 2—the psychologist's office.
Scene 3—outside the judge's chambers.
Scene 4—Joe and Conrad's bedroom.
Scene 5—the psychologist's office.

Scene 6—Joe and Conrad's bedroom.
Scene 7—a courtroom.
Scene 8—the bridge.

THE MOON AWAY IN HISTORICAL PERSPECTIVE

In the mid-1980s, hysteria swept the country. People in disproportionate numbers were using children to add fuel to what had become mass-hysteria to destroy the lives of others. Prosecutors and social workers coerced children to make false accusations of sexual molestation and satanic rituals involving the sacrificing of cats, dogs, rabbits and other small animals.

Day care workers, ex-marital partners and homosexuals became targets for shocking charges of rape, devil worshipping sodomy, etc. These were high profile cases that daily made the front pages of newspapers and in the endless reports on evening TV. Parents wore buttons that warned *"Believe the Children." "Listen to the children"* and *"children don't lie"* became the mantra of the day. Every adult was at risk. The mere accusation kept men and women imprisoned without bail. Jobs were lost, marriages wrecked, lives destroyed from unsubstantiated accusations. Innocent individuals spent years in prison without ever having committed a crime. All the high-profile defendants, after months and years of hellish pain, were found not guilty. The number of children who would eventually recant was an alarming high percent when compared to the accusations made.n What began this hysteria is anybody's guess, but it grew like wildfire making its way into every city, town and hamlet—eventually making its way into Hobbs, New Mexico. The population of Hobbs was around thirty-five thousand souls at that time. Its only newspaper ran a front page story questioning the demonic significance of the Arm and Hammer logo. Hobbs, New Mexico was ripe to become the epicenter for the perfect storm.

It is against this backdrop *The Moon Away* is set.

—E.C.W.

ACT ONE—*Scene 1*—*a bridge in Joe's dream*

AT RISE: the stage is in darkness. A single LIGHT begins to fade JOE into view before spreading as it intensifies on the bridge fading into view. The bridge, seemingly, goes nowhere. There are steps leading up to and down from the bridge.

JOE: *(On the bridge, speaking directly to the audience.)* This is the dream . . . or nightmare. You decide. I am on a bridge. Suddenly, the sun goes down as quickly as if someone had switched the lights off. This sudden shift—this darkness—does not seem out of the ordinary. I somehow have the knowledge that there is a force with specific form that I cannot grasp visually. Yet, I know it exists. I know it has form and shape within its own dimensions . . . dimensions for which I have no sense to put them into perspective. This force—this inexplicable entity —has the power to eclipse the sun by sheer will, enfolding me in the shadow of its omnipresence. *Is it God?*

I am overwhelmed by the thought of such an entity, so I fly. I fly just above arms beginning to reach up for me, trying to pull me down. Slowly, I descend toward the ground beneath the bridge.

(The TORMENTORS—three hooded and cloaked figures—ominously sinister and ghost-like, appear and move hauntingly through the fog and shadows beneath the bridge. They hiss and, in rasping voices, call: "Joseph, Joseph" etc.)

JOE *(Continued.)*: They drag me underground . . . into the dark, damp regions of their underworld. I recognize the futility of any effort to resist. Soon, after resigning myself to my captors, I try to remember where I was before I fell into their clawing, grabbing, clutching hands. I am horrified.

Horrified at the faceless faces of these demons. Horrified because I cannot remember any prior existence beyond suddenly finding myself on that bridge. Every attempt to remember causes unbearable pain . . . a savage anguish. I understand it only as a feeling; a sensation of being dissolved in the face of infinity when one has come too close to its realization; that last conscious moment of *I am* before melting into the enigma of the eternal world without end—overwhelmed by the incomprehensible magnitude of it. Have you ever felt that? I have.

(The TORMENTORS continue to whisper and hiss.)
JOE *(Continued.)*: The shock of that impending oblivion causes me to wake, not from sleep, but rather into another time and once again on that very same bridge.

(The TORMENTORS point accusingly at JOE.)

JOE *(Continued.)*: I hear voices accusing me of . . . *what?* Whatever it is, I feel the weight of its guilt. I think about flying to safety and I wonder about the direction to take, but I cannot move under the force of this guilt that restrains me from flight. I come to realize that my very ability to fly, the fact that I am able, is proof of my guilt.

(The TORMENTORS continue to whisper and hiss.)

JOE *(Continued.)*: Then, someone approaches. I can't make out his face. We struggle. There is one thought on my mind. *Kill him!* His death will be my absolution. *Kill him!* I push him from the bridge. I watch him fall silently to the ground below.

(The TORMENTORS watch the invisible body as it falls, pointing to it before surrounding it.)

JOE *(Continued.)*: I think there ought to be a thud. But, there is only silence. I wonder . . . What if he isn't dead? There must be no evidence of his ever having existed! I see a large rock on the bridge. I pick it up, raising it high above my head, and aim it at his face before hurling it with all the force that I can muster. Suddenly, he disappears. The rock strikes the empty ground and bounces, soundlessly, out of sight.

(The TORMENTORS disappear into the shadows.)

JOE *(Continued.)*: I fly away. Not very fast. Not very high. But, I fly just the same.

(JOE descends from the bridge and walks downstage.)

JOE *(Continued.)*: Then I am awake, soaked with sweat and feelings mixed with sorrow, guilt and remorse . . . a painful and complete sense of being utterly alone in all of time and space. And I wonder . . . Can absolution be won through the trials of men in their search for Truth? And I wonder . . . Was there ever innocence? Or is there, indeed, an original crime for which Man can never be absolved? Is there no redemption?

That's it. That's the dream . . . or the nightmare. You be the judge.

END ACT ONE—*Scene 1*

ACT ONE—*Scene 2*—*a visiting room in the city jail*

THE PSYCHOLOGIST: *(A thoughtful, pleasant, professional woman who appears as if from nowhere while finishing an entry in her notebook.)* I am not here to judge, Joe.

JOE: Well, I'm certainly not in any position.

THE PSYCHOLOGIST: Of course you are. You know there's been a substantial change.

JOE: Has there?

THE PSYCHOLOGIST: Don't you see it, Joe?

JOE: It's always the same. Nothing's changed.

THE PSYCHOLOGIST: What about the man on the bridge?

JOE: What about him?

THE PSYCHOLOGIST: Any idea who he is . . . whom he represents?

JOE: I told you, I couldn't see his face.

THE PSYCHOLOGIST: No, but in the past it was always you who fell from the bridge. *(Reading from notebook.)* "I am on a bridge. Someone turns the lights out. Someone approaches. He grabs me. We struggle. I fall from the bridge. I wake." *(Thumbs through notebook.)* The following session: *(Reads.)* "I am on a bridge." *(Looking through notes.)* Here it is. *(Reads.)* "I fall. I see the bridge as I fall. I think I am about to hit the ground. I wonder why I cannot wake. I am on the ground. I look up and see someone on the bridge looking down at me. He disappears."

JOE: That's right. We've changed places. What does that mean?

THE PSYCHOLOGIST: I really can't say. What do you think it means?

JOE: I don't know. It's a struggle with myself, maybe.

THE PSYCHOLOGIST: Maybe.

JOE: Why? Why would I want to hurt myself? Why should I want to destroy myself . . . so completely—so finally?

THE PSYCHOLOGIST: I don't know. Why should you?

JOE: Well, I don't.

THE PSYCHOLOGIST: Good. Joe, I want you to start writing down these dreams in more detail, along with how you feel about them at the time of the dream and then again upon reflection.

JOE: I can't.

THE PSYCHOLOGIST: Why is that?

JOE: Because they don't let me have a pen, paper—nothing in this place. I have to ask for my toothbrush every morning. They won't let me keep it with me.

THE PSYCHOLOGIST: I wasn't aware of that.

JOE: Yeah . . . well, I guess they're afraid I'm going to do myself in . . . disembowel myself with my multi-tufted Doctor Good-Dental.

THE PSYCHOLOGIST: I'm certainly glad to see that you're

keeping your sense of humor.

JOE: And my sanity?

THE PSYCHOLOGIST: Was there ever any doubt?

JOE: I think . . . no, I feel . . . I feel that I'm going to lose it in here.
Oh, God. I'm so afraid.

THE PSYCHOLOGIST: You're doing very well, Joe. I'm proud of you.

JOE: Yeah . . . well . . . I wish I were.

THE PSYCHOLOGIST: Do you want to talk about it . . . what you're feeling?

JOE: I hate the kid! I hate his mother! I hate the whole stinking idea of it!

THE PSYCHOLOGIST: What are your thoughts about the boy . . . his mother?

JOE: I'm sorry. I'm really not up to this.

THE PSYCHOLOGIST: All right. We don't have to if you don't want to. But, sooner or later you'll have to deal with it, Joe.

JOE: I know.

THE PSYCHOLOGIST: Good. Any word about when you're being transferred to the county jail?

JOE: If Conrad can't come up with the bond money . . . in two days, I think. *(A pause to control his mounting panic.) Oh, God.* I'm not going to make it, Doctor. I'm not going to make it.

THE PSYCHOLOGIST: Yes, you are. You'll be just fine.

JOE: No, I won't.

THE PSYCHOLOGIST: Joe, you've held together better than should be expected of anybody going through what you've been going through.

JOE: I'm not through it yet . . . not nearly.

THE PSYCHOLOGIST: No, but this is no time to lose control. *(Glances at her watch.)* I have an appointment at the hospital. Will you be all right?

JOE: *(Hesitantly.)* Yes.

THE PSYCHOLOGIST: Good. Is there anything I can do?

JOE: Talk to Conrad. Tell him to come up with the money. Rob it, if he has to.

THE PSYCHOLOGIST: Seriously.

JOE: Seriously? Seriously, I don't know. I just don't know.

THE PSYCHOLOGIST: I'll do what I can.

JOE: I know you will. Thank you. *(THE PSYCHOLOGIST turns to leave.)* Wait.

THE PSYCHOLOGIST: Yes?

JOE: No. Nothing. Just . . . just know that I am innocent.

THE PSYCHOLOGIST: I believe you, Joe. *(She disappears.)*

END ACT ONE—*Scene 2*

ACT ONE—Scene 3—*the same*

CONRAD: *(Appearing suddenly.)* I love you, Joe.

JOE: Then, how can you leave me here?

CONRAD: I'm doing everything I can.

JOE: I'm scared.

CONRAD: I know you are. Look, in a few days I think we can raise the money.

JOE: How? You tell me how we're going to come up with enough money to cover a hundred thousand-dollar bond. *Huh?* Tell me, Connie, tell me!

CONRAD: I don't know yet. We're working on it.

JOE: Working on it. I may be dead in a few days!

CONRAD: You're being unreasonable.

JOE: Go to hell!

CONRAD: Joe, I can't talk to you when you get like this.

JOE: They're going to kill me, Connie.

CONRAD: Who? Who's going to kill you?

JOE: You'll see. You'll see that I'm right.

CONRAD: No. I won't. You're just being paranoid.

JOE: *(Mimicking.)* You're just being paranoid. *(After a pause.)* You don't love me. You never loved me.

CONRAD: Stop talking nonsense.

JOE: Nonsense? Nonsense is it? Connie, they're shipping me off to the county jail in two days. You should hear what the guys in the cells on either side of me have to say about that place. Last month they found a guy hanging. Hung himself, they said. I mean, he had his hands tied behind his back, but he hung himself! The talk is they'll cut my balls off when they find out what I'm in here for.

CONRAD: Nobody's going to cut your balls off.

JOE: It's not like here in the city jail. Up there it's different, Connie. They throw you in with all kinds of criminals. Do you know what they do to child molesters?

CONRAD: You're not a child molester, Joe.

JOE: I know that. You know that. But, do you think they give a shit? *Christ.* Wait until they find out I'm a faggot.

CONRAD: That has nothing to do with anything.

JOE: You know, Connie, you're perfectly stupid sometimes.

CONRAD: *(Obviously hurt.)* Thanks. Thanks a lot, Joe. I'm sure you think I deserve your abuse. I'm sorry you feel that way. *(Turns to leave.)* Maybe when I come back you'll be in a better mood.

JOE: Don't bother. Just leave me alone. *(After a pause.)* Wait!

CONRAD: *(Turning back. Tired and drained.)* What? What, Joe? What do you want from me?

JOE: Understanding. Patience. Love.

CONRAD: You've already got that, Joe. Did it ever occur to you that I might want the same?

JOE: You get it.

CONRAD: From you? That's a joke. When you want something maybe.

JOE: No, not just when I want something.

CONRAD: It sure seems that way.

JOE: Well, I'm sorry.

CONRAD: Yeah . . . me, too.

JOE: I'm scared, Connie. I'm scared.

CONRAD: I know you are. So am I.

JOE: But, you're not the one in jail.

CONRAD: No. I'm not the one in jail. I'm the one left to pick up the pieces.

JOE: Oh, poor shat-upon Conrad.

CONRAD: Look, Joe, I'm doing what I can—all I can. I can't do anymore.

JOE: You think I'm guilty.

CONRAD: No. I don't think you're guilty. I'll do what I can to get you out of here as soon as possible.

JOE: *(After a pause.)* I know you will . . . I love you, Connie.

CONRAD: And I love you. Joe, you need to take things one day at a time.

JOE: Oh, thanks for the platitude. *(CONRAD disappears.)* Don't you think I know that? I take things one minute at a time in here.

END ACT ONE—*Scene 3*

ACT ONE—*Scene 4*—*the same*

THE LAWYER: (*Appears. Scribbles throughout scene on a yellow legal pad.*) Take it step by step, Joe.

JOE: I'm trying. For God's sake—I'm trying.

THE LAWYER: All right. Calm down and get hold of yourself. (*Pause.*) Are you okay?

JOE: Yes.

THE LAWYER: Why did you have the kid naked?

JOE: I told you.

THE LAWYER: A twelve-year old boy, Joe, naked?

JOE: I didn't want to get any oil on his posing-briefs.

THE LAWYER: Come on, Joe. Do you expect a jury to buy that?

JOE: Yes. It's true.

THE LAWYER: Okay, answer me this: Had it been a twelve year old girl would you have had her naked?

JOE: Of course not.

THE LAWYER: Why not?

JOE: Obviously . . . because . . . because it wouldn't be right. I mean, a grown man and a twelve year old girl. What do you take me for?

THE LAWYER: But, a boy makes it all right?

JOE: In hindsight, I guess not. But at the time . . . yes . . . I thought it did.

THE LAWYER: Even though you're homosexual?

JOE: What should that have to do with it?

THE LAWYER: Come on, Joe. Who do you think you're kidding? It has everything to do with it.

JOE: I told you there was nothing sexual about it. I didn't think, that's all.

THE LAWYER: Well, you'd better start thinking now because the Assistant D. A. already is.

JOE: Believe me, I'm not turned-on by little boys. That's not my thing. I was thinking about what I had to do to get the job done. I was thinking about poses . . . about lighting and about props, but I wasn't thinking about anything sexual with that kid. I mean, we were both males and I didn't see anything wrong with it. If the kid got horny and thought there was something more to it than there was, then it was in his head—not mine

THE LAWYER: That may well be. The jury may see it otherwise.

JOE: Don't you believe me?

THE LAWYER: That's beside the point.

JOE: That *is* the point. If you don't believe me, how can a jury? How can you defend me?

THE LAWYER: Try and understand what I'm going to tell you. You and Conrad came out here five years ago from New York. Right?

JOE: Yes. Right. So what?

THE LAWYER: This is another world, Joe. You've never really understood that. You came to town and got yourself involved with the little theatre, the arts council and—

JOE: *(Interrupts.)* What's wrong with that? I thought I had something to offer.

THE LAWYER: Let me finish. You did have something to offer. You and Conrad have contributed greatly. I know that and some of our friends know that. But this is Lea County, New Mexico. Most of the people here look askance on outsiders who blow into town and try to change things overnight.

JOE: Is that how you see it?

THE LAWYER: It doesn't matter how I see it. I'm telling you how things are. Three of your photographs were removed last year from an exhibition at the public library by the City Manager.

JOE: There was nothing wrong with them. You've seen them. They're hanging in my studio. I'm a first-rate photographer. It's not my fault if some stupid, narrow-minded people thought they were "too suggestive."

THE LAWYER: No, I suppose it isn't, but that is exactly what I'm trying to make you understand. Your fault or not, it doesn't matter. Are you listening?

JOE: I'm listening.

THE LAWYER: That jury will be made up of oil field workers, ranchers, farmers, and their wives. Can you identify with them? Can you understand where they're coming from?

JOE: I wasn't hatched, you know.

THE LAWYER: Damn it, Joe! I'm trying to tell you what you're up against.

JOE: So, if I'm to listen to you, I'm already convicted, aren't I?

THE LAWYER: You're not listening to anybody. I didn't say that. I just want you to understand what it is we are up against here—with what it is we have to deal.

JOE: Yeah, I get the picture. These good church-going, family-oriented fundamentalist hypocrites are going to bury my ass.

THE LAWYER: *(Losing his patience.)* Stop playing the fool. If we have to go to trial, you can be sure the Assistant D. A. is going to play up to that jury like the good ol' boy he is. He's nobody's fool. Now, tell me: Why did you have the kid naked?

JOE: Look. I made a mistake—a stupid, regrettable mistake. I usually wait in the reception area while my client is changing, but he was late. I had an appointment across town in less than an hour and I hadn't set the lights or the backdrop. So, I told him to go ahead and change while I set up. The next thing I know he was standing there naked and I said, "Let's put the oil on now so we don't stain your posing-briefs anymore than we have to." *That's it.* It was stupid and I'm sorry, but I'm telling you that there was nothing sexual whatsoever about it.

THE LAWYER: Then, you applied baby oil to his body. Correct?

JOE: Yes. I told you that already.

THE LAWYER: Tell me again.

JOE: Look. I had to cover him with baby oil. That's what his mother wanted. She came to the studio. She said that she wanted—

THE LAWYER: *(Stopping him.)* When? When did she come to the studio?

JOE: A couple days before the shoot.

THE LAWYER: Go on.

JOE: She came to the studio. She said that she was entering her son in a photogenic contest and wanted me to take the pictures. She said she wanted . . .

END ACT ONE—*Scene 4*

ACT ONE—*Scene 5*—*the photography studio*

THE PSYCHOLOGIST appears as THE MOTHER. She is wearing running clothes and a sweatband around her forehead. She is quick to speak, slow to listen, uncommonly affected in a rather common way.

THE MOTHER: *Something different.* Oh, nothing common at all. I can't tell you how much I loved your show at the library last year. Was it last year? Yes. I'm sure it was. Wasn't it? *Imagine.* Your best work removed by you-know-who. Junior! Junior! Stop picking your nose and come over here so Joseph can get a good look at you.

(CONRAD appears as JUNIOR and reluctantly moves toward THE MOTHER with his finger lodged in his nose.)

THE MOTHER: *(Continues.)* Isn't he handsome? Just like his father. But, he's got my chin, poor thing. Junior, if you don't take your finger out of your nose we won't be able to see that handsome face of yours and then what will Joseph think of us? *Huh? Huh?* Do you suppose you could give it a break and act your age or do you want Mother to show the nice man what we do to young men who don't behave themselves? *Huh? Huh?* This nice man doesn't have time to waste. He's an artist. Artists don't like bad manners. Tell him, Joseph.

JOE: Well . . . I . . . I . . .

THE MOTHER: You hear that, Junior? This nice man's time is valuable and he won't have you wasting it. So, put your frigging finger where it belongs! You must excuse us, Joseph, but you really have no idea what it's like being a mother.

JOE: No . . . I . . . I . . .

THE MOTHER: See, Junior? You've upset him. One must never upset an artist. Believe you me I know the artist's temperament. I've dabbled a bit myself. I'm not altogether uncreative, you know. I'm a mother, aren't I? So, don't upset him. He'll make you look ugly and then where will we be? *Huh? Huh?* I'll be out all that money and you'll never win anything. Unless, we enter you in an ugly little piggy contest. *(She snorts.)*

(JUNIOR removes his finger from his nose, wipes it on the side of his trousers, scratches his crotch.)

THE MOTHER *(Continued.):* Just like his father! Now, stand up straight, Junior, so the nice man can get a good look at you. *(Reluctantly, JUNIOR stands straight.)* There. Just look at that, Joseph. An hour every day at the gym. Show him your muscles, Junior. Don't be bashful. God knows we paid for them.

JOE: That's really not necessary, Missus—

THE MOTHER: But it is. We're going to make him look like a real little muscle-builder in our pictures. Aren't we, Junior? *(JUNIOR shrugs.)* Now, show the nice man your muscles. Now, Junior. *(JUNIOR makes a muscle.)* Oh, look! Look at Mother's little man. He's a . . . a . . . What's the word? Hunk? That's it. Don't you think he's a real hunk, Joseph? *Huh? Huh?* I mean, for his age. You can put your arm down now, Junior. *(JUNIOR drops his arm to his side, but not without first picking at the seat of his trousers.)* Just like his father!

JOE: How old is your son?

THE MOTHER: Tell Joseph how old you are, Junior.

JUNIOR: I . . . I . . . I'm . . . .

THE MOTHER: Twelve. Twelve years old and never been kissed. *(She cackles and snorts.)* He better not have or I'll give him what for! Won't I? *Huh? Huh?* Won't I? *(She pinches JUNIOR's cheeks and then gives him several, loud, pecking kisses.)* That's my sweet little hunkypoo. He's been taking karate lessons for over a year—just in case his father pulls something funny, if you know what I mean. *A real killer. (She cackles and snorts.)* Won't that be fun? So, tell me, Joseph, how do you get that shiny, sweaty effect like on the man in the photograph you-know-who removed from the library?

JOE: I use baby oil and then I spray it with a mist of water.

THE MOTHER: So, that's how they do it. I always wondered about that. Isn't that interesting? I swear, never a day goes by without learning something new. Well, that's what we want. Isn't it, Junior? I bought these for when you take the pictures. *(She holds up a scant posing-brief made of a silver metallic fabric.)* Sexy, huh? And don't tell me these didn't cost me an arm and a leg. The nerve of some people nowadays. And they call themselves businessmen. Funny business, if you know what I mean. *Huh? Huh? (She cackles and snorts.)*

JOE: I . . . I don't know what to say.

THE MOTHER: Of course you don't. Who does? I mean, really? *Huh? Huh?* I'm sure I don't. So, tell me, Joe—may I call you Joe?

JOE: Yes, certainly.

THE MOTHER: Well, tell me, Joey. *(She cackles and snorts.)* That's a joke. I ask if I can call you Joe and you say "yes" and then I go right ahead and call you Joey. That's called *schtick,* isn't it? Yes. You could use that over at the little theatre. Be my guest. It's yours. Free of charge. So, tell me, what kind of money are we talking about here? What's this going to set us back? *Huh? Huh?*

JOE: Conrad will give you all that information. Just stop by the reception desk on your way out and he'll have a form for you to fill out and—

THE MOTHER: *(Cutting him off.)* A form? What kind of form?

JOE: It's just a little questionnaire. Conrad will explain it to you. He'll also give you a list of our prices and set you up with an appointment.

THE MOTHER: Good. Good. Come along, Junior. Junior, now. *(JUNIOR has resumed picking his nose.)* One of these days that finger is going to swell up, turn green and rot off, young man. *(Moving toward exit.)* Remember Aunt Opal's toe? *Huh? Huh? (About to exit.)* Just like his father!

(JUNIOR and THE MOTHER exit.)

END ACT ONE—*Scene 5*

ACT ONE—*Scene 6—a visiting room in the city jail*

JOE: *(A sigh of relief. Directly to audience.)* Jesus . . . I never saw anything like it. She had him show me his muscles. Told me about his working-out at the gym—his karate lessons. Oh, and the posing-briefs. From Frederick's of Hollywood, no doubt. Look, my business is photography. I do a lot of work with models and pageants and stuff like that. She wanted him posed in briefs and shining like in muscle-building photographs she had seen. I had the gist of what she wanted and knew how to do it. She was crazy, of course. I knew that. It didn't take that proverbial rocket scientist to figure that out. But, after working with all those pageant mothers, I was used to crazy women. You've got to be in this business. It's all vanity and vanity's a bit crazy, you know. But, I didn't do anything sexual with that kid. I was just doing my job.

THE LAWYER: You said that you had her fill out a questionnaire?

JOE: *(Turns back to THE LAWYER.)* Yes. I have all my clients fill out a questionnaire at least a day before they're to come in. That way I've got a pretty good idea about how I'm going to approach the shoot.

THE LAWYER: On this questionnaire, did she write down what kind of photographs she wanted for her son?

JOE: In great detail. That's what the questionnaire is all about. It helps me determine how the client sees him or herself and how he or she wants to be seen. It really works. This is, after all, a fantasy business. Capturing an image of yourself in a photo that has nothing to do with who you really are or how you could possibly look at any given moment in day to day reality. *Fantasy.*

THE LAWYER: Do you keep these questionnaires on file?

JOE: Yes. At the studio. Conrad will get it for you. In fact, at the time, Connie and I had quite a laugh over it. She used words to describe how she wanted Junior to look . . . words like "hunk" and "he-man" and—

END ACT ONE—*Scene 6*

ACT ONE—*Scene 7*—*the photography studio*

CONRAD: *(Appears laughing and reading questionnaire.)* Macho. Do you believe this woman? *Straight out of hunger.*

JOE: *(Crosses to CONRAD.)* You should have to listen to her non-stop.

CONRAD: I did. I heard enough.

JOE: *(Reading.)* "If one word could describe the general spirit of your finished photograph, what would that word be?"

BOTH: "Stud!" *(They laugh.)*

JOE: That is one sick lady. The kid's only twelve. Can you imagine what kind of mess he'll be by the time he's twenty?

CONRAD: *(Affecting a thick West Texas drawl.)* Speaking of messes. Missus Emma Lou Shipp and little Heather Jo are in the waiting room a-waitin' the pleasure of your presence. So don't come a-rushin' on my account, she says, but I'm a-fixin' to take little Heather Jo to ballet class, so I hope he won't keep us a-waitin' too long, neither.

JOE: *Oh, God.*

CONRAD: *Oh, yes. (Resumes normal voice.)* So, how do you feel about re-shooting little Heather Jo's ballet pictures?

JOE: Shit!

CONRAD: No. Shipp.

JOE: So, what's wrong with the little shit's pictures?

CONRAD: Well, the big shit says that the tulle on the little shit's tutu is just too, too limp.
JOE: That's not my problem.

CONRAD: Of course it is. You want her to place an order, don't you?

JOE: I wish I knew exactly what in hell people expect of me.

CONRAD: Magic, honey. *Magic.*

JOE: Tell her I'll be out in a minute. *(A beat.)* When did you set up our little stud's appointment?

CONRAD: You mean Junior the nose picker? Thursday at three.

JOE: Damn it, Connie. You know I have a Cultural Council meeting at four on Thursdays.

CONRAD: It's money, honey. You'll just have to rush, rush, rush and click, click, click your little fingers to the bone.

JOE: I'm not happy about this.

CONRAD: I'm sorry, but don't you think a few extra bucks is more important than being a little late to your cultural affairs meeting?

JOE: That's not the point.

CONRAD: That *is* the point. You like the bills paid and you like to eat, don't you? What's the Cultural Council paying nowadays?

JOE: It's good for business.

CONRAD: Bullshit.

JOE: Well, call them Thursday morning and tell them not to be late.

CONRAD: Yes, master. *(He bows.)*

JOE: Fuck you.

CONRAD: Oh, thank you, massy. Thank you. What ever did I do to deserve you? *(Bowing while moving backward towards the exit.)*

JOE: Cute—really cute. *Just too fucking cute.*

CONRAD: *(At exit.)* He'll be out in a minute, Missus. . . . Shipp. *(Exits.)*

END ACT ONE— *Scene 7*

ACT ONE—*Scene 8*—*a visiting room in the city jail*

THE LAWYER: Do you get many requests for photographs of that nature?

JOE: From older would-be models, yes, but certainly not from a mother for her twelve-year old kid. That was a first.

THE LAWYER: Didn't you think it a bit odd?

JOE: Of course I thought it odd and more than a bit. I thought she was crazy.

THE LAWYER: She was on the police force. So was her husband.

JOE: *(Stunned.) What?*

THE LAWYER: They left the force last year to go into business with her father.

JOE: *A cop?*

THE LAWYER: You didn't know?

JOE: A cop? No. How would I know a thing like that? I know she was a space cadet, but a cop?

THE LAWYER: Joe, this is going to be a tough nut to crack. I don't know of a lawyer in this county who'd even consider handling this case.

JOE: You are going to be handling it . . . aren't you?

THE LAWYER: Yes, but, it won't be easy . . . for you . . . or for me. There'll be some rough road ahead, Joe. You can't fall apart on me. Understand?

JOE: *(Frightened.)* I understand.

THE LAWYER: Good. Now, our best hope is that we can keep your sexual preference out of this. We need to get a handle on what the D. A.'s office has come up with.

JOE: I'm not a screaming faggot, you know.

THE LAWYER: No. However, you haven't been the most discreet fellow, either.

JOE: I haven't been a liar if that is what you mean. I'm gay and I'm not ashamed of it. I've done nothing wrong. I'm proud of who and what I am.

THE LAWYER: Damn it, Joe! Put that pride of yours on the back burner.

JOE: *(After a pause.)* I'm scared.

THE LAWYER: You have every reason to be. No jury in Lea County is going to assimilate that kind of information and still give you a fair hearing.

JOE: Can't we get a change of venue?

THE LAWYER: It's too expensive and the county can't afford it. Besides, when it comes to this sort of thing, you're not going to find an impartial jury anywhere these days.

JOE: Then, I don't want to go to trial.

THE LAWYER: We'll cross that bridge when we get to it. First we have to see about getting you out of jail. We're meeting with the judge next week to try and get your bail reduced.

JOE: *Oh, God.* The county jail.

THE LAWYER: Just hang on a little while longer.

JOE: *(To audience.)* One hundred thousand dollars. How in hell can we ever come up with that?

THE LAWYER: We only need to come up with ten.

JOE: *(Ibid.)* It might as well be the moon.

THE LAWYER: We'll get it reduced.

JOE: *(Still, directly to audience.)* Conrad says business dropped off to zilch. He's getting threatening phone calls at the studio . . . and at home.

THE LAWYER: Just hang on. *(Moving toward exit.)*

JOE: When you're homosexual you're already guilty. It doesn't matter of what—*you're guilty.* I've had more Bibles thumped at me than I care to count. I mean, if you're queer —*you're guilty.*

THE LAWYER: Just hang on. *(He exits.)*

JOE: *(Alone onstage. Directly to audience.)* Guilty. Just plain guilty.*(Sighs.)* I never tried to hide the fact that I was gay. Well, there was a time when I did. I was younger and it was a matter of survival. At least, that is the way I experienced it. And, no doubt, I didn't fool anyone except myself. *(Pause.)* Shortly after coming out I met a black man with a Mississippi drawl who swore he was Black Irish. What in hell is Black Irish? He also swore he was "straight," but he had *had*—if you know what I mean—everybody I knew, including myself.

All over his apartment on the upper west side of Manhattan were these lovely, delicate doilies. They were everywhere, as fine as spiders' webs. And even though I had caught him at work spinning those lovely webs, he'd quickly bury the thread and crochet hook beneath him and swear with unabashed dignity, "No, no, no, a man don't fool around with what God didn't intend a man to fool around with. But have a look at my latest treasure. Like gossamer. *Heh,* Joe? Mother sent them from home—from Dublin." *(After a pause.)* Dublin. Sometimes it was Dublin. Other times County Cork or County Derry . . . or County something else. From one week to the next he could never remember where in Ireland he had told you he was from. This towering, three-hundred pound hulk of a man with a Mississippi drawl, with the sensitivity of an angel, died of a stroke on the men's room floor of The Great Northern Hotel where he had been an attendant for more than forty years—*and he died a liar.* *(Pause.)* What causes a man to lie?

END ACT ONE—*Scene 8*

ACT ONE—*Scene 9*—*the same*

THE PSYCHOLOGIST: *(Appears.)* Suppose you tell me.

JOE: I don't know. I don't know anything anymore.

THE PSYCHOLOGIST: Fear?

JOE: Yes. Fear of not being accepted. Fear of being different. Fear of someone actually discovering what it is you really are—who you are.

THE PSYCHOLOGIST: And that would be?

(On the bridge, a hooded figure appears in a ghastly, ghostly light. No longer THE LAWYER, the hooded figure sings.)

TORMENTOR 1: *(Sings.)* COME TO ME MY MELANCHOLY BABY

THE PSYCHOLOGIST: *(After a pause.)* What are you thinking?

TORMENTOR 1: *(Sings.)* CUDDLE UP AND DON'T BE BLUE

JOE: What?

THE PSYCHOLOGIST: You seem to be drifting.

TORMENTOR 1: *ALL YOUR FEARS ARE FOOLISH FANCIES*
MAYBE YOU KNOW DEAR THAT I'M IN LOVE WITH YOU

JOE: Drifting?

TORMENTOR 1: *EVERY CLOUD MUST HAVE A SILVER LINING*

THE PSYCHOLOGIST: Joe? Joe, are you all right?

TORMENTOR 1: *WAIT UNTIL THE SUN SHINES THROUGH*

(The LIGHTING FADES on the TORMENTOR and he disappears.)

THE PSYCHOLOGIST: Joe? Where are you?

JOE: *(No longer distracted.)* Here. Right here.

THE PSYCHOLOGIST: Where did you go?

JOE: I was thinking about my father.

THE PSYCHOLOGIST: What about him?

JOE: For a second he got caught in my mind.

THE PSYCHOLOGIST: Tell me about him.

JOE: If you don't mind, I'd rather talk about something else.

THE PSYCHOLOGIST: All right. Let's talk about you.

JOE: Sometimes I feel I've been a liar all my life.

THE PSYCHOLOGIST: Aren't you being a little too harsh on yourself?

JOE: I'm never sure if what I'm saying is really what I mean, or if I'm just repeating something I've heard before. I'm not always in the moment, you know?

THE PSYCHOLOGIST: Who of us is?

JOE: I was in my early twenties when I entered the gay scene. I was always gay, but I didn't have a word for it and I was beginning to discover that I wasn't the only one in the whole world who was gay. I knew no examples for how to be. Just stereotypes. I left the farm for the navy and the navy for New York City. I fell in with a crowd who used to cruise Forty-second Street. Teased hair, plucked eyebrows, make-up—the whole bit. Well, I didn't know any better. I thought if you're gay that's the way you were—that's the way you live, the way you behave. You just kind of fall into it—you lose yourself, you know?

THE PSYCHOLOGIST: But you grew out of it. You learned better.

JOE: Sure, with the help of Conrad I learned to be myself.

CONRAD: *(Appears on the bridge.)* You want the moon, Joe? It's yours. I'll wrap it up in cellophane and give it to you.

JOE: What color cellophane?

CONRAD: What color do you want?

JOE: Gold. I want the moon wrapped in gold.

CONRAD: It's yours.

JOE: Really?

CONRAD: Move in with me, Joe.

JOE: You want me? Really?

CONRAD: Really.

JOE: Why?

CONRAD: Because I like me better when I'm around you.

JOE: You make me feel special, too

CONRAD: *(A hearty laugh.)* Like an old chair.

(The LIGHTING FADES on CONRAD and he disappears. JOE chuckles, fondly.)

THE PSYCHOLOGIST: What's that?

JOE: I was remembering something Connie once said to me. He said I was like an old chair.

THE PSYCHOLOGIST: How so?

JOE: Comfortable. Just comfortable to be with.

THE PSYCHOLOGIST: You've been together fifteen years. Is that correct?

JOE: That's right.

THE PSYCHOLOGIST: Correct me if I'm wrong . . . but isn't that considered a long time for a homosexual relationship?

JOE: A long time, yes . . . for any relationship.

THE PSYCHOLOGIST: *(After a thoughtful pause.)* What do you want, Joe?

JOE: I want to be someone who can leave the world a better place than he found it. Is that too much to ask?

THE PSYCHOLOGIST: Not at all.

JOE: The man on the bridge in my dream is me, isn't he?

THE PSYCHOLOGIST: A part of you, perhaps.

JOE: I don't seem to like myself. *(Chuckles at his understatement.)*

THE PSYCHOLOGIST: Not all the time, Joe.

JOE: Not much of the time, you mean.

THE PSYCHOLOGIST: Don't be so hard on yourself.

JOE: *(To audience.)* Policemen tearing the place apart looking for child pornography—paraphernalia to arouse little children, hidden video cameras . . . tore the place apart—tore my life apart. *For what?* One spray bottle used mostly for misting plants and one bottle of baby oil in with the studio make-up. *Evidence. (Pause.)* Do they want me to say I did it? Do they want me to say I ran my hand down the crack of his little-boy ass? Is that what they want me to say? *All right.* I did it! I may have actually done it. How quick we are to judge. *The queer did it.*

THE PSYCHOLOGIST disappears.

END ACT ONE—*Scene 9*

ACT ONE—*Scene 10*—*the same*

CONRAD: *(Suddenly appears.) Stop it.* You stop it right now! You're only going to make yourself sick.

JOE: We make the world sick, don't we? A good queer's a dead queer,
right?

CONRAD: *Stop it.*

JOE: Why? I did it, didn't I? Guilty as charged. *(After a pause.)* One day—*everything.* The next day—*nothing.*

CONRAD: We'll get through this, Joe.

JOE: Will we? Will we really? Do you know the law in the state of New Mexico? A teacher can spank their little rumps and that's corporal punishment, legal discipline. But, just one little pat of approval on that rump and that's criminal sexual contact with a minor. And if you happen to be gay—God help you.

CONRAD: You didn't do anything wrong, Joe.

JOE: Didn't I? The fact is I may have actually done it. Not in any conscious sexual way, but rather, in a careless, reckless, disregarding, mind-elsewhere way.

CONRAD: That's different. It wasn't intentional.

JOE: We're not judging intent here. We're judging facts. We're judging actions.   And it is actions that count—not intentions.

CONRAD: In a philosophical debate you might have a case to argue there. But, we're not playing head games now. In the eyes of the law, intent is a very real consideration. It was not your intention to have sexual contact with that kid.

JOE: So, who's going to give a shit? I'm queer! Who's going to give a shit whether it was the premeditated act of a degenerate or the careless slip of the hand because my mind was elsewhere? *(Pause.)* I'm going to plead no contest. I don't see that I have a choice. Do you have any idea what a trial would cost us? And I'm not only talking about money.

CONRAD: You have a choice, but if that's the one you want to make—

JOE: Look, I'd never win a trial in this county. Don't you know that?

CONRAD: No. I don't know any such thing and neither do you. We can deal with this. We've gotten through rough times before and we'll get through this.

JOE: You think so, do you?

CONRAD: Yes, I do. Will you please stop feeling so sorry for yourself? *Christ!*

JOE: *Fuck you.*

CONRAD: Fuck you, too. You're not the only person affected by all this. Think of someone other than yourself for a change. You use being gay as an excuse—an affliction. It's an excuse for your shortcomings. Who could possibly feel sorry for you? You already hold a monopoly on that.

JOE: You think they won't drag you into court along with me? *(Pretending to be the prosecuting attorney.)* Oh? Forty? Ah, single. Never been married? You live with Joe? Well, what exactly is your relationship with the defendant? *Titter, titter.* Business partner. Oh, partners who live together. And good friends—*very* good friends. *Titter, titter.* And roommates for how long? Fifteen years. Now, isn't that quaint? *(A beat.)* No trial!

CONRAD: If that's your choice.

JOE: Don't say it like an accusation of guilt. Win or lose, we lose.

CONRAD: I believe you ought to think about it some more. *(After a pause.)* Did you eat anything today?

JOE: No.

CONRAD: You've got to start eating, Joe.

JOE: I can't. I want to die.
CONRAD: No you don't. You know, this isn't easy for me, either.

JOE: I know. *(After a pause.)* Are you all right?

CONRAD: I've been better.

JOE: Me, too.

CONRAD: I'm sure. *(After a pause.)* You'll be all right. We'll get the bail reduced and then we'll have you out of here in no time. It will all work out, you'll see.

(JOE tries to reach out and touch CONRAD, but there is an imaginary glass wall that separates them. And then, CONRAD disappears.)

JOE: I want to touch you . . . hold you. Hold me. I need you to hold me . . . someone to hold me. *Oh, God.*

(The stage slowly slips into DARKNESS.)

END ACT 1—*Scene 10*

ACT ONE—*Scene 11—the bridge*

The stage is in darkness except for a single LIGHT upstage center that slowly intensifies along with the haunting recorded MUSIC of a Gregorian chant rising in volume. The bridge, slowly, fades into view. Regally posed, and an imposing presence (no longer THE LAWYER), stands THE POPE on top of the bridge, dressed in regal splendor. A moment to be properly awed – and then, the Gregorian chant fades into silence. JOE falls to his knees beneath the bridge.

THE POPE: *(With outstretched arms—a magnificent gesture—he sings.)*
COME TO ME MY MELANCHOLY BABY
CUDDLE UP AND DON'T BE BLUE . . . .

(JOE applauds.)

THE POPE: *(Con't. Speaks, booming with pontifical fervor.)* Ex post facto. Gloria in excelsis. In extenso. In perpetuum. In toto. Meum et tuum. De profundis. De facto. Ad infinitum. *(JOE rises to speak.)* Not now, boy! I haven't finished. *(JOE kneels.)* Quid pro quo. Pro et con. Pro tanto. Pro tempore. Now, boy. Now. Now I'm finished!

JOE: *(As a twelve year old – through remainder of scene.)* Can you help me?

THE POPE: I am the fire-breathing, flying whatchamacallit! Of course I can help you.

JOE: I lost my . . . my . . . I don't know. I don't know what it was I lost until I find it.

THE POPE: Sounds a bit cryptic for my taste. It might make sense to a complete idiot.

JOE: Guess what?

THE POPE: What?

JOE: I can fly.

THE POPE: The devil you say.

JOE: I can. I can. I really can fly!

THE POPE: Don't you ever let me hear you say that again, young man. You hear me?

JOE: Yes, sir.

THE POPE: Flying is against the Holy rolling Church. Against the begets . . . the begotten and the begone. Against the beguine. Against the Great Inert Thingamajig, Himself. *(Takes out a cigar and lights it.)* We'll make a man of you yet. Did you kill any niggers today, boy?

JOE: No, Daddy.

THE POPE: Faggots?

JOE: No, Daddy.

THE POPE: No niggers or faggots?

JOE: That's a bad thing to say.

THE POPE: I'm the Pope! I can say what I please.

JOE: Forgive me.

THE POPE: Nope! What kind of kid are you? If I told you once I told you twice, a nigger a day keeps the doctor away and a faggot a day keeps the nurse at bay.

JOE: An apple. An apple a day.

THE POPE: Correct me once more and I'm going to split your skull with a two-dollar whore!

(No longer THE PSYCHOLOGIST, THE MOTHER SUPERIOR dressed in the black and white habit of her order rushes onstage and coddles JOE.)

THE MOTHER SUPERIOR: You will do no such thing, Big Papa!

THE POPE: Speaking of two-dollar whores. The kid said he could fly.

THE MOTHER SUPERIOR: Of course he can fly!

THE POPE: You hadn't ought to be putting ideas into his head.

THE MOTHER SUPERIOR: He'll fly to the moon one day. He'll be the moon away and you won't be able to touch him. *(To JOE.)* Now, don't you let that mean old bogeyman frighten you. I am the Earth and I will protect you.

JOE: Thank you, Mommy.

THE POPE: But, I am the sun and the stars and all that jazz, boy. I'm hot, boy. Hotter than hell. Hotter than lightning and twice as fast. OUCH! A scorcher! Hot as Easter!

THE MOTHER SUPERIOR: You will do no such thing! Not on Earth, you won't. From ashes to ashes he is mine—*mine*.

THE POPE: No! I will cause floods and famine and little razor-toothed creepy-crawling things. I will cause mind-boggling enigmas to grow and fester with putrefied pus and corruption. Every time you blow your nose you lose your brains! *Ha, ha, ha!* I will cause inter-galactic thermonuclear fireworks! And then where will you be?

THE MOTHER SUPERIOR: Better off.

THE POPE: You never loved me.

THE MOTHER SUPERIOR: How can you say that? I cook for you, clean and sew for you . . . do your laundry.

THE POPE: Big deal.

THE MOTHER SUPERIOR: Go to hell!

JOE: Mommy . . . Mommy . . . *please* . . . .

THE MOTHER SUPERIOR: *(Slaps JOE to the floor.)* Shut up! You stupid know-nothing! Just shut up before your father gives you a beating you won't soon forget. I'm only doing this to protect you from your father. So, thank me, you stupid thing! I never wanted you in the first place. *(Points an accusing finger at THE POPE.)* He made me have you—you useless thing. I prayed for a miscarriage.

THE POPE: That's right. Turn the kid against me. *(Puffing on cigar. Comes down from the bridge.)* You're the one who put the coat hanger up the old kazoo. Blood all over creation, but the kid came plopping out anyway. Well, let me tell you something, lady. You stink! *(Slaps her, punches her, beats her to the floor.)* Stink, stink, stink, stink. *(Each "stink" is punctuated with a blow to her body.)* Stink, stink, stink, stink!

THE MOTHER SUPERIOR: *(Hysterical.)* Help! Help! He's killing me! Joey! Joey! Help me! Your father's trying to kill me! Help! Help! Joey! Joey! Aren't you going to help your mother? For God's sake, what kind of a kid are you?

(JOE rises, clutching a long, shining butcher's knife high above his head and crosses, with cautious apprehension, towards the two fist-flying bodies entangled on the floor.)

JOE: You leave my mother alone! You hear me? I said leave my mother alone, please, Daddy. *Please.* I don't want to kill you.

(There is a terrible SILENCE while THE POPE slowly rises, staring menacingly at JOE who is beginning to back away.)

THE POPE: *(Breaking the silence.)* What's that, Sonny Boy?

THE MOTHER SUPERIOR: You leave my baby alone. *(To JOE.)* Kill him. Kill the sonofabitch if you have to. It'll break my heart, God knows . . . but kill the fucker anyway!

THE POPE: Shut up, you silly old cow!

THE MOTHER SUPERIOR: *(To THE POPE while grabbing onto his legs.)* I love you! I love you! I love you!

THE POPE: *(Pulling himself free of her.)* I'm going to teach that boy a lesson he'll never forget. You hear that, boy?

JOE: *(With knife poised for attack.)* Don't make me do it, Daddy. Please. Don't make me do it.

THE POPE: I love you, son . . . and the fishes and the loaves . . . and your mommy's thighs. Does Joe-Joe love his mommy's thighs? *(Moving towards JOE who is backing away.)*

JOE: Leave me alone.

THE POPE: Does Joe-Joe want to smell his mommy's thighs? How about your daddy's? You'd like that, wouldn't you?

JOE: Don't come any closer!

THE POPE: *(Cupping his crotch with his hand.)* Want to taste something good, boy?

JOE: Leave me alone.

THE POPE: I'm all for you, boy. I love you.

JOE: And I love you.

THE POPE: And that's why I've got to teach you a lesson you'll never, ever forget. Now, give your daddy the knife.

JOE: No.

THE POPE: You don't want to go to the orphanage, do you?

JOE: *(With fear and trembling.)* Na...na...no, Daddy.

THE POPE: Or the closet? Do I need to tie you up and put you in the closet—*again?*

JOE: Pa...pa...pa...pa...please, Daddy. Na...na...not again.

THE MOTHER SUPERIOR: He pissed himself the last time you put him in there, Big Daddy. Aren't you going to punish him? Beat him with your belt? Slap the little fucker around a bit?

THE POPE: I get a hard-on when I do that, Big Mama. I get a great big hard-on.

THE MOTHER SUPERIOR: *(Rubbing her breasts.)* I want to see the little bastard squirm. I love it when he squirms. Squirm, you stupid know-nothing!

JOE: I . . . I . . . I'm . . . sa . . . sa . . .sa . . . sorry.

THE POPE: Sorry what?

JOE: Sa . . . sa . . . sir, Daddy.

THE POPE: You won't piss yourself again . . . will you, boy?

JOE: Na . . . na . . .na . . .

THE POPE: Answer me when I speak to you!

JOE: Ye . . . ye . . . yes, Daddy. Na . . . na . . . no, Daddy.

THE POPE: Which is it? Yes or no?

JOE: Ye . . . na . . . I . . . I . . . I . . . I don't na . . . na . . . know, Daddy.

THE POPE: Give me the knife. Don't let me have to take it from you, boy. You know what'll happen if you make me have to take it from you, boy?

THE MOTHER SUPERIOR: Go ahead, Joey. don't just stand there like a nincompoop. Tell your father what he's going to do to you if you don't give him that knife. Somebody could get hurt, Joey. Don't be afraid. We only want to help you. We love you, Joey. JOE: I . . . I . . . I . . . da . . . don't want him to hu . . . hu . . . hurt me, Mommy.

THE MOTHER SUPERIOR: Oh, don't be such a silly goose. He's your father. He's not going to hurt you. Just tell your father what he wants to know.

JOE: He . . . he . . . he'll have my brains for breakfast.

THE MOTHER SUPERIOR: That's right, dear—and your

what for lunch, Joey?

JOE: An . . . an . . . and my ass fa . . . fa . . . for lunch.

THE POPE: That's right, boy. Now, give me the knife.

JOE: *(Stands his ground.)* No! Just stay away. Stay away and you won't get hurt.

THE POPE: You wouldn't hurt your old man, would you?

JOE: Ye . . . yes, I would. Sa . . . sa . . . so stay away or I'll kill you. *(Moving toward THE POPE who is backing away toward the bridge.)* I swear, I'll kill you if I have to.

THE MOTHER SUPERIOR: Don't swear, Son. I taught you better than that.

JOE: I will if I have to, Mommy.

THE MOTHER SUPERIOR: Well, if you have to you have to. It's your choice. Don't mind me. I'm only your mother.

JOE: He's a bad daddy. Didn't you say he was a bad daddy?

THE MOTHER SUPERIOR: I might have. Nobody's perfect, Joey. God knows I've tried. If you're going to kill him, kill him. Do it and be done with it, for God's sake.

THE POPE: *(To THE MOTHER SUPERIOR.)* This is your doing. You poisoned the little bastard against me.

THE MOTHER SUPERIOR: The little bastard didn't need my help for that. Every little thing that goes wrong you blame me for it. Be a man for once in your life.

THE POPE: *Yeah? Yeah?* How come every time you don't get your way you shove the kid's head in the oven along with your own and turn on the gas? *Huh? Huh?* If I'm not a man, what are you? Queen of the funny farm?

THE MOTHER SUPERIOR: I am Mother Superior. Divine daughter of Our Lord King of Kings, Lord of Lords. Tape up the door and windows real good, son. We're on our way to Jesus!

JOE: Ma . . . Ma . . . Mommy, please. You're scaring me.

THE POPE: Kill her, boy! See what she's doing to our lives? Take a good look at your mother, boy.

JOE: Na . . . na . . . no! THE POPE: Look, boy! Look!

JOE: *No.* She's my mother.

THE POPE: All the more reason you should look and learn. The truth shall set you free.

JOE: No!

THE POPE: You better take a good, hard look. She'll be dead soon.

JOE: Na . . . na . . . no!

THE POPE: Don't you remember, Joe? She does it on a warm Indian summer afternoon—with sleeping pills.

JOE: No.

THE POPE: You go downstairs and you get the glass of water. Remember? *(Ascending the bridge.)* A classic case of denial, boy. She takes the sleeping pills and then she wraps her green plastic-beaded rosary around her wrists and then she—

JOE: *(Cutting him off.)* They weren't plastic.

THE POPE: What's that, son?

JOE: The beads were green cut glass. They weren't plastic.

THE POPE: But, the crucifix was. Cheap plastic with a gold spray-painted Jesus clutched to her breasts. And then she was dead. *Dead, dead, dead.* The dead bride of Jesus. *(Puffs on cigar.)*

JOE: And Jesus—all the gold paint just peeled away.

THE POPE: *(On top of the bridge.)* That's right. It will happen in a few more days.

THE MOTHER SUPERIOR: I did it for you, Joey. *(She takes from out of the folds of her garment a set of rosary beads and a large plastic crucifix.)* I did it for you and I did it for your father. And I did it for the love of Jesus.

JOE: But, Jesus isn't gold anymore, Mommy.

THE MOTHER SUPERIOR: Well, what is?

THE POPE: Say goodbye to your mother, Son.

JOE: Don't do it, Mommy.

THE MOTHER SUPERIOR: The razor didn't work. The exhaust from the car out in the garage didn't even kill the cockroaches. The kitchen stove doesn't work for beans. So, what's a mother to do? Sleeping pills—that's the ticket.

JOE: Why, Mommy? Don't you love me?

THE MOTHER SUPERIOR: What kind of silly question is that? It's because I love you. Forever and ever—you'll be mine. You'll never forget me, I promise you that. *(She lies on the floor on her back. her arms enfolded.)* Mine. *(She is motionless.)*

THE POPE: *(After a pause.)* What a bitch! *(He snuffs out his cigar.)* Say goodbye to your mother, son.

JOE: *(Kneeling over her lifeless body.)* Mommy, Jesus is peeling all away. He isn't gold anymore, Mommy. All the gold's just peeling away. Jesus is turning green and gray and ugly, Mommy. Can't we paint him again and make poor Jesus all pretty again, Mommy?

THE POPE: Wake up, boy! Jesus doesn't give a piss ant's fart about you!

JOE: He does!

THE POPE: He doesn't and he doesn't because he can't.

JOE: But, he has to. He's got the key.

THE POPE: *Nope. (Holding up a silver key suspended from a silver chain.)* I've got the key.

JOE: *(Rises, crosses to bridge.)* How did you get it?

THE POPE: That's a mystery, my son. God loves a mystery. He always did and He always will. He's a slippery old goat, He is. Now, say goodbye to your mother, boy.

JOE: No. I've got to find what I've lost.

THE POPE: I've got the key. *(He spins the key on the chain as an airplane propeller.)* No key, no flying.

JOE: I'll kill you! *(Brandishing knife.)* I'll kill you, you son of a bitch!

THE POPE: That's your answer for everything, isn't it? Kill, kill, kill. Don't they teach you kids anything else in school anymore? First you go and murder your mother and now you want to kill your old man. What is this world coming to? You'll be the death of me yet, you . . . you . . . you juvenile delinquent!

JOE: I didn't murder my mother. *You did. (Begins to climb bridge.)* You killed my mother and now I want the key. *(He has reached the top of the bridge with the knife firmly in his grip.)* I don't want to have to kill you, Daddy.

THE POPE: You want the key?

JOE: Yes.

THE POPE: I loved her, son, and I love your mother. That's the key. *(JOE begins to close in on THE POPE.)* Do you know what love is, boy?   No, I suppose you don't. Who does? What's the matter with children nowadays? You sweat and sweat to put a meal on the table. You give them the shirt off your back and what's the thanks you get for it? Just a knife in the back . . . *(JOE plunges the knife into THE POPE's back. THE POPE then slumps to the floor of the bridge, gasping for breath.)* Wake up, boy. Wake up! Kids—who can figure them?

THE POPE's arm stretches out beyond the bridge. The key dangles in the air from his lifeless fingertips. A moment of SILENCE before the key drops to the floor below. JOE rises, goes down from the bridge and crosses to the body of THE MOTHER SUPERIOR. He silently slumps into her body like a child The stage LIGHTING falls into darkness.

END ACT 1—*Scene 11*

ACT ONE—*Scene 12*—*a visiting room in the city jail*

The LIGHTING returns to the stage. JOE is alone and in the same position as he was at the end of Scene 11.

JOE: *(Rises. Directly to audience.)* I don't know. I guess you could call my family dysfunctional. We were right there in the mainstream of American life—*dysfunctional. (Pause.)* My mother just lay there—dead. No. Actually that's not exactly true. She didn't die there. Eventually I did call someone. I telephoned my grandmother and she phoned for the ambulance that soon came to take my mother to the hospital to have her stomach pumped. Only, she never made it to the hospital. She died in the ambulance. *(Pause.)* After she ingested the sleeping pills, I crawled into bed and lay next to her, listening to the sounds of her breathing. At some point I determined that she was asleep. Then, I went to sleep myself. It was late afternoon and hours later before I awoke and, in a panic, called my grandmother to tell her what had happened. I just told her I found the empty pill bottles and the letter she had written. Oh yes, there was a letter. Only, the odd thing is I don't remember her writing it. I think, as I look back on it now, that she must have awoken while I slept and wrote it then. That's the only explanation I have since I am certain it wasn't there when I crawled into bed beside her.

THE PSYCHOLOGIST: *(Appears.)* This letter—what did it say?

JOE: The police took it. I never read it—or if I did I don't remember. I spent years afterward going to the police station from time to time asking for that letter . . . my mother's last words. I came home on leave from the Navy years later and went to the police station one last time to inquire about that letter. I was told it had been destroyed.

THE PSYCHOLOGIST: And your father?

JOE: After my mother's suicide I went to live with my grandparents. And he just took off. Flew away. Who knows where? Two years ago I received word that he was dead. Lung cancer. That's it. That's all. That's show biz. And I don't want to talk about it anymore.

THE PSYCHOLOGIST: All right. *(After a pause.)* I'll be out of town for the next couple weeks, Joe. I won't be seeing you at the county jail.

JOE: *(Frightened by this sudden shift into the Here and Now.)* Oh, God....

THE PSYCHOLOGIST: Keep your wits about you, Joe. You'll come through just fine.

JOE: *Oh, God....*

THE PSYCHOLOGIST: Be strong. You'll be all right. *(JOE seems miles away and continues to mumble, "Oh, God.")* It isn't fair. I know that. We were making such good progress until this unfortunate incident with the boy.

JOE: *Oh, God....*

THE PSYCHOLOGIST: It isn't fair to either one of us, but it'll be over one day soon. Then we can get back to helping you become a whole person again. *Again.*

JOE: *Oh, God....*

THE PSYCHOLOGIST: Nothing is as bad as it seems. *(More to herself – heavenward.)* Oh, shit! What am I saying?

JOE: *Oh, God....*

THE PSYCHOLOGIST: I care about you, Joe. I know that sometimes you don't think I do, but I do. I care very much. You must believe that. Do you hear me, Joe?

JOE: Our Father who art in heaven hallowed be thy name . . .

THE PSYCHOLOGIST: You must stay in control, Joe. Do you hear me?

JOE: Thy kingdom come. Thy will be done on earth as it is . . . as it is . . . as it is—

THE PSYCHOLOGIST: I know it won't be easy for you.

JOE: In heaven. Forgive us our trespasses and give us our bread . . . .

THE PSYCHOLOGIST: But, it won't last forever. Can you hear me?

JOE: Lead us not into temptation and forgive us our trespasses as we forgive them . . . Deliver us from evil . . . *No!* That's not it! I can't remember—

THE PSYCHOLOGIST: Joe, listen to me.

JOE: Deliver us . . . no . . . give us . . . give us our bread . . . give us our daily bread. I can't remember!

THE PSYCHOLOGIST: I've spoken with Conrad. He thinks he can come up with the bail money. So, you won't be there for very long. Remember that. Can you hear me?

JOE: As we give those who give us bread . . . blessed is the fruit of thy womb . . . world without end . . . *I can't remember!*

THE PSYCHOLOGIST: A few more days, a week, two at most. Will you be all right?

END ACT ONE—*Scene 12*

ACT ONE—*Scene 13*—*the psychologist's office*

CONRAD: *(Appears. Angrily.)* Well? Will he? Will he be all right, Doctor?

THE PSYCHOLOGIST: I don't know.

CONRAD: What do you mean you don't know? You just let them throw him into the sheriff's car and haul him off to the county jail?

THE PSYCHOLOGIST: There was nothing I could do.

CONRAD: You're a doctor, for Christ's sake.

THE PSYCHOLOGIST: I'm a psychologist. I pleaded with the sheriff's deputy to send for a medical doctor so we could give Joe something to calm him down.

CONRAD: And?

THE PSYCHOLOGIST: And he advised me that Joe was having a normal reaction, considering the circumstances.

CONRAD: *(Incredulous.)* A man has lost touch with reality, doesn't know where he is or who he is. He is blathering "The Lord's Prayer" like a goddamned lunatic and you take advice from a know-nothing sheriff's deputy who says Joe's having a *"normal reaction."* And you call yourself a doctor!

THE PSYCHOLOGIST: Your getting hostile with me isn't going to help Joe. We've got to think of him now.

CONRAD: *(Enraged. Almost in tears.)* For fifteen years I've done nothing but think of Joe. All his life Joe's done nothing but think of Joe. Well, fuck Joe! It's time we thought of somebody else for a change. *What about me?* I could go out that door . . . *(Indicating exit.)* . . . right now . . . get in the car and go—turn my back on this whole mess and go!

THE PSYCHOLOGIST: Where?

CONRAD: I don't know where. *Just away. (He storms out.)*

THE PSYCHOLOGIST: *(Calling after him while crossing toward exit.)* Conrad, are you going to be all right? *Conrad! Conrad! (She exits, leaving JOE where he's been kneeling downstage.)*

END ACT ONE—*Scene 13*

ACT ONE—*Scene 14*—*a cell in the county jail*

The shadows of prison bars stretch across a dimly lit stage. THE LAWYER, dressed in the garb of a PRISONER, enters and crosses to JOE.

PRISONER: Hey, bro! Waddaya in for?

JOE: I killed someone.

PRISONER: *Nooo.* You're shittin' me, right?

JOE: I killed someone.

PRISONER: Who'dya kill?

JOE: I don't know.

PRISONER: Ya don't know?

JOE: No.

PRISONER: Ya mean ya killed a perfect stranger? *Hooooleeee shit!* Go on! They ain't gonna put no murderer in with the general population. You're shittin' me, man. Waddaya really in for?

JOE: I don't know. I can't remember.

PRISONER: *Hey!* I knows who you are. I knows you. I recognized you from the get-go. You're the one who diddles little boys.

JOE: No.

PRISONER: *Yeah.* We all heard you was comin'. Been the talk of the town.

JOE: No! That's not me!

PRISONER: Oh, it's you all right. Ya even look like queer bait, sucker! Wait till the guys hear about this. *Sheeeet!* Your ass won't be worth two cents, motherfucker. Hey, bitch! *(Bellowing with laughter.)* I'm gonna have your brains for breakfast and your ass for lunch!

(The PRISONER raises his foot to kick JOE in the stomach. He swings his foot and just as he is about to connect there is a BLACK OUT.)

END ACT ONE—Scene 14

ACT TWO—*Scene 1*—*the bridge*

AT RISE: the three hooded-cloaked TORMENTORS move menacingly through the shadows and fog beneath the bridge.

TORMENTOR 1: Rocco was here.

TORMENTOR 2: Sonny was here.

TORMENTOR 3: Kilroy was here.

ALL: *(In loud, rasping whispers.)* Joseph . . . Joseph . . . Joseph . . .

TORMENTOR 1: *(Searching the fog and shadows.)* Come out. Come out, wherever you are.

TORMENTOR 2: *(Ibid.)* We know you're here.

TORMENTOR 3: *(Ibid.)* Where are you?

TORMENTOR 1: Anything?

TORMENTOR 2: Nothing. You?

TORMENTOR 3: Nothing. Keep searching.

TORMENTOR 1: You don't suppose he flew?

TORMENTOR 2: Not a chance. Too dark. Keep searching.

TORMENTOR 3: Where are you, Joseph?

TORMENTOR 1: Come out. Come out, wherever you are.

TORMENTOR 2: Maybe he doesn't know.

TORMENTOR 3: He never did and he never will.

ALL: Poor Joseph.

TORMENTOR 1: Rocco was here.

TORMENTOR 2: Sonny was here.

TORMENTOR 3: Kilroy was here.

TORMENTOR 1: He doesn't know his way through the dark.

TORMENTOR 2: There is no way.

TORMENTOR 3: No way but every way with nowhere to go but everywhere . . . through darkness. *(A snake-like hissing.)*

TORMENTOR 1: We'll tie you in knots.

TORMENTOR 2: And twist you inside-outside-in.

TORMENTOR 3: Ancient knots.

TORMENTOR 1: Forget-me-nots *(A snake-like hissing.)*

TORMENTOR 2: Knots upon knots with open-ended connections.

TORMENTOR 3: There's a tidy bundle for you.

TORMENTOR 1: Tightly bound.

ALL: We are the light. *(Hissing.)* We are the way.

TORMENTOR 2: Hear us. All who enter here cannot return.

TORMENTOR 3: Hear us. All who enter here can never

return.

ALL: *(Hissing.) Joseph . . . Joseph . . . Joseph . . . .*

TORMENTOR 1: Rocco was here.

TORMENTOR 2: Sonny was here.

TORMENTOR 3: Kilroy was here.

TORMENTOR 1: Without the light you are lost.

TORMENTOR 2: Forever lost.

TORMENTOR 3: Come out. Come out, wherever you are.

TORMENTOR 1: We've games to play.

TORMENTOR 2: Come play with us, Joseph.

TORMENTOR 3: Eternal games.

TORMENTOR 1: Immortal games.

TORMENTOR 2: Games you cannot lose.

TORMENTOR 3: Games you cannot win.

TORMENTOR 1: Games that never end.

ALL: *(Hissing.) Joseph . . . Joseph . . . Joseph . . . .*

TORMENTOR 2: *Joooooe . . . seeeeeph.*

TORMENTOR 3: JOSEPH! JOSEPH!

TORMENTOR 1: Rocco was here.

TORMENTOR 2: Sonny was here.

TORMENTOR 3: Kilroy was here.

(Slowly, the LIGHTING rises on the bridge where we see JOE slumped in the shadows.)

JOE: *(Slowly stands. Directly to the audience.)* In jail. In a place that serves and services the needs and the discards of its surrounding society. The essential aura of the place is primitive to medieval. The stale, musty odor seems to ooze like sap through the oppressive atmosphere. And the walls! The khaki-painted cement walls that cry out with the scribblings

TORMENTOR 2: Sonny was here.

TORMENTOR 3: Kilroy was here.

JOE: These walls, scabbed and encrusted with the soundless screams of incarcerated souls, peeling and chipping away in quiet, unending condemnation. *In jail.*

TORMENTOR 1: Jose Gonzales betrayed me!

TORMENTOR 2: My wife betrayed me!

TORMENTOR 3: My lawyer betrayed me!

TORMENTOR 1: Jose Gonzales is screwing my wife.

TORMENTOR 2: My wife is screwing everybody.

TORMENTOR 3: My lawyer is screwing me.

TORMENTOR 1: Chickie Valdez gives good head.

TORMENTOR 2: Sally D. gives good head.

TORMENTOR 3: Detective Brodsky gives good head.

TORMENTOR 1: Rocco loves Chickie.

TORMENTOR 2: Sonny loves Sally.

TORMENTOR 3: I never loved Lucy.

JOE: *In jail* . . . where the cockroaches come and go with certain and quick decisiveness on legs that take them nowhere.

TORMENTOR 1: *Nowhere. (Hisses.)*

TORMENTOR 2: *Nowhere. (Hisses.)*

TORMENTOR 3: *Nowhere. (Hisses.)*

JOE: *In jail.*

(THE TORMENTORS hiss and taunt JOE.)

JOE: Somewhere between nowhere and midnight.

TORMENTOR 1: Life is hell.

TORMENTOR 2: Only the good die young.

TORMENTOR 3: Born to be bad.

TORMENTOR 1: Bad to the bone.

TORMENTOR 2: Badder than Brando.

TORMENTOR 3: Badder than yo' mama.

TORMENTOR 1: Death to Jorge Martinez.

TORMENTOR 2: Jake Early is a stool pigeon.

TORMENTOR 3: Bubba is a motherfucker.

TORMENTOR 1: Mary, mother of Jesus, save me.

TORMENTOR 2: Jesus saves.

TORMENTOR 3: Jesus is my savior.

TORMENTOR 1: Love is a four letter word.

TORMENTOR 2: Bad to the bone.

TORMENTOR 3: Bite the big one.

TORMENTOR 1: My mother made me a homosexual.

TORMENTOR 2: Could she make one for me?

TORMENTOR 3: Death to all queers!

JOE: *In jail* . . . where the fingers of ghosts, long gone, carved away countless hours upon these stinking walls begging to be remembered.

TORMENTOR 1: Remember me.

TORMENTOR 2: Remember me.

TORMENTOR 3: Remember me.

TORMENTOR 1: I was framed.

TORMENTOR 2: Here sits an innocent man.

TORMENTOR 3: And I'd do it again!

TORMENTOR 1: Rocco was here. *(Exits.)*

TORMENTOR 2: Sonny was here. *(Exits.)*

TORMENTOR 3: Kilroy was here. *(Exits.)*

JOE: *In jail . (Descends from the bridge.)* In jail for three weeks, two days—*an eternity.* The bail was reduced to twenty-five thousand and Conrad, bless his soul, finally came up with enough money to post bond, and not a minute too soon. How I dealt with my time in jail I cannot say. My memory of it is much the same as that of a dream that escapes your grasp upon waking and then quickly slips into that place where dreams tease your memory, but never show themselves again.

Just pieces of dreams remain to dance through uncertain memories—the persistence of a memory of something certain and yet uncertain. The dilemma of the butterfly man.

END ACT TWO—Scene 1

ACT TWO—Scene 2—the psychologist's office

THE PSYCHOLOGIST: *(Appears.)* Butterfly man?

JOE: Yes. I'm sure you've heard it. *(Quotes.)* "Last night I dreamed I was a butterfly. Today I am not sure if I am a man who dreamed he was a butterfly or a butterfly who dreamed he was a man."

THE PSYCHOLOGIST: Ah, yes. I have heard it. Given a choice, would you be a butterfly or a man?

JOE: What kind of a dumb question is that?

THE PSYCHOLOGIST: Forgive me. You've never asked a dumb question?

JOE: Of course I have. All the time. *(After a pause.)* A man. A man who could do or be anything he damn well pleased.

THE PSYCHOLOGIST: And you feel you can't?

JOE: Of course I do. I mean I can't. You have a knack for confusing me, Doctor.

THE PSYCHOLOGIST: I don't mean to. *(Pause.)* You've come through the ordeal of jail all right, haven't you?

JOE: I suppose.

THE PSYCHOLOGIST: You suppose?

JOE: I'm here, aren't I? I'm alive and well enough to face whatever comes next.

THE PSYCHOLOGIST: What was it like for you?

JOE: What? Jail? *(THE PSYCHOLOGIST nods in the affirmative.)* I told you. I don't remember. *Really.*

THE PSYCHOLOGIST: You mean, you don't want to talk about it.

JOE: I mean, I don't remember. I have lost nearly all recollection of it. Honest. It was like a dream . . . a dream I can't remember. Call it denial. Call it what you will. I don't care. All I remember is that I stayed to myself most of the time—stayed in my bunk mostly. At night, when no one seemed to be awake, I'd go to the toilet and then I'd crawl back into my bunk. I pretended to sleep when I couldn't sleep and I slept when I could. *(After a pause.)* My back . . .

THE PSYCHOLOGIST: Your back? What about your back?

JOE: I remember always thinking about my back. Even in my sleep, I remained aware of my back. It had a sense all its own. An awareness, always aware of where anyone was in relation to me. Always sensitive to the slightest movement of others. Always on guard. Even in my sleep . . . always on guard.

THE PSYCHOLOGIST: Well, as you said, you're here. You're alive. You're well enough to face whatever comes next.

JOE: I said that?

THE PSYCHOLOGIST: Not more than a minute ago.

JOE: *Huh.* Imagine that.

THE PSYCHOLOGIST: What comes next, Joe?

JOE: There's supposed to be a hearing in a few weeks—some sort of pre-trial hearing. I don't know what it is, really.

If the judge will just hear me out—let me explain to him exactly what happened—I don't see any reason why it should go to trial.

(THE PSYCHOLOGIST disappears.)

END ACT TWO—*Scene 2*

ACT TWO—*Scene 3*—*outside the judge's chambers*

JOE: I mean, if he'd just listen to me he'd understand that there was nothing sexual about what I did. I don't want to go to trial.

THE LAWYER: *(Appears.)* All right. However, the state is requesting that you submit to certain tests.

JOE: What kind of tests?

THE LAWYER: If there is to be any plea bargain, the D. A. is recommending you submit to ninety days of testing to determine whether or not you would be considered a candidate for further rehabilitation.

JOE: If I refuse?

THE LAWYER: If you refuse and still plead no contest, the judge can order the tests anyway.

JOE: I don't want to go to trial. *I'm gay.* They'll crucify me.

THE LAWYER: I'm only telling you how it is. These are hysterical times, Joe, when it comes to charges of this nature. If you pass these tests and get a clean bill of health—

JOE: I will. What kind of tests?

THE LAWYER: Wired-sensors to the penis. Pictures of children. That sort of thing.

JOE: You've got to be kidding! I'm not going to get my dick wired-up to satisfy the prurient interests of the state.

THE LAWYER: Look at the alternative—you could be sentenced to a maximum of three years in the state penitentiary.

JOE: I don't believe this! You mean to tell me that without even being proven guilty, the judge wants to send me to the state mental hospital for ninety days?

THE LAWYER: That is the recommendation of the D. A. However, you would be sent to the state prison in Santa Fe.

JOE: *What?*

THE LAWYER: Not in with the general population. It would be a separate treatment facility for sex offenders.

JOE: But I'm not a sex offender.

THE LAWYER: That would be determined at the end of your ninety days.

JOE: No. No way. Absolutely not. That's out of the question!

THE LAWYER: Then we'll have to go to trial.

JOE: *Fine.* Then we'll go to trial. I'm not going to the state prison for ninety days to prove I shouldn't have been sent there in the first place. That doesn't make one bit of sense to me.

THE LAWYER: Let's get this straight. Are you saying that you want me to go back into the judge's chambers . . . *(Indicates some place offstage.)* . . . and change our plea from no contest to innocent?

JOE: Absolutely.

THE LAWYER: If we lose, Joe, you could be facing three years.

JOE: I'd be facing certain death in Santa Fe. I'd rather take my chances in court. *(Pause.)* Does it have to come out in court that I'm gay?

THE LAWYER: That would depend on how the trial goes. Unless you admit to it, or the prosecution can produce somebody with whom you've had sex—as it pertains to the case—it shouldn't be an issue. However, without it ever being brought up directly, if the jury smells it, it could be very damaging to our defense. *(After a pause.) So?* What do you want to do?

JOE: *(Determined.)* We go to trial.

THE LAWYER: If you're sure that's what you want.

JOE: It is, I'm sure. *(After a pause to exhale.)* Don't look so worried. I'm the one who's supposed to be worried. They're not going to put me away, wire me up, or do anything to me ever again without due process of law. Okay?

THE LAWYER: Okay. *(Crossing to the judge's chambers.)* Boy, the last thing I needed was a trial like this! *(Exits.)*

JOE: *Yeah . . . me too.*

END ACT TWO—*Scene 3*

ACT TWO—*Scene 4*—*Joe and Conrad's bedroom*

CONRAD: *(Appears.)* And what about me?

JOE: What about you?

CONRAD: You've made up your mind, just like that?

JOE: It's my life.

CONRAD: Don't I count for something? It's my life too, you know.

JOE: This doesn't concern you.

CONRAD: You self-centered son of a bitch!

JOE: I'm the one facing prison!

CONRAD: You won't go to prison—not if you tell the truth.

JOE: I will deny any accusation of being gay.

CONRAD: You want me to perjure myself. Is that it?

JOE: You do what you want, Connie. But, if I'm asked about my sexuality, I've no intention of giving them ammunition to use against me. Besides, unless you say anything, there's no way anybody could prove I'm gay.

CONRAD: Everybody who knows us knows we're gay. Everybody in this town knows we're gay.

JOE: No. They don't. They think and they assume. But, they don't know.

CONRAD: Whatever happened to, "I want to be an

example?" Whatever happened to, "I think all gays ought to be out of the closet because they do a disservice to the entire gay community?" *Huh?* Whatever happened to, "The worst kind of liar is the one who lies to himself?"

JOE: You know, I really hate you.

CONRAD: Sometimes, I hate you too. But, you just remember one thing, smart-ass, that studio was mine, too. *Mine.* My money went into it. My income came out of it. I hated to see it close, too. I poured a lot of myself into it, too. So, if I don't know how you feel, excuse me! I know how I feel, and I don't feel like listening to your bullshit!

JOE: *(After a pause.)* Where did everybody go?

CONRAD: You ought to know how people are by now, Joe.

JOE: Some bunch of friends they all turned out to be!

CONRAD: Then, they were never your friends. They certainly weren't mine.

JOE: All those free sessions. All those free portraits.

CONRAD: You can't buy friends.

JOE: I'm not interested in your aphorisms!

CONRAD: *Sorry.*

JOE: Thousands of dollars just in materials. Not to mention my time. All those photographs I did just to show how I cared. Do you know I've done more work gratis than I ever did for money?

CONRAD: I always thought that was a bad idea.

JOE: *(After a pause.)* You blame me for this. It's all my fault, isn't it?

CONRAD: No, Joe. It's not all your fault. If it's anybody's fault it's the kid's. The mother's. I don't know. It's . . . it's just the way it is. That's it. That's all. It's just the way it is.

JOE: But you blame me, don't you?

CONRAD: Will you just let it rest, *please?* I don't want to argue. Can't we go twenty-four hours without some kind of drama in our lives?

JOE: *(After a pause.)* And when, may I ask without risking a bit of drama, must we have our stuff packed and out of here?

CONRAD: Three weeks.

JOE: *Christ!*

CONRAD: I'll do the packing, Joe. You don't have to worry about it.

JOE: Would you stop making a martyr of yourself!

CONRAD: Joe, if you want to pack, be my guest.

JOE: We lost our business! We lost our house! What's next? What in hell is going to happen to us now?

CONRAD: After the trial we'll go somewhere else and start again.

JOE: After the trial? Suppose they send me to prison?

CONRAD: They won't.

JOE: You don't know they won't.

CONRAD: And you don't know they will.

JOE: They will if they find out I'm gay.

CONRAD: I'm going to tell you something and I mean it. If you go into that courtroom and deny being gay, should the question arise, I'm going to leave you, Joe.

JOE: Is this a threat?

CONRAD: I'm not going to make a liar of myself and I'm not going to watch you make a liar of yourself, either.

JOE: Do what you want!

CONRAD: I will. For once in my life, I will.

JOE: What is that supposed to mean?

CONRAD: It means, I'm tired of living for both of us! I'm going to start living for me from now on! And to hell with you!

JOE: *(Charges CONRAD, pushing and punching.)* Desert me! Go ahead; desert me, you fucking sonofabitch! You goddamn fucking piss elegant queen! Desert me! I always knew you would! Who the fuck do you think you are?

CONRAD: *(Blocking himself from JOE's fists.)* Stop it! Stop it! You're crazy! *(He lands a solid punch on JOE, knocking JOE down. After a pause.)* Are you happy now? Is this what you wanted?

JOE: *(After a pause.)* I get crazy sometimes. It's like I really want to hurt you. I want to hurt you and I want to see your pain.

CONRAD: Then look. *Look.* Look at my pain, goddamnit!

Look at me.

JOE: *(After a pause.)* I'm sorry. I'm afraid I'm going to wake up one day and you're not going to be there.

CONRAD: *(Crosses to JOE and helps him up. They embrace.)* We've come this far, haven't we? And I'm still here.

JOE: *(Breaking away.) Oh, God!* When will this all come to trial?

CONRAD: Soon.

JOE: Six months of waiting. How much longer do they intend to keep us on the hook?

CONRAD: Why don't I make us some breakfast?

JOE: Don't they care?

CONRAD: Probably not. How many pancakes do you think you can eat?

JOE: I don't know. Four. No, six. No. Make it two . . . It's like limbo. You know, where they keep souls on ice.

CONRAD: Who keeps souls on ice? Are we into some Catholic thing of yours, Joe? Haven't they dumped enough guilt on you for one lifetime?

JOE: I suppose. But, it is like limbo. You know, where they keep those poor bastards who haven't been baptized, souls too good to got to hell, yet not good enough to go to heaven. Neither dead or alive nor here or there. *On hold.* Just on hold. Do you know what I mean?

CONRAD: *Yeah*, you're in a rut. Do you want sausage with

your pancakes, or bacon? *(Moves toward exit.)*

JOE: Bacon. No. Sausage. And can I have some blackberry preserves on my toast?

CONRAD: Indeed, you can. And if we have any, you may. *(Exits.)*

JOE: *(Alone onstage. After a pause.)* He is such a literal son of a bitch.

CONRAD: *(His voice from offstage.)* I heard that!

END ACT TWO—*Scene 4*

ACT TWO—*Scene 5*—*the psychologist's office*

THE PSYCHOLOGIST: *(Appears.)* Is he? Is he "a literal son of a bitch?"

JOE: Sometimes. What, in my day, I'd call a piss elegant queen. But, only sometimes.

THE PSYCHOLOGIST: *(Amused.)* I've never heard that term before – "piss elegant queen." I don't mean to make fun, but I find the vernacular filled with images far more amusing than in "a literal son of a bitch."

JOE: You're putting me on.

THE PSYCHOLOGIST: No. I'm not. *Really.* You've got to remember that I grew up in Roswell, New Mexico. I haven't been around all that much.

JOE: What about college?

THE PSYCHOLOGIST: Los Cruces and Albuquerque. I wouldn't call that "getting around."

JOE: No. Neither would I. I'm at a loss for words.

THE PSYCHOLOGIST: Why?

JOE: Because you're so easy to talk to. I never thought of you as coming from . . . well, you know . . . *here*. These parts.

THE PSYCHOLOGIST: We don't all have horns, Joe. Some of us are the good guys Isn't Conrad originally from "these parts?"

JOE: Originally, yes. Now, you've shamed me.

THE PSYCHOLOGIST: Good. Why do you say, "In my day?" Do you mean to say that this isn't your day now?

JOE: It's just a phrase. Like when I was in New York and young and tomorrow was something I looked forward to with great expectations. That was my day.

THE PSYCHOLOGIST: And these days?

JOE: These days? I honestly don't know.

THE PSYCHOLOGIST: What don't you know?

JOE: Where I'm going. Why I'm going. Will I be going there with Connie? Will we ever stop bickering and fighting each other? Will I make it through the trial? Will I be free? Was I ever free? *Oh, God!* When I was young and stupid—*was I ever free.*

THE PSYCHOLOGIST: Seriously.

JOE: Seriously? Doctor, these days are about as serious as anything I will ever hope to know. New York is gone. For me, it might as well be the moon away. There's not one single soul I kept in contact with. *Not one.* I've never been good with keeping friends for very long, especially over long distance. Right now it's just Conrad and me.

THE PSYCHOLOGIST: No gay friends?

JOE: Not since leaving New York. I know they must exist around these parts, but I haven't met any. I've seen their calling cards etched into the walls of the men's room over at the state line rest stop.

THE PSYCHOLOGIST: How sad?

JOE: Is it?

THE PSYCHOLOGIST: Isn't it?

JOE: What's their choice? A little town in the middle of nowhere, how else are gays going to meet one another?

THE PSYCHOLOGIST: But, public restrooms? It's nothing but illicit sex.

JOE: Perhaps we could take out an ad in the local paper and hold a luncheon in one of the banquet rooms over at the country club.

THE PSYCHOLOGIST: We're being flip.

JOE: No. *I'm* being flip. I'm trying to say that as much as I believe all gays ought to be out of the closet, there are times and there are places where to do so is extremely hazardous to our health. This town, at this time, is one of those places.

THE PSYCHOLOGIST: How do you cope? I thought you were pretty open. Who are your friends?

JOE: I've spent the last five years with straight couples and singles and some who don't know what they are and probably never will. Five years to learn what I already knew the day I left the farm to join the navy.

THE PSYCHOLOGIST: And that is?

JOE: I don't fit. I never did fit. I never will fit. And, frankly, I no longer want to fit.

THE PSYCHOLOGIST: It sounds like a lonely life.

JOE: I'm used to it.

THE PSYCHOLOGIST: But, you did make the choice.

JOE: There was never any choice to be made. I was born this way. I am one hundred percent genetically homosexual.

THE PSYCHOLOGIST: That's been a subject of much speculation.

JOE: Of course it has. As long as conservative fundamentalist Christians can keep everybody believing that homosexuality is a choice, we will continue to be denied our human rights. For them to accept us as being born homosexual would mean that somehow God had something to do with it. It would mean that we'd have to be accepted as having minority status. And if they were faced with having to accept that we are genetically predisposed, and it could be determined before birth, abortion opponents would go mute. The fact that you even suggest there's a choice shows a bias on your part. Your fundy background, no doubt.

THE PSYCHOLOGIST: That's quite unfair, Joe. I'm a trained psychologist.

JOE: Well, you seem to have a general lack of understanding. I mean, a girl who comes from Roswell, New Mexico, goes to college and earns herself a Ph.D. in psychology ought to understand that kind of defiant pride from a woman's perspective.

THE PSYCHOLOGIST: According to you, what would that perspective be?

JOE: I am sure there were times when your just being a woman was an obstacle getting in your way. But, you don't want to be a man, do you?

THE PSYCHOLOGIST: I am proud of what I've done with my life. No. I don't want to be a man.

JOE: Even when you have to work harder than a man does

just to prove your worth? Even when you do not get paid as much as a man does for equal work?

THE PSYCHOLOGIST: No. I wouldn't choose to be anything else.

JOE: Exactly. That's just how I feel. I wouldn't choose to be anything else.

THE PSYCHOLOGIST: But, you said you had no choice.

JOE: I could choose not to be gay, but I'd still remain homosexual?

THE PSYCHOLOGIST: Joe, you've got me totally confused. Is there a difference between being gay and being homosexual?

JOE: In my mind, I imagine a distinction. There are homosexuals living in heterosexual marriages. They're miserable and disappointed with everything in their lives. They're homosexuals, but they're not gay. Gay is a point of view. A lifestyle. Gay is the choice made when one chooses to be true to oneself. I was born homosexual. T here was no choice in that. The choice comes in choosing to accept it, in choosing to be gay, in choosing to be true to oneself.

THE PSYCHOLOGIST: Then, why all the anxiety surrounding your decision to deny being homosexual if it comes up during the course of the trial?

JOE: That's another matter.

THE PSYCHOLOGIST: Listen to you. You can't have it both ways, Joe.

JOE: I'm trying to save my skin.

THE PSYCHOLOGIST: By lying? By self-denial?

JOE: If that's what it takes.

THE PSYCHOLOGIST: You see no hypocrisy there?

JOE: I know who I am. It's not necessary that I broadcast it to the world. Especially when the world we are talking about is Lea county, New Mexico, and is about as hostile toward gays as hostile can get. *(After a pause.)* I've been thinking and I don't think I'll be coming back here anymore. So, I want to thank you for all you've done. You've been a tremendous help and I'll never forget you for it.

THE PSYCHOLOGIST: I'm surprised. You think you've worked it all out, do you?

JOE: I've worked out all that I can here. The rest I'll have to do on my own.

THE PSYCHOLOGIST: If that's your choice.

JOE: It is.

THE PSYCHOLOGIST: *(Extends her hand for JOE to shake.)* Good luck.

JOE: *(Shaking her hand.)* Thank you. Well—goodbye. *(Exits awkwardly.)*

THE PSYCHOLOGIST: *Goodbye . (Alone onstage. To audience.)* I guess that's it. I haven't seen Joe since. About three weeks later I received a telephone call from Joe's lawyer declining my offer to testify on Joe's behalf. He thought—and I concurred—that the decision of the jury might be clouded by the fact that Joe had been in therapy for more than a year and a half. Much of our work had to do with his learning to accept himself as he is, and with learning to accept his homosexuality without guilt. That was, of course, at the core of most of our sessions. Therefore, the decision not to testify. As of Joe's last session, he had displayed more confidence in himself and more self-control than I had previously observed. His nightmares had subsided. They were less intense—less threatening. Still, I had my doubts. After all, in all honesty, Joe would not be tried by a jury of his peers. How could he? One week later the trial would begin. I would remain in my office, see some clients . . . and pray. Yes, pray. Maybe that all had something to do with that little girl from Roswell, New Mexico and her fundy Christian background. *(She exits.)*

END ACT TWO—*Scene 5*

ACT TWO—*Scene 6*—*Joe and Conrad's bedroom*

JOE enters. We see him preparing for the trial. He buffs his shoes, combs his hair, slips into a jacket, etc. CONRAD enters.

JOE: Connie, whatever happens at the trial . . . *whatever happens* . . . well . . . you know.

CONRAD: I'm with you, Joe. Whatever happens, I'll still be with you.

JOE: Aren't you afraid?

CONRAD: Of course I'm afraid.

JOE: Me, too. *(After a pause.)* Connie, about our being gay . . . .

CONRAD: I've said all I'm going to say in that regard. You do what you have to do.

JOE: About your leaving—I have to know.

CONRAD: You already know how I feel. There's nothing more to say.

JOE: But, if it comes up.

CONRAD: If it comes up, you'll do what you know is best.

JOE: That's not an answer.

CONRAD: It's the best I can offer.

JOE: What will you do? I mean . . . if it comes up.

CONRAD: The same—what I know is best.

JOE: (After a pause.) Well . . . how do I look?
CONRAD: Fabulous.

JOE: You, too. (THEY embrace. A gentle kiss. After a pause.) April the first! What a day to have a trial. God must be laughing His head off.
CONRAD: One can always hope.

END ACT TWO—*Scene 6*

ACT TWO—*Scene 7*—a courtroom.

JOE and CONRAD cross to opposite sides of the stage. THE LAWYER enters and crosses to JOE.

THE LAWYER: Relax.

JOE: I'm trying.

THE LAWYER: No matter what happens . . . no matter what the outcome . . . control yourself.

JOE: I feel sick.

THE LAWYER: No nonsense. Just stay calm.

JOE: *Oh God!* I'm going to be sick.

THE LAWYER: Here we go . . . ALL RISE! *(Crossing downstage. To audience.)* This court is now in session!

CONRAD: *(Aside.)* Oh, God, don't let Joe do something stupid.

JOE: Oh, God, please help me.

THE MOTHER: *(Enters, takes the stand and raises her right hand.)* So help me, God!

THE LAWYER: *(To audience.)* Help me. Help me sort through this mess. *(Turning toward THE MOTHER.)* Did someone say "victim?" *(Turning back to the audience.)* Yes. The prosecutor said "victim."

THE MOTHER: *(Points an angry, accusing finger at JOE.)* As the victim's mother, I, too, have suffered for what HE DID! *(She continues with all the pathos of a grade-B movie.)*

I haven't been the same since. My doctor had to prescribe medication for me ever since he did what he did! *(Again, she points at JOE.)*

CONRAD: *(Aside.)* I'm going to be ill.

JOE: *(Aside.)* I wish to hell she would stop that pointing. Who is this woman? This is not the same woman who came to the studio. What is she trying to do? What kind of act is this?

THE MOTHER: He forced my little boy to strip naked! And when he had him naked he . . . he . . . *(She breaks down, sobbing.)*

JUNIOR: He said to go ahead and change while he got ready to take my picture.

JOE: The boy had already taken his clothes off without my being aware. I was setting lights and arranging barbells and weights in front of the backdrop. You would not believe some of the things I go through for clients.

THE LAWYER: Just the facts.

JOE: When I noticed him he was standing there completely undressed.

JUNIOR: I asked him if I should put my posing-jock on.

JOE: I told him to leave them off until after I had applied the oil.

THE MOTHER: So he could perform his disgusting sex act!

JOE: So I could avoid staining his posing-briefs.

JUNIOR: So he wouldn't mess them up with oil. They cost

my mommy a lot of money.

JOE: Yes. Of course it was a mistake. It was the biggest mistake of my life.

CONRAD: I was in the hallway outside the studio working on a display.

THE MOTHER: I couldn't stay. I had errands to run. I was only gone about forty minutes. When I came back for Junior they were already done. *Oh! My poor, poor baby!*

CONRAD: Forty . . . forty-five minutes. Joe had a meeting to get to. I'd say it was a fairly quick session considering how much time it takes to shoot thirty-six poses.
JOE: Yes. I used a thirty-five millimeter camera. I took a lot of shots that day. Good shots.

THE MOTHER: How can I live with what he did to my little boy? *(She points at JOE.)* Every time I think of it I . . . I . . . I can't help blaming myself for leaving my baby alone with that queer.

CONRAD: *Oh, shit.*

JOE: *Oh, God.*

THE LAWYER: I OBJECT!

THE MOTHER: Everybody knows he's a queer.

THE LAWYER: I object!

THE MOTHER: Him and that partner of his! We had to get ourselves tested for AIDS. God only knows what kind of horrible diseases they carry! I hope he burns in hell! I know I shouldn't wish that on anybody because I'm a Christian. And if the truth be known, I love them. That's my Christian duty.

It's what they do that I hate. But, these aren't people. Not people like you and me. They're wicked and despised in the eyes of the Lord. Forgive me. I hope the jury understands a mother's pain and sorrow.

CONRAD: *(Aside.)* What a performance! The envelope please . . . .

THE LAWYER: *(To the invisible judge.)* That is hearsay! Sheer gossip, Your Honor. And irrelevant! *(To the audience.)* The seed is planted. I can represent and defend Joe to the best of my ability and with good conscience. But, can I defend Joe's sexuality?

THE MOTHER: It's true! Everybody knows it! But faggots are usually pretty good when it comes to artistic things, aren't they?

THE LAWYER: I OBJECT!

THE MOTHER: His father and I both told Junior to keep an eye out and make sure he didn't try any funny business.

JUNIOR: *Yeah.* If he tried anything funny I was to make sure and let mommy know. Daddy didn't want him to take my picture, but mommy said that his pictures win all the contests so we should give him a chance . . . even if he is queer.

THE MOTHER: It doesn't pay to give that type a chance!

THE LAWYER: I OBJECT!

THE MOTHER: A mother and her son have their rights, you know. How do you compensate a child who will carry the scars for the rest of his life? How do you compensate for my suffering?

THE LAWYER: *(Heavenward. Sardonically.)* A tragedy for

which the court is lacking in its ability to compensate. Sadly, our hands are tied. We can only do what the law will allow. Your suffering, however, has hardly gone unnoticed.

THE MOTHER: I object! Your Honor, is he being a smart-ass?

THE LAWYER: *(To audience.)* This is it in a nutshell. Joe is charged with criminal sexual contact with a minor under the age of thirteen. A felony in the state of New Mexico and punishable by a maximum of three years imprisonment and/or probation and rehabilitation at a state mental health facility. The State must prove that a felony has been committed and they must prove it beyond a reasonable doubt. What have they proven? Junior had some photographs taken. He was also prejudiced by the alleged nature of the defendant, and so was psychologically predisposed to any number of erroneous conclusions. Thirty-six exposures were taken in forty minutes. The contact sheet shows thirty-six distinctly different and carefully posed photographs. Hardly enough time for "funny business." But, the mother made certain that her opinion of the defendant be known in no uncertain terms, and in the court's record.

THE MOTHER: Well, he's queer, isn't he? He told the arresting officer that if he wasn't gay this never would have happened.

JOE: *(Aside.)* Did I say that? I don't remember saying that?

THE LAWYER: *(To THE MOTHER.)* There is no mention of that in the arresting officer's report.

THE MOTHER: Irregardless, he said it! *(She points at JOE.)*

THE LAWYER: Regardless of the fact that it does not appear in the report?

THE MOTHER: That's right.

THE LAWYER: *(To the audience.)* And exactly how did the mother know what Joe may or may not have told the arresting officer?

THE MOTHER: He's a good friend of the family. We attend the same church and we were on the force together.

THE LAWYER: On the police force doing undercover work.

THE MOTHER: Sometimes. We busted some heavy-duty drug dealers and broke up some gambling scams in the south part of town. We worked together on several major operations.

CONRAD: *(Aside.)* Jesus Christ. Next we'll discover she was a hit man for the CIA.

THE MOTHER: Well, once. *Just once.* I only shot a man once. I caught him in the chest. But, they got the bullet out and he lived to go to trial.

JOE: *(Aside.)* I'm sure that was a major disappointment.

THE MOTHER: He was scum. Why should I feel sorry? I was acting
in the line of duty, protecting our children from the criminal element. We've let low-life run our lives for too long! It's time we took our country back! Besides, I thought the perpetrator was armed. How was I to know? So the jury found him innocent. I don't care. I know better. He was scum. No. I'm not sorry. I'm not sorry at all. *I'm a mother, aren't I?*

CONRAD: *(Aside.)* Was there ever any doubt?

THE MOTHER: I was a police officer acting in the line of

duty. No. That was not why my husband and I left the force.

THE LAWYER: *(To the audience.)* No, indeed. She and her husband had come into a large sum of money that they, along with her father, invested in an oil well servicing company.

THE MOTHER: *(To the audience.)* And there was a little extra left over which I used to open a little boutique in the mall with, along with my sister.

THE LAWYER: *(Ibid.)* Where she sold ladies' negligees and other sorts of informal attire for "her" to wear for "him" in the privacy of the bedroom. And the name of that establishment?

THE MOTHER: *Scant Fantasies.*

CONRAD: *(Aside.)* Which, of course, was her idea.

THE MOTHER: The name was my idea. God knows we all agonized hours over it. But we all decided that *Scant Fantasies* was the best of all the names we came up with. The whole family. We're a very close Christian family. Unlike some, we still believe in family values.

THE LAWYER: *(To the audience)* And where did all this money come from?

THE MOTHER: I have been advised not to discuss it.

THE LAWYER: *(Ibid.)* Undoubtedly she had been advised not to discuss it. In fact, in the terms of their settlement, both she and her husband agreed not to disclose the amount. This undisclosed amount was an out-of-court settlement with a national chain of daycare centers where, for a very short time, Junior attended for a few hours each day after school.

THE MOTHER: I told you I can't discuss it!

JUNIOR: The director of the center touched my private parts.

THE MOTHER: *(Pointing at JOE.)* That doesn't change what he did! What business did this so-called photographer have stripping my son naked and rubbing oil all over his body? *Huh? Tell me that.*

JOE: She understood two days before the shoot exactly what the procedure would be.

THE MOTHER: I don't know what he's talking about. All I wanted was a picture of my little boy to enter in a photogenic contest. I never consented to child pornography!

THE LAWYER: Child pornography is not in question here. The photos all look perfectly normal to me and, no doubt, to the ladies and gentlemen of the jury.

THE MOTHER: It's what went on between the photos.

JOE: Yes. She did fill out a questionnaire.

THE MOTHER: I don't remember.

JOE: On it she wrote exactly what she wanted.

THE MOTHER: I don't recall. *(After a pause.)* Yes. That is my handwriting, I think. Yes, now I remember. But, don't they have girls to do that sort of thing?

THE LAWYER: What sort of thing is that?

THE MOTHER: You know, rub oil on his body and stuff like that. I was sure he had a girl who took care of things like that. I mean, wouldn't that be more natural?

THE LAWYER: Natural?

THE MOTHER: *Normal.*

THE LAWYER: You mean, a woman would be more suited to the task of applying oil to the body of a young man?

THE MOTHER: Yes, of course. I'm sure you would agree.

THE LAWYER: No, ma'am. I would not.

THE MOTHER: I was sure he had a female assistant who did that sort of thing. You know, like in a doctor's office.

THE LAWYER: My understanding is that a female assistant in a male doctor's office is there for the female patients.

THE MOTHER: I never dreamed that he would do it himself. I never dreamed . . . knowing what I know about him.

THE LAWYER: MOVE TO STRIKE!

THE MOTHER: *(Pointing at JOE.)* He's guilty! Guilty as sin!

JUNIOR: *Yeah.* He touched my butt-hole!

JOE: His what?

THE LAWYER: His anus. Did you put your finger on or in his anus?

JOE: No.

THE LAWYER: Did you fondle or touch his genitalia?

JOE: No.

THE LAWYER: Tell us what happened during the time you

were applying the oil.

JOE: He got an erection.

JUNIOR: I pulled a boner.

JOE: When I noticed it I told him to put his briefs on.

THE LAWYER: Did he?

JOE: Yes.

THE LAWYER: What was his reaction? Did he say anything?

JOE: He said something about when he grew up and got married he was going to have his wife give him oil massages.

THE LAWYER: What did you take that to mean?

JOE: That he was aroused by my putting the oil on him.

THE LAWYER: Were you sexually aroused?

JOE: No. I was amused. I had to restrain myself from laughing.

THE MOTHER: My son's erection is no laughing matter!

JOE: Look, it didn't seem so out of the ordinary at the time. It's just something that happens. That's all. I was amused because I knew that I had just filled the spray bottle with cold water and that the cold spray would get rid of it in a hurry.

THE LAWYER: What was the cold water spray for?

JOE: We had him pumping iron in the first few pictures and the spray would make it look like he was sweating. That's what he and his mother wanted. At the time, I didn't question it. My mistake.

THE MOTHER: No. I didn't go directly to the police. We went to the sheriff. He used to be our police captain when I was on the force. I could always go to him for advice. *(Pause.)* Yes. I did. I did call on the judge who set the bail. Why not? He and my father have been best friends ever since I can remember. He used to bounce me on his knee. My concern was for my child and for all the children he may have already victimized. *(Pointing at JOE.)* God only knows what he's capable of. Isn't one defenseless victim enough?

JUNIOR: *Yeah.* I know karate and I could've given him a good chop if I wanted to.

THE MOTHER: His father and me want to make sure our little boy can protect himself. *(Pointing at JOE.)* But, look at the size of that brute! He might have murdered my little boy right then and there so he could hide his dirty shame! His type are capable of that sort of thing. Everybody knows that. And then what? *Huh, huh?*

JUNIOR: *(Pointing at JOE.)* He did it! I know he did it! He touched my butt-hole! I know he did 'cause I was waitin' for him to try somethin' funny just like mommy said he would. And he did! He did! *I felt it!* Don't tell me I didn't feel it 'cause I did! I know how it feels when somebody touches your butt-hole. You can ask mommy if you think I don't 'cause I do!

THE MOTHER: And that's the truth!

THE LAWYER: Thank you. You may step down. *(THE MOTHER steps down from the stand and exits. CONRAD, also, exits.)* The defendant will please take the stand. *(THE LAWYER exits.)*

JOE: *(Crosses to the stand. Raises his right hand.)* So help me, God. *(Lowers his hand. Directly to the audience.)* I have told you exactly what happened that day in the studio and I have told you the truth. So, if there are any doubts left concerning my sexual preference let me make it perfectly clear who and what I am . . . I am homosexual and I am proud that I am homosexual I am who I am. For me, being homosexual is far more than just a way for having sex. It is a kind of sensibility—sensitive to the thoughts and words left unsaid by others. When seemingly good people hide behind the religions of the world to threaten, not only your existence here on Earth, but your immortal soul—you learn to listen. And if you fail to hear and respond to the dangers hidden in another man's heart, then today's subtleties can very quickly become tomorrow's atrocities.

To be homosexual is to know the pain of a prejudice so ingrained in our society that it can turn our families and loved ones against us. Who but us—the dregs of society— could know better how to judge and accept a man on his own merits? I am tired of rolling over and playing dead or playing the fool for all those who think I don't belong. *I do belong.* I am not sick, perverted or condemned. I am tired of listening to prejudice of any kind. And, when it comes under the banner of religious and moral doctrine—of family values—I am ashamed for Humanity itself. Family values without Human values are of no value at all.

I am tired of pretending I don't hear all the slurs and innuendo in conversations that make me blush with shame for not having the strength of my convictions to stand up for myself and others who are at the brunt of those disparaging remarks. Here I stand, gay and proud, tired of remaining silent. A slur about a Jew, an Arab, a Mexican, a Native American, or an Afro-American is a slur about me. To dishonor any man's or woman's heritage is to dishonor my own. *Here I stand.*

Is this planet so small that there is no room for us all? What have we done to deserve so many slurs and fists that would chase us and beat us out of existence simply for being who we are? I have cried and cried for an answer. *Well, no more tears!* No one, any longer, will determine how I feel about myself. I am tired of running and I am tired of hiding. *Here I stand. Here I am. Here. Now. Forever. I am homosexual.* I have lost my house, my business, my income, those friends I thought I had—and I almost lost my lover, but I have not lost nor will I lose my dignity. All that I am . . . all that I own . . . stands before you. I am homosexual and I am, in no way, guilty.

The LIGHTING slowly fades to BLACK OUT.

END ACT TWO—*Scene 7*

ACT TWO—*Scene 8*—*the bridge*

The three hooded-cloaked TORMENTORS appear and mill about in the shadows and fog beneath the bridge. In rasping whispers they call JOE'S name. JOE becomes aware of their presence and slowly rises and approaches them. He moves with them and around them and yet they do not seem to be aware of his presence. Blindly, they continue calling out his name. JOE waves his hands in front of their unseen faces and still they do not respond. The TORMENTORS continue to haunt the shadows and fog as JOE ascends the bridge.

JOE: *(From the bridge, he removes a silver key on a long silver chain from his pocket. To the audience.)* The key. My father's key. It was in my pocket all this time. *(He holds the key, watching it dangle from its chain before letting it drop to the floor below.*

(The TORMENTORS scramble to retrieve it. When one does, they disappear into the shadows, greedily fighting among themselves for possession of it.)

JOE *(Continued.):* Love. All it was—was love. That's all there is, really.*(After a pause.)* Connie and I will leave tomorrow to begin a new life. Tomorrow. Tomorrow is only a dream away . . . the moon away.

As the LIGHTING slowly dims a large golden moon rises behind the bridge before fading to BLACK OUT.

END OF PLAY

DESERT DEVILS

SYNOPSIS: (4W, One Set, Full Length.) Set in the formerly oil-rich desert Southwest, *Desert Devils* explores the lives of three generations of women living under one roof. The story centers on Jo who, after her father dies, takes in her feisty mother. Jo's daughter, Leota Ruth, a self-mutilating poet approaching middle-age, is also in her mother's care. The dialogue between them and with a long-time neighbor is, at once, outrageously funny and heart-breakingly tragic. These women tear and rip into one another's psyche with reckless abandon and something barely resembling love. The cookies in question may or may not be poisoned, but just beneath the surface these women hide a more potent poison—the deadly venom accumulated over years of unfulfilled dreams mixed with the sudden and bitter acceptance of a life unrealized.

1st place winner of the Panhandle Playwrights Festival, *Desert Devils* directed by Boone Smith was produced by the Amarillo Repertory Company in Amarillo, TX where it premiered May 30, 2008 with the following cast:

JO – Jessica Burton
Billie – Terri Morgan
Leota Ruth – Sarah Freeman
Mamma – Lorie Kiehl

"Without giving away the ending, Desert Devils leaves audiences questioning how they impact others in their own lives, and what we can all be driven to through the destructive nature of others. Edward Crosby Wells leaves us with a deeply interwoven plot full of twists and uncertainties, convincing both young and old to challenge the very core elements of the play.
—Nathan Furry, *Yass Tribune, New South Wales*

THE SETTING: *Jo*'s kitchen/dining room. A lower middle-class motif. Extremely clean and well organized. Lots of plastic: a plastic napkin holder, salt and pepper shakers, food storage containers, canisters and plastic mixing bowls, plastic ornaments on the walls, plastic fruit in a plastic bowl. And little wooden do-dads: A wooden memo pad holder, a wooden rack from which to hang keys – a souvenir from some past summer vacation. More souvenirs of questionable worth, although of an utilitarian nature: A toothpick holder from Carlsbad Caverns, a straw dispenser from Corpus Christi, and a bread box from El Paso. On the walls hang scenic plates: An oil well from Midland, Texas, the White House and the Alamo. There is one plate with the face of Jesus painted on it and another with the face of Elvis Presley. Downstage – looking out over the audience – the curtained window of the kitchen hosts no live potted plants; organic life other than human would only serve as breeding ground for germs and other things considered by Jo as "dirty." However, a neat arrangement of plastic flowers with glitter glued on their petals sits fading in the center of the dining table. Somewhere stands an ironing board and near it is a plastic basket bulging with clothes to be ironed.

THE PLACE: Hobbs, New Mexico—a small city in southeastern New Mexico, a mile from the West Texas border.

THE TIME: Late 1980s—mid-morning on a Monday in August. The weather is sunny and hot.

THE CHARACTERS:
JO: A woman in her fifties or sixties.
BILLIE: Jo's friend and neighbor, the same age as Jo.
LEOTA RUTH: Jo's daughter, late thirties to early forties.
MAMMAW: (pronounced ma'am-ah) Jo's Mother.

ACT ONE

AT RISE: Perhaps "Don't Be Cruel" sung by Elvis Presley is playing on the radio.

BILLIE, a large bulk of a woman with her hair in rollers is seated at the kitchen table, painting her toenails and sometimes knitting.

JO is slender and bony by comparison and prone to move about the kitchen bird-like—pecking here and there, searching for something to clean or polish, something to do. In JO's forever-scrutinizing eyes it is her duty as a housewife to see that all the household chores are done and when they are, it is her duty to create new ones; however mundane they may be. She wears a cobbler's apron filled with all sorts of cleaning supplies that she uses, more often than not, throughout the course of the play.

JO: *(Running her hands down along the curtains hanging on the kitchen window. Sighs, nodding her head negatively.)* I don't know. Honest to God, I really just don't know.

BILLIE: *(Stops polishing her toenails.)* Well, what kind of material did you have in mind?

JO: Don't know that I had any kind in mind, Billie. *(Crosses to turn off radio.)*

BILLIE: You'll be wanting something cheery.

JO: Why?

BILLIE: All right. You want something gloomy and dingy and ugly as sin, right? *(Picks up her knitting.)*

JO: You go to such extremes.

BILLIE: You want my input or not?

JO: *Input?* I don't even like the sound of that! *(Dusts something.)*

BILLIE: Input is a perfectly good word. It means putting in ones—

JO: *Two cents?*

BILLIE: *(Unruffled.)* Putting in one's . . . ideas about a thing.

JO: You mean *opinion.*

BILLIE: Well, yes. You could say that.

JO: Then, why didn't you?

BILLIE: What's wrong with the ones you got, anyway?

JO: Whoever said there was anything wrong with them?

BILLIE: Excuse me, but I'm sure I heard somebody say not two minutes ago in this very room that she wanted to change out the curtains in that there window. J

JO: That don't mean there's got to be something wrong with them. I'm just tired of looking at them, that's all.

BILLIE: *(Studying curtains.)* Hmmm. Oh, well maybe you're right, Jo. I don't know.

JO: *(Polishing something.)* You don't know what?

BILLIE: I don't know if I'm tired of looking at them or not.

JO: Why should you be?

BILLIE: I see those curtains often enough, don't I?

JO: Not half as much as me.

BILLIE: No . . . not nearly so much.

JO: Then, who cares? I'm the one who's got to look at them day and night. Not you. You can go next door and look at your own curtains. You don't got to live with them like I do.

BILLIE: No. Not like you do. *(Rises and goes to cabinet, searching for something.)*

JO: Who cares? That's all I've got to say . . . *who cares*. *(Watching BILLIE.)* Now what?

BILLIE: Something to nibble on with my coffee—*acid*. One should never drink too much coffee all on its own—too much acid.

JO: *(Reaches into a nearby cabinet and removes a plastic container filled with sugar cookies – handing BILLIE the cookies.)* Here. I made them yesterday.

BILLIE: Sugar cookies! My favorite!

JO: You say that about *all* cookies.

BILLIE: I do not.

JO: You do too. Last week peanut butter cookies was your favorite. The week before that it was tollhouse.

BILLIE: I love tollhouse.

JO: See what I mean?

BILLIE: Well, next to tollhouse, sugar cookies are my absolute favorite.

JO: Rats', too.

BILLIE: Rats?

JO: That's what I put down for the rats. *(Gets coffeepot.)*

BILLIE: You feed your rats?

JO: I don't have any rats . . . not anymore. *Coffee?*

BILLIE: Please. *(Polishing off a cookie.)* Delicious. You must give me your recipe.

JO: *(Pouring coffee.)* The one for people or the one for rats?

BILLIE: The one for people, of course. I don't have rats.

JO: You don't?

BILLIE: No. The very idea—

JO: They had to come from somewhere.

BILLIE: If you're hinting that I have rats and that they somehow carpet-bagged their way over here under my fence, you're sadly mistaken. What about Clara on the other side? They could've come from her, you know.

JO: As clean as she is? Don't be silly.

BILLIE: Well, I don't have rats. I never did have rats. And, I certainly don't intend to get any! But, if I did, I wouldn't be feeding them cookies. *Poison.* I'd feed them poison. *(Pauses to examine cookie.)* Jo, what's the difference between the people recipe and the rat recipe?

JO: Margarine instead of butter.

BILLIE: Practical.

JO: *Imitation* vanilla extract.
BILLIE: Smart. Why waste the real thing on rats.

JO And an extra cup of sugar.

BILLIE: They like them sweet, huh?

JO How would I know? The extra sugar counteracts the taste of the poison.

BILLIE: How would you know that? I mean, it could be sweet already. It seems to me, if you're going to make a poison, you're going to make it attractive to the thing you wanna kill.

JO: You think so, huh?

BILLIE: Maybe the extra sugar counteracts the taste of the cheese.

JO: What cheese?

BILLIE: In the rat poison.

JO: There ain't no cheese in the rat poison.

BILLIE: How do you know? Did you taste it?

JO: No. I didn't taste it.

BILLIE: *(Pause.)* Well, you ought to. *(Beat)* I bet it tastes like cheese.

JO: It could taste like chicken fried steak, for all I care.

BILLIE: *That's it.* I'll make chicken fry for dinner. Thanks, Jo.

JO: Don't mention it.

BILLIE So, instead of sugar on the top, you sprinkle on a little rat poison. . .
JO: No. I mix it in with the batter—a lot of rat poison.

BILLIE: *(Spitting out cookie. Soggy crumbs fly across the table.)* What?

JO: *Look at the mess you're making.* You don't really think I'm going to feed my best friend cookies I baked for the rats, do you?

BILLIE: *(Thinking.)* No. I guess not.

JO: Then stop acting like a retard. Look what you went and did. You got coffee and crumbs all over my arrangement. *(Examines the arrangement of plastic flowers setting on the table.)* Something else to clean.

BILLIE: I'll do it.

JO: You just stay put. *(Rises and crosses to drawer under counter.)* I'll take care of it . . . just like I have to do everything else around here.

BILLIE: Whatever. *(Removing the rollers from her hair. After a pause.)* Any news about H.O.?

JO: *(Searching through drawer.)* Nothing more than I told you yesterday. *(Removes metal Band-Aid container, closes drawer.)* They're going to send him home tomorrow. That's all I know. *(Crosses to table, sits and removes Q-tips from container and begins to clean plastic floral arrangement, meticulously.)* Ugh. What a filthy mess.

BILLIE: That's not all me.

JO: Billie, did I say it was?

BILLIE: No.

JO: Then don't go putting words in my mouth.

BILLIE: Did they find out what made him take such a fit?

JO: Some kind of stomach thing, that's all I know.

BILLIE: Well, something ain't right. I mean, a man just don't start foaming at the mouth in the middle of Tootie's and take to ripping all the plastic off all the chickens in the meat case.

JO: He said he wanted to set them free.

BILLIE: Free? Free to do what?

JO: I don't know! Fly away, maybe.

BILLIE: Jo, chickens can't fly away.

JO *(More to herself.)* I suppose H.O. will be moping around the house all week, expecting me to wait on him hand and foot.

BILLIE: They hop.

JO: What?

BILLIE: *Hop, hop.* Chickens kinda run and hop. I'm sure they don't fly. *(Demonstrates.)*

JO: What on Earth are you talking about?

BILLIE: Chickens. You said ol' H.O. took the plastic off so they could fly away.

JO: I didn't say any such thing.

BILLIE: *Oh,* I could've sworn—

JO: 'Sides, they was quartered.

BILLIE: *Quartered?* That pretty much puts an end to hopping, too, don't it?

JO: What is wrong with you this morning? You take a stupid-pill or something?

BILLIE: No. Took a water pill . . . bloat.

JO: Well, you better be careful. You're liable to end up with brain-rot!

BILLIE: I know you don't mean to hurt me, Jo, but you do sometimes. You know that, don'tcha? *(No response.)* Jo, is something bothering you this morning? I mean, more than usual.

JO: *(Returns to table and sits – resumes cleaning plastic floral arrangement with Q-tip.)* Ain't nothin' bothering me.

BILLIE: Well, you're not yourself.

JO: Who am I?

BILLIE: Don't you know?

JO: I know I'm someone who's tired. Just tired.

BILLIE: I didn't sleep well last night, either. Sanford dog barked all night. Did you hear it?

JO: No.

BILLIE: When Georgie's home, dogs don't bark all night.

JO: Course they do.

BILLIE: Oh, no. Georgie gets out there and yells once and you don't hear another yap all night.
JO: Well, it ain't got nothing to do with sleep. I'm just tired. Tired of taking care of people. Tired of living. Tired of not living. Tired. Just tired. Don'tcha get it?

BILLIE: How dense do you think I am, Jo? I understand more than you think.

JO: When's my turn, *huh?* I thought when we retired we were gonna do things—travel maybe. Visit some of H.O.'s folks up north.

BILLIE: You can still do that.

JO: Sure, with mother to take care of—

BILLIE: Mammaw can take care of herself. She's got more energy than any two people I know.

JO: And then there's—poor thing—Leota Ruth. Couldn't tie her own shoelaces on a bet.

BILLIE: Of course she can.

JO: It's a figure of speech, Billie. *Honestly.* She's been three times over in that mental health unit this year alone.

BILLIE: Maybe she'll have no cause to go again.

JO: A lot you know. Once you got it you got it for life. All you can do is medicate it.

BILLIE: What exactly has she got?

JO: She's crazy, Billie. She sees things and hears things that don't exist.

BILLIE: Maybe she's one of those psychics.

JO: You mean psychos.

BILLIE: No. I mean, like special extra-terrestrial gifted or something like that.

JO She ain't no such thing! Where do you get your crazy ideas?

BILLIE: There's solid proof that people like that exist.

JO: Not in Hobbs, New Mexico.

BILLIE: Well, maybe she'll meet someone real nice, get married, and move on.

JO: *Yeah ...* and maybe Publisher's Clearing House will give me ten million dollars.

BILLIE: Stranger things have happened. You never know.

JO: *(Disregarding the last.)* And, Howie Boy—sending him all our extra money so he can eat and pay his rent.

BILLIE: He's over forty, Jo. He hadn't ought to be drainin' you so.

JO: He's a songwriter. It takes time to break into the business.

BILLIE: Still, he's too tied to his mama, if you ask me.

JO: *(Warning.)* Ain't no one asking you, Billie.

BILLIE: Sorry. You got all the cotton plumb wore off that Q-tip. *(JO frowns and takes out a fresh Q-tip. A pause.)* What do you suppose the "Q" stands for?

JO: What?

BILLIE: The "Q" in Q-tip. What do you suppose it stands for?

JO: It don't stand for nothin'.

BILLIE: It's gotta stand for something.

JO: Why? Because you say so?

BILLIE: Quick. Quick-tip, that's it!

JO: I got things to do, Billie. I can't sit around all day like some people I know.

BILLIE: What is that supposed to mean?

JO: What is what supposed to mean?

BILLIE: You think I sit around all day and do nothing, don'tcha?

JO: Why does the world always have to revolve around you, huh? You always think I'm talking about you. There are other people walking around this planet, too.

BILLIE: Then, who? Who, Jo? Who? Who did you have in mind?

JO: I don't know who. Honest to God! *Miz Astor. That's who.* (Rises and throws Q-tip onto table.)

BILLIE: You meant me. You had me in mind.

JO: *(Squirts back of chair with cleaner taken from out her cobbler's apron and proceeds to wipe chair dry.)* I didn't have nobody in mind, Billie. Nobody. H.O.'s coming home tomorrow and there's things to get done. You know how men are. Get a little tummy ache and it's "get me this" and "get me that." There ain't nothing more helpless than a grown man outta sorts.

BILLIE: Still, it's nice to have a man around the house.

JO: Why don't you just die and stay stupid!

BILLIE: You're not as humorous as you think, Jo. You can abuse me all you like, but what goes 'round comes 'round.

JO: So you say.

BILLIE: It's a fact, Jo. As ye sow so shall ye reap.

JO: Don't you quote to me, missy. You wanna do that kind of thing you go down the street corner and quote to somebody who cares. Not to me—not in my house.

BILLIE: *(Demurely.)* Elvis would have agreed.

JO: How dare you? How dare you?

BILLIE: Well . . . he would have.

JO: Don't you ever disgrace the name of Elvis Presley while you're sitting under my roof again! Elvis was a saint! *(Crosses to 'Elvis' plate.)*

BILLIE: For God's sake, Jo, he weren't nothin' but a singer.

JO: A singer? A singer? *(Holding 'Elvis" plate – with maniacal restraint.)* An instrument of God, Billie! A saint among men, martyred! Taken to the Lord's breast in his prime . . . murdered!

BILLIE: Nobody murdered him, Jo. He did it to himself.

JO: How dare you?

BILLIE: Drugs, Jo. He took drugs.

JO: He was murdered! Cut down by the American Medical Association—a branch of the Mafia!

BILLIE *(Resigned.)* All right. Whatever you say.

JO: No. No, it's not all right because I say it. It's all right because it's the truth! *(Dusts 'Elvis' plate.)*

BILLIE: Okay, okay.

JO: Don't you ever disgrace the good name of Elvis Presley in this house ever again.

BILLIE: All right. I'm sorry. Okay?

JO: Never again. *(Replaces the 'Elvis' plate and gives the 'Jesus' plate a quick flick of the duster, almost as an afterthought.)*

BILLIE: *(Anxious to change the subject.)* I found a penny head's up this morning. That's good luck, isn't it?

JO: *(Returning to table – sits.)* It ain't nothin' but superstitious junk. How a grown woman can believe in that kind of nonsense is beyond me.

BILLIE: I never said I believed in it. *(Gathers up her knitting and hair rollers.)* I think I'll be heading home.

JO: Why? Got something better to do?

BILLIE: Maybe.

JO: I'm sure it ain't housework. B

BILLIE: *(Dropping her belongings back onto the table.)* Jo, my house is my business! You can clean, scrub, make a fool of yourself all you like. I don't care. Who've I got to clean for? Georgie ain't home but three or four days a month.

JO: Well, that's what you get for marrying a rodeo man.

BILLIE: *Humph—*

JO: But, since you bring it up, you can't exactly eat off your kitchen floor, can you?

BILLIE: I don't know. Do you need an answer right away?

JO: You can eat off mine.

BILLIE: Yes, Jo. You can eat off yours. I'll stay at the table if you don't mind.

JO: It's just a figure of speech.

BILLIE: *(Stands.)* Of course it is. It's your quaint, not to say "bitchy", way of telling me I'm dirty.

JO: I never said any such thing.

BILLIE: Not directly, no. You don't know how to be that honest.

JO: *(Stands – face to face.)* Honest? You want honest? Your house is a pigsty.

BILLIE: That's not honest. That's cruel, unnecessary, and rude. *(Sits.)*

JO: You asked for it. *(Sits and starts cleaning flowers with Q-tip.)*

BILLIE: This compulsive addiction you have for housewifery is a sickness, don'tcha know.

JO: So is living in filth.

BILLIE: Look at yourself polishing that there bunch of plastic flowers with a Q-tip. That's sane?

JO: It's my job.

BILLIE: Only because you make it so. Why don'tcha just dump it in the sink and run water over it?

JO: Because that's not the way it's done.

BILLIE: That's the way I'd do it.

JO: Well, that's your problem, isn't it?

BILLIE: *(Suddenly.)* Cushion!

JO: What?

BILLIE: Cushion-tip! That's what the "Q" stand for—cushion-tip.

JO: Cushion don't start with a "Q". It starts with a "C", stupid.

BILLIE: Oh, that's right. I wonder what I could've been thinking of?

JO: There's no telling.

(LEOTA RUTH enters from outside with the laces of her walking shoes dragging along the floor, untied. There is something fragile, haunting, and haunted about her. She appears as a frightened animal – always on the lookout for some hidden, silent predator. Whatever she is wearing must have long sleeves. She is carrying a bouquet of wild flowers.)

BILLIE: Well, I'm sure I was thinking of something.

LEOTA RUTH: *(Announces.)* Getting warm out there. *(Looks for confirmation. None comes.)* Three dimensional. Almost surreal. Silent . . . except for the sound of dragonfly wings . . . and the unremarkable sounds of uncaring, unknowable distance. And in the silence rocks languish while life spins and sputters by. They do nothing. They know nothing. They are rocks.

JO: *(Sotto voce.)* Oh, for God's sake.

LEOTA RUTH: *(Turning to BILLIE. After a pause.)* Morning, Missus Patterson. And how are you today?

BILLIE: *(Through a nervous, forced smile. She is not comfortable around LEOTA RUTH.)* Fine, thank you.

LEOTA RUTH: *(Finding a tall water glass for the flowers. After a pause.)* And I am fine, too, thank you. (Arranging flowers in glass.) Do you think flowers feel? Do they scream with pain as you gather them up into a bouquet? *(She looks about the room for an answer. There is only SILENCE.)* No. I suppose not. How could they? They are too beautiful.

Beautiful things do not feel. *(No response. After a pause.)* Others feel for them. Do you think?

JO: Leota Ruth, you know I don't want those filthy things in the house!

LEOTA RUTH: They are not filthy, mother. They are as clean as something proverbial. Honest. I shook them really well. I will put them in my room where they cannot bother you with their untamed and natural essence.

JO: Don't you have enough junk in your room already?

LEOTA RUTH: Is that rhetorical?

BILLIE: (Suddenly.) I know! I was thinking of quiet. Quiet-tip! You know, like cushion-quiet?

JO: Oh, for God's sake! I live in a loony bin.

LEOTA RUTH: That is inspired, Missus Patterson. *(Creating a poem extemporaneously.)*
The calico cat
On cushion-quiet feet
Leapt into her waiting heart
Looking for love
But love was never there
And the calico cat died of despair
(BILLIE and JO share a hopeless look. After a pause.)
Perhaps, it should be leaped into her waiting heart. No one says leapt anymore. What do you say, mother?

JO: About what?

LEOTA RUTH: Leapt or leaped?

JO: Did you take your medication today?

LEOTA RUTH: Yes. With my orange. Leaped is, of course, more prosaic, isn't it?

JO: I don't know what on Earth you're talking about.

LEOTA RUTH: Maybe I'm not talking about anything on Earth. Just abstractions. Wild things. Divine things. Ultimately, beauty is an affliction and the consciousness of it cannot endure its own demise. How sad.

JO: For the love of God, Leota Ruth, they ain't nothin' but stupid old weeds!

BILLIE: No. I was right the first time. Quick-tip. I bet the "Q" stands for quick.

LEOTA RUTH: You can only grow a weed in a garden, mother. In the desert there are only flowers—free and wild.

JO: Are you sure you took your medication?

LEOTA RUTH: Quite sure.

JO: I didn't see you.

LEOTA RUTH: One seldom sees more than one wants. Is that not right, Missus Patterson?
BILLIE: Excuse me?

LEOTA RUTH: My shoes. They seem to have come untied. *(While holding the glass of flowers, she puts her foot on the chair next to BILLIE.)* Would you mind? My hands are full at the moment. *(BILLIE ties the shoelace.)* Thank you. Thank you so much. *(Switches feet.)* This one, too, I'm afraid. *(BILLIE ties the other lace.)* Sometimes, mother worries needlessly. I mean, I know how to tie my own shoes, of course. But, I must be a constant source of doubt for her, nonetheless. Sometimes, when your hands are full, you need the help of others. Do you think? *(BILLIE forces a smile.)* I worry so, too. I worry that I will trip over my own laces one day, step outside of time and space, and life will stroll on down that endless and tedious road without me—forgetting I was ever here. Not a trace. Gone. Where does it all go, Missus Patterson—those little variations in time and space we call our lives?

BILLIE: *Huh?*

LEOTA RUTH: Time. The times of your life. *(After a pause.)* Do you ever remember the future, Missus Patterson?

BILLIE: Well, I . . . I don't see how that's possible.

LEOTA RUTH: Most people don't. *(Crosses to window.)* But it is possible. Quite possible.

JO: Will you stop bothering Billie with your silliness.

LEOTA RUTH: Are we going to the fabric store this morning?

JO: I don't know. I haven't made up my mind.

LEOTA RUTH: Nor I. But, I don't think so. I cannot remember clearly. Maybe it's the fabric store, or maybe it's somewhere else. I wonder what that means—to make up ones mind.

JO: For pity's sake, Leota Ruth, it means you make a decision and you stick to it. It don't mean nothin' more than that.

LEOTA RUTH: Is that a good thing?

JO: Look, if you need me to call your doctor, I will.

LEOTA RUTH: Why, mother?

JO: Well, you seem . . . *troubled.*

LEOTA RUTH: Do I trouble you, mother? Are you afraid I am going to slash my wrists again?

JO: *(Irritated.)* That's not what I meant.

LEOTA RUTH: *(Looking out window.)* There's a whole lot of nothing out there. Nothingness stretching into the horizon —unaware, unknowing, uncaring. There is so much in life that has nothing to do with life. One wonders why it exists. *(Crosses to exit to her room with the glass of flowers.)* You needn't worry, mother. I shall put a towel under the flowers to collect anything you might find disagreeable. *(She exits.)*

JO: *(Watches her exit. After a pause.)* She does it on purpose.

BILLIE: It?

JO: Goes out of her way to make me feel guilty.

BILLIE Guilty of what?

JO: *(After a scrutinizing pause.)* Is that a trick question?

BILLIE: No, Jo. You said you felt guilty.

JO: Well, I'm not! I'm not guilty of anything!

BILLIE: We're all guilty of something.

JO: Speak for yourself, Billie. *(After a pause.)* She gets crazier by the day.

BILLIE: Oh, I don't think so. She's just . . . well . . . a bit peculiar, that's all.

JO: I suppose slashing her wrists is just a bit peculiar, too, huh?

BILLIE: That was nearly a year ago, Jo. I thought you said the doctor said she was all right now.

JO: Are you deaf? Does she sound all right to you?

BILLIE: Well . . .

JO: She carves on herself with razor blades.

BILLIE: What?

JO: You heard me. She carves on herself with razor blades—her arms, her legs.

BILLIE: Jo, I can't believe—

JO: Why do you think she dresses the way she does—covering her arms in this heat?

BILLIE: I'm sure I don't know, but—

JO: I'm telling you. A few weeks ago I walked into her room and caught her. She was sitting on the end of her bed with a razor blade, carving on her arm.

BILLIE: What kind of razor blade?

JO: What does it matter what kind of razor blade? A razor blade, Billie!

BILLIE: Well, that sort of thing is hard to see. Maybe you were mistaken.

JO: I wasn't mistaken.

BILLIE: What did you do?

JO: I dropped her laundry and ran out.

BILLIE: What did she say?

JO: Nothing. She never mentioned it. It was like she was in a trance or somethin' and never even seen I was there.

BILLIE: Didn't you confront her about it?

JO: No. She'd only deny it anyway.

BILLIE: But the proof is there. It doesn't matter if she denies it. Did you call her doctor?

JO: What good would that do, huh? All that bitch doctor does is help her find more excuses to hate H.O. and me—more ways to make us guilty for her craziness. I swear, Billie, the next time she takes a razor to her wrists I won't care if she . . .

BILLIE: *(Stopping her.)* Don't say it, Jo.

JO: Why not? It's the truth, ain't it?

BILLIE: No. It's not the truth. You're her mother.

JO: Am I?

BILLIE: Well, of course you are. I was there, remember?

JO: *(Disregarding the last.)* Sometimes I wish I was dead.

BILLIE: No, you don't. Life's too short for those kinds of thoughts, Jo.

JO: Why don't you just shut up? I'm sick to death of your stupid sayings. I've heard them all a thousand times before.

BILLIE: Well, maybe you needed to hear them a thousand times. *(JO glares. After a pause.)* You're turning into an old lady, you know that?

JO: Look. I'm fixing to say something spiteful. 'Sides, I am an old lady. *(Crosses to ironing board – begins ironing a pair of H.O.'s boxer shorts.)*

BILLIE: By choice. You don't need to be. *(Bites into cookie, sips coffee.)* You were the sweetest thing in grade school.

JO: Weren't we all.

BILLIE: *(Resumes knitting.)* No, Jo. You were different. Everybody liked you . . . then. And in high school you were a regular hell-raiser and, still, everybody liked you. All those boys chasing after you. You. Not me. You . . . always you. I didn't even have a date for the prom.
JO: Yes, you did. H.O. took you, as I recall.

BILLIE: I took him.

JO: Same difference.

BILLIE: No, it's not. Do you know how humiliating that was? I had to buy my own corsage.

JO: He was broke.

BILLIE: He was saving up to marry you come the end of June.

JO: You knew we was engaged. And if I hadn't broke my leg falling off the running board of that Packard of yours, you wouldn't have had H.O. to go with.

BILLIE: Well, who asked you to go and try to jump on it just as I was pulling out of the driveway?

JO: You always put on the brakes before.

BILLIE: Maybe I was in a hurry that time.

JO: Ain't never been in a hurry before.

BILLIE: We've been over this time and again and we already decided it was your fault.

JO: I'm not saying it wasn't and I'm not saying it was.

BILLIE: Well, it was.

JO: I'm just saying, be thankful you had somebody to go to the prom with. I mean, considering. You know, Billie, you ought to count your blessings. 'Sides, if you had the good sense to push yourself away from the table a bit more often, maybe some of the boys might've taken a keener interest . . . if you know what I mean.

BILLIE: Oh, I know what you mean all right. Maybe I just didn't want to end up an old lady, waxing and polishing and Q-tipping my life away.

JO: You married George Patterson, didn't you?
BILLIE: He's different. We're more friends than anything else.

JO: Friends?

BILLIE: That's right . . . friends.

JO: Billie, a husband ain't supposed to be your friend. He's supposed to be someone you cook for and clean for. Wash and iron for. Mend for. Call the boss up for and lie for. Raise children for. Get your hair done for. If you want friends, you join the Mormons!

BILLIE: Georgie never expects anything from me but me.

JO: And that's how you picked up your filthy ways.

BILLIE: He doesn't want a house-slave, if that's what you mean.

JO: Is that what you think I am?

BILLIE: Well, I wasn't referring to the Queen of England.

JO: *Humph.* You're dumber than the day you were born.

BILLIE: Then, so are you!

JO: *(After a pause to glare, she turns toward the window.)* Yellow.

BILLIE: What?

JO: Yellow! Yellow! Something wrong with your hearing? I think I want something in yellow.

BILLIE: What? A dress?

JO: No, stupid. Curtains. We was talking about curtains, weren't we?

BILLIE: Oh. Well, yellow's nice.

JO: That's what I said, isn't it? *(The TELEPHONE RINGS.)*

BILLIE: *(After it rings a couple times.)* Telephone.

JO: I got ears, don't I? *(Crosses to telephone.)* I wonder who could be botherin' me now?

BILLIE: Maybe it's H.O. calling from the hospital.

JO: *(Into telephone.)* Yeah? Yeah . . . Yeah . . . No . . . No . . . No. Wouldn't you like to know! Suppose I don't want to have a nice day? Goodbye to you, too! *(Slams down telephone.)*

BILLIE: Who was that?

JO: Computer.

BILLIE: Didn't think it was H.O. What did it want?

JO: Information.

BILLIE: What kind of information?

JO: The nosy kind!

(MAMMAW enters. In spite of her age – maybe because of it – it is her spunky youthfulness that strikes us. LEOTA RUTH follows her.)

MAMMAW: *(Entering from the direction of her room. To LEOTA RUTH.)* Now watch if she don't lie about this one. *(To JO.)* Was that for me?

JO: Was what for you?

MAMMAW: The phone.

JO: No, mother. It wasn't for you.

MAMMAW: *(To LEOTA RUTH.)* She wouldn't tell me if it was.

JO: You know that's a lie, mother.

BILLIE: Good morning, Mammaw.

MAMMAW: *(To JO.)* You never tell me when Howie Boy calls. *(To BILLIE.)* Mornin'. Stuffin' your face again, I see. *(To LEOTA RUTH who is staring out the kitchen window.)* She never tells me when your brother calls.

JO: I do too! Only sometimes he don't ask for you. Sometimes he only wants to speak to his mother.

LEOTA RUTH: Did Howard call?

JO: No, he didn't call.

MAMMAW: Funny thing when a boy don't want to talk to his Mammaw.

JO: Well, sometimes he's in a rush.

MAMMAW: *(To BILLIE.)* That's her story. Gained some weight since I seen you last.

JO: It ain't a story, mother!

BILLIE That was only yesterday. I took a water pill. I lost some since yesterday.

MAMMAW: That's your story. *(To JO.)* Then, who called? *(To LEOTA RUTH.)* See if she don't lie about this.

JO: For your information it was a computer that called.

MAMMAW: Did it ask for you?

JO: No, mother. It didn't ask for nobody.

MAMMAW: Then how do you know it wasn't for me? *(To BILLIE.)* She does this all the time.

JO: No, I don't, mother.

MAMMAW: *(To BILLIE.)* She hoards all the mail what comes for "occupant." *(To JO, while going through discarded mail in waste basket.)* Now don't lie about that, sister.

JO: I don't know what you're talking about.

MAMMAW: That's never stopped you before. *(To BILLIE.)* She's got something to say about everything. Don't know a dang thing—never did. Thinks she knows more than Dan Rather, she does.

LEOTA RUTH: Mammaw met some aliens up in Roswell.

JO: There's aliens all over, Leota Ruth. You don't need to go up to Roswell. Just go to the supermarket. They're generally the ones usin' food stamps.

LEOTA RUTH: Not that kind of alien. Real aliens. The kind that come from outer space—or maybe from another dimension right here on Earth.

BILLIE: *(Making fun.)* Really? Little and green?

MAMMAW: That shows how much you know, Miss Smarty Always Feeding Her Face. They was yellow—like a ripe banana. They smelled a bit ripe, too.

LEOTA RUTH: Tell them what they wore, Mammaw.

JO: Am I the only sane person in this house?

LEOTA RUTH: Tell them, Mammaw. Tell them.

MAMMAW: Hawaiian shirts and sunglasses.

JO: Aliens don't wear Hawaiian shirts and sunglasses.

MAMMAW: How do you know? You ever seen one?

JO: No, of course not. But if there was such a thing, they ain't gonna be wearin' Hawaiian shirts and sunglasses.

BILLIE: Well, maybe sunglasses, Jo.

JO: Shut up, Billie!

LEOTA RUTH: They were incognito. They were trying not to be conspicuous.

MAMMAW: That's right. *(To JO.)* Tryin' to hide from nosy people like you, sister.

BILLIE: When was this, Mammaw?

JO: For pity's sake! Don't egg her on!

MAMMAW: Now let me think. Summer of '57, I believe. Yeah. I was helping Rosie and Kirby at the truck stop. That was the summer Rosie dislocated her shoulder. No . . . hip. Somethin' anyway. She was always dislocating something.

JO: Mother, you don't know what you're talking about.

MAMMAW: Don't tell me. She stepped into a prairie dog hole and liked to fall to China. Threw her back out—got dislocated.

BILLIE: That's terrible.

MAMMAW: They always was lousy rodents.

BILLIE: *Aunt Rosie and Uncle Kirby?*

MAMMAW: Prairie dogs.

BILLIE: Mean little buggers.

MAMMAW: That ain't the half of it. I saw a family of 'em chew the leg off a hobo once.

JO: Aliens?

MAMMAW: Prairie dogs. But that was over in Brownfield. Stupid man. He was doing some day labor for Burty Babcock who paid him in prickly pear moonshine. Drunk as a skunk, he was. Anyway, ten years earlier some of their friends crash-landed somewhere 'round Roswell and they was sent to find them.

BILLIE: Rosie and Kirby?

MAMMAW: Aliens. You really ought to learn to pay attention.

LEOTA RUTH: Ten years and they still hadn't given up. One could learn a lot from the compassion of an extraterrestrial. They must have come from a very caring civilization.

JO: *(To LEOTA RUTH.)* They didn't come from no such place. There ain't no such thing as a caring civilization. Out of your Mammaw's head, that's where they came from.

MAMMAW: *(To JO.)* Sister, I know what I saw. I was the one to wait on 'em. They ordered pancakes with a side order of Rosie's gut-buster chili. *(Nudging BILLIE.)* You'd like that 'stead of those poison cookies of sister's.

JO: Mother!

MAMMAW: They was . . . Leota Ruth, what's that called when people can talk to you inside your head?

LEOTA RUTH: Telepathy?

JO: *(To BILLIE.)* Told you it was in her head.

MAMMAW: *(Ignoring the last.)* That's right. Telepathy. We had this long conversation using telepathy 'cause they didn't have any mouths. Just a little slit not big enough to stick your pinky in.

BILLIE: What about the pancakes and chili?

MAMMAW: What about 'em?

BILLIE: Well, if they didn't have any mouths, why did they order pancakes and chili?

MAMMAW: You got me. Maybe they was just bein' polite. Anyway, after they left Rosie snarfed it up. That ol' gal could eat anything you threw at her. Know what I mean? *(Pours some coffee. After a pause.)* Pit bulls are eating people up left and right, don'tcha know.

BILLIE & JO: *WHAT?*

MAMMAW: Munchin' people up to beat the band.

JO: Mother, they ain't doing any such thing.

MAMMAW: Don't tell me. I got eyes don't I? *(To BILLIE.)* She thinks I'm senile. She'll be senile long before me, I'll tell you that. *(Pulls her "special" chair to the table and sits.)*

JO: You never saw a pit bull eat nothin' or nobody. You don't even know what a pit bull looks like.

MAMMAW: *(To BILLIE.)* See how she talks to me? Showed the kid being eaten right there on TV—in front of God and everybody!

BILLIE: Really? Why didn't somebody do something about it then?

MAMMAW: They was busy takin' pictures. That's show biz, don'tcha know.

JO: No, mother. They never showed anything like that on TV.

MAMMAW: How do you know? Were you there? They show people gettin' eaten up by all kinds o' things all the time on TV. *(To BILLIE.)* It was on the news last night.

JO: I saw the news last night and there wasn't anything about pit bulls eating people.

MAMMAW: You got up.

JO: No, I didn't.

MAMMAW: *(Sips coffee. To BILLIE.)* She got up.

LEOTA RUTH It was me. I got up. I always get up during the news. It's very unbalanced, you know.

JO: Ain't the only thing unbalanced around here. 'Sides you weren't even there. You was busy in your room writing your poetry.

LEOTA RUTH: Yes, that's right. *(Recites.)*
Alone
I reach into rarefied air
Embrace the evening clouds so fair
Upon the horizon with fingers bare

Pulling at the hem of God Who doesn't careHe cannot care for He is not there
As I reach into His rarefied nothingness
Alone

JO: *(After a pause. To LEOTA RUTH.)* I don't know why you have such thoughts.

LEOTA RUTH: I don't know either, mother. I just do.

JO: More's the pity.
LEOTA RUTH: It is called Alone.

JO: I figured somethin' like that.

BILLIE: I think it's beautiful. *(Looking at JO who frowns disapprovingly.)* Really. Honest. I know that feeling.

LEOTA RUTH: Then you might need some of my medication, Missus Patterson.

JO: She don't need none of your medication!

MAMMAW: *(Undaunted. To BILLIE.)* She got up.

JO: I didn't get up.

MAMMAW: You got up and went to relieve yourself.

JO: I did not relieve myself during the news, mother.

MAMMAW: Oh, you relieved yourself all right . . . just when they was about to show them pit bulls eating that little kid. Now, don't tell me different 'cause I know better.

BILLIE: Seems to me I heard something about that.

JO: Don't you start!

BILLIE: Up in Roswell, wasn't it?

MAMMAW: That's right. And then there was that ball player what got himself hit by a bolt of lightning and it never did come back out.

JO: Mother, for the love of God, you don't know what you're talking about.

MAMMAW: I do too!
JO: I saw it too, mother. They took him off the field where he was playing that there new kind of game they got . . . soccer, they call it.

MAMMAW: Baseball.

JO: No, mother. They don't kick a baseball.

MAMMAW: That's right. They use a bat. And they got him under lock and key just in case that lightning decides to come back out and strike a nurse or something.

LEOTA RUTH: *(While looking out window.)* There are devils in the desert.

JO: Leota Ruth, you're scaring Billie.

MAMMAW: She don't look scared to me. Are you scared, Billie?

BILLIE: No, Mammaw. I don't believe in devils.

MAMMAW: You believe in angels?

BILLIE: Well, maybe.

MAMMAW: If there's angels there's devils.

BILLIE: I'm not going to get scared about something I can't see.

MAMMAW: Big ol' horny things—devils. You ought to be scared—fat as you are.

JO: For the love of God, mother!

LEOTA RUTH: The love of God. Some say the only thing that separates us from Hell is the love of God. Without it, this planet would surely be Hell . . . some say.

MAMMAW: *(To BILLIE.)* And what do you say?

BILLIE: Some say it already is.

JO: Well, it ain't! It just feels that way. And it gets worse. The older you get the worse it feels.

BILLIE: Now I'm scared.

LEOTA RUTH: *(Looking out window.)* There goes one.

JO: There goes one what, Leota Ruth?

LEOTA RUTH: Desert devil.

JO: What on Earth are you talking about?

BILLIE: A dirt devil. Isn't that what you mean, Leota Ruth, a dirt devil?

JO: *(To BILLIE.)* That's a vacuum cleaner, stupid.

BILLIE: Dirt devils. Little whirlwinds of dirt—like tiny tornadoes.

LEOTA RUTH: Without love we just torture one another like devils in the desert stirring up sand and dirt—blowing it into our faces—blinding us. Desert devils stirring up trouble and sin. Little twisters of hot air blowing us all to Hell.

MAMMAW: Amen! *(Rises and searches about.)* I'll tell you, the moral fiber of America is worn thin and that's the truth!

JO: What are you prowling around for?

MAMMAW: *(Finding a loaf of bread.)* Something to eat. *(To BILLIE.)* She never feeds me.

JO: Oh, for pity's sake.
BILLIE: Would you like a cookie, Mammaw?

MAMMAW: I don't eat rat food. *(Sits – peels the crust from a slice of bread.)*

JO: It ain't rat food, mother.

MAMMAW: It's why H.O.'s in the hospital, ain't it?

JO: *(Through clenched teeth.)* No, it isn't, mother.

MAMMAW: *(To BILLIE.)* I wouldn't eat those cookies if I was you.

BILLIE: (Rises.) Excuse me.

JO: Where are you going?

BILLIE: To the bathroom.

JO: There ain't nothing wrong with those cookies, Billie!

BILLIE: It's the water pill. *(She exits to bathroom.)*

JO: Now see what you've done.

MAMMAW: I don't know what you're talking about, sister.

(From offstage we hear the SOUNDS of BILLIE throwing up. LEOTA RUTH crosses to sit on stool.)

JO: You made her sick.

MAMMAW: *(Rises – crossing to window.)* Well, you make me sick.

JO: Sometimes I could strangle you with my bare hands!

MAMMAW: You could chew on a Brillo pad for all I care. *(Examining curtains.)* Thought you was going to change out these here curtains today?

JO: Yes, mother. Billie and I are going to the fabric store soon as I get 'round.

LEOTA RUTH: Me too . . . maybe.

MAMMAW: Can I come?

JO: If you want.

MAMMAW: No. I'll just stay to home . . . in my room . . . all alone.

JO: Do what you want, mother.

MAMMAW: You'd like that, wouldn't you? Leave me alone so I can fall and break my bones while you're out gallivantin'. Maybe I'll be stretched out on the floor dead . . . or worse.

JO: Then come with us for God's sake!

MAMMAW: The way you drive? Be safer on roller skates.

LEOTA RUTH: I'll stay with you, Mammaw.

MAMMAW: *(To LEOTA RUTH.)* You're the only one who cares about old Mammaw, aren't you?

LEOTA RUTH: *(Nervously.)* I am sure that I am not the only one.

JO: Mother, how can you be so ungrateful?

MAMMAW: I'm sure I don't know what you're talking about. *(Looking out window.)* Tut! That ol' Tom's in the backyard again. Shoo, shoo! (A beat.) Remember the McGreevy boy?
JO: Bobby Lee?

LEOTA RUTH: Tommy Lee.

MAMMAW: That's the one. He died of cat fever.

JO: He had the croup.

MAMMAW: From sleepin' with cats.

JO: You don't get the croup from sleeping with cats.

MAMMAW: Are you a doctor now?

JO: He had weak lungs, mother. He was born with weak lungs and that's what killed him. Weak lungs.

MAMMAW: Sleepin' with cats didn't help. *(Out window.)* Shoo, shoo! Go home! Scat! Tut! There's that nigger boy. Shoo, shoo! Don't you go climbin' over that fence! I'll get the police on you. See if I don't! *(Turning back to JO who is crossing to window.)* Call the police, sister.

JO: *(Looking out window.)* Oh, mother, he's just getting his ball.

MAMMAW: He ought to keep his balls on his side of the alley!

JO: There. He got it.

MAMMAW: What's that hangin' outta his pocket?

JO: I don't know, mother. Looks like a stick.

MAMMAW: Bet it's a jackknife!

JO: It's not a jackknife, mother.

MAMMAW: Looks like a jackknife to me. Liable to cut your throat in the dead of night.

JO: For God's sake, mother! Nobody's gonna cut anybody's throat. There. He's gone now.

MAMMAW: He'll be back. And the next time he'll bring the whole gang with him.

JO: What gang?

MAMMAW: They run in packs don'tcha know. Robbin' and killin' and rapin'. Wanna get raped?

JO: No, mother, I don't want to get raped.

MAMMAW: Some folks do, you know.

JO: Well, not me!

MAMMAW: No. Who'd wanna rape you? You better call the police before he gets back here with his gang.

JO: Where do you get this stuff from?

MAMMAW: It's the truth. *Tut!* There's that ol' Tom again—doin' his duty. Better be careful when you go to hangin' out the wash, sister. Pile of cat shit big enough to bury your shoes in.

JO: What are you talking about?

MAMMAW: *(Pointing out the window.)* There. See it?

JO: I don't see nothin'.

MAMMAW: Maybe you don't know what cat shit looks like.

JO: Of course I do. I just don't see it.

MAMMAW: That's 'cause you're blind.
JO: I ain't blind.

MAMMAW: Blind as a bat, sister. Always was. Don't know where it comes from. Not my side of the family, I can tell you that. We got eyes like hawks . . . my side of the family.

JO: Mother, I'm really tired. *(Goes for paper towels, a plastic bag, yellow rubber gloves.)* You've never had a good thing to say about me in your entire life.

MAMMAW: Of course I have.

JO: When? When was the last time you told me something good about myself, huh?

MAMMAW: I don't know. My memory's not as good as it used to be.

JO: Could've fooled me.

MAMMAW: Better hurry, sister, 'fore the flies start to swarm.

JO: *(About to exit house.)* Leota Ruth, I don't suppose you could make yourself useful.

LEOTA RUTH: Yes, mother. I suppose I could.

JO: *(Indicating one of the piles of clean laundry.)* Then suppose you separate what don't need ironing of yours and put them away.

LEOTA RUTH: Okay. *(JO exits. Crossing to laundry basket. After a pause.)* Mammaw, did you really see aliens from outer space?

MAMMAW: I can't really say for sure. What do you think?

LEOTA RUTH: I think you enjoy being provocative.

MAMMAW: *(Crosses to help LEOTA RUTH.)* I like to get her goat. But all that about Rosie steppin' in the prairie dog hole I remember true as true. Don't you go and let anybody tell you different. Nasty little buggers.

LEOTA RUTH: *(While sorting through clothes.)* Sometimes I wish I were from another planet. It sure would be convenient. It would explain a lot of things, wouldn't it?

MAMMAW: Like?

LEOTA RUTH: The way I feel.

MAMMAW: How's that?

LEOTA RUTH: Alienated. Removed. Don't get me wrong. I'm not complaining. In fact, I've become used to it. It's this terrible sense of self. Not really a part of anything . . . especially anything around here.

MAMMAW: Ain't nothin' around here to feel a part of, darlin'. 'Sides, everybody feels that way from time to time. You don't gotta be from outer space to feel those things.

LEOTA RUTH: No, but it would be beneficial—give me an explanation. It's a shame to feel so separate and apart while knowing that you are home. Home is the last place you should feel those things. Maybe, this is the last place. Sometimes, I think I might as well be invisible or dead.

MAMMAW: That's a bad way to think.

LEOTA RUTH: Do you think I am crazy, Mammaw?

MAMMAW: It doesn't matter what I think.

LEOTA RUTH: Of course it matters. Please. Tell me the truth.

MAMMAW: I don't always know the truth. It keeps on changing the older you get. But, I do believe that you don't always act in your own best interest.

LEOTA RUTH: Sometimes I feel I must be crazy—stark raving, loony mad.

MAMMAW: Sometimes you are.

LEOTA RUTH: I know. Other times, I feel everybody around me is and I am the only one who is not. That is when I realize I must be because I cannot be the only one. That would mean I really am. But, somewhere inside me, underneath it all, I am sure that I am not.

MAMMAW: You're not?

LEOTA RUTH: Crazy—*all* the time.

MAMMAW: Well, there you go. You answered your own question. You got the gift. I think you're one of those artists who hasn't found a way to express herself.

LEOTA RUTH: You mean, I haven't found my medium?

MAMMAW: I guess. You got all kinds of wonderful things in you. I don't know where they all come from. Not from your mother, that's for sure. And H.O., well his side of the family's a bit slow. Good people—just slow. You need to get away from this house—this dried-up, God-forsaken desert before you end up mean and bitter just like sister.

LEOTA RUTH: I would never—

MAMMAW: No, I don't suppose you would.

LEOTA RUTH: Where could I go?

MAMMAW: Go to Lubbock.

LEOTA RUTH: Why Lubbock?

MAMMAW: Then, try Dallas.

LEOTA RUTH: What's in Dallas?

MAMMAW: More of the same. But, you could have a home of your own.

LEOTA RUTH: *A home?* I wouldn't know how to act. Besides, my doctor is here in Hobbs. I must have my medication.

MAMMAW: *Bull.* You haven't taken your pills in two, three months that I know of.

LEOTA RUTH: How do you know that?

MAMMAW: True, ain't it?

LEOTA RUTH: Maybe.

MAMMAW: Ain't no maybe about it. Give your old Mammaw a little credit. I see things.

LEOTA RUTH: I see things, too, Mammaw.

MAMMAW: Of course you do. But, that's not exactly what I meant. *(They BOTH chuckle.)*

LEOTA RUTH: I'm afraid.

MAMMAW: Of?

LEOTA RUTH: I don't know.

MAMMAW: Life and shadows, maybe?

LEOTA RUTH: Maybe. I don't know much about life.

MAMMAW: Who does? It just happens and you go along with it. Fight it and you run into all kinds of complications.

LEOTA RUTH: I just question it, that's all.

MAMMAW: That ain't livin' it.

LEOTA RUTH: *(After a pause.)* Do you think we are really going to die?

MAMMAW: What?

LEOTA RUTH: Die. I am pretty much resigned to the fact that our bodies are going to die, but I mean us. That thing that makes us us.

MAMMAW: Us *us?*

LEOTA RUTH: I think all life is connected and that on some level, some deep level of consciousness, we all share the same "I" and that "I" is eternal. God, maybe.

MAMMAW: Does that include your mother?

LEOTA RUTH: Yes, of course.

MAMMAW: Then it ain't God.

LEOTA RUTH: Do you really hate mother?

MAMMAW: She's my daughter, ain't she?

LEOTA RUTH: That's not an answer.

MAMMAW: It's all the answer you're gonna get.

LEOTA RUTH: Please. You never talk to me about what happened between you and mother.

MAMMAW: Ain't nothin' happened. I don't know what you're talkin' about—always pryin'.

LEOTA RUTH: I'm sorry.

MAMMAW: Sometimes you just got to leave well enough alone. *(After a pause.)* Too much "yes."

LEOTA RUTH: Excuse me?

MAMMAW: Too much "yes."

LEOTA RUTH: I don't understand.

MAMMAW: There was always too much "yes" goin' on 'tween your Pappaw and your mother. The only one either of them ever said "no" to was me. Too much "yes" 'tween them. It wasn't natural. And, I don't wanna know nothin' more than that.

LEOTA RUTH: Are you saying that mother and Pappaw—

MAMMAW: I ain't sayin' nothin'. You understand? *Nothin'.*

LEOTA RUTH: Yes, Mammaw.

MAMMAW: *Nothin'.*

LEOTA RUTH: *(After a pause.)* Well, maybe it's all a dream anyway.

MAMMAW: What?

LEOTA RUTH: This. Life. Maybe, we just go on and on from one dream into another.

MAMMAW: Leota Ruth, what in blue blazes are you talking about?

LEOTA RUTH: Life. Maybe it's just a dream like the song says.

MAMMAW: Sweetheart, you don't know what you're talking about. Look at this body. Look at me. *Old.* Flesh hangin' like on one o' those Chinee dogs. Do I look like a dream to you?

LEOTA RUTH: Well, since you put it that way.

MAMMAW: Ain't no other way to put it.

LEOTA RUTH: *(After a pause.)* I had the telephone dream again last night. Its been coming now about two or three nights a week.

MAMMAW: It's just a dream. Put it out of your mind.

LEOTA RUTH: I don't seem able. It is really scary.

MAMMAW: Ain't nothin' scary 'bout telephone dreams. Telephone bills, now that's a whole other story.

LEOTA RUTH: *(Disregarding the last.)* It is as though I am lost. Far from home. I think I need a ride—a way back—a way home. So, I pick up a telephone and try to call you, daddy, mother—somebody at home. Home. But, I keep forgetting the number. And, when I do remember the number I am all thumbs. I dial it wrong. Over and over and over I dial it wrong. I cannot make a connection. Lost. I cannot reach anybody however hard I try—someone who can come and take me home. *(Cries.)*

MAMMAW: *(Hugging her.)* Shhh. Just a dream, child. Just a dream. You're gonna be right as rain. I promise. *(After a pause. Indicating clothes.)* Suppose you get these here things into your room before your mother has herself a hissy fit.

LEOTA RUTH: Mammaw, if I was of a mind to leave Hobbs —for Lubbock or Dallas—how would I go about it?
MAMMAW: Well, to start with, you'll be needing the money I got hidden in the back of my closet.

LEOTA RUTH: Really?

MAMMAW: Yup. There's enough to get you started anywhere you wanna go.

LEOTA RUTH: Where did you get it?

MAMMAW: Cashed in my life insurance.

LEOTA RUTH: But, mother thinks she is going to—wasn't that for mother?

MAMMAW: *Yup.* Won't she be surprised. *(Hearing something in the direction of the bathroom. To LEOTA RUTH.)* Put this stuff in your room, in a drawer or in a suitcase. It's all the same to me. I got a rat to catch.

LEOTA RUTH: A rat?

MAMMAW: A big fat rat. Now, you hurry along.

LEOTA RUTH: *(Starting toward her room with an armload of clothes.)* Thank you, Mammaw. *(Exits.)*

MAMMAW: *(Speaking towards bathroom.)* You can come out now! I hear you standin' back there wheezin' like a buffalo with asthma!

BILLIE: *(Entering.)* Who? Me?

MAMMAW: No. Flora Dora the one-legged fan dancer. You breathe one word of what you heard to sister and it'll be the last time the fat lady sings.

BILLIE: Whatever do you mean, Mammaw?

MAMMAW: Don't play innocent with me, missy!

BILLIE: You don't have to worry about me saying anything, Mammaw, because I happen to think her leaving would be for the best all 'round.

JO: *(Enters. MAMMAW heads for the window, BILLIE stands with a guilty look etched into her face. There is a long*

SILENCE while JO removes her rubber gloves. To BILLIE.) Well, don't you look like the cat that ate the rat.

MAMMAW: Found rat hair in the cat shit, did you?

JO: *No, mother.*

BILLIE: *(Nervously.)* Do you have any Lysol?

JO: Now what did you do?

BILLIE: A little accident.

MAMMAW: Rat food.

JO: Honest to God! If it ain't one thing it's another! *(Turns and exits.)*

MAMMAW: *(After a pause.)* Is she gone?

BILLIE: *(Sits at table.)* Yes.

MAMMAW: *(Crossing to BILLIE. Urgently.)* They beat me.

BILLIE: *(Incredulous.)* No.

MAMMAW: *(Showing BILLIE the bruises on her arms.)* See these? They didn't get there by themselves.

BILLIE: That's from the Prednisone.

MAMMAW: Prednisone my ass!

BILLIE: Yes, Mammaw. It's a side effect of the Prednisone. You don't really expect me to . . . I mean, I can't believe . . .

MAMMAW: *(Cutting her off.)* Believe it. It's true. *Call the police.*

BILLIE: What?

MAMMAW: Does that stomach of yours affect your hearing?

BILLIE: Of course not.

MAMMAW: Then, call the police.

BILLIE: I can't do that.

MAMMAW: Fingers gone bad? Arthritis, huh?

BILLIE: No.

MAMMAW: Oh, don't talk to me about arthritis. Look at these. *(Showing BILLIE her fingers.)* Sometimes they like to get knotted somethin' awful. I'll never play the harp, I'll tell you that! Let me see yours. *(BILLIE holds out her hands.)* Fat little piggies, ain't they? Call the police!

BILLIE: Mammaw, if what you say is true, why don't you call the police?

MAMMAW: I did. They don't believe me. Some know-nothin' woman cop came to investigate and ended up siding with sister. When you reach my age you don't have any rights, don'tcha know?

BILLIE: Well, what makes you think they'll believe me?

MAMMAW: You're my witness.

BILLIE: But, I never saw them beat you.

MAMMAW: That don't make no nevermind. Tell them you did.

BILLIE: That would be a lie, Mammaw.

MAMMAW: Have it your way. One day when you come over here, stuffing yourself with rat food, I'll be lyin' in my room all beat up and broken—dead, maybe. How are you gonna feel then?

BILLIE: I'd feel . . . is this the truth?

MAMMAW: You want it on the Bible?

BILLIE: No, of course not.

MAMMAW: Don't believe in the Good Book, huh?

BILLIE: I'll have a word with Jo about it.

MAMMAW: What good do you think that'll do?

BILLIE: I'll ask her if she's ever done what you said.

MAMMAW: Sure. Go ahead and sign my death warrant!

BILLIE: I won't ask her directly, of course.

MAMMAW: Directly or not, I'm telling you they beat me! They kick me! They punch me! They slap me! They . . . *(JO enters with Lysol and bucket.)* Have a nice day.

JO: What?

MAMMAW: I said, "Have a nice day."

JO: *(Hands BILLIE Lysol and bucket.)* Here.

BILLIE: Sorry. *(Exits to bathroom.)*

MAMMAW: She's sorry all right. If that ol' gal had to haul ass, it'd take her two trips.

JO: Now, mother, she's a child of God just like you and me.

MAMMAW: If you're a child of God, sister, I'm throwin' in with the one downstairs!

JO: Did you ever love me, mother?

MAMMAW: Did you ever love anybody but yourself?

JO: The problem is I love everybody too much.

MAMMAW: That's a problem, all right. All those Air Force boys you took in as boarders. You loved every one of them, didn't you?

JO: If you mean I loved them like they was my own boys—then, yes. Yes, I did love them.

MAMMAW: *(After a pause.)* They drown female nigger babies in Africa.

JO: What are you talking about?

MAMMAW: Unwanted offspring. They drown 'em in Africa.

JO: Well, thank God they don't do that in America.

MAMMAW: Yeah . . . aren't you lucky.

JO: Mother, what exactly are you saying?

MAMMAW: Got time to give me a perm this week, or do I got to go to that sissy-man on Gibson? *(Goes to ironing board and refolds JO's ironing.)*

JO: You don't need a permanent. You only had one a month ago. *(Gets scissors and magazine, clips coupons.)*

MAMMAW: Grew out.

JO: It didn't do no such thing!

MAMMAW: It did. I always was a fast hair grower.

JO: Oh, mother! Your hair grows like everybody else's.

MAMMAW: No, it don't!

JO: It most certainly does.

MAMMAW: It grows faster when you're older. The older you get, the faster it grows.

JO: Then, how come mine don't? I'm getting old, too, mother.

MAMMAW: You ain't normal, that's why. When you're normal it grows faster. Maybe yours is retarded.

JO: It ain't retarded, mother!

MAMMAW: They say when you get old enough you can hear it growin'. *(Crosses to counter, searching.)* It don't even stop when you're dead. Hair's awful funny that way.

JO: Are you looking for an excuse to be silly this morning?

MAMMAW: No. I'm looking for my teeth. Where did you hide them?

JO: I suppose they're where you left them, mother . . . in the bathroom.

MAMMAW: She probably threw up on them.

JO: She didn't throw up on them.

MAMMAW: People do, you know. *(Returns to ironing board.)*

JO: She didn't throw up on your teeth, mother.

MAMMAW: How do you know? Were you there? That doctor in Juarez what fitted me with those teeth said not to get foreign objects on them.

JO: You put foreign objects in your mouth everyday, mother.

MAMMAW: I do not! Have you gone daft?

JO: Your teeth are just fine! When Billie comes out you can go in there and get them.

MAMMAW: Make me sick! *(Spits on iron.)* This ol' iron ain't puttin' out steam again. *(Looking up toward ceiling.)* And that seems to be all that ol' swamp cooler's puttin' out —steam.

JO: When H.O. gets home I'll have him take another look.

MAMMAW: What about the iron?

JO: I'll have him look at that, too, mother.

MAMMAW: That's all he ever does is look. He ain't mechanical minded, I'll tell you that. Run some vinegar through the iron. That ought to break down the corrosion. *(A pause to scrutinize.)* What did you poison him for?

JO: What?

MAMMAW: You heard me.

JO: It was an accident!

MAMMAW: That's your story.

JO: I did not poison H.O.!

MAMMAW: Somebody did.

JO: Now you stop that! I didn't do no such thing!

MAMMAW: He got into the rat food just like you intended.

JO: *(Appearing hurt.)* How can you say such a thing?

MAMMAW: True, ain't it?

JO: No! It isn't true!

MAMMAW: How'd they get switched, then?

JO: Suppose you tell me. I'm not the only one who lives in this house.

MAMMAW: You're the only one in all of Hobbs who bakes cookies for rats.

JO: To get rid of them, mother, not for them.

MAMMAW: What's the difference?

JO: There's no use trying to make sense with you.

MAMMAW: No. Not when you're retarded. *(Re-ironing and "correcting" all of JO's ironing and folding.)*

JO: I am not retarded!

MAMMAW: Doc Sears said you was.

JO: Then, Doc Sears was a quack!

MAMMAW: Oh, you shouldn't speak ill of the dead, sister. Poor man killed himself. Treated Dickie Keefer for hemorrhoids—big as grapes, they were—then he went into the closet and hung himself. Tongue swelled up like an eggplant, big and purple. Terrible thing—hemorrhoids. That's why I don't eat eggplant.

JO: You don't eat eggplant because it gives you gas, mother.

MAMMAW: There was this travelin' show with a two-headed rattlesnake come through while I was carryin' you and it liked to scare me to death! Give me nightmares, it did.

JO: Oh, mother, you're making this up.

MAMMAW: Am not! It had two heads big as your fist!

JO: Well, what's that got to do with me?

MAMMAW: Told you. It marked you and that's why you're retarded.

JO: I am not retarded, mother!

MAMMAW: Not all the time, no. Just some of the time—like when you poisoned H.O.

JO: I didn't poison H.O.

MAMMAW: Tell it to the judge.

JO: You stop it! Stop it right now! *(Stops clipping coupons. Rises and, with scissors in hand, crosses towards MAMMAW.)*

MAMMAW: Sure is lucky Tootie ain't gonna sue. All that good chicken gone to waste. What a shame.

JO: You're crazy!

MAMMAW: And you're a murderer!

JO: *(Shaking her fist, with scissors, at MAMMAW.)* Sometimes I could . . . could *(BILLIE enters.)* . . . kill you!

MAMMAW: *(To BILLIE – with satisfaction.)* There . . . see?

BILLIE: Jo, what's going on?

JO: Nothing!

MAMMAW: Don't you say you didn't see that, Billie Patterson! *(Slams down iron and starts to exit – turning back.)* There better not be puke on my teeth. *(Exits to bathroom.)*

BILLIE: What was that all about?

JO: *(Staring out window. After a pause.)* I don't know. Honest to God, I just don't know.

BILLIE: You don't know what, Jo?

JO: *Curtains.* We was talking about curtains, weren't we?

(BILLIE and JO stand staring at each other as the LIGHTING slowly FADES revealing LEOTA RUTH standing near the entrance to her bedroom.)

LEOTA RUTH:
Deep within our soul burns an eternal flame
Through primordial mire it nurtures our Becoming
Till the end-times it lights our consciousness

Steering us toward the hidden
Into galaxies more numerous than
The sum of all of us
And all who ever were
And all who will ever be
Is
We are guided and driven toward the stars
Towards other hearts beating across the universe
Like lonely orphans abandoned
We wait and we listen
For the soul of God and all that
Is

The LIGHTING continues to FADE to BLACK.

END ACT ONE

ACT TWO

AT RISE – BILLIE and JO stand frozen as they were at end of Act One. LEOTA RUTH is standing near the entrance to her bedroom, unseen and unheard by the others. Her invisibility will apply throughout the remainder of the play with the exception of a brief passage in flashback.

LEOTA RUTH:
When night falls into deepest sleep
I float tethered from silver threads
As a flame fears the approaching moth
I fear the burning of a brilliant truth
To guide me on my journey home
Heavenward towards God
Where promises are kept
And words left unsaid
Are heard and understood
Then morning comes and my astral form
Slides back into me as I awaken
Famished for the Love that feeds the spirit
and gives us strength to sail the midnight air

(She disappears into her bedroom.)

JO: (Suddenly animated.) Curtains. We was talking about curtains, weren't we?

BILLIE: *(Nervously. Showing concern.)* Yeah—sure. Yellow, wasn't it?

JO: That's right . . . yellow. *(Pause.)* I didn't poison H.O.

BILLIE: What?

JO: She blames me.

BILLIE: Who blames you?

JO: Mother. She blames me for trying to murder H.O.

BILLIE: *(After a pause.)* You're not serious?

JO: Of course I'm serious. Mother thinks I poisoned him.

BILLIE: Did you?

JO: You can go lay down on the highway right now, Billie Patterson!

BILLIE: I don't mean on purpose.

JO: On purpose or otherwise, I did not poison H.O. *(After a pause.)* I'm going to tell you something and I don't want it to leave this house. You better brace yourself.

BILLIE: This has something to do with the rat poison in the cookies, doesn't it? *(Sitting.)* What? What are you going to tell me?

JO: I think my mother switched the cookies.

BILLIE: Oh, my God! I'm going to die, aren't I?

JO: No, stupid! Not on you—on H.O.

BILLIE: Then, I'm all right?

JO: Yes, Billie. You're perfectly fine. I already threw the poisoned batch out. *(A beat.)* She's trying to kill me, Billie. She wants me dead.

BILLIE: But, *I'm a*ll right?

JO: Of course you're all right. It's me she's trying to kill, not you.

BILLIE: Jo, I can't believe that.

JO: Believe it. She's been trying to kill me for over fifty years!

BILLIE: Well, she couldn't have been trying very hard.

JO: Would you shut up and listen to me! I think she switched the cookies around, knowing I like a snack every now and again. Only, she didn't count on H.O. getting into them since he's always braggin' about not having a sweet tooth.

BILLIE: Surely, they would have discovered that at the hospital, wouldn't they?

JO: Not if they weren't looking for poison.

BILLIE: What are you going to do?

JO: I don't know. I can't go to the police because she's my mother. 'Sides, I'm the one who baked them in the first place. She's an evil woman, I'm telling you that.

BILLIE: Oh, I'm sure it's all just an innocent mistake.

JO: You really want to die stupid, don'tcha?

BILLIE: I am sick to God with the way you talk to me sometimes.

JO: You love it.

BILLIE: No, I don't. In fact, I wonder why we're friends at all.

JO: Because I'm it! You don't got anybody else.

BILLIE: What a terrible thing to say. I had lots of friends, Jo. Lots.

JO: Not in this lifetime.

BILLIE: *(Undaunted.)* But, one by one, you drove them all off with your jealousy.

JO: Bull shit.

BILLIE: If somebody took the slightest interest in me, you had to put the kibosh on it. Jealous. Jealous and afraid you were going to be shut out—left alone.

JO: I don't know what you're talking about.

BILLIE: Of course you do.

JO: 'Sides, there ain't a thing to be jealous about when it comes to you, missy. I can tell you that.

BILLIE: Does cruelty really come that easy to you?

JO: If you lost any so-called friends, it weren't because of me.

BILLIE: You butt in, you take over, then you run everybody off. My God, Jo! What happened to you?

JO: Nothing's happened to me, Billie. *Nothing.* That's what's happened.

BILLIE: You strike out at the least little thing. Remember Lennie?

JO: Ain't never knowed any Lennie.

BILLIE: You most certainly did! Lennie King. My God! You tried to kill her with a pair of pruning shears.

JO: I don't remember.

BILLIE: Oh, yes you do. That's not something one would likely forget.

JO: I said, I don't remember.

BILLIE: You can be as selective as you like with that memory of yours, but it was my birthday party and I'm not about to forget it anytime soon.
JO: When did you ever have a birthday party?

BILLIE: Last year, the year before, the year before that.

JO: More like last minute back yard get-togethers than parties.

BILLIE: Lennie came all the way over from Amarillo to spend my birthday with me. She was my friend and you were jealous.

JO: Well, like I said, I can't imagine of what.

BILLIE: It was when somebody remarked how much prettier the birthday cake was over any they could remember. She had just finished that decorating course and was so proud and you had to go and ruin it.

JO: Ah, yes. Now, I remember.

BILLIE: Thought you would.

JO: And who was it made your birthday cake the year before, and the year before that, and the year before that all the way back to Moses?

BILLIE: You know perfectly well who.

JO: But what thanks did I get? I don't remember having to force-feed anybody.

BILLIE People were just being kind to Lennie.

JO: At my expense.

BILLIE: I don't think anybody meant it that way, Jo.

JO: *(After a pause.)* Honest to God! The things you choose to remember.

BILLIE: Jo, the shears went an inch deep into my new siding.

JO: It was still under warranty, wasn't it? I seem to recall that Sears came out and took care of it. Free of charge.

BILLIE: That's not the point.

JO: Then what the hell is the point, Billie?

BILLIE: *Friends.* Every time someone shows me the slightest bit of interest—some small token of affection—you either insult them or try to kill them!

JO: You really do exaggerate.

BILLIE: I don't know why I've remained your friend all these years. I really, truly don't. Nobody deserves all your abuse.

JO: You do! You stuff yourself with food till you're fat as a heifer! Nobody could begin to abuse you as much as you abuse yourself! You love abuse. You thrive on abuse. You marry a man who's never to home and when he is home you say he's more a "friend" than anything else. When was the last time you had sex with a man, Billie Patterson?

BILLIE: You go too far! I think we've known each other too well for too long! I think we're too familiar—at least, *you* certainly are. I think we don't really like each other. We don't know how to be friends. And, what is worse, we don't know how not to be friends. It's like we're condemned in Hell with each other.

JO: *(After a pause.)* Did somebody die and leave you their subscription to Reader's Digest?

BILLIE: *(Not amused.)* Maybe I'll put my house up for sale.

JO: What?

BILLIE: You heard me. Georgie and I have been thinking about moving to Amarillo. Got some friends in Amarillo . . . not to mention Lennie King.

JO: Fine. Good riddance to you.

BILLIE: I mean it, Jo.

JO: Me, too! *(After a pause.)* Well? Shouldn't you be home packing?

BILLIE: Why are you like this?

JO: Like what?

BILLIE: Mean. Ornery.

JO: Look, Billie! My mother is trying to kill me. My husband is in the hospital from something I believe my mother did. My son can't find himself and I can't afford to help him keep up the search. My daughter has up and gone to another planet. And you're acting like the ninny of the month. I don't have time for your silly nonsense. You ain't selling your house. 'Sides, who'd buy that pigsty? And you ain't going to Amarillo. You were born in Hobbs, America and you will die in Hobbs, America!

BILLIE: Oh, joy. So, what are you telling me? You fed me poisoned cookies and now I'm about to keel over dead? Is that what you're trying to tell me?

JO: I already told you that you're perfectly fine.
BILLIE: I don't feel fine. I feel much maligned. I feel like I'm having some dark and awful hallucination brought on by rat poison and you're in it. You're standing over me with a whip and you're drooling blood.

JO: The only hallucination around here is the appearance of everyday normality.

BILLIE: Well, that's about as profound as anything I've ever heard you say. *(After a pause.)* So, do you really think she switched the cookies?

JO: I most certainly do. She wants me dead.

BILLIE: Well, what proof do you have?

JO: She murdered my father. What more proof do you need?

BILLIE: Jo, Pappaw *(Pronounced Pap-paw)* died of heat stroke.

JO: Who knitted him that sweater in the middle of July, huh?

BILLIE: That's hardly murder.

JO: Not in the eyes of the law, maybe. But, murder just the same. She knew what she was doing.

BILLIE: I think you're being a bit unfair.

JO: You think so, huh? Daddy always loved me better than her and she knew it. She knew it and that was her way of getting back at me.

BILLIE: Jo, you're being stupid.

JO: You think so, huh?

BILLIE: I've heard you say some pretty dumb things, but that takes the cake, the blue ribbon and the best of show, hands down.

JO: Side with her all you like, it don't change a thing.

BILLIE: I'm not siding with anybody, Jo.

JO: As soon as H.O. gets out of that hospital she's going in a home. I don't care if it takes every last cent we've got. She's not staying here!

MAMMAW: *(Enters – followed by LEOTA RUTH.)* My mouth tastes like Lysol.

JO: What are you on about, mother?

MAMMAW: Those motor vehicle people took my license away!

JO: What has that got to do with anything?

MAMMAW: I could get in the car and get out of here, that's what! Go somewhere where people don't go throwing up on other people's teeth. *(To BILLIE.)* I drove a covered wagon 'cross Texas and now they won't even let me drive across the street.

JO: It's for you own protection. You'd only get yourself killed like you almost did last time.

MAMMAW: Because you went and bought me them slippy shoes for my birthday. I told you they was no good. Slipped right off the brakes and onto the gas pedal. Who told you to buy me them anyway?

JO: Nobody, mother. I just thought I was doing something nice.

MAMMAW: Why?

JO: What do you mean, "Why?"

MAMMAW: You ain't never done nothin' nice in your whole life.

JO: How can you say such a thing?

MAMMAW: Read my lips, sister. You want me dead, don't tell me different. You bought me those slippy shoes on purpose.

JO: I bought you those shoes because you was complaining about how you didn't have any shoes to wear.

MAMMAW: I had plenty of shoes.

JO: That's what I told you.

LEOTA RUTH: *(To no one in particular.)*
This is how it starts time after time
The cycle of our lives
There seems no way to break
This spinning wheel existence
Living day to day on hand-me-down thoughts
And hand-me-down beliefs

Where words are stuffed into our mouths
Then forced to repeat time after time
Never changing yet pushing us onward
Toward ends with neither rhyme nor reason
Toward ends of inarticulate suffocation

JO: *(Ignoring the last.)* Only you went on and on about how nobody ever does anything for you.

MAMMAW: Well? Do they?

JO: I've given up my life for you, mother, and I've had about all I can take!

MAMMAW: *(To BILLIE, who is nervously knitting.)* They was cheap, slippy, catalog shoes. 'Sides, they never fit me right, anyhow.

JO: *(To MAMMAW.)* Can't you let me love you?

MAMMAW: Now you stop that! You stop that right now. You hear me, sister?

LEOTA RUTH: *(To no one in particular. With all the gravity of sincerely.)* Can't you let me love you? I just want to love you. *(Recites.)* You cannot stop me from loving you
You cannot stop me from touching you
Once I sail forth upon my invisible fingers
Reaching out to touch your Humanity
You cannot stop the embrace
Of one you do not know exists

JO: *(Pleading.)* I just want to love you.

MAMMAW: Stop it, I said! Don't you go play-actin' for Billie's sake. She knows better.

JO: I gave up my life for you.

MAMMAW: And I gave you life. Remember that, sister.

JO: *(Holding back tears.)* Then, why are you trying to kill me?

MAMMAW: You ain't shed a sincere tear in your life, sister. So, forget about it. Ain't nobody gonna buy it. 'Sides, you got it backwards. *(To BILLIE.)* Don't let her kid you. She knew they was slippy shoes when she bought them.

JO: I didn't know any such thing, mother!

MAMMAW: That's your story.

JO: What is going on around here! Are you all trying to drive me insane?

MAMMAW: Sister, you can stand there and lie all you like. It don't change a thing. God knows how you hate me. *(Crosses to window.)*

JO: *(To MAMMAW.)* I don't hate you.

MAMMAW: Oh, yes, you do. Ain't no doubt about that.

LEOTA RUTH: *(To the open air. To no one in particular.)* Sometimes there are dueling voices in my mind . . . rattling swords . . . screaming for attention . . . vile and hateful. *Noise.* There is a mirror up ahead. I think I ought to be reflected in it. But, the noise of those voices gets in the way and keeps me from seeing where I am—who I am. The noise is thick and dense and leaves a dark, sap-like stain deep inside me. I cannot see myself clearly. There is too much noise. Just too much noise. Am I the reflection?

MAMMAW: *(Shouting out window.)* Get outta that apricot tree, you Mexican hoodlum! Go! *Shoo, shoo!* Damn wetbacks!

JO: *(Crosses to window.)* That's the Martinez boy, mother.

BILLIE: Dorella's boy?

JO: That's the one.

MAMMAW: I don't care if it's the boy on the milk carton! It's still a wetback!

BILLIE: Oh, no. Dorella's a teacher.

JO: No, she ain't.

LEOTA RUTH: *(Aside.)* But, of what? Of what am I a reflection?

BILLIE: Yes, she is.

JO: You're thinking of Manny's wife. *(Crosses to ironing board and proceeds to once again fold the laundry that MAMMAW had previously refolded.)*

BILLIE: No, I'm not. Manny's wife is a secretary over at the high school. Dorella teaches.

LEOTA RUTH: *(Aside.)* There is God in unlikely voices.

MAMMAW: *(Yelling out window.)* Go back to Pango Pango!

JO: Mother! Will you stop making a spectacle of yourself.

MAMMAW: Thievin' hoodlum!

JO: He ain't but six or seven years old.

MAMMAW: They teach 'em young. They got three-year-old pickpockets roaming the streets of Juarez. Steal everything you got if you don't keep an eye on 'em. Knife you for a chew of bubble gum.

JO: Nobody knifes anybody for bubble gum, mother.

MAMMAW: No? *(To BILLIE.)* What do you say?

BILLIE: Well, I think that's a bit extreme, Mammaw. Don't you?

MAMMAW: If I did, I wouldn't have brought it up. *(Sits and rearranges the order of JO's coupons.)* Remember the Flowers girl?

JO: Peggy?

BILLIE: June.

JO: Peggy. Peggy Flowers.

BILLIE: No. It was June. I'm absolutely certain.

MAMMAW: Christie Mae. Christie Mae Flowers.

BILLIE: Ah, yes, that was her name.

JO: Well, whoever! Died of scarlet fever.

BILLIE: Measles.

JO: Scarlet fever.

MAMMAW: Bubble gum. She swallowed bubble gum.

JO: Oh, mother!

MAMMAW: She did! She swallowed bubble gum. Got herself bound. All stuck up. Died. Some say it was suicide. *(To BILLIE.)* What do you say?

BILLIE: I don't know enough to say anything, Mammaw.

MAMMAW: Of course you don't. Never thought you did.

JO: Mother, why don't you go and lay down for awhile?

MAMMAW: No! You're gonna sneak off to the fabric store while I'm not looking.

JO: No, I'm not, mother. Please, just for a little bit while I fix us some lunch.

MAMMAW: I don't want any lunch.

JO: Then, lay down anyway!

MAMMAW: I might not wake up.

JO: Of course you'll wake up.

MAMMAW: You don't know that.

JO: *(Crossing towards MAMMAW.)* Go and lay down!

MAMMAW: *(Rises. Backing away.)* No! I'm afraid.

JO: There's nothing to be afraid of.

MAMMAW: People die in their sleep. I'm not going!
JO: Nobody's gonna die in their sleep, mother.

MAMMAW: *(Crosses to ironing board.)* How do you know? Are you a fortune teller now? *(Proceeds to, once again, refold the ironing.)*

JO: Oh, for God's sake— *(BILLIE rises.)* And just where do you think you're going?

BILLIE: *(Obviously feigning an excuse to get out of the room – away from the mounting tension.)* Well . . . I . . . I thought . . . ah . . . the bathroom.

JO: Sit down!

BILLIE: I . . . I took a water pill and I—

JO: I don't care if you took an enema!

MAMMAW: She's not going to pee on the floor, is she?

BILLIE: I really need to—

JO: SIT DOWN! *(BILLIE sits.)* Thank you.

MAMMAW: Sister, if she's got to pee, let her pee.

JO: She doesn't have to pee.

BILLIE: I do. I really, really do, Jo.

MAMMAW: You hear? She does. She really, really does.

JO: She don't!

BILLIE: I do.

MAMMAW: Best to believe a bloated woman, sister.
JO: She don't gotta pee! She wants to get away from you! You're making her crazy. *(Sits and proceeds to rearrange the order of the coupons.)*

MAMMAW: *(Crossing to BILLIE.)* Am I making you crazy?

BILLIE: No, Mammaw. It's these water pills I've been taking for the bloat.

MAMMAW: See, sister? Bloated like a blimp. It's those water pills making her crazy.

JO: It's not the water pills. It's you!

MAMMAW: I ain't never, in all my life, made anybody have to pee! Remember Harvey Monroe? He had bladder problems, too. They had to hook a plastic bag to him.

JO: Mother! Go and lay down!

MAMMAW: No! And you can't make me.

BILLIE: What's that poem called?

JO: What poem?

BILLIE: Leota Ruth's. The one about the devils.

LEOTA RUTH: *(Aside.)* The poem is called *Desert Devils* and it is dedicated to God.

BILLIE: *(To JO.)* Devious Devils—something like that. Do you remember that poem? How did it go?

LEOTA RUTH:
Desert Devils spin round the buried Soul
While the Mind flies on Ancient wings
And the Body by Gravity bound
Wanders chained to the desert ground

Mother, Goddess of the Earth, let her soar
Where Time is stopped and Space is naught
But the spinning fibers of her thought

Father, God of the invisible Mind
Teacher of revelations Divine
Let her drink deep the atmosphere sublime
Then take away Space
Then take away Time
Take her to where thought upon matter revels
To the tune and to the dance
of the Desert Devils

BILLIE: I don't know what made me think of that poem, but —

MAMMAW: Sister used to write poetry.

JO: I ain't never wrote a poem in my life.

MAMMAW: You used to come home with poems all the time. There was one about roses and violets, and then there was one about the three men in a tub. *(To BILLIE.)* When sister was a little girl she was just full of poetry.

JO: I was never full of poetry, mother.

MAMMAW: Sure sounded like poetry to me.

JO: Well, it wasn't!

MAMMAW: She was full of somethin'. You can go to the bank on that. Leota Ruth's poems were very beautiful and I'm sure God was pleased.

LEOTA RUTH: *(To no one – just the air.)* Thank you, Mammaw.

JO: Mother! Go lay down!

MAMMAW: No! You just don't want me around when Howie Boy calls.

JO: Howie Boy ain't gonna call today

MAMMAW: How do you know?

JO: 'Cause it's Monday. Howie Boy never calls on Monday. 'Sides, he called last night.

MAMMAW: Liar.

JO: He called last night, mother.

MAMMAW: Liar. He didn't call last night.

JO: He did too. After you went to bed.

MAMMAW: You called him.

JO: No, I didn't.

MAMMAW: Yes, you did.

BILLIE: *(Trapped between them.)* I have to pee.

MAMMAW: You thought I was asleep, but I wasn't. You called him.

(LEOTA RUTH goes to cabinet and begins to search.)

JO: Well, he had a right to know that his daddy was in the hospital, didn't he?

LEOTA RUTH: *(To herself.)* My medication. Where is my medication?

(LEOTA RUTH finds the full bottle of pills. During the dialog to follow, she fills a glass with orange juice and then – still unseen by anyone in the kitchen – proceeds to take the entire bottle, one pill at a time.)

MAMMAW: You waited for me to go to bed so you could have him all to yourself.

JO: That's not true.

MAMMAW: It is so true. You don't want him to talk to his Mammaw.

LEOTA RUTH: *(To audience.)* The funny thing about my particular kind of illness is that during those times of pure lucidity—of sane and normal consciousness—the afflicted person wants, more than anything, to be once again engulfed in the illusions of the disease. It is of rare and ironic comfort to the tormented party. *(Ingests some pills.)*

MAMMAW: You don't want him to talk to his Mammaw because you know he loves me more than he does you! Just like your daddy loved you more than he did me!

JO: How can you say such a thing? You're sick!

MAMMAW: I'm not the one that's sick around here, sister.

LEOTA RUTH: *(To audience.)* To be sane in a sane world is difficult enough, but to be sane in an insane world—well, there's the rub. *(Continuing to ingest pills.)*

BILLIE: *(Rising.)* Look, I really need to . . .

JO: *(Stopping her.)* Sit down! *(BILLIE sits.)*

MAMMAW: *(To BILLIE.)* Remember all those Air Force boys sister used to take in after Howie Boy left for college?

BILLIE: Yes, Mammaw.
JO: Don't listen to her, Billie.

MAMMAW: I can't tell you how many times poor, stupid H.O. would come cryin' to me whiles sister was doin' somethin' nasty with one of those boys.

JO: That's a filthy lie!

MAMMAW: Don't talk to me about filthy, sister! Ol' H.O. got to be the weakest man alive or the biggest fool for love I've ever known.

JO: You don't know what you're talking about! They was boarders. We were just trying to make ends meet. I loved them like they was my own sons.

MAMMAW: You'll get no argument from me, sister. *(To BILLIE.)* Do you know why Howie Boy never comes around?

LEOTA RUTH: *(To audience.)* You might not want to listen to this. It gets a little scary. I generally tune out. But, then I've heard it all before.

BILLIE: I just want to go to the bathroom, Mammaw.

JO: *(To MAMMAW. Warning.)* Mother, stop it. *(To BILLIE.)* Go to the bathroom.

MAMMAW: Stay put! *(Blocks BILLIE's way.)*

JO: She's got to go to the bathroom.

MAMMAW: I don't care if she's got to go to the emergency room. *Sit! (BILLIE sits.)*

JO: Mother, I'm gonna have you put away.

MAMMAW: Put a zipper on it, sister.

LEOTA RUTH: *(To audience.)* Fair warning. There is much violence of the spirit to follow.

MAMMAW: *(Picking up plastic floral arrangement – to BILLIE.)* See this ugly flower thing?

BILLIE: Yes.

MAMMAW: Well, I'm gonna bust it over your dumb skull if you budge one inch! Now, do you know why Howie Boy never comes around here anymore?

BILLIE: *(Resigned.)* No, Mammaw. Why?

JO: That cinches it! You're going today!

LEOTA RUTH: *(Sotto voce.)* Please stop. MAMMAW: *(Putting floral arrangement on table.)* He told me.

JO: Mother, stop it! Stop it right now!

(JO and MAMMAW begin a pattern of going around the table – like two cats about to pounce. LEOTA RUTH appears more and more frightened - more stressed.)

MAMMAW: Told me how sister runs around in front of him in her under things.

JO: That's not true!

MAMMAW: In front of a grown man in her bra and panties.

JO: That's a lie!

LEOTA RUTH: *(In pain.)* Please stop. You're hurting me. *(Frantically, takes the remainder of the pills.)*

MAMMAW: Trapping him in her bedroom.

JO: You goddamned liar!

MAMMAW: Seducing her own son.

JO: You're crazy.

MAMMAW: Crazy like a fox, sister. No wonder he prefers men to women.

LEOTA RUTH: I can't breathe.

JO: You don't know what you're talking about!

MAMMAW: Oh, I know what I'm talking about all right. *(Sits.)*

JO You'd do anything to get between us! You was always interfering—trying to poison him against his own mother—just like you tried to poison daddy against me. Well, he's my son, not yours. You wanted a son, but you had me and you couldn't stand that, could you? So, when I had a son you tried to take him away, poison him against me—make him your own.

MAMMAW: You had a daughter, too.

JO: I never had a daughter! I had another retard just like you!

(LEOTA RUTH walks to the window.)

MAMMAW: And you were so busy telling her that. No wonder Leota Ruth killed herself.

JO: *(After a long, uncomfortable SILENCE.)* That had nothing to do with me.

MAMMAW: Nothin' ever does. *Murderer!*

JO: STOP IT!

MAMMAW: Murderer! Murderer! I should've drowned you!

JO: I know. You've been telling me that all my life. Why didn't you, huh? Why, mother, why?

MAMMAW: Because you're my daughter.

LEOTA RUTH: *(Looking out the window. Almost a chant.)* Take away time. Take away time. Take away time. *(She produces a razor blade and carefully examines it.)*

JO: Since when has that ever meant anything to you?

MAMMAW: You ain't nothin' but an ingrate.

JO: *Me? Me?* Who takes care of you, mother? Who took you in when daddy died? You sat over in that old drafty shack and didn't eat a thing for nearly a week. You'd be dead now, if it weren't for me.

MAMMAW: It weren't no shack. It was good enough for you at one time, wasn't it?

BILLIE: *(Timidly.)* Can I go now?

JO: Shut up! *(Crosses behind MAMMAW who is seated at the table.)* I should have left you there to die.

MAMMAW: Like you did Leota Ruth?

JO: You goddamned bitch! *(Grabs towel and begins to strangle MAMMAW.)* I hate you! I hate you! I hate you!

LEOTA RUTH: Take away time. *(She raises her arm and slowly, carefully, begins to carve on her flesh. Each "Take away time" is punctuated by a fresh slash to her arm.)* Take away time. Take away time. Take away time. Take away time . . .

(The action freezes. JO has the towel wrapped around MAMMAW's throat. BILLIE is about to jump up and stop JO from strangling MAMMAW. LEOTA RUTH, her eyes glazed over, ceases to cut herself. The LIGHTING FADES while LEOTA RUTH is bathed in her own "special" LIGHTING.)

LEOTA RUTH: *(Taking on the persona of a thirteen-year-old.)* Mommy, mommy! Come quickly!

JO: *(Moving out of the frozen shadows, comes down to the window and to her daughter. She takes on the persona of a much younger woman.)* What is it, sweetie?

LEOTA RUTH: *(Looking out window.)* Look. Isn't it beautiful?

JO: Oh, yes.

LEOTA RUTH: I knew you'd like it.

JO: I do.

LEOTA RUTH: Isn't that about the most beautiful sunset you have ever seen?

JO: I believe it is. Yes, I think it is. Now, isn't it about time you got yourself ready for bed?

LEOTA RUTH: Soon. Let me just look until it goes down—until it is all over.

JO: All right, just a little while longer.

LEOTA RUTH: Just till when it is all over.

JO: Yes. When it's all over. You look and I'll finish putting up the supper dishes. But as soon as the light fades, you go to bed. Okay?

LEOTA RUTH: Stay with me. Please. Just until the light fades.

JO: I've got work to do, sweetie.

LEOTA RUTH: I know. But, it is very, very sad to look at something beautiful when you are all alone without anybody to share it with. Ugly should be seen when you are all alone, but beauty has to be shared.

JO: You say the strangest things sometimes. *(They BOTH stare out the window as the LIGHT shifts on the faces. After a pause.)* There. See? It's almost over.

LEOTA RUTH: Not yet. *(After a pause.)* Why couldn't it always be like this?

JO: Like what, sweetie?

LEOTA RUTH: Like now. Full of love and kindness.

JO: You think there is no love and kindness?

LEOTA RUTH: Oh, yes. Yes, I do—*now. (A sigh.)* But *now* will not always be.

JO: Won't it?

LEOTA RUTH: No. That's why I have to leave, mommy.

JO: You're a strange duck. And exactly where will you be going?

LEOTA RUTH: I don't know exactly. *Somewhere.* Outside of time, I expect.

JO: And just how does my little girl plan to do that?

LEOTA RUTH: The sun. I'm going to leave with the sun.

JO: *(Kisses LEOTA RUTH on the forehead.)* You're such a strange little creature. But, I love you.

LEOTA RUTH: *(Begins the metamorphosis back into the woman she is.)* I love you, too, mother. If only we were able to continue loving . . .

JO: *(Reverting back into the woman she is.)* You changed. You're not my little girl anymore. I don't know who you are, Leota Ruth.

LEOTA RUTH: Why don't you look? Why don't you try, mother?

JO: I don't like what I see.

LEOTA RUTH: What do you see?

JO: Something I'm ashamed of.

LEOTA RUTH: What, mother? What?

JO: I don't know! I don't want to know! It's in your eyes and I don't want to be reminded of it.

LEOTA RUTH: Who do I remind you of, mother?

JO: *(After a pause. Tearfully.)* All that I rejected in my own life. You remind me of all that I struggled against becoming. You remind me of who I can no longer be—what I threw away a long time ago.

LEOTA RUTH: Goodbye, mother.

JO: Goodbye?

LEOTA RUTH: I need to follow the sun now.

JO: Then follow the sun. I won't stop you.

LEOTA RUTH: *(As the LIGHT fades on their faces.)* Mother?

JO: Yes?

LEOTA RUTH: Be careful. There are devils in the desert.

JO: I know, Leota Ruth. I know.

(The LIGHTING fades and LEOTA RUTH exits outside of Time, outside of Space. The LIGHTING slowly rises as JO returns to where MAMMAW sits frozen with the towel still around her neck. JO grabs the towel. The LIGHTING is back to where it had originally been. The SOUND of BILLIE's and MAMMAW's screams!)

JO: *(Strangling MAMMAW with towel.)* I hate you! I hate you! I hate you!

MAMMAW: *(Sinking to the floor.)* Help . . . help . . . *(Obviously struggling to breathe.)*

BILLIE: *(Pulling JO from off MAMMAW.)* Jo! Stop it! You'll kill her! *(The TELEPHONE RINGS.)* Stop it, Jo! Stop it! *(Manages to get JO away from MAMMAW.)*

(BILLIE comforts MAMMAW. JO staggers around in a rage. She grabs the plastic flowers and hurls them across the kitchen. She throws the folded ironing in all directions.

Things fly – the laundry, the iron, the ironing board, this and that, etc. The TELEPHONE continues to RING.)

JO: *(While in her rage.)* When's my turn, huh? When's my turn?

MAMMAW: *(To BILLIE.)* She never was any good. Now, will you call the police?

(The TELEPHONE continues to RING.)

BILLIE: Nobody's gonna call the police, Mammaw.

JO: Oh, she's had the police here before, don't think she hasn't.

BILLIE: Are you all right, Mammaw? *(Helping her back into the chair.)*

JO: Is she all right? Is she all right? What about me, huh? What about me? Jesus Christ! What about me?

BILLIE: *(Grabs JO in an effort to calm her.)* Jo, get hold of yourself. *(JO pulls away.)* Why don't you answer the phone, Jo?

JO: When I'm good and ready! I'll answer the goddamned phone when I'm good and goddamned ready! *(Crosses slowly to telephone. Answers.)* Yeah?

BILLIE: *(Comforting MAMMAW.)* Do you want to go to your room?

MAMMAW: No. Now do you see what I have to put up with?

BILLIE: Yes. Mammaw. Do you want something to drink— to eat?

MAMMAW: Is that Howie Boy she's talkin' to?

BILLIE: I don't know, Mammaw.

JO: *(Into telephone.)* When? Are you sure?

MAMMAW: I bet that's Howie Boy. *(To JO.)* If that's Howie Boy, you better let him talk to his Mammaw!

JO: *(Into telephone.)* Yes, I understand.

MAMMAW: Don't you hang up that phone without me talkin' to him!

JO: *(Into telephone.)* Thank you. *(Hangs up telephone.)*

MAMMAW: *(To BILLIE.)* See? She did it again!

JO: Did what, mother?

MAMMAW: Talked to Howie Boy and pretended I didn't exist.

JO: That wasn't Howie Boy, mother. It was the hospital.

MAMMAW: Was it for me?

BILLIE: *(To JO.)* Is everything okay?

MAMMAW: I bet it was for me.

JO: It's H.O. They're operating on him right now.

MAMMAW: Now what did you do to him?

JO: I didn't do anything, mother. That stomach thing turned out to be appendicitis. Will you drive me to the hospital, Billie? My nerves have had all they can stand for one day.

BILLIE: Certainly. You want to go right now? JO: If you don't mind, yes.

MAMMAW: Since you're not driving, can I come?

JO: Yes, mother. If you want to come, come.

MAMMAW: *(Rises to exit.)* Just let me get my bag. Remember Piggy Smith?

JO: No, mother. Who's Piggy Smith?

MAMMAW: Oh, just someone I knew once. He used to charge a nickel to let you see his appendix scar.

JO: *Mother—*

MAMMAW: All right, all right. I'll just be a minute. *(Exits to her bedroom.)*

BILLIE: *(Gathering up her knitting and her hair rollers.)* Is H.O. going to be all right?

JO: Yes, I think so.

BILLIE: And you?

JO: I'm fine, Billie, just fine. Let's go. *(BOTH start to exit. JO turns back and looks toward the window.)* Maybe we'll wait till the spring, Billie.

BILLIE: The spring? What are you talking about, Jo?

JO: *Curtains.* We were talking about curtains, weren't we?

BILLIE: Yes. Yes, we were, Jo.

JO: Well, we'll hold off on new ones. For awhile, anyway.

BILLIE: Sure, Jo. Anything you say.

JO: Leota Ruth, bless her soul, picked out the material for these curtains. *(Pause.)* Why did she have to go and kill herself?

BILLIE: I don't know, Jo. Why does anybody?

JO: Sleeping pills, ripped arteries, slashed jugular. Why, Billie, *why?*

BILLIE: I don't know, Jo. *(A pause.)* We best be going.

JO: Yes.

BILLIE: Yes. *(After a pause.)* I always liked those curtains. *(A pause.)* Well, I'll go get the car. *(Exits.)*

JO: *(She crosses to the window and gently touches the curtains. LEOTA RUTH enters and gently rests her hand on JO's shoulder. Perhaps, JO feels her presence.)* Maybe. Maybe in the spring. I mean, they're not bad—not really—not all bad. A little worn, perhaps. A little frayed. But, they're familiar—comfortable. Easy to come home to. Easy on the eye. I mean, they still have some wear in them—some life. Don'tcha think?

Slow FADE to BLACK perhaps to the MUSIC of Elvis Presley's "Don't Be Cruel."

END OF PLAY

THE PROCTOLOGIST'S DAUGHTER

SYNOPSIS: *The Proctologist's Daughter takes* a comedic look at the film noir of the 1940's. Baroness Von Cobra is the epitome of the "dragon lady" of the particular genre. She is a spy for the Third Reich and from her mansion high atop the Hollywood Hills she runs her spy operation and reports directly to Berlin. Her residence is a nest of Nazi, a gorilla and a cobra named Adolph. Otto Papschmier, her ever-faithful servant, and Frau Schnapps, her deviously clever housekeeper, assist her in her villainy. The Baroness is assigned to uncover the whereabouts of a secret weapon the the Third Reich is anxious to get its hands on, but all attempts are foiled by Dick Palmer, the cool secret agent for the Allied Secret Service (ASS) and his girlfriend, Velma Lombard the Woolworth's saleslady and wannabe movie star. All the characters are pretty much Hollywood stock. In face, there is not an once of realism, just cliché and a lot of fun-filled shtick.

NOTE TO DIRECTOR: The costumes, the set with all its furnishings, the makeup and the lighting works best in black and white and all the shades in between.

The Proctologist's Daughter (under the title of *Curse of the Snake Woman*) opened at the Raw Space, 543 W. 42nd St., NYC, October 29, 2002 under the direction of Sean Cassels with the following cast:

TOMMY BARZ—Dick Palmer
ANDREA HOFFMAN—Velma Lombard
SCOTT PETCHE—Otto Papschmier
NATASHA YANNACANEDO—Baroness von Cobra
BREANA MURPHY—Frau Schnapps
MICHAEL DULEV—Adolph, Kongo
Stage Manager—Gary Phillip Russo
Set Design—Tommy Barz
Sound Engineer—Peter Vipulis
Costumes, Make-up & Hair—Amada Wade

THE CHARACTERS:

DICK PALMER: A secret agent for the Allied Secret Submarine Service (ASSS).
VELMA LOMBARD: Dick's love interest, a shop-girl and wannabe actress.
OTTO PAPSCHMIER: Baroness Von Cobra's faithful henchman.
BARONESS VON COBRA: The consummate *femme fatale*, played by a man in drag.
FRAU SCHNAPPS: The mysterious housekeeper with a wandering mole.
ADOLPH: A cobra.
KONGO: A gorilla.
THE TIME: Halloween in the early 1940s.
THE PLACE: Hollywood.

ACT ONE

Scene 1—a bench in a park.
Scene 2—the living room of the Von Cobra mansion is ornate and overdecorated. Somewhere there is a table covered with a floor length cloth and holding a large basket. This basket is home to Adolph the cobra which, as a sock puppet, must be manually animated.
Scene 3—the lingerie department of Woolworth's.
Scene 4—the living room of the Von Cobra mansion.

ACT TWO

Scene 1—the living room of the Von Cobra mansion
Scene 2—the living room of the Von Cobra mansion
Scene 3—a bench in a park

ACT ONE – *Scene 1*

AT RISE: A park. DICK PALMER, wearing a fedora and a trench coat, is seated on a bench reading the Los Angeles Times. He folds the paper, lays it on the bench and stands.

DICK: *(Directly to audience.)* Halloween . . . it's when the ghouls and gorillas come out. . . the real heart stoppers. No, not the little kids in costumes, masks or made-up faces, but the real McCoy on the sleazy underbelly of the City of Angels. The kind of horror show that you can only see 'round midnight in the filth and shadows near Hollywood and Vine. The angels and the sinners tread these treacherous streets; these streets where stars and tramps walk side by side; where perfumed dames are lookin' for good-time Charlies and the good-time Charlies are lookin' for . . . well, lookin' for a good time. These are my streets. This is my city. This is my beat. My name is Dick Palmer and I'm a secret agent man.

Boy, if this bench could talk! It was right here on this bench a few years back when me and my ladylove, Velma Lombard, first talked about marriage. Velma Lombard is a big star now, but she wasn't then. Then there was a war on. You know, the big one; WW II. We were all doing what we could for the war effort, only some of us were doing more than others. We could have lost that war if it wasn't for me and Velma back then on that fateful Halloween. The Germans were breathing down our backs and if we hadn't squashed the evil Baroness Von Cobra dead in her tracks, we might all be eating blood sausage pudding.

We had just finished lunch, Velma and me, right here on this very park bench on that fateful Halloween.

(VELMA LOMBARD, a platinum blonde bombshell, enters and sits on the bench. When she speaks, she has a high-

pitched voice and is incredibly naïve. She probably chews gum and, when she's finished, sticks it under things. Hiding behind a fake tree that he carries is OTTO PAPSCHMIER.)

VELMA: *(Her hands all over DICK.)* Dicky, Dicky, Dicky. I've waited so long. I'll be an old maid before we get married. Say you will take my hand.

DICK: *(Taking her hand.)* What do you want me to do with it?

VELMA: I want you to marry it. I mean *me*. Say you will marry me, Dicky. Say you will take my hand in marriage.

DICK: *Ah,* Velma. I can't. I can't say that I will take your hand in marriage because I can't.

VELMA: Oh, say it. Say it, Dicky. Say you will. Say you'll be mine, sweetheart. We're closer than ham and cheese. Closer than tomato and lettuce. Closer than franks and beans, and cream cheese on a bagel. We belong together. Say you love me.

DICK: Ditto, Babe. But I can't.

VELMA: You can.

DICK: I can't. There's my career to think about. I don't want you worrying every time I leave home to go to work.

VELMA: Oh, why can't you stop being a secret agent man?

DICK: Because I'm a red-blooded, loyal, faithful, all-American boy who loves his flag and will defend it till death do us part.

VELMA: Sounds like you're married to it.

DICK: In a way, sugar, I am.

VELMA: Well, where does that leave me?

DICK: Next, Babe. Next.

VELMA: I wouldn't let my movie career get in the way of our getting married.

DICK: You can't get killed making a movie, sweetheart.

VELMA: In this town? You've got to be kidding!

DICK: Besides, you don't have a movie career.

VELMA: Not yet, but I will as soon as I am discovered.

DICK: In Woolworth's?

VELMA: This is Hollywood, ain't it? Stranger things have happened.

DICK: But not at Woolworth's.

VELMA: Suki Salome was discovered in Woolworth's.

DICK: Who's Suki Salome?

VELMA: She was a stand-in for Maria Montez. She used to work in the cosmetic department. She's the one who actually got to jump into the smoldering volcano.

DICK: Isn't she lucky!

VELMA: Yes and no. She's back at Woolworth's. Only this time she's working in the hardware department until they remove the bandages.

DICK: Bandages?

VELMA: From the burns.

DICK: I see. Fame is a fleeting flame, ain't it?

VELMA: Yeah, and it can be short too.

DICK: There's a war on, babe, a big ugly world war with an ugly little man with an ugly little mustache with an ugly attitude who means to conquer the world and make it into something as ugly s himself.

VELMA: *Gads!* What an ugly mess.

DICK: You got that right, sister. How can I think about marriage while the Germans are breathing down our necks?

(OTTO quickly backs away, tree and all.)

VELMA: Say yes. Throw caution to the wind. Say you will marry me, my beloved.

DICK: I can't. We got to end this big bad war before I say yes. I'm doing what I must for the war effort.

VELMA: I know you are, Dicky, and I think that's just swell. But why can't I marry a G-man. A secret agent? It's a good job. You pay taxes. You're doing what you can to preserve the American way, aren't you?

DICK: You bet I am, babe. But that's the thing. My kind of work is dangerous. There's danger around every corner, around every bend in the road, around everywhere there's someplace to hide and lurk in the shadows.

VELMA: *Gads!*

DICK: There's danger all around us, sweetheart, and I will not put you in the middle of it.

VELMA: I don't care. I'm very proud of you. And when people ask me what my husband does for a living, I can raise my chin and stand tall when I tell them that my Dick is a secret agent. My Dick works to protect justice and freedom and the American way. My Dick works for ASSS.

DICK: You gotta spell it, Velma. A-S-S-S. The Allied Secret Submarine Service has my body, but you will always have my heart.

VELMA: Oh well, one can't have everything. I'll just have to be content with your heart for now and wait till after the war for the rest of you.

DICK: Shucks! We've got to win this war, Babe, and soon.

VELMA: And we will. We've got to put our trust in President Roosevelt and in the American way because the American way is the right way and the right way is our way; therefore, we should get our way, right?

DICK: *(Bewildered.) Ah,* right.

VELMA: *(Glances at her watch.)* Oops, my lunch hour is almost over. While you figure out how we're going to win this big ugly war I have to get back into ladies' lingerie or I'll be out on my. . . *(OTTO sneezes from behind a slowly advancing tree.)* Bless you.

DICK: What?

VELMA: I said, bless you.

DICK: Bless you, too, Velma.

VELMA: Thank you, Dicky, but I didn't sneeze. *(She rises to leave.)*

DICK: I thought you did.

VELMA: Nope. Wasn't me. *(Gives him a quick peck on the cheek.)* Happy Halloween, darling. Gotta go. Can't be late for work. I really just can't. Don't forget we're going trick-or-treating this evening.

DICK: I won't. See you later. Here's lookin' at you, kid. *(An afterthought.)* Wait.

VELMA: What?

DICK: I almost forgot. I've got something for you, Babe.

VELMA: You do? What is it, Dicky?

DICK: *(Removes a long-stemmed red rose from one of the pockets of his trench coat.)* A rose. An American Beauty rose for the most beautiful girl in America.

VELMA: *(Taking the rose.)* Thank you, Dicky. Aren't you too sweet. OUCH!

DICK: What happened?

VELMA: I think I pricked myself on your rose, Dicky.

DICK: Here, let me see. *(He takes her hand and kisses it.)* There, all better.

VELMA: *Ooh,* it feels better already. I guess in the garden of life there has always got to be a little prick.

DICK: My mother's words, exactly. Now you hurry along and I'll meet you right here after work.

VELMA: Bye-bye.

DICK: Bye-bye. *(VELMA leans in to kiss him.)* Ixnay on the isseskay. We're in a public place.

VELMA: Sorry. Bye again. *(She exits.)*

DICK: Bye again. *(OTTO sneezes.)* Bless you.

OTTO: *(From behind the tree.)* Thank you.

DICK: What the . . . *(Starts to rise. OTTO, wearing a tuxedo and red sash, comes out from behind the tree and drops a cloth sack over DICK's head.)*

BLACK OUT.

END ACT ONE – *Scene 1*

ACT ONE – *Scene 2*

AT RISE: The living room of the Von Cobra mansion. BARONESS VON COBRA is alone onstage talking into the microphone of a short-wave radio. She is wearing something dark and sexy; perhaps a slinky, snake-like, floor length, black satin dress with a long slit on the side and with lots of sparkling beading and a cape with a turned-up collar in the shape of a cobra's head. Perhaps she is wearing something else. She smokes cigarettes using a long ornate holder.

BARONESS: *Ya. Ya ya. Ya ya ya!* My manservant, Otto Papschmier *(pronounce pap shmeer)*, is taking care of that as we speak, Herr Lipshitz. Vhat? Very vell. Let me schart from the beginning and work my way toward der middle. It is the only way to get to the bottom of things, *yah? (Still speaking into microphone.)* It was late last night. It was dark and it was stormy. One might even say, gloomy.

(A flash of LIGHTNING followed by the SOUND of THUNDER.)

BARONESS: *(Con't.)* Shortly after receiving a radio call from Herr Hitler, *heil,* Otto came into the living room of my beautiful mansion high in the Hollywood Hills for his nightly orders.

(OTTO enters.)

BOTH: I am waiting for my orders.

BARONESS: He said. And then I said . . . *(No longer speaking into microphone, but rather in the moment.)* Of course you are, Otto, darling.

OTTO: *(Throws himself to his knees.)* Beat me! Kick me!

Give me orders! I live to look up to the soles of your shoes!

BARONESS: Of course you do, Herr Papschmier. *(She pronounces it pap-shmeer.)*

OTTO: *(Correcting her.)* Sha-my-er. Otto Pap-sha-my-er.

BARONESS: How many times have I told you, Papschmier, you are who I say you are!

OTTO: Of course. I cannot imagine what came over me.

BARONESS: A lapse in judgement, I presume. Although I am not one to presume. I am one who knows. Neither presumption nor assumption in my little *Mein Kampf*. Struggles you could never imagine.

OTTO: I must read it someday.

BARONESS: Tonight after your hot cocoa.

OTTO: I am looking forward to it.

BARONESS: Now get up before you sink to levels beneath yourself. By the way, I just spoke with der man.

OTTO: Der man? You mean?

BARONESS: I do.

OTTO: *(Salutes.)* Heil.

BARONESS: *Heil.* It seems there is a submarine about to leave the Port of Los Angeles. It contains a top-secret weapon that the Third Reich must get its hands on.

OTTO: Right. Third Reich. Hands. Der man?

BARONESS: Der man.

OTTO: *Heil.*

BARONESS: *Heil.* He needs to know when the schnitzel schleps.

OTTO: The schnitzel schleps?

BARONESS: Leaves port. We must know vhich schnitzel contains das sauerbraten before it schleps to sea.

OTTO: Vhich schnitzel contains das sauerbraten before it schleps?

BARONESS: That's what I said! Das secret weapon is the sauerbraten.

OTTO: Das sauerbraten is der secret weapon?

BARONESS: *Ya, ya, ya!* You keep repeating me and I will need to burn the wax out of your ears. We must know what we must know. Und ve must get our hands on that secret weapon.

OTTO: Yes! We must get our hands on that schnitzel.

BARONESS: *Nein!* We must get our hands on das sauerbraten after we have boarded der schnitzel. Our leader will not rest till we have it in our hands.

OTTO: The sauerbraten.

BARONESS: *Ya vohl.* The secret sauerbraten. I mean, the secret weapon. Sauerkraut is most anxious.

OTTO: Sauerkraut is anxious?

BARONESS: *Ya,* sauerkraut must get his hands on das sauerbraten.

OTTO: You mean . . . ?

BARONESS: I do.

BOTH: *(Salute.) Heil!*

BARONESS: The future of der pumpernickel depends on it.

OTTO: Der pumpernickel?

BARONESS: You're doing it again! *(She slaps his ear.)* Das Third Reich!

OTTO: *(Rubbing his ear.)* Now, I see. Der future of der pumpernickel, which is headed by de sauerkraut, depends on knowing when de schnitzel containing das sauerbraten schleps to sea, *ya?*

BARONESS: *Ya.* You can say that again.

OTTO: Der future of der pumpernickel, which . . .

BARONESS: *(Cutting him off.) Nein!*

FRAU SCHNAPPS: *(Enters. She is dressed more like a gypsy than a housekeeper. She has a thin mustache.)* You called, Baroness Von Cobra?

BARONESS: *Nein.*

FRAU SCHNAPPS: I distinctly heard my name.

BARONESS: No one called your name, Frau Schnapps. Now go about your rat catching!

FRAU SCHNAPPS: I'm finished with the rat catching, Madam.

BARONESS: Good. Feed them lots of cheese. I want them nice and plump when I give them to Adolph.

OTTO: *Heil!*

BARONESS: Not *that* Adolph, *dumkoph!*

OTTO: Ah, you mean das snake Adolph.

BARONESS: *Ya*, das schnake Adolph. *(Turning to FRAU SCHNAPPS.)* Well? Haven't you something to do?

FRAU SCHNAPPS: I'm making pretzels, Your Ingratiatingness.

BARONESS: I beg your pardon?

FRAU SCHNAPPS: Pretzels, Your Good Graciousness. I am making pretzels.

BARONESS: How charming. Go. And get a shave, Schnapps!

FRAU SCHNAPPS: I'm gone. *(Exits.)*

BARONESS: Now, where were we, Otto?

OTTO: Getting our hands on der sauerbraten for der sauerkraut after we've boarded der schnitzel in order to save das pumpernickel.

BARONESS: Otto, it is best you watch your "ders" and your "dases." We are in America and we should not vant to arouse suspicion. Know vhat I mean?

OTTO: *Oh, ya* . . .

BARONESS: *Ah,* yes. Herr Hitler said . . .

OTTO: *(Salutes.) Heil!*

BARONESS: *Heil! (A beat.)* As I was saying, Herr Hitler . . .

OTTO: *Heil!*

BARONESS: Schtop it! Schtop it, schtop it, schtop it!

OTTO: Yes, Madam.

BARONESS: Now where was I, Papschmier? *(Mispronounces, as always.)*

OTTO: *(About to correct her but thinks better of it. After a pause.)* You were saying, Herr Hitler *(He gets in a quick, short, sotto voce.) Heil,* said.

BARONESS: Ah, yes. Und vhat he said vas: we must find the man from ASSS.

OTTO: Ass, Madam?

BARONESS: Allied Secret Submarine Service. *(She spells it out.)* A-S-S-S.

OTTO: *Ah,* that kind of ass.

BARONESS: *Dumkoph!* We must get our hands on Dick Palmer. He is ASSS's top man. He knows where the secret weapon is hidden and he knows vhen the submarine leaves port and vhere it is headed, and he knows . . . he knows everything und ve know nothing! You must bring him back to me for interrogation, if you know what I mean, dear Otto.

OTTO: *Ya,* Madam. I know exactly what you mean. I will go and get Dick from ASSS and bring him back for interrogation.

BARONESS: And I will inject him with the secret truth serum made from the venom of the king cobra.

OTTO: I live to grovel, Baroness Von Cobra.

BARONESS: *(Handing OTTO a slip of paper.) Of course.* This is where you will find Agent Palmer tomorrow at noon where he will be having lunch, as he does every weekday, with his lady friend Velma Lombard. Undershtood?

OTTO: *(Falls to his knees.)* Yes, I understand, my Baroness. Tomorrow at noon I will invite Agent Palmer for a nice cup of tea and some strudel. Then, after the strudel, the sauerkraut will have the last laugh as the sauerbraten and the schnitzel hit der fan. Long live der pumpernickel!

BARONESS: *Wunderbar!* And then I will inject him with the truth serum of the king cobra.

OTTO: So you said, Madam.

BARONESS: It bears repeating.

OTTO: You make my life so delicious, Baroness. Could you kick me once before I retire to my room, please?

BARONESS: Oh, how I spoil you, Herr Papschmier.

OTTO: *Pap-sha-my-er.*

BARONESS: Of course. *(She kicks him.)* And for correcting me you get an extra kick. *(She kicks him again.)* Now go! And may your dreams be filled with the scent of black boot leather. *(OTTO gets up, bows and backs out and exits.*

BARONESS returns to the short-wave radio and speaks into the microphone.) So, as I was saying, Herr Lipshitz, Papschmier left to fetch Palmer directly after breakfast this morning. Shortly afterward our housekeeper, Frau Schnapps, came stumbling in *(FRAU SCHNAPPS stumbles in.)* screaming something about das tricks und das treats.

FRAU SCHNAPPS: Baroness Von Cobra! Tonight is Halloween and I don't know what to give de trick-or-treaters.

BARONESS: Give them nothing. They are filthy, dirty, nasty, vile, foul little beggars. I never begged for anything in my life. What I got I got from honest, hard work. Halloween is just an excuse to exploit the masses and to rot de teeth of de little children. If you ask me, Frau Schnapps, Halloween was invented by a greedy, evil dentist! *(After a pause.)* You still have not shaved, Schnapps. I gave you an order!

FRAU SCHNAPPS: It is a beauty stash.

BARONESS: If one were to stretch ones imagination to such an improbable degree I suppose one could call it that. Shave it anyway!

FRAU SCHNAPPS: Yes, Your High Horse.

BARONESS: What was that, Schnapps?

FRAU SCHNAPPS: Yes, Your Highness. I will shave my beauty stash. Can I wait until tomorrow. I have so much to do today.

BARONESS: Like what?

FRAU SCHNAPPS: Well . . . The pretzels. The strudel.

BARONESS: *What!*

FRAU SCHNAPPS: The Strudel. The apples to peel . . . the pastry . . . .

BARONESS: *Ah.* That kind of strudel.

FRAU SCHNAPPS: Yes, that kind of strudel. And the children. We must give the children something or they'll put soap on our windows and toilet paper up our trees.

BARONESS: Soap on our vindows? Toilet paper up our twees?

FRAU SCHNAPPS: Something like that. It's old American custom. I will give them pretzels.

BARONESS: *Ya*, pretzels. We lived on pretzels, mother and I. Pretzels were our salvation. Father was an outdoorsman. He was also a proctologist, but got himself into a lot of trouble for practicing proctology without a license. Anyway, one day father went hunting for bear in the backwoods of the Black Forest with Bertha the Bavarian barmaid and neither were ever heard from again. He left mother and me to struggle and to starve. *Ya, ya.* I was a poor little girl in Heidelberg who sold pretzels my mother made to university students with scarred faces. That was our only source of income.

FRAU SCHNAPPS: But you are a Baroness.

BARONESS: *Ya,* now. But not then, Frau Schnapps, then I was poor little Helga Schmidt the proctologist's daughter in das schwein tails.

FRAU SCHNAPPS: Schwein tails?

BARONESS: *Ya, ya,* schwein tails. *Oink, oink!*

FRAU SCHNAPPS: Ah, pigtails!

BARONESS: *Ya,* und schwein tails The Baron was very fond of little girls with der schwanz of das schwein.

FRAU SCHNAPPS: *Ya,* so I've heard.

BARONESS: It was the Baron Von Cobra who took me away from the squalor of Heidelberg. The first Baroness Von Cobra died quite suddenly after some radical experimental surgery and I happened to be in a position to comfort the poor bereaved Baron.

FRAU SCHNAPPS: And what position might that have been, Your Swineness?

BARONESS: I beg your pardon?

FRAU SCHNAPPS: I was wondering what happened to the Baron Von Cobra, Your Highness?

BARONESS: Adolph bit him.

FRAU SCHNAPPS: The Fuhrer?

BARONESS: Das Schnake.

FRAU SCHNAPPS: On purpose?

BARONESS: The late Baron was a small man with a big appetite. He had just finished his third platter of sausage and noodles when he bumped into Adolph's basket, passed gas, and got himself bit on der arsch. Perhaps, Adolph mistook him for a large farm animal.

FRAU SCHNAPPS: *Ya,* I can see how that could happen. How sad.

BARONESS: Is it?

FRAU SCHNAPPS: Oh, yes, I think it is.

BARONESS: *Guten.* In that case, remind me to tell it to you again sometime. Now go and make more pretzels! *(FRAU SCHNAPPS stumbles out. The BARONESS returns to the short wave-radio and speaks into the microphone.)* Now go and make more pretzels, I told Frau Schnapps. What's that? *Ah,* yes, Herr Lipshitz, der whole kitchen is filled with de pretzels. Little ones, big ones, salted, unsalted, you name it. I certainly don't want soap on my vindows or toilet paper up my twees. Und any minute I am expecting Otto to return with Agent Dick Palmer. Our plan is right on schedule. I will contact you as soon as I've got the lowdown on das sauerbraten in das schnitzel. I pledge allegiance to de pumpernickel. Heil Sauerkraut! I mean, Heil Hitler! *(She carefully replaces the radio into its hiding place, surveys the room, and then yells towards the kitchen.)* Frau Schnapps!

FRAU SCHNAPPS: *(Comes running into the room wearing strings of pretzels around her neck ?She no long sports the mustache.)* Trick or treat? I got a hot treat for you!

BARONESS: *Nein, nein, nein.* Not yet! It is time to feed my baby Adolph. Bring me a nice plump rat.

FRAU SCHNAPPS: Yes, madam. *(She turns to leave.)*

BARONESS: *Wait!*
FRAU SCHNAPPS: *(Turning back.)* What?

BARONESS: Come here. *(FRAU SCHNAPPS approaches her.)* Where is your beauty *stash?*

FRAU SCHNAPPS: It is on my bosom.

BARONESS: Which one?

FRAU SCHNAPPS: I will give you three guesses.

BARONESS: I only need two.

FRAU SCHNAPPS: Are you sure?

BARONESS: Of course I am sure. How did das beauty stash get on your bosom?

FRAU SCHNAPPS: I don't know, Madam. It may be afraid of razors. It seems to have a mind of its own. *(She turns and exits.)*

BARONESS: *(Calling after her.)* Hurry with the rat! *(She puts a cigarette into her cigarette holder and lights it. Aside.)* I am surrounded by *dumkophs*. Oh vell, good servants are so hard to find nowadays. It is a manner into which one needs to be born. So few hear the calling and fewer still will answer. Wherever will tomorrow's servants come from? I foresee a world to come where none will be fit to shine my shoes! How sad. How very, very sad. I live to step upon others. Where would we be without der scum of the earth? *Der abschaum der menschlichen gesellschaft.* Herr Fuhrer will see that there's lots of scum for people like me. *(Pause.)* Now, where is that Papschmier? He should be back with our guest by now.

FRAU SCHNAPPS: *(Enters, carrying a caged rat.)* Here is your rat, Your Rodentness.

BARONESS: I beg your pardon?

FRAU SCHNAPPS: Your rodent, Baroness.

BARONESS: Thank you, Frau Schnapps. *(Takes the cage.)* By the way, I may need you to do das Dance of de Seven Veils of Truth. So you will change into your dance clothes immediately.

FRAU SCHNAPPS: Yes, Your Despised.

BARONESS: I keep hearing things?

FRAU SCHNAPPS: I'm sorry. I asked if I will be dancing for anybody I know or will it be a surprise?

BARONESS: A surprise, I suspect. We will be entertaining an agent from ASSS.

FRAU SCHNAPPS: Is that an object or a place, Baroness?

BARONESS: *Nein.* It is a position. Now go. And see that no one disturbs me while I am feeding my Adolph.

FRAU SCHNAPPS: Yes, Madam. *(Turns and exits.)*

BARONESS: *(To herself.)* I never heard of a mustache with a mind of its own. *(Crosses to Adolph's basket and begins to sing. At some point during her singing the lid to the basket slowly rises as Adolph the cobra begins to rise up and sway to the singing of his mistress.)*
LET ME CALL YOU SCHEETHEART
I'M IN LOVE VIT YOU
LET ME HEAR YOU VHISPER
THAT YOU LOVE ME, TOO
(She hums awhile then speaks, stroking and kissing her pet.) How is my little darling? I've got a present for you my liebchen. Oh, yes I have. Look what mama's got for you. *(Removes rat from cage and feeds it to Adolph.)* A nice fat roly-poly rat. *Yummy, yummy.* Eat the nice fat roly-poly rat.

(There is the SOUND at the front door of OTTO entering with his captive DICK PALMER. NOTE: The front door cannot be seen as it is upstage, to the side and at the end of a hallway.)

BARONESS *(Con't.):* Ah, what do I hear, my little pet? I do believe it is Otto and our houseguest, Agent Dick. You go back to sleep, my pretty one. I will need your services later.

But for now, mama's got work to do. (She laughs. ADOLPH sinks back into his basket. The BARONESS closes the cover.)

(Atop a hooded DICK PALMER rests a fedora as he is escorted into the room by OTTO who has a gun pointed at his back. OTTO removes DICK'S hat and then his hood and pushes him into the room.)

OTTO: Madam, our guest has arrived for tea and strudel.

BARONESS: Welcome to my humble mansion high in the Hollywood hills, Herr Dick. The room you are standing in was personally decorated by *moi*. I have impeccable taste. You look a bit anxious, a bit limp, Herr Dick. I've always been one to bend over backwards for my guests. Can I offer you some refreshment, Herr Dick?

DICK: I ain't no Herr, fraulein!

BARONESS: I ain't no fraulein, dear boy. I am the Baroness Helga Von Cobra at your service.

DICK: Take a gazunt hike, lady! Suppose you tell me what this is all about.

BARONESS: I like a man who comes right to the point.

DICK: Then you're gonna love me, Toots.

BARONESS: Otto, my precious, please help our guest feel at home.

OTTO: Your coat, sir.

DICK: Thank you, but I'll leave it on if you don't mind. I don't plan to stay very long at this altitude.

BARONESS: *(While removing a syringe from a box, holding*

it up and examining its contents.) Otto, show Herr Dick to a chair.

(OTTO pushes DICK into a nearby chair. The BARONESS crosses to DICK and plunges the needle into his arm.)

DICK: *Ouch!* What in blue blazes was that?

BARONESS: The truth serum of the king cobra. Otto, you can put your gun away. Herr Dick won't be going anywhere for quite some time. This takes effect quite suddenly and renders the patient incapable of even the desire to escape. Besides, it instantly puts de feet to schleep. *(To DICK.)* How do you feel, Herr Dick?

DICK: With my hands, lady!

BARONESS: *(Examining DICK'S hands.) Ya, ya,* and what big hands you got. You must be a man with a great big *feeling, ya?*

DICK: Yeah, it could make you cry, lady.

BARONESS: Papschmier, go!

OTTO: *Pap-sha-my-er.*

BARONESS: Whatever! Go!

OTTO: Go?

BARONESS: Away!

OTTO: Where?

BARONESS: Go and make sure Frau Schnapps is ready for das Dance of de Seven Veils of Truth.

OTTO: You want Frau Schnapps to do das Dance of de Seven Veils of Truth?

BARONESS: If it becomes necessary. And vhile you are gone melt der wax out of your ears. Now go and attend to business.

OTTO: Let us hope the agent from ASSS cracks before we have to go that far.

BARONESS: But, if he doesn't, tell Frau Schnapps to be ready.

OTTO: Yes, my Baroness.

BARONESS: Now go! I must be alone with Herr Dick so we can have our little tea party.

OTTO: Very well. But if you need me for anything you know where to find me.

BARONESS: *Ya, ya.*

OTTO: *(Approaching, as a shy child.)* Madam, could you, would you—

BARONESS: Oh, very well. *(She slaps OTTO.)* There! Now go! You're a dirty little boy with a dirty, dirty, dirty little mind! If you don't straighten out I will tie you up and beat you silly! Now, what have you got to say for yourself?

OTTO: Oh, thank you! Thank you, my Baroness. *(Backing toward exit.)* I live to grovel. *(To DICK,)* Were I you, Herr Dick from ASSS, I would tell the Baroness what she wants to hear. You really don't want Frau Schnapps to do das Dance of de Seven Veils of Truth. *(Exits.)*

DICK: Nice dog you got there, princess. Take long to train

him?

BARONESS: He came that way.

DICK: From where? A box of Cracker Jacks?

BARONESS: I must know about the secret weapon.

DICK: What secret weapon? I don't know sauerbraten from schnitzel, lady.

BARONESS: Sauerbraten from schnitzel? Then you do know when it schleps.

DICK: When what schleps?

BARONESS: Das schnitzel. Where is das schnitzel und vhen does das schnitzel schlep?

DICK: When the moon is full? What are you talking about, lady?

BARONESS The submarine containing the secret weapon. You said you didn't know sauerbraten from schnitzel. How did you know not to know what you know so well?

DICK: Huh? Look lady, you can force-feed me sauerkraut on pumpernickel and I won't spill the beans.

BARONESS: Sauerkraut on pumpernickel? So, you know about sauerkraut und
pumpernickel? Und beans? Vhat is das beans?

DICK: It means I ain't gonna talk, sister. You can dose me with truth serum till the cows fly back to Capistrano and I ain't gonna talk. It's my training, lady.

BARONESS: I have some training too, mister.

DICK: Yeah, the kind of training you can only get from Barnum and Bailey.

BARONESS: What's das Barnum und Bailey?

DICK: It's the circus, lady. It's where you ought to take your act. You're doin' the high trapeze without a net, sister.

BARONESS: The high trapeze?

DICK: You're flyin' high and you're gonna crash like a cast-iron Hindenburg, sister. You're hard and you're tough, but you're all bad air.

BARONESS: We shall see about that!

DICK: Really? So I guess the rolling pin is next?

BARONESS: Vhat rolling pin?

DICK: C'mon, don'tcha read the funny papers?

BARONESS: Vhat papers? You got papers? Vhat kind of papers?

DICK: The Sunday papers. The Katzenjammer Kids. Always gettin' chased by the old lady with a rolling pin.

BARONESS: I don't know old lady with rolling pin. How common and vulgar.

DICK: That's me, Toots, common and vulgar. I ought to keep my pie hole shut, huh lady?

BARONESS: *Ya, ya.* You Americans, you can talk de talk but you can't dance de polka. *(Crosses to phonograph and turns it on. German lederhosen dance MUSIC plays.)* Perhaps this will change your mind.

DICK: What? You're gonna kill me with Om-Pa-Pa? Sorry, I didn't bring my lederhosen.

BARONESS: *(Calling to kitchen.)* Frau Schnapps!

DICK: I ain't thirsty, lady.

BARONESS: *Ah,* but this is a very different kind of schnapps, Herr Dick.

DICK: Hey! I thought I told you ixnay on the herry Dick stuff?

FRAU SCHNAPPS: *(Enters, followed by OTTO. She is dressed in veils. She is a frightful sight.)* You called?

BARONESS: It is time we gave our honored guest das floorshow. *(To OTTO.)* Otto, just in case we need to persuade our guest a bit more I think you should go and pick up the linguini.

OTTO: The linguini?

BARONESS: Plan B, Otto. *Plan B.*

OTTO: *Ah,* the dish of linguini. *(Hesitates before exiting.)* Before I leave, Madam, would you give me a slap for good luck?

BARONESS: Otto, I'm busy! Slap yourself, you nasty little boy!

OTTO: *(Slaps himself while moving toward exit.)* Nasty boy. Little nasty boy. Nasty, nasty. *(Exits.)*

DICK: *(Calling out to OTTO as he exits.)* That's little Nazi boy Otto

BARONESS: Now, where were we?

DICK: *(Tries to rise.)* Look, sister, you and Brunhild here better make tracks for
Berlin 'cause I'm about to bust this operation wide open. *(His legs are rubber and his feet are asleep.)* Hey, what's this?

BARONESS: A side effect of the truth serum! We don't play around, Mister Dick. *(She puts on a different record and turns up the volume. DICK wobbles some more then falls back into his chair.)* Now, Frau Schnapps, show our guest vhat you got.

(FRAU SCHNAPPS begin her dance as the LIGHTING and the MUSIC fade.)

BLACK OUT.

END ACT ONE – *Scene 2*

ACT ONE – *Scene 3*

AT RISE: the counter at the lingerie department of Woolworth's. A single red rose is in a bud vase is setting on the counter. VELMA LOMBARD has just finished with a customer and she is waving "goodbye."

VELMA: Thank you. Happy Halloween. On behalf of the family and staff of
Woolworth's may I wish you and yours a swell day. *(A beat.)* Bless you! *(To herself.)* I don't know. Seems like "have a swell day" ought to be nice enough. Oh, well . . . I'll put it in the suggestion box. *(OTTO enters.)* Good afternoon, sir. Welcome to Woolworth's Department Store. May I interest you in some ladies' lingerie? Of course lingerie is only for ladies, isn't it? So maybe I should ask if I may interest you in lingerie? I mean, did you ever hear of men's lingerie? What do you think? *(OTTO sneezes.)* Bless you. Geez, that sneeze sounds familiar.

OTTO: Your perfume.

VELMA: That's the next aisle over.

OTTO: No. Your perfume . . . it makes me sneeze.

VELMA: Oh, it makes everybody sneeze. Except my Dicky. It's hard to get my Dicky to sneeze. He doesn't smell much.

OTTO: Your Dicky doesn't smell much?

VELMA: Nope. Thick hairs . . . up the nose . . . they filter everything out. Runs in his family, I think.

OTTO: I see.

VELMA: You do?

OTTO: Perfectly. But why do you wear der perfume that makes everybody sneeze? That is, everybody but your Dicky.

VELMA: Because it's all the rage. Did you know that Joan Crawford wears this very perfume? That's not to say I'm a huge fan of Joan Crawford, but she is a real sweet lady – I mean, adopting those little kids and all. Anyway, I read in one of my movie magazines that she wears this very same perfume. It doesn't seem to have done her any harm. *(OTTO appears bewildered.)* Anyway, she does and if it's good enough for Joan Crawford it is good enough for me. It's called *Voodoo*.

OTTO: *Voodoo?*

VELMA: *Yeah* . . . like that voodoo that you do so well?

OTTO: I don't do voodoo. Who is telling you these lies?

VELMA: No, silly. I didn't mean to say that you do "do voodoo." It's a song. You'll stop after three sneezes. Everybody does. Now what may I interest you in?

OTTO: I can't really say.

VELMA: Then you came to right place.

OTTO: I will be picking something up.

VELMA: What did you have in mind?

OTTO: *(Carefully eyeing her, taking mental measurements.)* Something not too heavy. *A bit frivolous. Perhaps, a little schtupid.*

VELMA: Schtupid?

OTTO: *Ya,* not too schmart.

VELMA: Not too schmart?

OTTO: *Ya.*

VELMA: *Ah, smart.* You'd have to go to Gimbals or Macy's for that. Nothing too smart here. Then this is for your wife.

OTTO: *Nein.*

VELMA: Was that a "no?"

OTTO: *Ya.*

VELMA: Perhaps it is for your mistress? You can talk to me. I'm very modern.

OTTO: *Nein,* she is not exactly my mistress. She tells me what to do. She gives me orders. She beats me and she whispers nasty things in my ears. She calls me names und she makes me feel good all over. Sometimes when I am blue and lonely and feeling lost and alone in der soulless streets of Tinseltown she gets out der whip—

VELMA: *(Cutting him off.) Whoa.* You're not talking about Mother Mavis over atSaint Gertrude's Catholic School for Girls, are you? We used to call her Mad Mother Mavis. Jeepers creepers! You didn't want to cross that mean Mother.

OTTO: *Nein, nein, nein.* I know nothing about mean mad mothers.

VELMA: Aren't you lucky? Then are you sure we're not talking about your wife?

OTTO: I am not married.

VELMA: Like I said, I'm very modern.

OTTO: She is of royalty. I am a mere commoner. I am not fit to lay down and let her schtep on my face and squish my nose and leave sticky bubble gum all over my face from off the soles of her shoes.

VELMA: Ah, a Princess! I know exactly what you mean. So many Princesses
nowadays. Me, me, me . . . that's all they think about, isn't it?

OTTO: She is a Baroness.

VELMA: A Baroness . . . Oh, you do have it bad, don't you? Well, let's see . . .
something not so smart for a Baroness . . . how about something in black?

OTTO: Black is her favorite color.

VELMA: Somehow I knew that.

OTTO: You are a very perceptive young lady.

VELMA: Likewise I'm sure. *(OTTO sneezes.)* Bless you.

OTTO: Thank you.

VELMA: Are you sure I don't know you? You have a very distinctive sneeze. I seem to have heard it before. Oh well, it'll come to me. So, does your Baroness have a castle?

OTTO: In Heidelberg she has biggest castle in all of Deutschland.

VELMA: Really?

OTTO: No, not really. But she likes to think so. The Kaiser's . ... his is bigger. I play along because she plays along with me.

VELMA: But she is a Baroness, right?

OTTO: *Ya,* she has the papers to prove it.

VELMA: Papers?

OTTO: Of pedigree.

VELMA: Pedigree? You mean like a Chihuahua?

OTTO: Maybe. I know nothing of Chihuahua. She also has a mansion high up in the Hollywood hills. It is the biggest and it is the best mansion in all of Hollywood.

VELMA: Really?

OTTO: I don't know. I don't get around much anymore.

VELMA: Well, I'm sure I'd love to see it.

OTTO: Maybe you will . . . *ya,* maybe you will.

VELMA: I know!

OTTO: What? What do you know?

VELMA: A teddy! Every Baroness needs a black teddy.

OTTO: I don't think she would like a bear.

OTTO: *(Examining and fondling the teddy.) Ooh,* vhat a nice piece of merchandise. This *would go so good with der whip.*

VELMA: I suppose it would. *(OTTO sneezes.)* Bless you.

Hey! Now I remember.

(OTTO quickly swoops the teddy over VELMA'S head.)

BLACK OUT.

END ACT ONE—*Scene 3*

ACT ONE – Scene 4

AT RISE – The living room of the Von Cobra mansion. All is as it was before. The MUSIC rises with the LIGHTING as FRAU SCHNAPPS is about to remove one of the remaining veils.

DICK: Stop! Stop! I've had enough! I can't take it anymore! I've seen my share of bad
floorshows, but this one's worse than the Tijuana donkey serenade.

BARONESS: Then you vill talk?

DICK: Sister, I'll sing like a hundred and seventy-five pound canary with a hair lip if she promises to cease and desist. (The BARONESS turns off the phonograph.) Just when I thought I saw everything there was to see, there they were *three*. Count 'em—*three*. How did you get three bosoms, lady?

FRAU SCHNAPPS: Herr Doctor Fleischspeiler. It was an experiment und I was a volunteer. He wanted to make de perfect woman and I am das perfect result.

DICK: Looks to me like an experiment gone bad . . . really bad. Bad like a month old hardboiled egg. Bad like a three day old sardine sandwich.

FRAU SCHNAPPS: *Nein.* The boy with three hands liked them. *Ya,* he'd come to me in his tight little lederhosen under the light of the gypsy moon as the violins was playing and the trees was swaying to der sweet gypsy music . . . und he was feeling frisky und with those big hairy hands of his he would reach up for my—

BARONESS: *(Cutting her off.)* That will be enough, Frau

Schnapps! You may go now. It is almost time for der tricky treaters.

FRAU SCHNAPPS: Yes, Your Arbitrariness. We certainly don't want soap on our windows.

BARONESS: Good, good. Und we don't want toilet paper up our twees . . . it gets all wet and soggy and impossible to get it out, if you know what I mean. *(FRAU SCHNAPPS exits. To DICK.)* So, we are alone at last.

DICK: Yeah, ain't this the bee's knees? It's just you and me, kid. My heart is goin' all pity-pat, and so is my gall bladder.

BARONESS: I am waiting to hear the canary singing.

DICK: I don't chirp on an empty stomach, lady.

BARONESS: You are schtalling and you are wasting precious time! *(The SOUND of the front door closing.)* Ah, delivery! It looks like you'll get your wish, Herr Dick. I sent out for a very special dish.

(OTTO enters with gun in hand, pushing VELMA into the room. VELMA still has the teddy over her head. The BARONESS crosses to VELMA and pulls the teddy from off her head.)

BARONESS: *(Con't. To DICK.)* I do hope you approve.

VELMA: *(Runs to DICK.)* Oh, Dicky! This terrible man with a funny accent abducted me right out of Woolworth's. You think they'll dock my salary? I hope not. I used up this month's supply of ration stamps, but then this month is pretty much over, isn't it? Anyway, it was almost closing time. Oh, I could spit. I could just spit.

BARONESS: Put a zipper on it, sister!

VELMA: Likewise I'm sure.

BARONESS: *(Pushes VELMA into the chair next to Adolph's basket.)* Well, it looks like *the floorshow isn't quite over yet.*

VELMA: There's a floorshow?

DICK: *(To the BARONESS.)* You never give up, do you?

BARONESS: Not when the fate of the Third Reich is at stake.

OTTO: De pumpernickel.

BARONESS: *Ya,* de pumpernickel.

DICK: I'll have mine on rye with a side of potato salad, sister.

BARONESS: It is not all the same with me, Herr Dick. You vill see very soon that this is not all fun and games. This is a battle of vills und the German vill is der vill that vill out!

DICK: Ya-ya and a yippy ki yay to that, sister.

VELMA: Is this some kind of weird Hollywood Halloween party? 'Cause if it is I really didn't come dressed for it.

DICK: I'm afraid not, sweetheart. We seem to be in the dirty, slimy, blood-soaked hands of secret agents for Adolph Hitler.

BARONESS & OTTO: *(Salute.) Heil!*

VELMA: Adolph Hitler? You mean *the* Adolph Hitler?

BARONESS & OTTO: *Heil! Heil!*

DICK: *Yup!* There ain't none other, sweetheart. It is safe to surmise that they are going to use and abuse you to get at me. But I wouldn't let it bother me were I you.

VELMA: Use and abuse me? I don't want to be used or abused, Dicky. How are they going to use and abuse me?

DICK: Maybe the old Chinese water torture routine, maybe the bamboo slivers under the fingernails, or toothpicks to hold the eyes open, or the limburger cheese up the nostrils, or another dance by the three-bosomed lady.

VELMA: *(Confused and then to the BARONESS – extending her hand.)* Hi. I'm Velma Lombard. I'm an actress. You may not have heard of me. I haven't done very much yet. In fact, I haven't done anything really. But I'm gonna be the next big thing, only nobody knows it yet. I mean big. Big like Veronica Lake, or maybe Merle Oberon. Anyway, Miss. What a pretty dress. Is it off the rack? What did you say your name was?

BARONESS: Clam up, blondie. The next act is about to begin.

VELMA: What do you mean . . . the next act? I think I missed something here. Could you fill me in on the first act?

BARONESS: What's the matter, creampuff? You didn't get a program at the door?

VELMA: No, I just came right in with this . . . this . . . *(Indicates OTTO.)* I'm sorry. I never got your name. I'm Velma Lombard. I'm an actress.

BARONESS: Shut up! You're making me crazy!

DICK: Somebody else did that long ago, sister.

BARONESS: Little Dicky here doesn't want to sing so I've got a little ditty that is sure to
make him change his tune. *(She begins to sing.)*
LET ME CALL YOU SVEETHEART

(A GORILLA suddenly is seen lurking in the shadows.)

I'M IN LOVE VIT YOU

(The GORILLA moves about the room unseen by all.)

LET ME HEAR YOU VHISPER THAT YOU LOVE ME, TOO

(The lid to Adolph's basket slowly opens.)

KEEP THE LOVELIGHT GLOWING IN YOUR . . .

(She sneezes.)

EYES SO TRUE.

VELMA: Bless you.

BARONESS: Thank you. *(Continues singing.)*

LET ME CALL YOU SVEETHEART *(The GORILLA sneezes.)*

ALL: *(None actually pay attention to whom it was who sneezed - they respond merely out of habit.)* Bless you!

(The GORILLA grunts. By now Adolph has risen high over his basket.)

BARONESS: *(Continues. Sings.)*
I'M IN LOVE VIT YOU

(ADOLPH sneezes.)

VELMA: *(Turns to Adolph.)* Bless you. *(Adolph proceeds to bite her on the neck and then retreats back into his basket.)* Ouch! What was that?

BARONESS: That, girlie, was der bite of Adolph!

VELMA: Adolph sure looked like a snake to me.

BARONESS: *Ya,* a king cobra . . . und without de antidote I'm afraid you have less than an hour to live. *(She laughs. To DICK.)* So what have you got to say for yourself now?

VELMA: Less than an hour? I'm going to be a movie star. Do something, Dicky!

DICK: *(Looks over toward VELMA.)* I'm sorry, Velma, but I can't.

VELMA: You can't?

DICK: I can't. I really can't. I am sworn to secrecy.

VELMA: What are you – crazy ? You would choose ASSS over me?

DICK: Sorry, babe, but a man's gotta do what a man's gotta do.

(The GORILLA sneezes.)

ALL: Bless you! *(ALL turn and see the GORILLA which causes them all to scream!)*

(As the LIGHTS slowly dim to the screams of ALL, we see the GORILLA beating its chest. A Flash of LIGHTNING followed by the SOUND of THUNDER.)

BLACK OUT.

END ACT ONE

ACT TWO – *Scene 1*

AT RISE: The living room of the Von Cobra mansion. Everything is as it was at the end of ACT ONE. All are frozen in place as the LIGHTING rises. When it has fully risen, ALL continue screaming.

FRAU SCHNAPPS: *(Removes the head from off her gorilla costume. The screaming of the others stops.)* What? What?

BARONESS: Frau Schnapps! What do you think you are doing?

FRAU SCHNAPPS: I was trying on my Halloween costume.

BARONESS: Well, take it off! You look like a gorilla.

FRAU SCHNAPPS: I'm supposed to look like a gorilla. When the little children come for der tricks und der treats they like a little scare. A good scare from time to time is good for them. Herr Doctor Sigmund Freud said it helps der little wisenheimers to grow and to be strong eight ways. I think he said eight ways. Maybe that was somebody else. I wonder?

BARONESS: Just throw water in their dirty little faces and they'll grow just as strong as scaring them with all this monkey business. Und where did you get das gorilla suit?

FRAU SCHNAPPS: I rented it.

BARONESS: Well, take it back! It is ugly! You vill not wear this for der twick or tweaters. I don't care how much it makes der children grow and I don't care in how many ways. They grow fast enough and in too many ways as it is.

VELMA: Excuse me for interrupting but if you all don't

mind I've got less than an hour to live, and you certainly do look like a gorilla. No offense. My Aunt Louise on my mother's side spent a fortune on electrolysis. It's all the rage don'tcha know? My name is Velma Lombard and I'm an actress.

FRAU SCHNAPPS: *(Extending her gorilla hand.)* Pleased to meet you.

VELMA: Likewise I'm sure. *(Shakes hand.)* Geez. I never shook hands with a gorilla before. Did you know that Kongo the killer gorilla escaped from the zoo this morning? They made a special announcement on the loudspeaker over at Woolworth's. Pretty much cleared out the store, but what the hey? For a moment I thought you were he . . . you were him . . . he was you . . . it was him . . . or, is it he?

BARONESS: *(Looking at watch and then at VELMA.) Tick, tick, tic—*

VELMA: Anyway, if it had of been Kongo we'd probably all be dead by now, or worse.

FRAU SCHNAPPS: What could possibly be worse?

VELMA: They say he never met a female he didn't . . . well, you know.

FRAU SCHNAPPS: *Nein,* I don't know.

VELMA: Yes, you know. *(Timidly demonstrates using finger gestures to suggest sexual intercourse.) Ewingscray* the old down and *irtyday umpinghay.*

FRAU SCHNAPPS: *Ah, ya.* I get it. *Ya,* I believe I do know. But then I have always had a good imagination.

OTTO: What? I want to know. Somebody tell me.

FRAU SCHNAPPS: Monkey love.

OTTO: Monkey love? *Ah*, I understand. Monkey love.

BARONESS: Schtop it! *Schtop it, schtop it, schtop it!* You understand nothing! *(To VELMA.)* What is wrong with you, girlie?

VELMA: Well, to start with, I've got less than an hour to live.

BARONESS: *Ya,* and that's a fact. *(To FRAU SCHNAPPS and OTTO.)* Haven't you two got something to do?

FRAU SCHNAPPS: Come with me, Otto. You can help arrange pretzels on der trays for das trick or treaters.

BARONESS: And take that silly costume back from where you got it! You will not wear it in my mansion. My beautiful mansion high up in der Hollywood hills. *(A beat.)* I hate monkeys! I have always hated monkeys!

VELMA: *(Starts to rise.)* May I go now?

BARONESS: Sit down! *(OTTO and FRAU SCHNAPPS exit.)* What is the matter with you? You were bit by Adolph der king cobra and you have less than an hour to live. Unless I am mistaken, he did not also give you a lobotomy! *(Turns to DICK.)* How do you feel about that, Herr Dick?

DICK: Is he a licensed surgeon?

BARONESS: *Dumkoph!* Adolph is a schnake!

VELMA: Of course he's a schnake. I could tell that the minute I saw him.

DICK: Then I'm sure he only bit her. *(To VELMA.)* Ain't

that right, Velma? Did he just bite you or did he try something funny?

VELMA: No, he bit me and that's about all. I'd say that's funny enough. And I don't mean funny hah-hah.

DICK: I wouldn't worry about it then.

VELMA: It wasn't you who got bit, Dicky.

DICK: Remember the little prick this afternoon?

BARONESS: *(A disappointed sigh.)* But such big hands.

VELMA: You bet I do. It still stings, Dicky.

BARONESS: What little prick?

DICK: The thorns of a rose I gave Velma were coated with the antidote to cobra venom. We knew all about your little Adolph here. *(To VELMA.)* You ain't got nothing to worry about, Sweetheart, you've been vaccinated.

VELMA: You mean I'm not going to die?

DICK: Not today, sweetheart.

BARONESS: Vaccinated? What are you talking about?

DICK: Seems old Adolph here is a little weak in the venom department. Long in the tooth too.

VELMA: How did you know, Dicky?

DICK: It's our job to know. ASSS prides itself on covering its . . . well, all its bases.

BARONESS: Weak venom? Long in der tooth? *(Takes one*

of her high heel shoes off and starts beating Adolph's basket.) Hello! Hello in there! Why didn't you tell me this, you, you non-Aryan schnake. *(Adolph rises from the basket.)* How could you betray me? You will never be part of der master race! *Nein!* You've gone soft and schmushy. You'll never march side by side for the glory of Deutschland. You can forget about that right now you . . . you Aryan wannabe! *(Shaking shoe at Adolph.)* And remember all those times I said it was *wunderbar?* Well you can forget about that too, Mister. It wasn't *wunderbar.* It wasn't *wunderbar* at all . . . I was faking it! You impotent limp biscuit! *(Adolph grabs the shoe and sinks back into his basket—shamefully, if that is possible.)*

DICK: ASSS has been on your tail for months, lady.

BARONESS: Vhat kind of talk is that, you nasty little boy?

DICK: On your tail like a fly on last week's liverwurst. We've been watching your every move and monitoring your radio conversations with Berlin. We have transcripts of every one of your conversations.

BARONESS: *Ya, ya!* So what?

DICK: We've got the goods on you, Baroness Helga Schmidt Von Cobra from Heidelberg.

BARONESS: *Ya, ya,* das ist my name. That and a quarter vill get you a free lunch.

DICK: The proctologist's daughter. Only your daddy never had a license to practice. The apple never falls far from the tree does it, sister?

BARONESS: I don't know vhat you're talking about, Mister.

DICK: Of course you do, lady. Your father was up to his

elbows in dirty business and your hands are just as filthy from doing the Furor's business.

BARONESS: Der Furor's business is my business, Herr Dick. I am a daughter of Deutschland! *(Salutes.)* Heil Hitler! *(Grabs gun from somewhere.)* Und now de games *is over.*

VELMA: Did I miss the games?

DICK: It shoots blanks, sister, just like your little limp friend in the basket. Herr Adolph the spineless wonder. No more moonlit nights for the two of you, *heh?* A woman and her snake; sort of tugs at the old heartstrings, don't it?

VELMA: I'm a modern girl, but that's a little too modern for me.

BARONESS: What are you talking about?

DICK: I told you. We've had you under surveillance for quite some time. You don't think we'd leave a loaded gun laying around, do you? You might hurt yourself.

(A GORILLA enters, pounding its chest and grunting. Suddenly it sneezes.)

VELMA: Bless you.

BARONESS: Go back to the kitchen, Frau Schnapps! I don't like das monkey business! I told you to take that suit off and take it back from where you got it!

(The GORILLA approaches VELMA and touches her in some unseemly, lurid way.)

VELMA: Don't get me wrong. Like I say, I'm a very modern girl. Maybe later. I've got a headache right now. So, amscray!

(OTTO and FRAU SCHNAPPS enter. FRAU SCHNAPPS is carrying a large box with "SUNSET COSTUMES GORILLA SUIT" printed on it. OTTO is carrying a tray of pretzels that he places on a table.)

VELMA *(Continues.)* Up until a minute ago I thought I had less than an hour to live.

FRAU SCHNAPPS: Here is the gorilla suit, Your Meanness. *(She sets the box down somewhere.)*

VELMA: *(Seeing FRAU SCHNAPPS.)* Frau Schnapps! Then who? It's Kongo!
(ALL ad-lib "Kongo" and scream etc. Strobe LIGHTING. VELMA jumps up hitting the phonograph that begins to play "oom-pah" music. ALL continue to ad-lib as everyone runs in all directions as in some wild game of hide-and-seek. The BARONESS shoots her gun at KONGO but soon realizes that it is indeed loaded with blanks. The BARONESS, having one shoe, hobbles in and out of closets, behind drapes and doorways. DICK, still recovering from the effects of the truth serum, moves with floppy legs on feet that have gone to sleep. KONGO seems intent on capturing VELMA, the BARONESS or FRAU SCHNAPPS. It is obviously a woman that he wants. At one point KONGO corners FRAU SCHNAPPS. With her back to the audience, FRAU SCHNAPPS exposes her unique breasts to KONGO who appears momentarily stunned and bewildered; he then counts to three on his fingers before becoming horrified and runs away from her. KONGO now only pursues VELMA and the BARONESS and runs from FRAU SCHNAPPS whenever they are in close proximity. At one point, OTTO stands on a table or a bench, swishing his hips, trying to entice KONGO with some pretzels and some sexual innuendo. KONGO considers OTTO for a moment and then dismisses the idea. OTTO ends up frustrated and eats the pretzels himself. Every

time the BARONESS and VELMA come into close proximity they take turns punching each other. Finally, the BARONESS has had enough and turns off the phonograph. The LIGHTING returns to normal as the BARONESS musters all her available strength.)

BARONESS: *(Shouts.)* Schtop it! Schtop it, schtop it, schtop it! *(ALL freeze in their tracks. To OTTO.)* Otto! Sit down! You look like a namby-pamby sissy boy! I will not tolerate such behavior. *(OTTO sits.)* You're all acting like a bunch of wild animals. *(To KONGO.)* Especially you! *(KONGO grunts.)*

VELMA: Kongo *is* a wild animal.

BARONESS: Shut up, blondie! *(Turns to KONGO and makes loud, ferocious animal sounds which causes him to cower, retreat and exit.)* Now for you, Mister Dick. I'm not done with you yet.

DICK: I think you are, sister. I think your day of reckoning has finally arrived. It's time to pay the piper.

FRAU SCHNAPPS: *Hallelujah.*

BARONESS: Der piper pays me, Mister. *(To FRAU SCHNAPPS.)* And where is your mustache now?

FRAU SCHNAPPS: It's on vacation. Gone south for the winter. *(Cupping one of her breasts.)* Way south. You want I should show you?

BARONESS: *Nein.* I've seen enough of you already. Go. Get out of my sight. You're fired!

FRAU SCHNAPPS: *Nein,* I don't think so, Helga Schmidt—daughter of a proctologist.

BARONESS: What is this obsession everybody has about my father's line of work? So what if he got his hands a little dirty?

FRAU SCHNAPPS: You are not the Baroness Von Cobra.

BARONESS: I certainly am.

FRAU SCHNAPPS: *Nein,* the Baron was already married when he wed you.

BARONESS: I know that, but she was dead.

FRAU SCHNAPPS: She was not dead, Your Wretchedness. He thought she was dead after he threw her to der starving pigs so he could be with you, but she was tougher than pigs! She crawled her way out of that filthy schwein muck and joined a band of traveling gypsies until she could devise a plan to take back her rightful title. Then, after you and der snake Adolph murdered the late and loathsome Baron, she and her new boy friend, the three-handed boy, took employment in your household where they waited for their day to arrive. *Hallelujah!* Today is das come and get it day!
BARONESS: What are you talking about? I never hired a boy with three hands.

FRAU SCHNAPPS: Maybe he had one of them surgically removed by Herr Doctor Fleischspeiler while his girlfriend held a gun to the good doctor's head?

BARONESS: Nonsense! I have never hired anybody other than Otto and you.

FRAU SCHNAPPS: *(Coyly.) Ya,* just Otto and me.

DICK: *(To the BARONESS.)* Looks like the jig's up, sister.

FRAU SCHNAPPS: As it turned out, the Baron couldn't

handle a woman with three titties. I was too much of a woman for him. He wanted a Catholic schoolgirl in der plaid skirt and der schwanz of das schwein.

VELMA: *Huh?*

FRAU SCHNAPPS: Pig tails.

BARONESS: I was young and beautiful. You were last week's chopped liverwurst. You are das freak of nature.

FRAU SCHNAPPS: Nature had nothing to do with it, *Herr Helmut Schmidt—son* of a proctologist.

(ALL gasp.)

BARONESS: What? What did you say?

FRAU SCHNAPPS: Don't think I didn't know about your little surgical procedure.

BARONESS: No. Nobody knows.

FRAU SCHNAPPS: I know. I know, Herr Helmut Schmidt, because I was the attending nurse.

BARONESS: *Nein!* Das is not true.

FRAU SCHNAPPS: It's true all right.

VELMA: You mean that she's a he?

BARONESS: I am all woman, sister! I was poor and I wanted to marry a Baron. Der operation was my only chance for the good life. I, too, knew Herr Doctor Fleischspeiler. He and my father were very good friends. They were like that. *(She crosses her fingers.)* They were bosom buddies, as you Americans say. It was Herr Doctor Fleischspeiler who removed my you-know-what.

FRAU SCHNAPPS: Small loss.

BARONESS: It was not a small loss. In fact, he used my you-know-what on another patient. I recognized the beauty mark on your middle bosom.

(ALL gasp.)

DICK: *Only in Hollywood.*

FRAU SCHNAPPS: It was der Baron who insisted on my operation. He told me that it was a fantasy of his all his life to have a woman with three bosoms.

OTTO: Am I hearing that one of her bosoms is made from the Baroness' you-know-what?

DICK: That's about the size of it, Papschmier. *(He also pronounces it incorrectly.)*

OTTO: *Sha-my-er! Sha-my-er! Otto Pap-sha-my-er!*

BARONESS: It was just the foreskin of my you-know-what. It was no small matter! He never wanted a woman with three of those there what you got. He wanted a nice Catholic schoolgirl in a plaid skirt und white blouse with a little blue tie und black patent leather shoes and little lace Robert socks.

VELMA: I think she means bobby socks.

FRAU SCHNAPPS: Dream on, Your in Denialness. *(Reaching into her breasts.)* Let's see. Down here between one of these . . . .

(Unknown to all, KONGO sneaks back in.)

BARONESS: What are you doing? Schtop it!

FRAU SCHNAPPS: It's in here somewhere. *(Pulls out folded sheet of paper.)* Ah, here it is. My marriage license to the Baron Von Cobra. Signed, sealed und delivered.

(The BARONESS grabs a nearby vase and breaks it over the head of FRAU SCHNAPPS causing her to pass out cold on the floor. VELMA gives the BARONESS a punch that throws her into the waiting arms of KONGO.)

BARONESS: *(Struggling.)* Let me go you big hairy monkey! *(Struggling less.)* Ooh, what big arms you got. *(Submitting.)* What big muscles you got! What a big . . . *(Sings.)* LET ME CALL YOU SVEETHEART . . . (etc.)

(The BARONESS continues to sing as KONGO carries her off like a prize trophy. DICK'S attention is drawn to the short-wave radio with its flashing light. He then runs over to FRAU SCHNAPPS and slaps her a few times trying to wake her.)

DICK: Wake up, Baroness. I need your help. Berlin is calling. *(He slaps her.)* Wake up!

OTTO: Will the real Baroness be all right?

DICK: She'll be just fine, Otto. All she needs is some time with the sandman to sleep it off. The question is, will the world be all right?

VELMA: This is the best floorshow ever.

DICK: *(To OTTO.)* You take the Baroness to her room while I figure out how to save the world.

OTTO: I want you to know that it's been good working with you, Agent Palmer. Thank you for trusting a poor three-handed boy.

DICK: You're a man, Otto, and you no longer have three hands.

OTTO: I know, but I still see myself reaching for three things at once.

DICK: I can see how that could happen.

OTTO: Thank you and good luck.

DICK: You're very welcome, Otto.

OTTO: The future of America and all der free world depends on you, sir.

DICK: I know it does. And don't think it doesn't weigh heavy on my shoulders. Heavy like a Sherman tank filled with overweight soldiers. Heavy like Kate Smith.

OTTO: That's heavy, boss. *(Drags FRAU SCHNAPPS from the living room and exits.)*

VELMA: You mean that the two of you have been working together all this time?

DICK: Of course. *(DICK goes to the radio.)* Velma, quick! I've got an idea!
VELMA: What is it, Dicky?

DICK: You are about to give the performance of a lifetime.

VELMA: I am?

DICK: You must take this call from Berlin or else they will know something is afoot. You must pretend you are the Baroness.

VELMA: I can't do that.

DICK: Of course you can.

VELMA: I can't.

DICK: You can. You must.

VELMA: How will I know what to say?

DICK: I'll help you. There are only a few things you need to remember.

VELMA: But he'll know I'm not the Baroness. I don't sound one bit like the Baroness.

DICK: Are you or are you not an actress, Velma?

VELMA: But, Dicky, I . . . I . . . YES. I am Miss Velma Lombard—actress!

DICK: Then show us your stuff! Show us the stuff that dreams are made of!

VELMA: Okay! I'll make you proud of me, Dicky. Now, what do I need to know?

DICK: You need to know that a submarine is a schnitzel and when it leaves port to go out to sea it schleps.
VELMA: Submarine is schnitzel. Leaves port it schleps. Gotcha.

DICK: The sauerbraten is the secret weapon and the sauerkraut is Adolph Hitler.

VELMA: Sauerkraut—Hitler. That's easy enough to remember.

DICK: Don't forget the sauerbraten.

VELMA: Right. The sauerbraten is, is, oh dear. What's the sauerbraten, Dicky?

DICK: The sauerbraten is the secret weapon.

VELMA: What is the secret weapon?

DICK: I can't tell you that, Velma.

VELMA: Right. So, I don't know what the sauerbraten is because the sauerbraten is a secret.

DICK: Right, and it is kept in a secret hiding place until it is put in a schnitzel and it is not put in the schnitzel until just before the schnitzel schleps to sea underwater and under the cover of night to destroy the pumpernickel.

VELMA: The pumpernickel is underwater?

DICK: No, the pumpernickel is the Third Reich.

VELMA: Third Reich . . . got it.

DICK: Are you sure?

VELMA: *Yup.* Let's do it.

DICK: One more thing.
VELMA: One more thing is about all I can handle, Dicky.

DICK: You must let them think that the schnitzel with the sauerbraten schleps tonight at midnight from pier eighteen. They will send all of their local operatives and ASSS agents will be waiting there to wipe them up.

VELMA: Okay, I got it. But you don't want me to tell them

about the ASSS agents wiping them up, right?

DICK: Right. *(VELMA holds the earphones to her ears and readies herself to speak into the microphone.)* The outcome of this war is in your hands, Miss Velma Lombard. Good luck.

VELMA: Break a leg. You're supposed to say, "Break a leg." "Good luck" is bad luck so you better say, "Break a leg."

DICK: Sure thing, Velma. Break your leg. *(He turns a knob on the short-wave radio.)* You're on. The future of the world depends on you.

VELMA: *(Looking heavenward.)* Mary Astor, this is for you. *(To DICK.)* Now, amscray! *(She takes charge as she speaks into the microphone, sounding remarkably like the former Baroness.)* Ya, ya, ya. Hold your lederhosen on! I vas on der throne. So who is this anyway in such a hurry? Ah, Herr sauerkraut! Heil to you. How's things in de old pumpernickel? Got everything under control? Good, good. Ya got to show them who's who, who's the boss, if you know vhat I mean. So, how's tricks? Lampshades? Nein. I got plenty of lampshades, but tell her good luck in her new business venture. Vhat? Did I hear the one about who? Ya, ya. Nein. Ya. Nein. Und what did she say? Ya, ya. Und what did Goebbels say? Really? really? Oh, schtop it! Schtop it, schtop it, schtop it! You're killing me! That's funny. Vell, like I always say, if they can't take a joke, shoot them. Der Schnitzel? Ya, I was vondering when you were going to get down to business. Dick Palmer? He squealed like a stuck pig. Pig. Pig. Oink, oink. Ya, ya, das schwein. Nein, not schtoop. Stuck. Stuck with a sharp object. Schtoop a pig is something very different. Ya, ya. Ask Goebbels. He should know about that. Linguini? What linguini?

DICK: You! You are the linguini! I mean, Velma is the linguini.

VELMA: *Ah,* the linguini. Vell, Herr sauerkraut, let me tell you about the linguini. You know she is quite a dish, that linguini, und a very famous and talented actress. *Ya, ya.* Miss Velma Lombard, star of stage and screen. Vell, when she is not working at Woolworth's she is really quite famous. She was pasta putty in my hands. But in the end our little noodle bent just like Dick did and ve got all der information ve need. *Ya, ya.* You got a pencil und paper? *Wunderbar!* Here goes: Der schnitzel is in pier . . . pier . . .

DICK: *(Whispers loudly.) Eighteen.*

VELMA: Pier eighteen. You got that, Herr sauerkraut? Good. Das sauerbraten is in der schnitzel and it schleps . . . *schleps.* Am I going too fast for you? Are you getting it all down? Good, good. It schleps tonight at midnight. *Wunderbar! Auf wiedersehen. Danke shoene. Gesundheit. Heil you.* Thank you for shopping at Woolworth's. *(Turns off the radio and puts down the microphone.)*

DICK: Terrific, Velma! Now we've got to get out of here. We've got to let ASSS know that the snake is in the bush.

VELMA: The snake is in the bush? I love it when you talk secret agent talk, Dicky.

DICK: All in a day's work, sweetheart. A man's gotta talk the talk of the road he walks upon in his journey through life.

VELMA: Wow, that's deep, Dicky. *(A beat.)* What about trick or treating? You
promised we'd go trick or treating.

DICK: *(Picking up the box with the gorilla suit.)* I've got an idea.

BLACK OUT.

END ACT TWO – *Scene 1*

ACT TWO – *Scene 2*

AT RISE: The living room of the Von Cobra mansion, a couple hours later. FRAU SCHNAPPS is dressed in a black tuxedo and top hat. She has a bandage on her forehead. She is smoking a cigarette from a long cigarette holder. She is posed on a wooden chair reminiscent of Marlene Dietrich. She is also holding a whip or has one nearby. OTTO is dressed in boots and a black teddy; presumably the one from Woolworth's. The mustache that was once FRAU SCHNAPPS' is now worn by OTTO's. ADOLPH is risen high over his basket and is swaying to the singing of FRAU SCHNAPPS.

FRAU SCHNAPPS: *(Singing.)*
LET ME CALL YOU SVEETHEART
I'M IN LOVE VIT YOU
LET ME HEAR YOU VHISPER THAT YOU LOVE ME, TOO
KEEP THE LOVELIGHT GLOWING
IN YOUR EYES SO TRUE
(Speaks.)
Okay. You can give him a rat now, Otto.

OTTO: Whatever you say, Baroness. I live to grovel.

FRAU SCHNAPPS: Of course you do.

OTTO: *(Tries to feed a rat to ADOLPH who shakes his head "no.")* He doesn't seem to *want the rat, Madam. Poor Adolph. He looks so sad.*

FRAU SCHNAPPS: *Ya,* the proctologist's daughter, son, whatever, called him some pretty nasty names. You would be sad too if somebody said the awful things to you that she said to him. Let him sulk for awhile. Schnakes are very sensitive creatures.

OTTO: *Ya, ya.* Schnakes are very sensitive. But I am not. You can call me anything you like, Baroness.

FRAU SCHNAPPS: *(Cracks whip.)* Schtinker. You dirty schtinker.

OTTO: *Ya, ya!* I'm a dirty schtinker.

FRAU SCHNAPPS: Maybe you need mama to whip your little behind, ya?

(NOISES OFF: The SOUND of trick or treaters at the front door.)

OTTO: It's time!

FRAU SCHNAPPS: Ya! Here. You take der pretzels Take both trays. I got der whip. Isn't this exciting?

OTTO: *(Struggling with trays of pretzels.) Ya,* but I wish I had three hands again.

FRAU SCHNAPPS: *(While walking toward exit.)* Vell, we could look up Herr Doctor Fleischspeiler und see what he's doing these days.

OTTO: Good idea.

(BOTH exit.)

LIGHTING slowly dims except for a pin spot on ADOLPH's basket. The lid slowly rises and ADOLPH stands tall and spits out the shoe that the former BARONESS had fed him.

BLACK OUT.

END ACT TWO – *Scene 2*

ACT TWO – *Scene 3*

AT RISE: A bench in a park. DICK is wearing the gorilla costume and fedora while holding a large model airplane. To the side of the bench is a large cardboard cut-out of the Empire State Building. There is a Woolworth's shopping bag on the bench filled with candy and other Halloween treats.

DICK: *(Removing the gorilla head and putting on his fedora. He speaks directly to the audience.)* We saved the world that night, Velma and me. And many more nights since. That's what I do. That's my job. I'm the man from ASSS and I save the world from the ghouls and gorillas. The job of a secret agent man is to make the world a place where you can sleep soundly and without fear in your beds at night. Or, if you work nights, you can sleep soundly in your beds during the day.

Velma and me went our separate ways. She's a big star on the silver screen now. She got what she wanted and I got the memories of the good times we had.

In case you're wondering about what happened to the evil Baroness and Kongo . . . well, they got what was coming to them. After Kongo dragged Helmut Schmidt, the proctologist's son, off into the mean streets of the City of Angels they were picked up in The Brown Derby where they were demanding to be served. They should have known better. They don't serve gorilla at The Brown Derby. Kongo was taken back to the zoo where he died six months later of a broken heart. And as for Helmut . . . well, he got what he always wanted; he became a resident of the biggest house in all of California—Alcatraz. After the war he got released, got married, and became an American citizen.

BARONESS: *(HELMUT SCHMIDT comes out in drag from behind the Empire State Building.)* Are we about ready to go home, mein liebchen? My dogs are tired and this building is getting pretty heavy.

DICK: Sure thing. I'm putting the wraps on this case and tying it up with a pretty bow. Now where was I? Ah, yes. If you ever find yourself lost and alone 'round midnight where Hollywood meets Vine, along the streets of broken dreams, where nobody knows your name and if someone comes up and sings in your ear, "Let Me Call You Sweetheart" you better listen and listen good. It could be a proctologist's daughter wooing you. Here's lookin' at you, *sveetheart.*

BLACK OUT.

END OF PLAY

ECW, Denver, Colorado
2020

edwardcrosbywells@yahoo.com

Printed in Great Britain
by Amazon